# Life of a College Bandsman 2
## Is This Love

# Also by Jaxon Grant

Crimes of the Heart

Crimes of the Heart 2: The Aftermath

Crimes of the Heart 3: The Resurrection

Bad Religion

Bad Religion 2: A Sinner's Denial

Incidental Contact

Incidental Contact 2: EX-Factor

Incidental Contact 3: Deadly Intentions

What Webs We Weave

What Webs We Weave 2: Nobody Knows

What  Webs We Weave 3: Finding Your Love

What Webs We Weave 4: Don't Look Back

What Webs We Weave 5: Old Terror

What Webs We Weave 6: Could This Be

Life of a College Bandsman

# Life of a College Bandsman 2
## Is This Love

Life of a College Bandsman Series #2
A *BnTasty* Novel

# JAXON GRANT

@jaxon_grant

ISBN-13: 978-1518740541
ISBN-10: 1518740545

# DEDICATION

This book is dedicated to one of my most loyal readers, Jammon R. Meeting you in New Orleans back in September 2015 was one of the most exciting times I've had as an author. I enjoyed the conversation and it's something that I'll never forget as long as I live. Thank you for your continued support and passion in regards to my books. I really appreciate it. Thanks for showing me so much love!

# Life of a
# College Bandsman 2
## Is This Love

# Part One:
## Summer 2003

# 1

# *Zachariah T. Finley*

*Orlando, Florida*
*July 2003*

I was so fucking excited! I wasn't a damn freshman anymore! If I could stand atop Mount Everest and scream at the top of my lungs, I would. I'll never forget the memories and bonds that were created last year, but I'm ready to move on. I'm ready to fuck with the new freshmen, the same way Quinton, Jared and the crew fucked with me.

The 2003 FAMU Summer Band Camp was coming up and I was beyond eager to get back to Tallahassee for that event. I had been a member of the camp for the past two years and now I have the opportunity to be on the other side—I was now in position to be the person that the campers looked up to for guidance. More importantly, I had been home in Orlando all summer and I was looking forward to getting back to Tallahassee. I missed it.

I spent the summer working at Universal Studios Islands of Adventure theme park. I had that job in high school. Thankfully, they kept me on their roster as a seasonal worker while I was away at college. Those extra dollars in my pocket has made a huge difference this summer.

When I wasn't at work, I was at home practicing my instrument or watching television. The NBC soap opera, Passions, was my favorite show and I would die if I missed it. Luckily, for me, I had the VCR step up to record the show every day. Theresa Lopez-Fitzgerald was my girl.

Life is a funny thing, and you never know where you may end up.

11

# Jaxon Grant

To say I didn't enjoy my freshman year would be a complete understatement. I loved my freshman year! I experienced a lot, but I think that all helped make me a better person. A lot of crazy things happened, but you know you have to go through something to have a testimony. I still can't believe Chaz fucked me over the way he did. When it first happened, I felt so stupid. Then I thought about my grandma. She once told me, "When someone shows you who they are the first time, believe them!" Chaz showed me his true colors plenty of times. I just didn't see them—no, I didn't want to see them. Despite everything that happened around me, I still finished my freshman year strong. I had a great overall GPA (3.47) and I'm looking forward to taking this achievement to greater heights for the upcoming school year.

Finally reaching my destination, I walked into the corner store. My grandma had a headache and asked me to drive up to the store to get her a box BC powders. *I never understood how she took that nasty, bitter shit—whatever.* Instead of driving, I decided to walk. I needed the extra exercise, especially with marching band season coming up.

I grabbed the fifty-pack box of BC powder and a pint of praline and crème ice cream for myself. I saw a bag of pork skins and got that for my grandma. She loves those things. After I paid for everything, I headed back outside. I sighed as the heat slapped me in the face like a pimp slapping his two-dollar whore. It was just hot for no fucking reason. *What the fuck was I thinking walking over here at two o'clock in the afternoon?*

As I walked back home in my orange basketball shorts, black wife beater and my black Nike slides, I removed the wife beater and placed it around my neck. When I got back home, a quarter mile later, my grandma looked at me as if I were crazy.

"What?" I said, looking at her.

"Where are your clothes?" she asked, offended.

"Grandma, it's hot out there. I'm about to go take a shower anyway."

"Umm, hmm," she rolled her eyes. "Bring me my glass of water out of the refrigerator."

"I got you a bag of skins, too," I said, placing the skins on the table before putting my ice cream in the freezer.

"Oh, thank you," she smiled, as I brought her the glass of water.

"No problem," I said, as I turned around and headed for my room to prepare for my shower.

# Life of a College Bandsman 2: Is This Love

Once out of the shower, I dressed in another pair of green basketball shorts and a black wife beater. I walked back into my room and my phone started ringing. I smiled when I saw the name. Excited, I quickly answered, "What's up, man?"

"It ain't shit, freshman bruh," Dwight said. "How are things down in O-town?"

"Boring as hell," I stated.

"I can't wait for y'all to get back up here, Shawty," Dwight said.

I replied, "Hell, I can't wait, either. I feel like I've been gone forever."

"Man, Tally is so fucking dead in the summer," Dwight stated.

"I can imagine," I said, sitting down on my bed. "How is practice going?"

"It's cool," he said. "We just got the camp music the other day, so you ain't missed too much of nothing. Dr. Burton said that if y'all ain't here by Wednesday, y'all can't perform on stage for orientation."

"I'll be up there tomorrow," I said, excited. "I can't wait!"

"I bet you can't," Dwight sarcastically stated.

"What's that supposed to mean?" I asked, as I stared at my green wall.

"Nigga, don't act stupid," he said. "You know you ain't seen old boy in a few months."

"Yeah," I thought about my dude. "I can't wait to get up there for that, too."

"Yeah, whatever," Dwight said, as I could imagine him rolling his eyes. "Just hit me up when you get back in town."

"Ight," I said.

He said, "I get out of class tomorrow at noon, so I'll have the afternoon free."

"Ight, I'll hit you up," I said, as I hung up the phone.

When I got off the phone with Dwight, I started to think about my dude. I missed my man and I couldn't wait to get back up with him. Tomorrow is going to be a great day!

"ZACHIE!" my grandma yelled from the living room.

"MA'AM!" I yelled back, as I headed towards her.

"The mailman just came; go get the mail," she stated, as she continued to watch her soaps.

"Ok," I went outside.

My grandma had been doing a whole lot better health wise. That excited me because my grandma was my heart. If she left me, I don't know what I would do.

"Zach, have a seat," she said, as I came back in the house.

"What's up, Grandma?" I said, handing her the mail.

I sat down and she looked at me kinda funny. She turned off the TV and said, "Zach, I want you to be honest with me for a second."

I started to get nervous. She never turns off the TV during soap opera time unless it's lightning. I stared at her and said, "What's wrong, Grandma?"

"Nothing's wrong with me, but I want to ask you something."

"Ok," I said, trying to figure out where she was going with this conversation.

She took a deep breath and seriously said, "Is there something you wanna tell me?"

"Not that I know of," I said, looking at her like she was crazy.

"ZACHARIAH!" she sternly said. "LOOK…AT…ME!"

I stared at her and, based on the look in her eyes, I realized what she was talking about. She was referring to my sexuality.

"I'm looking at you," I said back to her, hoping my internal thoughts were wrong.

"Well, is there something you wanna say?" she asked.

"No, ma'am," I shook my head.

She said, "Well, I'm your grandmother. I raised you and I love you. Whatever we talk about will say between us. I mean that. I won't tell a soul."

"I don't have anything to say."

"Ok," she said. "Well, when *you* are ready to talk, I'm ready to listen."

"Ok, Grandma," I left the living room.

When I got in my room, I closed the door and jumped on the bed.

"FUCK," I said to myself, as I thought about what just happened. I don't do any *gay* shit around my family. I'm very masculine acting and in no way shape or form could you look at me and tell that I was gay.

*What the fuck am I doing wrong?* I took some time and I thought about everything. *As long as they don't catch me in the act, then they have no proof. It's my word against theirs.*

After a few more minutes of pondering about everything, I decided that I needed to get out of the house.

# Life of a College Bandsman 2: Is This Love

"I'll be back," I said to my grandma, as I grabbed my car keys.

"Where are you going?" she asked.

"I don't know," I said. "I just need to go for a drive."

When I got in the car, I didn't know where I was going—I just drove. Before I knew it, I had taken a forty-five-minute trip over to Daytona Beach. When I got there, I parked my car and walked on the beach.

It wasn't that many people out on the beach today, so that helped me clear my mind. Sitting out on the sand and looking at the water was relaxing. For some reason, that night when Chaz told me that Genevieve was two months pregnant with his second child continues to play in my mind. It's been nearly seven months since that conversation and I can't get that scene out of my head. As I continued to think about Chaz, my phone started to ring.

"Hello, Antonio," I answered the phone.

"Damn, this nigga calling me by my government name," Tony said laughing. "What's good, Z?"

"Nothing much," I said. "Just trying to clear my mind."

"Oh, ok, where you at?"

"Daytona."

"What you doing all the way over there?" he asked.

"I said I was clearing my mind."

"I guess, Z," he said.

"What's up with you?" I asked.

"Nothing really," he said. "Just getting ready for the baby."

"When is he due?"

"Next week."

"Oh, ok," I sighed. Both Tony and Chaz's baby were due around the same time.

"Yeah and practice starts on the first of August," he stated. "So, yeah, we're gonna be in Tally together."

I didn't respond to his statement.

After a few awkward moments of silence, Tony said, "What, you don't want me up there with you?"

I sighed, "Tony, I don't feel like getting into this with you right now."

"Yeah, yeah, whatever," he said.

In an effort to change the subject, I asked, "So, what are you gonna do about the baby?"

"What do you mean?"

"How are you gonna be a father to the boy if you ain't there."

"April is moving up to Tallahassee, too," he said in reference to his baby mama.

"Really?"

"Yeah, she has a brother who graduated from FAMU and two sisters that currently attend FAMU. She is gonna move in with her two sisters. They're getting a three-bedroom apartment."

"Oh," I said.

"Yeah, so I still get to be around my son."

"Oh, ok," I sighed, as I stared at the waves.

Tony said, "I really miss you, Zach. You've been here two months now and we really haven't spent much time together."

"Tony, I have a dude!" I snapped.

"Ok?" he said, unbothered. "What the fuck does that have to do with us?"

"I'm not cheating on my dude," I said in a matter-of-a-fact type tone.

"Why does everything gotta be about sex with you?" he said. "We're supposed to be boys."

I answered, "Because every time I get around you, it turns into some sort of sexual act. Tell me I'm lying, Tony."

He paused for a second and then said, "Well, I've changed."

"Whatever, Tony."

"I'm serious, Z," he said. "I miss our companionship."

"I gotta go," I said.

"Whatever, man," he said upset. "You always do this shit to me!"

"Tony, when I wanted you—when I wanted to be in a relationship with you, you weren't ready for that. You just wanted to fuck. You used me for sex. Now, I'm just supposed to stop living my life because you've decided that you wanna play husband? Get the fuck out of here with that bullshit!"

Upset, he yelled, "I told your ass before why I couldn't do that shit! I told you why I couldn't be in a relationship with you! Don't play me, Zach! Talking about it was just sex. I just used you for sex? Seriously? I fucking loved you and you know that. I still love you. I wanna do this. I want this relationship with you. I'm at a different place. I'm ready now, Zach!"

"It's always on your terms," I said. "People move on, Tony."

"I bet it's that fuck nigga you brought here last year, ain't it?" he said, upset.

# Life of a College Bandsman 2: Is This Love

"Who? Dwight?"

"Yeah, that tall ass muh'fucker!" he said.

"Dwight ain't down," I said in reference to the DL lifestyle. "That's just my homeboy."

"Whatever," he said. "When I get to Tally and when I meet this new nigga, he just better be worth it."

"Whatever, Tony," I said. "People move on. Besides, you're talking all this shit, but when I called you the other day, you didn't answer my phone call."

"I was in West Palm Beach," he said.

"What's down there?" I asked.

"We went to visit my mom's sister who lives down there. I wanted my cousin to come home because I hadn't seen him in a lil minute, but he was in school. His sister was home though."

"What school does he goes to?" I asked.

"Florida State," Tony said.

"Oh, ok. That's what's up. You have family in Tally, too," I said.

"Yep," he said.

"Ight, Tony, I need to get off this phone so I can start to make my way back to Orlando."

"Ight, just get at me, Z."

"Ok."

"I'm serious, Zach. Get at me!"

"Ok," I hung up the phone.

When I got back home, my grandma had finished cooking some beef stew with rice and cornbread—which was one of my favorite dishes. Once I finished eating, she spoke to me again. She said, "Don't forget what I said—when you're ready to talk, I'm ready to listen."

"Ok, Grandma," I said, as I washed my dish.

When I got back to my room, I grabbed the rest of my clothes that I would need for the week. As I was packing, I got a text that said, "Call me if you're free."

After a few rings, he answered. I smiled and said, "What's up?"

"I can't wait to see you tomorrow," my dude said.

"I know. I can't wait to see you, too. It's been months. I miss you," I said.

"I miss you, too, baby," he replied.

"Has the baby come yet?" I asked.

"Naw, but it's getting close. She went to the hospital last night with contractions, but they sent her back home."

"Oh, ok," I said.

"Are you staying with me while you're up here in Tally?" he asked.

"Well, I can tomorrow night and on Friday, but when the campers get in town, that's a no go," I said.

"Cool, I can't wait!"

"You sound excited," I said.

"I am!"

"Why?" I asked.

"For one, you're coming into town," said, my boyfriend, Eric McDaniel. "And for two, I just got off the phone with my mom."

"What did she say that got you so excited?" I asked.

"She told me that my aunt came down a few days ago and that my cousin was coming to FSU in a few weeks," Eric said.

"That's what's up," I said.

"Yep," he said. "He's trying out to be the starting quarterback on the football team."

"What?" I asked, as I realized what Eric was telling me.

"My cousin is about to be big, nigga!" he said, excited.

"Ummm?"

"What's wrong, babe?" Eric asked, calming down.

"Eric?"

"Yeah?"

"What's your cousin name?" I asked.

"Antonio," he said. "But he just goes by Tony. Tony Shaw."

# 2

# *Zach*

I couldn't get what Eric told me out of my mind. During the entire ride to Tallahassee, I was on stuck on what he revealed. "THEY ARE FUCKING COUSINS!" I told myself.

Of all the years I have known Tony, he never mentioned anything about Eric—hell, or Chaz for that fact.

*How the fuck is this possible?*

My thoughts were interrupted by my vibrating phone. When I answered it, Dwight asked, "Where you at, Big Z?"

"On I-10," I said.

"Nigga, you were supposed to be here an hour ago," he said.

"Damn, I didn't know I had a fucking bodyguard," I replied.

"Whatever, Shawty. I was just worried about you," Dwight said.

"Aww," I teased. "I didn't know you cared so much."

"Whatever, Shawty."

"Naw, but I left a lil bit late and I got stuck in some traffic along the way," I said.

"Oh, ok," he said. "How long you got before you get here?"

"About another hour."

"Ight, hit me up when you get in town, nigga."

"Ok, Dwight," I hung up the phone.

When I got off the phone with Dwight, I started to think about some of the good times that we had. I was put in an awkward situation because Eric and I are working on something real. The truth of the matter was that I really liked Dwight. Even though I had Eric, I *still* liked Dwight. We spent a lot of quality time together in the spring semester. During that period, I started to catch *real* feelings for him. I've always liked Dwight, but it was more on a lustful type of way before. Once I got past the physical and got to know Dwight personally, I really started to fall for him. He may not admit it, but somewhere deep down inside, I think he feels the same way about me—even though Dwight claims he is straight.

Before I knew it, I was safely in Tallahassee. I called my grandma first to let her know that I was in town and then I called Dwight. Once he answered, I said, "Nigga, where you at?"

"In my room."

"Nigga, where is that?"

After he told me his campus apartment name and number, I said, "Ight."

"You here in Tally?" he asked.

"Yeah, man," I said.

"Cool."

"I should be over there in like fifteen minutes. I just got off the interstate."

"Ight, hit me up when you're outside."

After I got off the phone with Dwight, I called Eric. He answered, "Hey, babe, what's up?"

"I'm just letting you know I'm in town," I said.

"Oh, ok. Are you coming by now?" he asked.

"Naw, I gotta run and do something first," I lied. *I had to see Dwight.*

"Oh," he said, bothered.

"I mean I'm coming, I just gotta do this first."

"Ight, man," he said, upset. "I just ain't seen you in months."

"I know, Eric," I sighed. "I'm gonna come right over when I'm done."

"Yeah, man," he hung up the phone.

I sighed, as I hung up the phone. I started to feel bad. Eric was the dude I was in the relationship with, but I was rushing to go to see Dwight. Hell, I even called Dwight before calling Eric. Something wasn't right with that picture.

Despite that, it felt good to be back in Tallahassee. Before I made my way over to Dwight's crib, I drove through campus, taking in the beautiful sights.

"Man, I missed this place," I told myself when I got to Dwight's apartment.

"BIG Z, MY NIGGA!" Dwight yelled, when he saw me get out

of the car.

"What's up, Dwight?" I said, as we dapped each other up.

"Damn, fool, you're bulking up some," he said, as he punched me in the chest.

"Ouch, that shit hurt," I said, as I started to laugh.

"I'm starving. You hungry, Shawty?" he asked.

"Yeah, I can eat," I said.

"Shit, let's go cop something before practice."

"Cool," I said. "Where we going?"

"It doesn't matter because you're driving," he said, as he went over to the passenger side of the car.

"I don't have that much money to spend, so it has to be something reasonable," I said.

"Nigga, you're driving," he repeated.

I stated laughing and said, "Ight, man," as we pulled off.

"This is nice, Shawty," he said, as he looked around my car.

"Yeah," I said. "I try to keep it up, but it is kinda old."

As I drove, Dwight started to tell me about this girl he was fucking. She joined the band a year before we did and she played clarinet.

"Nigga, Kiki is ugly as fuck!" I said, disgusted and disappointed at the same time.

"Yeah, but her pussy is good."

"Is Subway good?" I asked, changing the subject.

"Yeah, that'll work," he said, as he started to laugh. "You don't like me talking 'bout that, do you, Shawty?"

I looked over at him and said, "Subway it is." I parked the car.

When we got out, we saw a few other band members in there as well.

"What's up, y'all?" we said, as we entered.

"Zach, when did you got back in town?" one of my freshman brothers, Raheim Tyms, asked. He played saxophone.

"A few minutes ago," I said.

"That's what's up."

After they left, we ordered our food. We decided to eat at Subway. As I bit into my steak and cheese sub, Dwight said, "Yo, Big Z?"

"What's up?" I looked over to him.

"Do you remember when we saw Quinton and Ian here that night?"

21

I chuckled and replied, "Yeah, I do. Who would've thought that they were fucking?"

"Better yet, in a relationship," Dwight added, as he looked at me dead in my eyes.

I looked back at him, but didn't say anything. A nervous feeling overcame me. My stomach was balling up in knots.

"Are they still together?" Dwight asked, after a few seconds of silence.

"Last time I heard they were," I said, continuing my meal.

"That's good for them," Dwight said, taking a bite of his meatball sub.

"Yeah, it is," I said.

"So," Dwight said.

"What?"

"I guess I can tell you that we're in a relationship," he said.

"Who's in a relationship?" I asked concerned.

"Kiki and me," he said.

"WHAT?" I said upset, looking at him.

"Shawty, you heard me. Kiki and I are in a relationship."

"Whatever, man," I said.

"What you mad for? Don't you have a boyfriend?" he asked.

I stared at him. He was making my blood boil, turning this around on me. I swear he's always playing these fucking games. Why won't he just admit that he has feelings for me, too?

"You don't like that shit do you?" he asked. "You don't like the image of me being in a relationship, fucking bitches, do you?"

I replied, "You're a grown ass man, Dwight. You're gonna do whatever the fuck you want whether I like it or not."

"That is true," he laughed, as he took another bite of his sub.

I rolled my eyes.

*I'm ready to go see Eric!*

# 3

# Raidon Harris

*Norfolk, Virginia*

I sat in my mom's living room and exhaled. I looked over to the end table and grabbed the family portrait, from when I was teenager. Things were so different back then—well, except Ra'Jon. My older brother was always a bit *off*. After my mom's revelation to me that RJ was fathered by a different man than the rest of us—my dad's best friend—it all made sense. RJ didn't act like us because he had a different father. When my father finds out this information, hell is going to freeze over.

I looked at the rest of my siblings on that picture and smiled. Even though RJ was the oldest, everyone else always considered me, the second born, the more mature and responsible one. My next two brothers, Morgan and Micah, and my baby sister, Michelle, always sought out my expertise and advice. Nobody really fucked with RJ like that.

I placed the picture back down on the end table and sighed. I was trying everything possible to ignore the serious issue I was just presented. I wasn't trying to deal with that shit! My entire life could change if this didn't work out in my favor.

I could feel the tears trying to escape down my face, but I stopped them. I couldn't cry about this. I wouldn't cry about this.

My mom caught me off guard and walked in the living room. She looked at me and asked, "Baby, what's wrong?"

"Nothing, Mama," I said, clearing my throat.

"Boy, why are you lying to me?" she asked, standing next to me.

"I'm ok, Mama. I promise," I forced a smile.

"Yeah, whatever," she said, as she sat down next to me. "I would think that you would be excited that you got the job down at FAMU."

"I am happy, Mama. But the news that I just got was really devastating to me. I really didn't—don't—know what to do."

"I know you inside and out," my mom said, as she gripped my hand. "I know when something is wrong with my children and something is definitely wrong with you, Raidon. Now, I trusted you with my secret and I hope that you can do that same with me."

"Ma, I trust you," I said. "But I don't know why you're tripping. Everything is cool."

"If you say so, boy," she said, releasing her grip on my hand.

"But how are things with dad?" I asked.

"Nothing has changed," she said. "It's as if we are just living in a house together."

"How long has this been going on?"

She said, "A little over a year now. We haven't touched each other in over a year."

"What are you gonna do about the *other* thing," I said in reference to RJ's paternity.

"I don't know," she shrugged her shoulders. "I don't know what to do."

"Mama, this has been going on for too long and you need to do something about it. That's the only way your mind will be free," I said.

"But I'm gonna lose my family in the process," she said. "That's not something I want to risk. I was in college when I made that mistake. I was in college!"

"We're always gonna be here for you," I said. "And for how you talk about pops, he's already gone."

"Raidon!" she yelled, as tears started to roll down her face. "Don't talk like that!"

"Mom, I know it hurts, but let's be truthful here—the marriage ain't on good terms. Michelle is the last of your children in the house and she graduates high school this school year. When she goes off to college, you and pops can end this façade. I just want you to be happy and you haven't been happy in a while. The stress from this can cause serious medical issues. I don't want or need anything happening to you, Mama. You're my life. Y'all have been married a long time, but sometimes they just don't work anymore. You need

# Life of a College Bandsman 2: Is This Love

to accept that fact, Mama."

"I know, baby," she said. "But I don't wanna lose my husband. I love him but just I don't know what happened."

"I know, Mama," I said, as I consoled my mother. I really hated to see her like this.

I was startled when I saw Morgan coming down the stairs. He walked into the living room, looked at mama and then over to me. He asked, "Are you ok, Mama?"

"I'm ok, Morgan," my mom said, as she wiped the tears from her eyes.

Morgan looked to me and asked, "Raidon, what's wrong? Why is mama crying?"

"Everything's cool," I said.

"It's pops, isn't it?" Morgan said. "I know it's him!"

"Everything is ok, Morgan," she said again.

Upset, Morgan replied, "Mama, I know I don't be here much, but when I do come home from college, I can feel the tension in the house. What exactly is going on?"

"Everything is gonna be ok," she said, as she looked at him. "I just need you to focus on finishing college this school year and getting that degree."

Morgan looked at me before looking back at our mother. Unsurely, Morgan said, "Ok, but I'm just letting you know that I don't like seeing you like this."

"She's ok," I said.

"If you say so, but has anyone seen RJ?" Morgan asked.

"No," my mom said. "He left early this morning and he hasn't been back since."

"Hmm," Morgan said. "That's interesting."

"Yeah, it is," I said. "What is he up to now?"

# 4

# *Zach*

*Tallahassee, Florida*

I thought I would never say this, but it felt good to be at the band room. I missed being around my fellow band mates.

"Aww shit, Zach is in this bitch!" Omar yelled, as he saw me walk up with Dwight.

"What's going on, Omar?" I said, as we gripped each other up.

He smiled, "You know how it is—work and school."

"I feel you on that shit," I said.

"What's up, Dwight?" Omar said.

"Ain't shit, freshman bruh," Dwight said, as his phone started to ring. "I'll catch up with y'all in practice."

"Yeah," both Omar and I said.

As Dwight walked away, Omar turned to me and said, "You know he's fucking Kiki's ugly, ghetto ass."

"Yeah, he just told me," I said.

"And you're cool with that?" Omar asked.

"Shit, I don't have a choice," I said.

"Y'all just need to stop playing with each other and get this shit poppin'," Omar stated. "I don't know why y'all been playing with each other for this long. It's been a whole fucking year since y'all met."

"Nigga, you know I'm with Eric," I said.

"Yeah, whatever," Omar rolled his eyes. "Eric is there just to pass time until you and Dwight get y'all shit together."

"It ain't even like that," I said.

Omar, Jared and I became very close during the spring semester.

They always fucked with me about Dwight. Omar was very blunt with how I should get with Dwight, but Jared always brought some wisdom into the picture.

"Yeah, whatever," Omar said. "Don't wait too long or else some other faggot is gonna get what's supposed to be yours."

"It ain't even like that," I said again, as we started to walk into the band room.

I was greeted by a bunch of people. It really felt good to be an official member of the band—not a freshman anymore. Everyone treated you differently once you were official. I knew as an upperclassman, I was gonna have a shit load of fun this year. After a few minutes of talking to some people, I started to make my way over to my seat.

"My nigga," Jared said, as he came over.

"What's going, Jared," I said excited. I missed my buddy.

"Nothing much, man, just trying to get the section right for camp," he said. "I wish your ass were here in during the summer. I could have used you."

"I wish I were here, too, but I had to go home and make that money."

"I feel you on that shit," he said. "I'm working this summer, too, trying to save up for the fall, so I will be good financially."

"I know the feeling," I said. "So, you ready for this?"

"As ready as I'm gonna be," he said. "I am a lil nervous though."

"Man, you will be a good section leader," I said. "The freshmen will have someone good to model. You're nothing like Quinton's bitch ass!"

"I guess, Zach," he said.

A few minutes later, Ian came in and started the rehearsal. Ian was appointed at the band ball, by Dr. Hunter, to be the band's head drum major for the 2003-2004 school year. The band ball is the end of year event awards banquet, where the band comes together one last time. It is a formal event where the band eats dinner and the staff gives out band awards such as best marching section, best playing section, best dancing section, most improved section and best overall section. The staff also gives out individual awards such as most outstanding freshman, sophomore, junior and senior. Dr. Hunter then announces the new leaders for the upcoming year and he ends the event with the announcement of the new drum majors. Truth be told, the announcement of the new drum majors was the

# Life of a College Bandsman 2: Is This Love

main reason why a lot of people came to this event.

The night before the band ball, the new candidates for the position of drum major have an official "try-out" on the band practice field. The new candidates start "trying-out" for the drum major position a few weeks into the spring semester, but the official "try-out" is not until the night before the band ball. Chaz, the assistant head drum major from last year, along with my head drum major decided to call it quits, leaving two spots open on the nine-man drum major roster. I liked one of the new drum majors, but I really didn't care for the other one.

As Ian went through the warm-up, I noticed that he continued to look over at me. After I broke up with Chaz, I hadn't really been in much contact with Ian. I always thought Ian was a good dude, but I just didn't understand why he was looking over at me.

We spent about three hours in practice getting the camp music down for the band camp. When practice was over, Ian came over to me and said, "What's up, Zach?"

"Nothing much," I said, as I continued to put my things away.

"Cool," he said. "It's good to see you again."

"It's good to see you, too, Ian," I said. "Oh, and congrats."

"Congrats for what?" he asked.

"On being selected as the head drum major," I said. "That's a big deal."

"Thanks," he said. "I will just continue to be myself. That's all I can do."

"That's good. I don't like folks who get in high positions and then forget where they came from."

"Well, that ain't me," he said.

"That's good," I said again.

"You know Chaz talks about you a lot," he said.

"Good for him," I rolled my eyes.

"I'm serious, Zach," Ian said, as he looked around. He looked back to me and said, "That boy loves you."

"I'm sure he loves his new found family, too. When is the baby due?"

"Any day now," Ian said, overlooking my sarcastic statement.

"I'm serious, Zach. That nigga can't stop talking about how bad he fucked up and shit," Ian said.

"Well, that's something he's gotta deal with," I said. "I am through with him for good!"

Ian looked at me.

I continued, "I mean it! Tell your boy it isn't going to be no more us, so he can move on to the next gullible dude. I'm done with him. That *Genevieve is pregnant* shit was the last straw."

"Can I ask you something?" Ian said.

"Yeah."

"How did you and Eric get up?"

"It's a long story that I don't feel like talking about right now."

"You know that was fucked though," Ian said.

"What was fucked up?" I asked.

"Eric," he said. "That was Chaz's favorite person in the world. They are cousins. Chaz loved Eric, now their shit is all fucked up."

I sighed, "Chaz did that to himself. Chaz doesn't have anyone to blame for his mishaps but himself."

"You ready?" Dwight said, as he walked up, interrupting the conversation.

"Yeah," I said, as I stood up.

"What's up, Ian?" Dwight said.

"Chillin'," Ian replied.

"Ight, Ian," I said, as we walked away.

"What was that nigga talking to you about?" Dwight asked once we got in my car.

"Chaz," I said.

"I figured as much," Dwight said. He looked to me and said, "You're not going back to that nigga are you?"

"FUCK NO!"

"Shit, you need to leave his damn cousin alone, too," Dwight said, as he started to text somebody.

I didn't respond.

When we got to his crib, he turned to me and said, "You're not getting out and coming inside?"

"Naw, man. I need to go get up with Eric."

Dwight looked at me for a second and then replied with an attitude, "Whatever, man. Just get at me later then." He got out of the car and slammed the door.

"Yeah," I said, as I pulled off.

As I headed for Eric's place, I thought about the conversation with Ian and sighed. Chaz really fucked me over, but everything is

# Life of a College Bandsman 2: Is This Love

a learning process. I've learned that sometimes you have to take the good with the bad. I enjoyed the time I spent with Chaz, but after the second go around, I knew I wasn't gonna be the fool anymore. Chaz can say and do whatever he wants, but I wasn't gonna be part of that shit any more. I was over it!

*Fucking over it!*

# 5

# Zach

When I got to Eric's house, I thought about what I was gonna tell him. I mean, I knew I should have come and saw him first, but I had to see Dwight. *I had too.*

"I'm outside," I sent in a text message.

"The door is open," he replied.

It was very quiet when I entered the townhome. I don't think any one was home. I opened Eric's room door and he was lying on the bed watching TV. He looked to me and rolled his eyes.

"What?" I said smiling, as I came in the room. He had every reason to be upset with me.

"Hey," he said, as he continued to watch TV.

"What's up?" I said, as I walked over to the bed.

He looked over at me and in a nasty tone, said, "Shit, you tell me."

"What's wrong with you?" I asked.

"I thought *we* were in relationship," he said.

"We are," I replied.

"So, how is it that when you get to town, and mind you I haven't seen you since you left in April, you go somewhere else first and push me last?" he asked.

"I had to go to practice," I said.

"Zach, practice didn't start until three," he said. "You had more than enough time to come and see me before you went out with your friends. I see where I stand with you."

"Why are you acting like this?" I asked.

"Like what?" he said, pissed. "All I wanted to do was see my dude, but he wanted to see some other nigga first. Don't you think that's a fucking problem?"

"It wasn't like that," I said. "I told you I went to practice."

"Yeah, after you chilled with *that* nigga first!"

"Eric, what are you talking about?" I asked.

"Zach, you don't have to play dumb with me," he said. "I know you were with that Dwight dude."

"How do you know that?" I asked.

"I have a lot of friends," Eric said. "You don't know who I know."

"Eric, it wasn't like that," I said. "We were going to practice, but we just stopped to get something to eat, first."

"It's fine," he said. "That shit hurt my feelings though, Zach. Real talk!"

"I'm sorry, Eric," I said. "I wasn't thinking. How did you find out?"

"That's not important," Eric said. "Just forget about it and come give me a kiss."

Kissing Eric reminded me of the Eric I knew. I didn't like the person I just saw, and I hope that I won't see it again.

Eric was there for me when I ended things with Chaz. He was the person who didn't judge me. He was just a friend and that got us back on track again. We chilled for a while and then on February 20, 2003, we decided to make it official. Eric and I have been together going on five months, and believe it or not, but we have not had intercourse. We have been intimate and we have had oral sex, but when haven't gone all the way, yet.

I wanted to be with Eric in that way, but he said we should do it when the time was right. When he told me that, I was immediately drawn more into him. Eric wasn't all about sex; he was trying to develop a solid relationship built on real feelings other than just how good the sex was.

After we made out, we sat in the bed and talked about a few things. I started to think about the Tony situation again and I needed some answers fast.

"Eric?" I said.

"What's up, lil pimpin'," he said, as he looked over at me.

"You say your cousin's name is Antonio...Tony?" I asked.

"Yeah," he said.

"And he is from Orlando?" I asked.

# Life of a College Bandsman 2: Is This Love

"Yeah, he went to your high school. I know you've gotta know him," Eric said.

"Antonio 'Tony' Shaw?" I said.

"Yes, sir," he said.

"He lives down the street from my mom," I said.

"Wow," Eric said. "Small world isn't it?"

"Yeah, it is," I said. "How come you never mentioned him before?"

"I never really thought about it. I didn't have a reason to," he said. "To be honest, it never really crossed my mind."

"So, if y'all are cousins that means he is Chaz's cousin, too," I stated.

"Not exactly," Eric said, as he sat up.

"How not? Explain," I said.

Eric took a sip of water and then said, "Because Chaz's mom is my dad's sister."

"Ok," I said, still confused.

"Tony's mom is my mom's sister," Eric said.

"Ohhhhh, ok," I said. "You are the link between the two."

"Right," he said. "Tony is on one side of my family tree and Chaz is on the other side. Chaz and Tony don't even know each other."

"Ok, I got it. Your parents connect you to both of them," I said, as I started to see the image in my head. Eric's dad and Chaz's mom are siblings and Eric's mom and Tony's mom are sisters.

"Yep," he said. "I'm so excited for him though. I hope he makes it big."

"I hope so, too," I said, as I realized I just put myself in another potentially dangerous situation. How the fuck did I end up with two sets of cousins? This isn't gonna end well once Tony find's out that my boyfriend is his cousin, Eric. *What a fucking coincidence.*

We continued to watch TV until I noticed a worried look come across Eric's face. I turned to him and asked, "What's wrong, babe?"

"I'm just thinking about some stuff," he said.

"Like what?" I asked.

"Do you remember the dude that I said was my first?" Eric asked.

"Yeah, Micah's brother, Raidon," I said. "What's up with him?"

"Well, I was talking to him the other day and he told me that he was coming back into town," Eric said.

"Coming back into town for what?" I asked.

"He got a job here," Eric stated.

"Oh," I said.

"He's gonna be teaching at FAMU in the fall."

"Oh," I said again. I looked at Eric and he still had that look on his face. "Eric?"

"What's up?" he said.

"Why does that bother you?" I asked.

"It's not bothering me," he said.

"Eric, now *you're* lying," I said. "You look worried."

"I'm not worried."

"BULLSHIT!" I said. "You wouldn't look like that unless you still have feelings for him."

Eric didn't say anything.

"Eric," I said, as I looked at him.

"What?"

"Do you still have feelings for him? Are you still in love with Raidon?"

# 6

# *Eric McDaniel*

I looked at Zach as if he had lost his mind. He repeated himself, "Are you still in love with Raidon?"

"Why would you even ask me something like that," I said upset, as I got off the bed.

"Why would I ask you something like that?" Zach said, saddened. "I asked because I've been through a lot of bullshit with your fucking cousin and before I get any deeper in this shit with you, I need to know the truth! Period!"

"How many fucking times have I told you that I want you!" I pleaded. "If I wanted to be with Raidon, I would have slept with him when he came down for homecoming last fall!"

Zach just looked at me.

I continued, "Keep in mind that we—we as in me and you—weren't even together then and I didn't do it because I wanted something with you. Raidon is my past and you are my future." I took a deep breath, calmed down and said, "Zach, I know Chaz hurt you but I can promise you that I'm not my cousin." I walked towards Zach and held his hands. I said, "I won't do the things that he did to you. I promise you that. I'm a good dude, Zach and I want us to be good together."

"So, answer me this," he said.

"Anything," I replied, looking him dead in the eyes.

"Why were you looking like that?"

I answered, "Because Raidon is still my friend and he is going through a lot right now."

"What's wrong with him?" Zach asked, as I sat on the side of the bed.

"He's got a lot of personal stuff happening along with that of his family," I said, not really wanting to go in detail about Raidon's situation—both personal and family.

I think Zach got the hint because he said, "Ok," and then dropped the subject.

"You ok?" I asked.

"Yeah, I'm cool," he said.

"Ight," I said, as reached over and kissed him on cheek. "What do you want for dinner? I'm cooking!"

*****

# *Chaz McDaniel*

This couldn't be true. I couldn't believe what Ian was telling me. To make sure I wasn't tripping, I asked Ian, "What did you just say he said?"

"Zach said that he was through with your ass," Ian said, sitting on my couch. "He said that he wasn't gonna be the fucking fool anymore."

"Man, I can't believe this shit," I said to my best friend.

"Nigga, I told yo' ass a long fucking time ago that yo' shit was gonna catch up with yo' ass," Ian told me. "But you kept being stupid and look what yo' ass got now."

"I can't believe Eric did this shit to me," I said.

"Nigga, you need to drop that Eric shit," Ian said. "It's been damn near five months since that shit went down. You need to drop it."

"That was my fucking cousin," I said. "I loved that nigga!"

"And yo' ass still do," Ian said. "Y'all can't let no dude come between y'all relationship."

"Fuck that!" I said upset, as I jumped up from the couch. "Eric did that shit on purpose! He knew what was up and he still went after him! Fuck that nigga! Fuck Eric!"

Ian stared at me as I paced the room. He said, "Chaz, you need to grow up the hell up! Real talk. Grow up! Your second son is due any fucking day now and you're worried about some bullshit with

# Life of a College Bandsman 2: Is This Love

Eric and Zach? Drop it!" Ian sternly said.

"That's my fucking blood," I said. "That shit hurt worse than anything else!"

"Yeah, but think about how Zach felt during this whole thing," Ian said. "What about him?"

I sighed and said, "I'm not through with this shit. Eric's bitch ass is gonna wish he never crossed me!"

"Chaz, you're tripping," Ian told me. "That's your fucking cousin."

"Fucking cousin my ass," I said. "Cousins don't take their mates from them."

"You still don't get it do you?" Ian stated. "YOU DID THIS SHIT TO YOURSELF!"

"Whatever, man," I said.

"You need to drop this shit and take advantage of the good opportunity that you have with Genevieve."

"I know," I said. "But I just wanna get even!"

"LET IT GO!" Ian said.

"Yeah, man," I said to shut him up.

But the truth of the matter was that I wasn't done with this shit. Eric was gonna get exactly what was coming to him—exactly what was coming to him.

*Bitch ass nigga.*

# 7

# *Zach*

I was ready for camp. I had been in Tallahassee for a few days and I was back into the swing of things. Reporting time for Marching "100" members was at seven in the morning. We had to make sure that everything was in place for when the first band camper arrived.

The first half of the day was very hectic. It was a lot of running around, taking the kids all over the campus. As the day died down, I became excited because it was almost time for us do our miniature concert for the campers.

Being on that stage with other members of the Marching "100" while the campers looked on with excitement in their eyes, made me feel proud. I kept telling myself that this upcoming year was gonna be great.

When we finished the orientation for camp, the assistant band director, Dr. Burton, had all the section leaders take their band camp sections back to the band room for music rehearsal. When we got to the band room, one camper in my section just stood out to me. I knew he was gay, but he just looked scared. I was determined to make it my mission to get to know this kid before the camp was over. During music rehearsal, Omar pulled me to the side and said, "Do you see that kid?"

"Which one? It's five-hundred kids here."

"The gay one," he said.

"In our section?" I asked.

"Yeah, man," he said. "The tall light skinned one. Doesn't he just looked scared to you?"

"Yeah, he does," I said. "I had told myself earlier that I was gonna get to know the kid. Camp is supposed to be a fun experience and he has no reason to be scared."

"Yeah, I kinda feel sorry for him," Omar said.

As we continued to talk, Quinton came into the building. As soon as he walked in, I immediately got upset.

"What's wrong with you?" Omar asked.

"I really don't like that nigga," I said.

"Oh," Omar chuckled. "That bitch nigga don't faze me none."

"I'm just so happy that he ain't marching anymore. I don't know if I could have done another year with him," I said.

"He ain't that bad, Zach," Omar said, as he walked off.

During the practice, I saw Ian sitting on the balcony along with his fellow drum major, Devin. Whatever they were talking about got cut short. In the middle of their conversation, Ian answered his phone. A few seconds later he said something to Devin and he quickly left the building. He didn't come back.

When practice was over, we had to walk the kids over to the dorms. I was a dorm counselor, so I was responsible for about ten kids on my hall. I had to sleep in the dorms during camp to watch over the kids to make sure nothing happened.

Once the kids got showered, I saw the gay dude from my section again, so I made my way over to him.

"What's up," I said.

"Nothing," he said in a soft, shy tone.

"You like it here so far?" I asked.

"It's ok," he said. "I miss home."

"Where are you from?" I asked.

"A small town north of Atlanta," he said.

"Oh, ok. You sure you ok?" I asked.

"Yeah," he said. "This is just different for me."

"How so?" I asked.

"Well, the band I was in was a corps style band and we really didn't do the stuff that FAMU does."

"Oh, ok. So how did you end up here?"

"My mom said that I should come to get a feel for it," he said.

"Oh, do you plan on coming to FAMU?"

"Yeah," he said. "I just graduated and I will be here in the fall— well, next month."

"That's what's up," I said. "What's your name?"

# Life of a College Bandsman 2: Is This Love

"Keli," he replied.

"Zach," I said. "So you sure you gonna come?"

"I know I'm coming to FAMU, but I'm not too sure about the band yet," he said.

"Well, you should come," I said. "Trust me, you will fit right in."

"Trust me, I can tell," he smiled.

"Is that so?" I asked.

"Yeah," he said, "But I need to get to my room so I can get some sleep. I guess I will see you tomorrow."

"Ok, I just hope I see you next month," I said, as he walked away. *Yeah, he's definitely a gay.*

# 8

## *Chaz*

This was it. Genevieve was in that room about to give birth to my second child. I had a bunch of feelings, but I didn't know what to do with them. As soon as Ian came, I gave Xavier to him so I could go inside the room with Genevieve.

I had been in the room a few times, but the doctor said that it wasn't time yet. I stepped outside of the hospital to use my phone, but when turned it on I had a message: "I'm still shocked because I really didn't think I was gonna hear from you again. But I've thought about what you said, and if you really want me to go along, then I'm down for it. You just make sure you're one-hundred percent sure you're gonna do this before you get me involved in this shit. Call me back later."

When I hung up the phone, I didn't notice Ian standing behind me, holding my first-born, Xavier.

"Who was that?" Ian asked.

"Umm, nobody important," I replied.

Ian looked at me and said, "I just hope you ain't up to no crazy shit."

"I'm good, best friend," I said, as I reached down and kissed Xavier.

Xavier just smiled when I kissed him. I love my son with every breath in my body. When I got back in the hospital, I went straight to Genevieve's room.

"You ok?" she asked.

"I should be asking you that, Mommy," I said, as I kissed her.

"I'm just so happy that we're gonna be a family," she said. "I'm happy that you've changed and decided to do the right thing. This is what's best, Chaz."

"This is my family; y'all are my family," I said, as I touched her stomach.

"Oh, Chaz, I love you, sooo—AWWWWW SHIT!" she yelled.

"What's wrong baby?" I asked, as the nurse that was in the room rushed over to Genevieve.

"HE'S COMING," Genevieve yelled, as she gripped my hand.

"Fuck," I said to myself. That shit hurts.

The nurse called in the rest of the medical team. I stood by Genevieve as the doctor guided her to push. It was so intense in the room. I know I couldn't be a woman, because I could only imagine what that shit feels like.

She cried and yelled, as she continued to push.

"Just a little bit more," the doctor said. "Just a little bit more."

"C'mon, baby," I said. "He's almost here."

Genevieve continued to push our son out of her womb.

"I can see the head," the doctor said. "Give me one more big push!"

"AWWWWWWWWWWWW," Genevieve yelled, as I heard my son crying.

I immediately started to smile when I saw my son. The doctor allowed me to cut the umbilical cord. After they cleaned my son up, the nurses gave him to Genevieve. She held him close to her heart as he cried.

"This is our son," she said thrilled, as she looked up to me.

A few minutes later, Ian and Xavier came into the room to see the new baby.

"Congrats, y'all," Ian said, as he started to smile.

"That's your little brother," he said to Xavier, as he pointed at the baby. Ian looked to us and said, "So, what did y'all name lil man?"

"Well, since we named Xavier after Chaz, we thought that it would be nice to name this one after me," Genevieve stated.

"I hope y'all didn't name the boy Genevieve Elaine Nichols," Ian said laughing, as he recited Genevieve's full name.

"No, dummy," she said, as she started to laugh.

"It was kinda hard, but we came up with something," I said.

"Yeah, it was hard," Genevieve said. "We really couldn't find anything that would work since he was a boy."

"Enough with the explanations," Ian playfully said. "What's my godson's name?"

"Elijah Gene McDaniel," I said.

"Xavier and Elijah," Ian said as he looked at us. "That's cute."

\*\*\*\*\*

# *Raidon*

*Norfolk, Virginia*

My mind has been going in circles the last few days. After I received that news, I didn't know what to do. I confided in Eric and hoped before God that he doesn't tell anyone. Nothing was for certain yet, but I hope that everything works out for me.

I was supposed to be happy. I was recently offered the job that I wanted at FAMU. I was living the good life, but now this? *God, please let it work out in my favor!*

I decided to get out of the house and get something to eat.

"I can use the fresh air and the drive," I told myself, as I grabbed my keys.

I turned on the radio when I got in the car, but nothing wasn't playing that I wanted to hear. I turned the radio off and let my window down. I was just gonna enjoy the sound of the night.

I had the hardest time trying to figure out what I wanted to eat, but when I passed the Rib Shack, I knew that is what I wanted. I turned into the next shopping plaza so I could turn around and go back to get the ribs.

When I got to the Rib Shack, I turned my car off. As I was getting ready to get out, I saw my pops through the window. He was sitting at a table by himself.

"What is he doing here?" I asked myself, as I got ready to go in the place and eat with him. But as soon as I said that, someone joined him.

"Who the fuck is that?" I asked myself, as I looked at my pops dine with this person.

I stayed in the car, because I didn't want him to see me. After about ten minutes, they got up and left. My pops walked right past my car and didn't even see me. When they left, I went inside and ordered my food.

"Who the fuck was that?" I asked myself again, as I drove home.

When I got back to my place, I fixed a glass of sweet tea before putting the old school movie, Juice, into the DVD player. I needed to relax and that is what I intended to do. I hated plastic utensils, so I grabbed some real ones from my cabinet.

I started to get comfortable, as I ate my ribs, baked beans, and macaroni and cheese, while watching the movie. About half an hour into the movie, my phone started to ring.

When I looked at the phone to see who was calling, I thought about not answering it, but I knew I had to face the truth at some point or another. I took a deep breath, sighed and answered, "Hello?"

"Umm," he said.

"What is it?" I asked. "What happened?"

"You need to go ASAP," he replied.

"DON'T TELL ME THIS SHIT!" I yelled. "DON'T FUCKING SAY THAT SHIT!"

"You need to go ASAP," he said again.

"Do you?" I asked, as I feared the worst.

"Yeah," he said. "I do."

# 9

# *Zach*

Camp week was tough. When I was a band camper, I knew it was hard on me, but I now think its twice as hard on the Marching '100' members who help out with the camp. I was beyond tired. Today was the last day of camp and I couldn't wait to get these kids out of here.

I hadn't really had much contact with Eric since the week-long camp was an all-day affair. I told him that I was gonna spend the next few days with him before I went back home to Orlando.

In the midst of the week of camp, I really kept talking to Keli. It was something about him that I liked. Quinton bothered him the entire week of camp, and I knew it had to do with Keli's sexuality. That shit really disturbed me being that Quinton was gay, too. That was the main reason why Quinton and I got into that altercation last season. He always had something to say about gays, when I bet Ian was the one fucking him.

I knew that Quinton was getting to Keli, so I took the time to try and be nice to Keli and show him that there are nice people in the band as well. I don't know why, but I wanted this little kid to be part of the band and part of my section next year.

As the kids did their final performance, I looked over at Keli. I could see that he has so much potential. I really hope the dude comes back next month for pre-drill.

When the camp was over, everyone in the section went over to say the last good-byes to the campers. When I got to Keli, he spoke first. He said, "I'm coming. You don't have to ask me again."

I started to laugh and said, "I hope so."

"I am," he said, as he gave me a hug. "Thank you."

"For what?" I asked.

"For being yourself," he said, as he looked at me. "I really appreciate that."

"That's all I can be," I said, as Omar and Dwight made their way over to us.

"So, are we gonna see you next month?" Dwight asked Keli.

"Yeah," Keli said. "I will be here."

"Good," Omar said. "This season is gonna be great."

"Ight, y'all," Keli said. "My parents are waiting."

"Be safe, man," I said, as Keli walked away.

A few moments later when Keli was out of our vicinity, Omar said, "He's cute. Tall, very light-skinned. Even though his hair was braided up, I can tell it's long and beautiful. His skin is flawless. He had beautiful teeth. Nice slim, lean body with a phatty."

"Damn, are you trying to get with him?" I asked.

Omar replied, "He's a bit too fem for my liking, but I'm sure he'll make some top very happy."

Dwight laughed, "That Keli is sooo fucking gay!"

"Yeah, just like everybody else in this damn band," Omar said, as he walked away.

"NOT ME!" Dwight yelled to Omar.

"WHATEVER!" Omar yelled back, as he continued to walk away.

"I ain't gay, Shawty," Dwight said to me.

"I know Dwight, I know," I rolled my eyes. "You've told me that a thousand times."

"Well, shit, I'm not," he said. "I just need to put that out there."

"Ok," I said, as we left the stadium.

As we walked away, I saw Chaz.

"There goes lover boy," Dwight said, as we approached Chaz.

"I see," I said, as I looked at Chaz.

When Chaz saw me, he just stared at me. I hadn't seen Chaz since March. I must say he still looks damn good though. *Damn.*

"Yo," Chaz said, as we walked past him.

"What?" I snapped.

"You not gonna speak?" he asked.

I looked over at Dwight and he was heated. I could see it all over his face.

"Hi, Chaz," I sarcastically said, as I started to walk away.

# Life of a College Bandsman 2: Is This Love

"HOLD UP!" Chaz said, as he ran over to us.

"What?" I stopped walking. Dwight gave me an evil look.

"Can I holla at you?" Chaz asked.

"Big Z is cool," Dwight interjected.

"I didn't ask you," Chaz said to Dwight.

"Yeah, but I'm telling you!" Dwight said with authority, as he stepped closer to Chaz.

"You better get yo' boy," Chaz said pissed, as he looked at me. "Now is not the time or place, especially in front of these kids and their parents."

"What do you want?" I asked Chaz. "I've got shit to do."

"Man, just forget about it," Chaz said upset.

"Ight," I said, as I turned to Dwight. "Let's go!"

"I don't like that bitch ass nigga," Dwight said. "He's gonna make me have to hurt him."

"It ain't that serious. Just let that nigga be."

"I'm hungry," Dwight said.

"Me, too," I said, as we got to his car.

"What you want?" he said. "It's on me."

"Shit, let's hit up CiCi's Pizza," I said.

"Cool."

On the ride over to CiCi's, Dwight's phone started to ring, but he didn't answer it.

"Why didn't you answer the phone?" I asked. "You don't want me to hear who you're talking to?"

"No," he said. "I just didn't feel like talking to her ass."

"Who?"

"Kiki."

"Isn't that supposed to be your girlfriend?" I asked.

"Yeah, but I just don't feel like talking to her right now."

"I guess, Dwight," I said, as I listened to the radio.

When we got to CiCi's, we weren't the only Marching '100' members there.

"I guess us '100' members all think alike, huh?" Dwight said, as we walked in.

"I guess so," I said, as we saw Omar and Jared and we made our way over to them. I looked at Jared and said, "You did a good job this week. You should be proud."

"Thanks," Jared said. "I guess that kinda helped me prepare for pre-drill."

"Yeah, I told him he would be fine," Omar said.

"Has anyone talked to Kris?" Dwight asked the table.

"Yeah, I talked to him a few days ago," Omar said. "He wanted to come to the camp, but had some family issues going on."

"That sucks," I added.

Jared caught the table off guard when he turned to Dwight and asked, "Why are you fucking Kiki?"

"Because the pussy's good," Dwight rolled his eyes.

"Yeah, but she's ugly as hell," Jared said. "It's a few people—well one in particular that I know is in love with yo' ass and they look a whole lot better than Kiki."

"Is that so?" Dwight said, as he looked at me.

Omar started to smile.

"Yeah, it is," Jared said.

"Well, who is it?" Dwight asked.

"Hmmm," Jared said. "I think you already know."

"Probably do," Dwight said. He glanced at me before he resumed eating his pizza.

In the midst of the conversation, Eric called me. After I answered, he said, "What's up, lil pimpin'?"

"Nothing much, just out eating," I said.

"Where?"

"At CiCi's with some members of the section," I said.

"Oh, ok," he said. "That's what's up. Are you still coming by the house?"

"Yeah, I'll be there later," I said.

"Cool," he said. "I just found out that Chaz had the baby."

"When?" I asked.

"Last Saturday," he said. "My brother told me."

"That's what's up."

"Yeah, but get at me before you come," Eric said.

"Ight," I said, as I hung up the phone. When I turned my attention back to the table, Jared was just shaking his head. "What nigga?" I said.

"I don't know why you're doing that shit," he said.

"What?" I asked.

"You know where you're supposed to be," Jared said.

"Umm, hmm," Omar added.

"Where is he supposed to be?" Dwight asked.

"You tell me," Jared said, looking at Dwight.

# Life of a College Bandsman 2: Is This Love

"Shit, I don't know, that's why I'm asking y'all," Dwight said, shrugging his shoulders.

"Nigga, you ain't stupid," Jared said, as he left the table to get some more pizza.

I sighed. *This shit was awkward.*

# 10

## Chaz

I walked into Ian's place and said, "Eric is turning him against me!"

"I thought I told you to drop this shit," Ian said, as I sat down at the breakfast bar.

"I am dropping it," I said. "But after today, I know he is brainwashing Zach."

"No," Ian said. "That boy is just growing the fuck up."

"Whatever," I said. "I know my cousin and Eric ain't everything he claims to be."

"Even if that shit is true, that's Zach's problem to deal with, not yours."

"I guess, Ian," I said, as I looked around his kitchen. "Nigga, you got something to eat?"

"Yeah, it's some chicken pot pie in the fridge," Ian said.

I opened the refrigerator, looked at the food and asked in disgust, "How old is this shit?"

"FUCK YOU," he said. "I just made that shit a few days ago."

"I'ma be back," I said, as I closed the refrigerator.

"Where you going?" he asked, as I headed for the front door.

"To get me something safe to eat," I said, as I left.

I couldn't keep my mind off Zach. I really wanted to be with that dude, and Eric fucked it up for me.

"Now, I'ma have to fuck him up," I said, as I picked up my phone. Within a few rings, Ra'Jon answered.

"What's up, man?" I said.

"Nothing really," RJ stated.

"So, you still down for it?" I asked.

"Yeah," he said. "I hate that lil bitch ass nigga and I will do anything to get my revenge on his ass."

"GREAT!" I smiled.

"I thought you liked the lil boy though," RJ said.

"I do like him."

"So, why are you doing this?" he asked.

"I'm not doing anything to Zach," I said. "It's my cousin that I wanna get."

"Yeah, but I will have great fun taking out the little bitch in the process," he said.

"I guess, Ra'Jon," I said, as I pulled up to Wendy's. "Hold on."

After I placed my order, RJ said, "That's still your favorite thing to eat from Wendy's, huh? A number two with no tomatoes, no onions and a fruit punch for the drink."

"Yeah, it is," I said.

"So?" Ra'Jon said.

"So, what?" I asked.

"What do I get out of this shit?" he said. "How am I supposed to trust your ass?"

"You can get whatever you want," I said, as I put a French fry in my mouth.

"Even you?" he asked.

"I'm not having sex with you," I stated.

"Well, I don't know," Ra'Jon said.

"Ight," I said. "Forget about the whole thing then."

"NO!" Ra'Jon yelled. "We'll just work out the details later."

"Ight," I said, as I got back to Ian's house.

"How's Genevieve?" Ra'Jon asked.

"She's good," I said. "She's at home with Xavier and Elijah."

"Oh, ok," he said. "I miss her."

"I guess," I said. "Well, I need to get off the phone."

"Ok," he said. "Call me later."

"Yeah," I rolled my eyes, as I made my way into Ian's crib.

*****

# Life of a College Bandsman 2: Is This Love

# Morgan Harris

*Norfolk, Virginia*

I stood outside RJ's door and eavesdropped on the tail end of his conversation. As he hung up the phone, I walked into his room and asked, "Who the fuck are you talking to?"

"None of your fucking business," he said, placing the phone on the charger.

"I'ma tell Raidon that your ass ain't up to no good," I said.

"What the fuck is he supposed to do to me?" RJ asked, looking at me as if I had lost my mind.

"You need to grow up, man," I said. "That's why your old ass is back at home in mama's house because you act to fucking stupid."

"You better watch how you talk to me," RJ said.

"Nigga, fuck you!" I said. "I swear something ain't right about you."

"If something ain't right about me, then something ain't right about you," RJ said. "All five of us—Me, Raidon, you, Micah and Michelle—all come from the same two people."

"Well, Raidon, me, Micah and Michelle do, but I don't know about you," I said. "You must be adopted or some shit because you don't act like the rest of us."

"FUCK YOU!" RJ said. "I'm the oldest in this family!"

"You may be the oldest, but you ain't one of us," I said, as I walked out the room.

"What's wrong with y'all?" Michelle asked, as she came out of her room.

"Nothing, baby sis," I said. "I was just telling RJ how very different he is."

"Oh, I guess," she said. "When are you going back to Tallahassee?"

"In a few days. Why?" I said, as I looked at my sister. She was definitely a head turner, almost resembling actress Nia Long.

"Because I wanna come a long for a lil bit," she said. "Micah said that he would bring me back up before school starts."

"I don't know, Michelle," I said, as I thought about my boyfriend, Devin. If she comes down, then she is gonna find out about my sexuality.

"Why not?" she said with sassiness in her voice. She placed her hands on the hips, rolled her neck and said, "You got something to hide?"

"No," I said. "It's just who's gonna watch after you?"

"I can watch myself," she said. "I'm seventeen!"

"Yeah, but you'll be in a place that you know nothing about," I said.

"You're stalling," she said. "What's the real reason why you don't want me to come?"

"No, I'm not stalling," I said. "I mean both Micah and I are working and you know Micah is in summer school. How are you gonna get around? We both need our cars. What are you gonna do all day?"

"Micah already told me that I can use his car as long as I take him to work and pick him up from work," she said.

"Who are you gonna stay with?" I asked. "Micah lives on campus and you can't stay with him."

"I can stay with you—unless you don't want me there with you," she said in a knowing tone.

"It's not that," I said.

"So, back to my original question—what are you hiding, Morgan? What don't you want me to know?"

"I ain't hiding nothing," I said.

"Why don't you have a girlfriend?" she asked.

"WHAT?" I said.

"Where is your girlfriend? Someone who looks like you have to have plenty of girls on yo' lil dick! Where are they at?"

"My dick ain't small," I said.

"Where...are...the girls?" she said.

I looked at her.

"Oops...I guess it ain't none," she said, as she went back into her room.

# 11

## *Zach*

I had a few more days in Tallahassee and I wanted to make the best out of it with Eric. When I got to his house, we sat and watched TV for a bit, talking about random things. The more we talked, the more Eric started to look like something was bothering him again. I thought about not asking him about it, but I wanted to see what it was.

"What's wrong, Eric?"

"What'cha mean, lil pimpin'?" he looked over to me.

"You've got that look on your face again. I know something is wrong."

"You know me, don't you," he said, as he smiled.

I smiled back, "I hope so. But stop trying to change the subject. What's wrong with you?"

"I was just thinking," he said.

"About what?"

"Honestly?" he looked to me with worried eyes.

"Yeah, I wanna know what it is," I said.

"It's Chaz," he admitted.

"Oh," I sighed.

He said, "Yeah. I started to think about Chaz a lot after talking to my brother today."

"What exactly are you thinking about?" I asked.

"I mean, that was my road dawg," Eric said. "I really miss being around him. That's my cousin, man."

I didn't reply.

He continued, "Ever since that shit went down, things haven't been the same."

"Yeah, I know," I said, as I thought back to what happened that night in January. Chaz found out about my involvement with Eric and the cousins got into a huge fist fight. They both were in pretty bad condition for a few days.

"I wish things can go back to being the same," Eric said. "I miss my cousin."

"I'm sorry," I said. I started to feel bad because I felt like I was the main reason for that night.

"It ain't yo' fault," Eric said. "You have no reason to feel bad. No reason at all!"

"If it wasn't for me then it would've never happened," I said.

"No, Chaz did that shit to himself," Eric said.

"I guess, Eric," I shrugged my shoulders, giving up.

"I missed the birth of the baby," Eric said. "I had to hear about that shit from my fucking brother."

"I know," I added. "What did they have?"

"A lil boy," Eric said, as he stared at the wall. "They named him Elijah."

"That's a nice name," I said.

"Yeah," he sighed.

Eric didn't say anything else for a few minutes. I didn't say anything either. I just wanted him to gather his thoughts. That night in January did change everything; I only hope they can go back to being close again.

"IGHT, enough about Chaz," Eric said, as he came over and kissed me. "Let's focus on us!"

I smiled and said, "I'm down for that!"

*****

# *Raidon*

*Norfolk, Virginia*

I was still bothered by the recent news that I had received. I knew what I had to do, but I was scared to do it for the obvious reasons. My mom continued to ask me what was up all week. It's hard lying to her, but I couldn't let her know what the real deal was.

# Life of a College Bandsman 2: Is This Love

I walked around my house, packing some things up for my move to Tallahassee next month. I was excited about that, but I couldn't focus on that because I had to deal with this situation first.

"Who is it?" I yelled, as I heard someone knock on the door.

"It's me," he said.

I took a deep breath and exhaled before opening the door. When I let him inside, I said, "What's up?"

"Nothing much," he said, as he made his way into the living room and sat down on the green sofa.

"You ok?" I asked.

"I'm managing," he said. "I mean it ain't shit else I can do."

I didn't say anything; I just looked at him.

"Have you went yet?" he asked.

"No," I said. "I'm not ready."

"Just go and get it over with," he said. "You will feel much better once it's over. Trust me."

"Hell, that's that problem," I rolled my eyes.

"What's that?" he asked.

"I FUCKING TRUSTED YOU!" I raised my voice.

As I continued to pack my things, he just sat there on the couch without saying anything.

I looked to him and said, "You can talk. It ain't the end of the world."

"I don't know what to do," he said.

I didn't want to dwell on this shit anymore, so in an effort to change the subject, I asked, "So, when are you going back?"

"Back where?" he asked.

"To school."

"The first of August," he said. "The new band freshmen arrive for pre-drill during that time."

"Oh, ok," I said. "What made you go there?"

"My folks," he said. "My mom went there."

"Oh," I said. "Kinda like my brothers, and hopefully my sister, going to FAMU."

"Yeah, just like that," he said. "It's a shame Norfolk State is right here and we go everywhere else but there."

"Yeah, it is," I said. "I wouldn't trade in my FAMU experience for the world."

"I wouldn't trade in my Aggie experience for the world, either," he said.

"What about your dad?"

He stared at me with evil in his eyes, deepened his voice and said, "What about that fuck nigga?"

I cautiously asked, "Is he an Aggie, too? Is he up here in Virginia?"

"That fuck nigga lives in Orlando with his new family. He's a pastor down there. I can't fucking stand that nigga. Fuck him!"

Seeing that mentioning his father was a sore spot for him, I changed the subject and asked, "So, was that your first trip down to Tallahassee when y'all band went last year?"

"Yep," he said. "I met some dude from FAMU's band when I was down there."

"Really?"

"Yeah, but thankfully nothing happened," he said.

"Yeah, that was God!" I said.

"Yeah," he said. "He was a young kid, a freshman."

"I thought you didn't like young kids?"

"I don't, but he was cute. I couldn't resist."

"So, why didn't it go down?" I asked.

"He got a call and he had to go ASAP. It was something with his section. He was a freshman, so he was probably about to get his ass beat."

"Oh, ok," I said.

"But I guess everything happens for a reason, huh," he said.

"Yeah, I guess so," I said.

"Ight, man, I just came by for a second. I gotta get back to my mom," he said.

"Ight," I said, as I walked him to the door.

"Make sure you go," he said, as he looked me in the eyes.

"I'm going, Phil," I said. "I'ma go next week."

"Ok," Phil said, as he left my house.

"I hope everything works out for me," I said, as I looked at Phillip Butler, Jr. drive away with his North Carolina A&T State University Aggies license plate on the back of his black Chevy Malibu.

# 12

## Zach

*Orlando, Florida*

I rolled my eyes. All I wanted to do was sleep, but I heard my grandmother yelling, "Get up! We've got somewhere to be!" *Oh, God.*

She continued with a raised voice, "Zachariah, if I have to come in that room, I know something!"

"I'm up, Grandma!" I yelled, as I sat up in the bed. *Damn.*

I looked over at the clock. It was 7:30 in the morning. *Where the fuck are we going so early in the damn morning?*

"I can't wait to get back to Tally so I can do what I," I said to myself as I went to the bathroom.

While in the bathroom, I thought about my time up in Tally. I really enjoyed myself and I couldn't wait to get back there next month. I started to smile as I thought about Dwight and Eric. "I really miss them," I told myself, as I exited the bathroom.

"Can you put some pep in that step?" my grandma said as I walked out. "I didn't tell you to stay up in Tallahassee so long!"

I loved my grandmother—I really do—but she was really irking my last nerve right now.

I stepped outside to see what the weather was like. "How in the hell is it this fucking hot this damn early in the morning?" I asked myself, as I walked back in the house. I had to find something to put on.

I wasn't really sure where we were going, so I just threw on a plain white t-shirt and my blue *And-1* basketball shorts.

"You ready?" I asked, as I walked in the living room.

"Yes," she said.

"Where are we going?" I asked, walking out of the house.

"You forgot?" my grandma asked.

"Yes, ma'am."

"I have to go to the doctor. I have an appointment at nine," she said.

"Ohhhhh," I said, as I remembered that she told me that before I left to go to Tallahassee.

"Why did you stay up there so long?" she asked me. "I thought you were supposed to be back a few days ago."

"I was, but I just wasn't ready to leave."

"Umm, hmm," she said. "Who was it?"

"Who was who?" I asked.

"I ain't stupid, boy," she said, sitting down in my car. "I know it was somebody that caused you to stay up there."

"I was just having fun," I replied, backing out of the driveway.

"I thought you had to work?" she asked.

"I did, but I switched with this girl so I'ma work the weekend for her."

"Oh, ok," she said. "So, you ready to talk yet?"

I looked at her and replied, "I don't have anything to say."

"Oh, ok," she stated. "Just know when you are ready to talk, I'm ready to listen."

"I don't have anything to say," I repeated.

"Ok."

When we got to the doctor's office, I sat down and watched CNN. They were talking about our troops being sent over to Iraq. I hated going to the doctor's office. Hell, I hated anything related to the medical field. I honestly didn't see how people could work in hospitals and shit. The smell of it just makes me sick. After a few minutes of sitting in the main lobby, the nurse called for my grandmother.

"I'll be back," she said.

When she left, I stepped outside.

"Damn, it's fucking hot!" I said, as I grabbed my phone and sent Eric a text saying, "I miss you."

He sent back, "I miss you too, lil pimpin…I'm in class…I'll call you when I get out."

I walked around the corner and had a seat on one of the benches at the adjacent hospital. A few minutes later, a doctor came out talking with a patient.

"You make sure to follow those instructions very carefully," the doctor said.

"Ok, I will do," the patient said, as he looked at the prescription form. He looked to the doctor and said, "I have one more question though."

I stared at the young brother. *Damn, he looks familiar.*

The young brother was a tad over six feet tall. He had a nice caramel skin tone followed by nice, neat, shoulder length dreads. His muscles were coming hard through his shirt. His eyes were very sexy with that hazel color. He had huge hands and huge feet.

"Whoever he is with is a lucky person," I said to myself, as I admired the young brother; he couldn't be any more than twenty-five or twenty-six years old. His voice was very deep and that added to his sexiness.

I was brought out of my trance when I felt my phone vibrating. I answered, "Hello?"

"What's up, lil pimpin'?" Eric said.

"Nothing really," I said. "Just out with my grandma."

"Oh, ok, that's what's up."

"Yeah, so what you up to?" I asked.

"Just got out of class. My other class was canceled, so I'ma just chill at home."

"That's what's up. I wish I was up there with you," I said.

"I wish you were here, too," Eric replied.

"I can't wait to get back," I said, as I started to make my way back into the office.

"You know I've been thinking," Eric said.

"About what?"

"About the Chaz thing," he said.

"What about it?" I asked.

"I think I'ma be the better man and try to work things out with him," he said.

"Wow, that's noble of you," I said, shocked.

He said, "Yeah, somebody has to do it. This shit has gone on for too long."

"Well, I support you in anything that you decide to do," I said.

"Thanks, babe," he said.

"Let me get back at you," I said. "I'm going back to my grandma now."

"Ok, get at me," he said, as he hung up the phone.

"Perfect timing," I said, as I got back upstairs. My grandma was walking out as I walked in.

"Everything ok?" I asked once we got back in the car.

"Yep," she said verbally, but her body language was saying something else.

"Grandma, what's wrong?"

"Oh, boy," she said. "It ain't nothing wrong. Y'all worry too much."

I knew my grandmother and she never liked to tell us the truth about her health. I just really hoped that everything was ok—even though, deep down, I didn't believe it.

# 13

## *Raidon*

*Norfolk, Virginia*

Today was the day—the day of truth. I tried to stay in the bed for as long as I could. I didn't want to face the truth.

"Ight, Raidon," I said to myself. "Just go and get it over with."

As I started to get myself together, I thought about everything. My life flashed before me. I could see everything—all my partners, all my sexual adventures.

"God, please let the results come back negative," I said, as I ran some bath water. "I need to relax myself before I go up there."

I drew blood for the HIV test a few days ago. Yesterday, I got a call from the doctor's office that my results had come back.

I sat in the bathtub and thought about how all this happened. I met Phil a long ass time ago. Phil was one of my regular sex buddies. We first met at a sex party back up in Richmond, a few years ago. That was my first time attending one of those things, and to be honest, I really enjoyed myself. The dudes that were there were fine as fuck. It was a fantasy come true.

When I first got there, I was shy, but after a while of watching dudes go at it, this dude, whom later became known as Phil, approached me. We kicked it there for that night and that was that. A few days later, I saw Phil at Walmart back in Norfolk, and that's when we really started kicking it. That's when I learned that he attended North Carolina A&T State University in Greensboro.

As the years passed, Phil and I became really good friends, despite the random sex that we had with each other. When I moved back to Norfolk after leaving Tallahassee, we really started kicking with each other. I would drive out to Greensboro, NC to see him some weekends and he would come back to Norfolk to see me. We were never in a relationship, but we just had an understanding that we were gonna be exclusive to each other.

Well, one night a while ago, we were at my house and got pissy drunk. We were fucked up and ended up having sex with each other. When I woke up the next morning, I realized that we didn't use any condoms. As time went on, we stopped using protection all together. Deep down in my mind, I knew that it was wrong, but what was the chance that I would become infected with the bug?

Phil called me two weeks ago to tell me that I needed to go to the clinic.

"Why?" I asked.

"Cause you just do," he said.

"What's wrong?" I said.

"Look, I just got a call!" he said.

"A call from who?" I asked.

"The clinic," he said. "Somebody that I slept with just found out that they were infected."

"What are you saying?" I said, as I got upset.

"They told me that I needed to come down to get tested to be on the safe side," he said.

"So, you're telling me that I might have that shit!" I yelled, upset.

"We don't know yet," he said. "I'm about to go down and get tested in a lil bit."

"Phil, I thought you weren't sleeping with anyone but me," I said. He didn't say anything.

"ALL THAT TIME WE WERE HAVING UNPROTECTED SEX AND YOU WERE SLEEPING WITH SOMEONE ELSE?"

"No," he said. "I didn't intend on it happening. It just happened a few times, but I cut it off."

"Phil, I trusted you!" I yelled.

"Look, I ain't trying to argue with you," he said. "I'm just trying to give you a heads up."

"I guess," I said.

"Go get tested!"

"Yeah," I said, as I hung up the phone.

# 14

## *Eric*

I was really falling for Zach and I'm sad that my relationship with my cousin had to suffer because of that. I really wanted to make things better. After that night in January, nothing has been the same.

I took a deep breath. I wanted to call Chaz, but I didn't have the guts to do it. I honestly don't know if I'm in the wrong, or if Chaz is in the wrong. I understand that Zach was Chaz's dude first and I guess I did kinda take Zach from him. But, on the other hand, Chaz ran Zach away with all his infidelities. Maybe the way Zach and I went about things was wrong, but I couldn't let Chaz know that I liked dudes. No one can know about my sexuality! My mom and brother would kill me if they found out. At least I know Chaz ain't gonna say shit because if he does, he would be outing himself in the process. I know that's something he isn't willing to do.

"Who is this?" I said, as I reached for my ringing phone. When I saw the name, I answered, "What's up, boy?"

"Nothing much," Raidon said.

"What you up to?"

"About to go over my parent's home."

"That's what's up," I said. "Did you go to the clinic yet?"

"Yeah," he said.

"Well?"

"I don't have the results yet. I'm gonna go get them later today."

"Good luck, man," I said.

"Thanks, Eric. I really appreciate it." He took a breath and said, "You know you are the only person that knows this."

"Really?" I said, shocked.

"Yeah, man," he said. "I really trust you."

"Thanks, Raidon," I said. "I'm sorry about that though."

"Did you go get tested?" he asked. "I mean I know we used protection, but you can never be too sure."

"Yeah, I did," I said. "I went the day after you told me."

"What happened?"

"I'm negative," I said.

"Oh, ok, that's good," he said. "You know I was thinking—"

"About what," I cut him off.

"That night back in October."

"You're talking about around homecoming when you came down?" I asked.

"Yeah, God works in strange ways, huh," he said.

"Why you say that?" I asked.

"Because had you slept with me, you might be in the same situation that I'm in," he said.

"Raidon, stop talking like that! You don't know the results, yet. Stop trying to give yourself that shit!"

"I'm just saying," he said.

I didn't say anything.

"You must really like that dude," he said.

"Yeah, I do," I said. "I really do."

"He may not know it, but he's got a good dude," Raidon said. "I wish I still had you."

"You wild, man," I chuckled.

"I know you're moving on with dude and I wish y'all all the luck," he said.

"Thanks, Raidon. I really appreciate that."

"What's his name?"

"Zach," I replied, as I heard a beep, alerting me I had another call coming through. I looked at the name and said to Raidon, "Yo, let me call you back. My brother is on the other line."

"Ight, do that," he said, ending the call.

I flipped over to my brother and said, "Hello?"

"What's up, lil bro," my older brother said. "You called?"

"Yeah, I called. I just got out of class not too long ago. I was just trying to see what's up with you."

"Man, keep doing what you're doing, Eric," he said.

"Blackwell, what are you talking about?" I asked my brother.

# Life of a College Bandsman 2: Is This Love

"You, nigga," Black said. "I'm real proud of you. You're doing the damn thing."

"Thanks, Black," I said. "I'm trying to make everyone proud."

"Don't do it for us," Blackwell stated. "Do it for you."

"Black?"

"What's up?" he said.

"Man, forget it," I said.

"What's bothering you, lil bro?" Blackwell asked.

"When did you get out of the hospital?" I asked.

"This morning," he said. "The doctor gave me some stuff to ease the pain."

"Are you sure you're ok?" I asked.

"Yeah, man," he said. "No need to worry. It's just some headaches."

"When did you go in?" I asked.

"I went to the ER last night," he said.

"Oh, ok, are you sure you're ok?"

"Yeah, man," he said. "How did you find out?"

"Mom called and told me."

"Oh," he said. "I'm good, though."

"Ight, Black, I'ma get at you later because I wanna take a quick nap."

"Ight, lil bro," Blackwell said. "I love you."

"I love you, too, Black," I said, as I hung up the phone.

I really loved my brother. Blackwell was twenty-three and he was really protective of me. He hated being called Blackwell, so everyone just called him Black, even though there was nothing *black* about him. That nigga was so light skinned, he could pass for white. *Not really, but he was very light skinned.* Black really loves me and my baby sister, and I believe that he would kill for us.

When I got in the bed, I started to think about Raidon again. When Zach asked me was I still in love with Raidon, that shit really hurt my feelings. Raidon and I were cool like that once, but that time has passed. Raidon and I are good friends, but that's all we'll be. Zach is who I want. I really do hope that everything works out for Raidon though. I would hate to be in his situation.

# 15

# *Raidon*

*Norfolk, Virginia*

I arrived at my childhood home. The garage was up, so I parked my car inside of it and headed inside the house. I was trying everything to avoid that clinic.

I walked inside and my baby sister, Michelle, was walking out with keys in her hand.

"Where are you going?" I asked.

She looked at me like I was crazy and said, "Tending to my business." She closed the door behind her.

I opened the door and yelled, "Where is mama?"

"At her office," she said with sassiness in her voice, as she got inside of our mom's car. Our mom was a professor of English at the historically black school, Norfolk State University.

I rolled my eyes and headed back inside. I love Michelle, but that attitude is out of control.

As I walked into the kitchen and grabbed a banana, I heard the garage coming down. It was eerily quiet in the house. Morgan was back in Tallahassee, along with Micah. RJ went away for a few days, but he wouldn't tell anyone where he was going. Michelle said mom was at her office, so I assumed dad was at the pharmacy.

I walked up to the computer room to do some browsing on the net. A few minutes later, I heard someone enter the house. I walked over to the window to see who it was.

"Oh, ok," I said, as I saw my father's car parked outside the garage. I stayed in the room, but told myself that I would make my presence known when he came upstairs.

I was caught off guard when I heard my mom yell, "What the fuck is your problem?"

"You better watch it!" my dad yelled back. "Rachelle, I'm really getting sick of your fucking antics!"

*They must have ridden together.*

My mom cried, "Why, Michael? Why are you doing this?"

"Rachelle, you're on that bullshit!" he said. "Bitch, you better watch it!"

My mom snapped, "Michael, you've got one last fucking time to call me a bitch!"

"Or what?" my father replied.

I started to make my way downstairs because I didn't want this to get out of hand. I damn near lost my balance when my mom yelled, "You're a fucking faggot! And all of my damn boys are fucking faggots, too, all because of your fucking faggot ass!"

The next thing I heard, shocked the shit out of me.

*Bam. Bam.* That was the sound of two slaps to the face.

I immediately ran downstairs. *I know my pops wasn't beating on my mother.*

"STOP IT, MICHAEL!" my mom screamed. "STOP HITTING ME! YOU CAN'T KEEP BEATING ON ME!"

"SHUT THE FUCK UP, STUPID BITCH!" my pops said, as I heard him hit her again. "CALL ME A FAGGOT AGAIN AND I WILL FUCKING KILL YOU!"

"WHAT THE FUCK?" I said, as I ran into the kitchen.

My pops had a deer-in-the-headlights look on his face before he up and ran out of the house. I started to run after him, but my mom stopped me.

"Let him go," she said. "Let him go!"

"Mama," I said, upset.

"Raidon! Let him go!"

I stopped pursing my dad and focused on my mother. We looked each other in the eyes before she said, "Don't ask no damn questions!" She ran upstairs. I followed behind her. I beat on her door, but she wouldn't open. I tried to talk to her, but she didn't say anything.

That shit really had me pissed, and now I had it out for the man I knew as my father. This man was beating on my mother. Who knows how long this shit has been happening.

An hour or so later, I grabbed my keys and left. As I headed down

# Life of a College Bandsman 2: Is This Love

the road, I saw Michelle coming back home.

I drove around Norfolk trying to find my dad's car, but I had no luck. I eventually ended up at the clinic. I hated going to places like this; I just wanted to get this over with.

After a few minutes, I was called to the back. The doctor looked at my file and took a deep breath.

"What is it?" I said. "Do I have it?"

"I'm so sorry, son," he said. "But you are HIV-positive."

# 16

## *Zach*

Tonight was my last night in Orlando. Micah was scheduled to move into our new apartment yesterday and I couldn't wait to get up there and get settled in our new place tomorrow. Jared wanted me to help him out with the freshmen during their pre-drill period, so I needed to get up there anyway to start getting myself in shape for the upcoming marching band season.

Tony has really been trying to spend some time with me before everything gets underway in Tallahassee, but I have been putting him off.

April finally had Tony's son, Tony Jr. last week. Tony said that April would stay in Orlando until the start of September and then she would make the move up to Tallahassee to live with her sisters.

I haven't had sexual intercourse…umm…penetration…in eight months and I really needed something inside of me. I couldn't wait to get back to Tally so I can finally do this thing with Eric. I wanted him bad!

Dwight continues to talk about that thing he's got going with Kiki, even though I really hate listening to that shit. I don't like her and he knows it. I think he gets off on my dislike of Kiki.

When I wasn't at work, I have spent the last few weeks at my high school helping out my band. There were a few kids from my high school band that was coming up to FAMU this year. I have been working with them, trying to get them right, the same way the people did for me last year. One thing I have learned at FAMU was to help someone else get to where you are, as someone helped you get there. That's how we as a people continue to strive for better things—we should help each other out.

As I was leaving my high school today, my mom called me and told me that she needed me to take something over to my grandmother's house. I told her that I would come by and get it as soon as I left the school.

I believed that our relationship was still on rocky terms. My mom was spending a lot of time asking me about why I don't have a girlfriend. Her new thing was that boys my age should be involved with a female. I really hated listening to her. Sometimes, I wished that we'd continued that conversation last year when she was asking me about my "relationship" with Tony.

"Maybe I should have told her that I liked dudes anyway," I said to myself, as I pulled up in her yard.

When I stepped outside my car, I looked down at Tony's house and his car wasn't there.

"Great," I said to myself, as I went inside my mom's house. "I really don't wanna deal with him right now."

I didn't spend much time at my mom's house. She gave me a package to give to my grandmother.

"What time are you leaving tomorrow?" she asked, as I walked to the door.

"Early," I said. "I've got some stuff to do when I get to Tallahassee."

"Ok," she said. "Well come by and see me before you leave."

"Why?" I asked, dumbfounded.

"Because I'm your mother and I want to see you off," she said, as she got upset.

"Ok," I coldly stated.

"You know I just don't understand you at times," she said, as she went in the kitchen.

"Likewise," I said, as I walked out the house. I rolled my eyes when I saw Tony's car pulling into his yard.

"Z!" he yelled, as I walked to my car.

"Be nice, Zach," I said to myself, as I walked down the street.

"What's that?" he asked, as he looked down at the package.

I shrugged my shoulders, "I don't know. It's something my mom wanted me to give to my grandmother."

"Oh, ok," he said. "Why are you avoiding me?"

"I'm not avoiding you," I said. "I've just been busy."

"Yeah, whatever," he said.

"I have."

"Well, you ain't doing shit tonight," he said.

"How you know what I'm doing?" I asked.

"Because I'm telling you that you're not," he said, as he looked me in my eyes.

"Whatever, Tony."

"No, but for real, we should get up one last time before we go up there."

"Get up how?" I asked.

"Nothing serious," he said. "Just as friends, because you know when I start practice and when you start practice, I ain't ever gonna see you."

"That's true," I said, as I looked at my watch.

"So, let's do it," he said, as he started smiling.

I thought about it for a minute, and then replied, "Ok. I'll call you when I get home."

"Bet that up," he said, as he started to walk up to his front door.

When I got to my car, I thought about it—*we're only going out as friends…right?*

# 17

## *Raidon*

*Norfolk, Virginia*

I was getting pissed the fuck off. Someone had been knocking at my door for the past few minutes.

"What the fuck?" I said to myself, as I turned over in my bed, snatching the sheets over my head. "Why won't they just get the fucking picture?"

Moments later, I heard a series of doorbells, followed by more knocking. I got out of the bed and stepped into my slides. I heard my mother yell, "Raidon, open this damn door right now!"

I took a breath and headed for the door. The moment I opened it, she barged in and said, "What is your problem?" She made her way over to my living room.

"What are you talking about?" I asked, closing and locking the door.

"Boy, don't play dumb with me!" she stared at me.

I looked at her.

"What is going on with you?" she asked.

"Ma, I'm ok." I said, as I took a seat.

She said, "Stop lying to me, Raidon. I'm your mother and I love you. Now, what is the problem?"

"I'm just doing me right now," I said.

"Umm, hmm," she said, as she started to look around my place. "I see you're almost ready to go."

"Yep, almost everything I'm taking is packed. I just gotta get it down to Tallahassee," I said.

"I'm gonna miss you when you leave," she looked at me. "You

know how much I love you."

"I know and I love you the same."

"But you don't love me enough to tell me what's going on," she sighed.

"Speaking of what's going on, how long has he been hitting on you?" I asked, staring her in the eyes.

"Excuse me?" she said, shocked.

"Now, don't you play dumb. I know exactly what I heard and what I saw."

She took a deep breath.

"How long, Ma," I asked again.

"A few months now," she said, as she looked down at the ground in shame.

"What? Why haven't you said anything?"

"What am I supposed to say?" she stared at me. "I love my husband! We're just going through some hard times right now!"

"Ma, no one that loves you will hit on you," I stated.

She sat down and said, "Raidon, things are complicated right now. But I have faith that they will get better."

"MA!"

"NO!" she yelled. "I caused that on myself."

"No, you didn't."

"Yes, I did. I shouldn't have called your father a faggot."

I paused for a second as I thought back to what she said to my father that day: *"You're a fucking faggot! And all of my damn boys are fucking faggots, too, all because of your fucking faggot ass!"*

"Did you mean that?" I asked her.

"Mean what, Raidon? What are you talking about?"

"You think the boys are gay?"

She paused for a moment, scratched her head and said, "Umm…umm…I was in the heat of the moment."

I knew she was lying, so I said, "Why are you lying? You think my brothers and me are faggots."

"No, Raidon," she said, as tears started to fall from her eyes. "I was in the heat of the moment."

"But there has to be some truth to that statement or you wouldn't have said it," I said.

"Why are you pushing this subject?" she asked.

"Because I wanna know what you really think. Do you honestly believe that we are gay?"

# Life of a College Bandsman 2: Is This Love

"I know your damn father is," she said, as she looked me in the eyes.

"How do you know that?" I asked.

"Don't worry about that," she said. "I just do."

"So, because you think he's gay makes us gay, too?"

"No," she said.

"That really hurt," I said.

"What hurt, baby?"

"To hear my mother call me a fucking faggot!"

"I know you're not, baby," she said. "Besides, faggots get that damn disease and are condemned to hell. I know you're not a faggot, baby."

I yelled, "WHAT? WHAT HAS GOTTEN INTO YOU? WHERE IS MY MOTHER?"

"I'm right here," she said. "I'm just sick of these fucking faggots ruining my damn life!"

"STOP SAYING THAT!" I yelled, getting frustrated.

"Damn faggots need to rot in hell!"

"STOP IT! STOP SAYING THAT SHIT!" I yelled, as I kicked the coffee table.

My mother jumped in fear; it immediately got quiet in the house.

I started crying. The truth of the matter was I have known that I have been HIV-positive for a few weeks now and I didn't know what to do with myself. I had been shut in my house, not really talking to anyone. I didn't understand how this shit could happen to me. I've always done everything right. I was a good kid, a good person. Why did this shit have to happen to me? I've just been in a slump after I got that news, and I didn't know how to effectively deal with it. Today was the first time I have cried. I have distanced myself from my family and I guess that's why my mom came over here today. I talk to her every day, but since I got that news, I may have talked to her twice in two weeks. And when I talk to her, it's no longer than a minute or two. I know I shouldn't feel sorry for myself, but FUCK...I'm HIV-positive. I'm a walking death sentence.

"Raidon," she calmly stated. "What's wrong?"

I couldn't look at her. I faced the wall and let the tears flow.

"Raidon, what is it?" she asked, as she walked over to me.

When she touched me, I lost it. That mothers touch is a bitch. I couldn't control my emotions. My mother held me as I cried. She never said another word. She walked me over to the couch and continued to hold me. She started to cry, too. In the midst of us crying, she started to pray.

"Heavenly Father, give us strength! GIVE US STRENGTH! I know I am close, so close to losing it, but keep us near the cross, Father. God, I don't know what troubles my son, but protect him, Father. Keep him close. Keep us close. Remind us that no matter what we may endure now, an unending joy awaits us in the future."

The more my mother prayed, the harder I cried. This was the first time, I really dealt with my problem.

When everything calmed down, no one said anything. I rested my head on my mother's chest like I was a child again. She held me tightly. I felt so safe in her arms. She started to hum old church hymns, as she rocked back and forth. I thought about my life and what was to come of it. Just like that, everything changed. I have to go do bloodwork to see where my numbers are at so I can start treatment. I just don't want to face the truth. I want to pretend this is all a dream.

It was time that I stopped feeling sorry for myself and got this shit together. The first step was admitting the truth to my mother.

"Ma," I said, as I sat up to face her. I wiped my tears.

"Yes?"

I paused for a second, got off the chair, stopped and said, "I can't do this."

"Yes, you can baby," she said. "You will feel so much better once you get it off your chest. I'm your mother. I'm here for you, regardless of how bad it may be."

Just the thought of it was starting to make me cry again.

"What is it, baby? What is troubling you?"

"First," I said, as I took a deep breath. It was hard for me to form the words to come out of my mouth. I sighed and continued, "I'm gay."

"Oh, God!" she cried.

"AND," I said.

"Oh, God, no. God, no," she said, as she started to shake her head. "GOD NO…PLEASE DON'T SAY IT!"

I knew that she knew by the way she looked at me. I took a deep breath and confessed, "I just found out that I'm HIV-positive."

"Why God, why! she yelled as *we* started to cry again. "WHY?"

# 18

## Zach

I really didn't know what to do, so Tony decided that we should go to the movies. We went and saw *Pirates of the Caribbean: The Curse of the Black Pearl*. It was a decent movie.

"You want something to eat?" he asked, as we got back in the car.

"Yeah, you paying?" I said.

"I can do that since I wanted to get up with you. What do you want to eat?"

"It doesn't really matter."

It was kinda quiet in the car. He glanced over to me a few times, as he drove. Being around Tony again, in this environment, started to bring back feelings—feelings that I really didn't want to come out.

"You ok, Z?" he asked, as we pulled up to Red Lobster.

"Yeah, I'm good," I said. "Just got a lot on my mind."

"Like what?" he asked.

"A lot of shit," I said. I really didn't want to talk about it.

While we ate, I noticed that he had *that* look in his eyes.

"Get it out of your head, Tony," I said.

"What are you talking about?"

"It's not happening," I said. I was not having sex with him.

"I don't know what you're referring to."

"How are your parents?" I asked, trying to change the subject.

"They're ok. They're still not too happy about Tony Jr., but they're dealing with it. I'm just happy they're gone so I can breathe."

"Where are they?"

"They went with the church on a trip and they won't be back

until sometime tomorrow afternoon."

"Oh, ok," I said, as I ate some more of my shrimp scampi.

"When are you coming up to Tally?" I asked.

"In three days," he said. "The coaches want the freshmen to meet first."

After we left Red Lobster, he drove me around the town. Tony started to talk about old times and the things that we used to do when we were little. I must admit, he had me laughing again.

"Where are we going?" I asked, as we passed my grandmothers street. "My grandma house is right down there."

"Just be patient," he said.

"Tony, I've gotta get up in the morning, so I can't be out all night," I said.

"Damn," he said. "You always talk to damn much. Just let the night flow."

I looked at him.

"I knew I should've drove," I said, as I looked out the window.

"But you didn't, so stop fucking complaining!"

I didn't say anything else after that. A few minutes later, he got on the phone and said, "Hey, what's up, Black...nothing much, you still gonna do it...great...oh, you already have it...damn, you the man, cuzzo...ight, I'm on my way."

"Who was that?" I asked.

"My cousin."

"What he got?" I asked.

"Something that I asked him to get for me," Tony said.

"What is it?"

"Nigga, you'll see," he said, as he turned up the radio.

A few minutes later, we arrived at this house that I assumed belonged to his cousin.

"C'mon," Tony said.

"I'll just wait in the car."

"Nigga, get yo' ass out," Tony said, as he turned off the car.

When we got up to the house, the door opened.

I paused. *He was the man I saw talking to the doctor when I took grandma to the doctor the other week.*

"Zach, this is my cousin Black; Black this my nigga, Zach," Tony said.

"What's going on, man?" Black said.

"Nothing much," I replied.

# Life of a College Bandsman 2: Is This Love

"Y'all be safe and don't get too fucked up," Black said, as he gave Tony a bag.

"You know we 'bout to go scoop up them hoes," Tony said.

"Hell yeah, cuz. Do that shit," Black said. Black looked at me and said, "Nice meeting you, man."

"Same here," I said, as we walked back to Tony's car. I looked at Tony and asked, "Is that liquor?"

"Yep," he said. "I couldn't get it, so I had Black get it for me."

When we got back to Tony's house, he wasted no time getting the drinks together. I wasn't too keen on drinking tonight, but then thought that it couldn't hurt too bad.

After Tony fixed the first drink, he went back to his room. He stayed back there for a minute, but when he came out, the only thing he had on was his basketball shorts.

We both were downing the drinks pretty fast and I was starting to feel a lil tipsy. I wasn't drunk, but I was just right.

We continued to talk about things from our past. Every so often, I noticed Tony looking over at me, and I couldn't help but notice his dick when he walked around the room. The way it slung in his basketball shorts was starting to get to me.

"I gotta use the bathroom," I stood up. I had to get out of the room and get myself together.

When I walked to the bathroom, the only thing I could think about was Tony and his dick. I know that's why I didn't want to be around him, because deep down inside of me, I knew that he knew how to push my buttons.

"Get it together, Zach," I said to myself, as I walked to the door after taking my long piss.

"Yo, Z!" Tony yelled, as I walked out the bathroom. "I'm in here!"

When I got to Tony's room, he was laying on the bed. He didn't have any lights on, but I could see because of the light from the TV screen.

"What's up?" I said, as I made my way over to the bed.

"I'm horny as hell, so I'ma watch this to get my mind off of it."

"Watch what?" I asked.

"Hold up," he said, as he got off the bed. He went to the closet and pulled out a bag. He looked through it for a second, and then he came back and put a DVD in the DVD player. When he turned around, I could see the hardness of his dick coming through his basketball shorts.

When he got on the bed, he pushed play and a straight flick started to play. I didn't say anything. He didn't say anything. We just looked at the screen.

After a few minutes of watching the porn, he started to put his hands in his pants. I immediately started to get hard watching Tony play with his dick. He didn't say anything. I didn't say anything.

Tony pulled his basketball shorts off, exposing his manhood.

"*Damn*," I said to myself, as I looked at his dick for the first time in a year.

He continued to play with his dick as I tried to look at the TV, but the more he played with it, the more I started to look in his direction. He didn't say anything. I didn't say anything.

The next thing I knew, Tony reached over and started to pull off my shirt. He didn't say anything. I didn't say anything.

He reached down and pulled off my jeans and my boxers. We were both sitting in the bed naked with hard dicks. Nothing was said.

Tony reached down and started to take my raging manhood into his wet, warm mouth. I knew this shit was wrong, but something about it felt so right.

Tony sucked me off for a lil minute. He then got off of me, and without saying a word, he laid back down. I knew what was next; it was my turn. I reached down, licked around his shaft and took his into my mouth. After a few minutes of that, Tony turned me around again and put me in the doggy style position. I felt the coldness of the lube hitting my ass. No words still weren't spoken.

A few seconds later, I felt Tony's dick piercing my hole. I don't know why, but it didn't hurt. I guess the liquor had something to do with that. Once he was inside of me, he went to work. He was fucking and fucking hard!

We never changed positions. He fucked me like a mad man for about ten minutes in the doggy style position. Throughout this whole fiasco, neither one of us had said anything. This felt like a fuck that we both needed. It was nothing special about it, just a fuck.

Without saying anything, he pulled out and nutted on my back. His breathing got heavy as the nut shot through his dick, but he never said a word.

When he finished, he wiped the nut off my back. I turned around and laid on the bed. He took my dick in his hand and jacked me off until I caught my nut. He took the towel and wiped the nut off of

# Life of a College Bandsman 2: Is This Love

me.

He walked out of the room without saying anything and a few minutes later, I heard the shower running.

When I came back to reality and I realized what I just did, I started to hit myself on the head.

"You're so fucking stupid!" I told myself.

I got out of the bed when I heard the water stop.

*You just cheated on Eric with his fucking cousin and you didn't use a fucking condom. What the fuck, Zach?*

I gathered my things to go get in the shower.

I sighed.

*You're so fucking stupid!*

# 19

# *Zach*

I couldn't believe I did that. *You're so fucking stupid! So fucking stupid!* Eric is too good for you to do some crazy ass shit. Get it together, Zach. Get that shit together.

"What's wrong with you?" Tony asked, as he took another sip of the liquor.

"What?" I said, as I came back into reality.

"Nigga, what's wrong with you?" he asked again.

"Why something gotta be wrong?" I asked.

"Because you just went into this daze," he said. "What's wrong?"

"A lot of shit," I said.

"Well, talk to me," he said, as he took yet another sip of the liquor.

"Look, I wanna go home," I said. I had to get out of there before I did something that I would truly regret. Thankfully, I was just dreaming about having sex with Tony. That liquor had me fucked up!

"C'mon, man," Tony said. "We had a good night out, why can't we just finish it out here with some drinks and shit. Take another sip, man."

"I'm good," I stood up. I went looking for my phone but I didn't see it. "Tony, where is my phone?"

"Shit, I don't know, where did you put it?"

"Nigga, stop playing and shit. Where the fuck is my damn phone?" I said, as I was starting to get irritated.

"Damn, have some fucking fun for a God damned chance!" Tony yelled, as he went into his room.

When he came back out, I saw his dick swinging through his basketball shorts. I knew I had to get out of there before I really did what I just imagined that I did.

"HERE!" he said, as he threw the phone on the couch. As soon as I got my phone, I called my cousin.

"What's up, Zach?" my cousin answered.

"You busy?" I asked.

"No."

"Can you come scoop me up?"

"Where you at?" he asked.

"Down the street from my mom's crib."

"Ight, I'm actually leaving the Walmart by Auntie Paula's crib, so I should be there in like five-to-ten minutes."

"Ight," I said. "I'll be outside, so you'll see me."

"Ight."

Tony was just staring at me as I hung up the phone.

"What?" I said, as I grabbed my take-out bag from our dinner at Red Lobster.

"I swear I don't understand you," he said.

"If you don't know me after all these years, then I guess you never will," I said, as I made my way to the door.

"Whatever, nigga!" Tony stated.

"Good luck at Florida State," I said, as I walked out of the house. *Goodbye and good riddance.*

# Part Two:
## Back in Tallahassee

# 20

## *Zach*

My alarm clock woke me up and I smiled. I sat up in the bed and said to myself, "Great, I can get this shit on the road!" "You up, Zachie?" I heard my grandmother yell.

"Yes, ma'am," I said, as I put on some shorts. I couldn't wait to get my shit and get on that interstate to make my way back up to Tallahassee.

While I took a shower, I thought about last night with Tony. I don't know how or why I started to think about having sex with Tony, but I knew I needed to get my ass back up to Eric before I really do some shit that I would regret. I knew if I would have stayed at Tony's house last night, we would've had sex and that is what scares me. I am not a cheater. I wasn't raised like that. That shit ain't in my fucking character, but I don't know what's been up with me lately. I have been having a lot of thoughts about sex. Maybe I really do just need some dick. Eight months is a long time for me. I've been having sex for years and this is the longest time that I have gone without something.

The more I thought about things, I really started to wonder why Eric really didn't want to have sex. I know he says that he wants us to get to know each other and build a strong relationship off of that, rather than how good the sex is, but fuck, he's a nigga, too. I know head and jacking off gets old after a while.

What is the real reason why he doesn't wanna have sex with me? What was really the situation with Raidon? I know Eric said that Raidon would be moving to Tallahassee because he got a job there, but I wonder what exactly will that do to our relationship. It's one thing to hide your feelings for someone when they are hundreds of miles away and you don't have to deal with them on a regular basis, but what do you do when the person that you fell in love with is right back in town? I know Eric says that the thing with Raidon is over and they are only friends now, but Raidon is a Harris and those Harris men cannot be trusted.

I've never met Raidon, but it's something about him I don't like. I guess I can say the only one I do like is Micah. Our relationship as friends could not have gotten better. I haven't heard from him in months, so I know he must be busy with school and work. I hope his relationship with Kris is still good.

"How the hell did I come in contact with that crazy ass family?" I asked myself, as I got out of the shower. The notorious Harris family from Norfolk, Virginia, had been a pain in my side and I wonder what life is really like for them in Norfolk. I guess since I will be staying with Micah again, I will get to know more about his family. It may sound crazy, but something about that family intrigues me.

After I put on my traveling clothes, I checked to make sure that I didn't leave anything in the room and then I headed out to the living room. That's when I heard my grandma talking to my cousin.

"What's up, cuzzo?" I said. "Thanks again for last night."

"It's cool," he smiled.

"You off today?" I asked.

"Yeah, I'm on a much needed vacation, so I'm just chilling for the week."

"That's what's up," I said, as I made my way to my car to put my last few things in there.

"You got everything?" my grandma asked, as I walked back in the house.

"Yes, ma'am."

"Ok," she said. "Be safe on the road and call me as soon as you get in."

"Ok, grandma," I said, as I gave her a hug.

"Ight, cuz," I said, as I dapped him up.

"Be easy, Zach."

When I got in my car, I put a mixed CD in the CD player, as I got ready to make that journey. Once I got a few houses down the street my car started to jerk.

"WHAT THE FUCK?" I said, as I eased off the gas pedal.

# Life of a College Bandsman 2: Is This Love

"DON'T DO THIS SHIT NOW! NOT NOW!"

The jerking got really bad and I knew that I had to turn the car around. I decided that I would just drive the car around the block and go back to my grandma's house. When I got back on my grandma's street, the car cut off.

"DAMN, MAN!" I yelled, as I tried to turn it back on but it was to no avail.

I took a deep breath and walked a few houses down to my grandma's place.

"What's wrong?" she said, as I came back in the house.

"The car cut off and it won't cut back on," I said upset.

"Dang, cuz," my cousin said.

"What happened?" she asked. "Where is it?"

"It stared jerking and when I turned it back around to come back here, it cut off."

"We need to go push it back up here," my cousin stated.

After we pulled the car back in the yard, I knew I was fucked. I didn't have any money, my grandma didn't have any money and I knew my mama didn't have any money. How the fuck was I gonna get my car fixed? I needed to be in Tallahassee today!

After talking and trying to figure out what was wrong with the damn car, I just gave up. I got mad and went to my room.

"I can drop you off, man," my cousin said, as he came back in the room.

"Really?"

"Yeah, man, I told you I was on vacation and I don't have nothing to do. Why not?"

"Dang, man, that's what's up," I said, as I got somewhat excited again. I knew I was gonna miss my car for the moment, but I just needed to get up to Tally.

After we loaded his car up with my stuff, we said our goodbyes to our grandma and we started our journey up to Tallahassee.

# 21

## *Eric*

I was beyond excited. My baby was coming back into town today and I couldn't wait to get up with him. Life without Zach sucks. He really does something to me that just puts me in places I've never been before. Everything about Zach really gets to me. The way he talks, the way he walks, the way he smiles, the simple conversation that we have—I love it all. Even though we never went all the way sexually, I feel like we've been doing it forever. Just being around Zach takes me places that I quite honestly thought no dude could do. After Raidon just up and left me, I was pretty much done with my experimentation with dudes. Zach just doesn't know what he does to me.

"Yo, Eric!" Quinton yelled from the kitchen.

"What?" I yelled back.

"Come here for a second!"

*"What the fuck does he want?"* I asked myself, as I made my way into the kitchen. When I saw him, I said, "What's up?"

"I was making some breakfast and I was wondering if you wanted some," he said.

"Yeah, that's what's up," I said, as I looked hard at him.

"Why are you looking at me like that?" he asked.

"Are you ok?" I asked.

"Yeah, why would you ask me that?"

"Because you've been acting really different around here lately."

"Oh," Quinton chuckled. "I'm ok, just been living the good life."

"Umm, hmm," I said, as I started to laugh. Ian was dicking his ass down good. I continued, "It has been really peaceful in this house this summer."

"Yeah, it has," Quinton said, as I sat down. "I think Amir is coming back today."

"Oh, cool. Amir is good people."

"Yeah, he is," Quinton said, as my phone started to ring.

"Hold on Q," I said, as I answered my phone. It was my brother. "What's up, Black?"

"Nothing much, lil bro. Everything ok with you?" he asked.

"Yeah, just living."

"That's what's up. Can you do me a favor, Eric?"

"What's up, Black?"

"You know Tony is coming up there."

"Yeah, mama told me," I said, as I watched Quinton finish up breakfast.

"I'ma need you to keep an eye on him," Black stated.

"Why, what's wrong with Tony?"

"Just keep your eyes open, Eric," Black said.

"What's wrong with Tony? What's going on, Black?"

"The lil nigga came by the house last night and he had this dude with him," Black explained.

"What's wrong with that?" I asked.

"Tony wanted me to get some liq for him, but when I got it I didn't think much of it. But when he came there with the dude, I started to wonder."

"What are you trying to say?"

"Eric, I don't wanna jump to conclusions, but I think our cousin fucks around with dudes," Black said.

"Oh," I said, getting a little nervous. "What would make you think something like that?"

"It was just something about those two. Something just wasn't right. Then Tony tried to throw in some shit talking 'bout they were going to pick up some bitches. I wasn't buying that shit."

"Was Tony's friend feminine or something?" I asked.

"No, not by a long shot. He was very much manly acting."

"So, what's the problem?"

"It was just something about those two together that made me think about this shit."

"But you know Tony just had that baby," I said.

"What the fuck is that supposed to mean?" Black said. "Any man can stick their dick in some pussy. A fucking baby doesn't mean shit."

"I guess you got a point."

"Shit, I know I do."

"Black, I think you're over analyzing that shit."

"That nigga is fucking around with dudes, Eric."

"You don't know that shit for sure. It's not good to judge the man like that. Black, that's a huge accusation."

"I just say what I feel and this is what I'm feeling," Black said.

"I guess, bruh."

"You know how much I hate that shit," Black said. "I can't stand men who like men. There are too many beautiful women out there for that crazy shit."

"Yeah, that's true," I said, as I wanted to get off the phone with my brother. "But I'll keep an eye out on Tony."

"Yeah, do that. Look out for our lil cousin," Black said. "I'ma get off the phone but get at me later, lil bro."

"Ight, Black."

"I love you, man," Black stated.

"I love you, too," I said, as I hung up the phone.

I love my brother with all my heart, but I knew this was bad territory. Anyone who knew Blackwell knew how much he hated gay and bi-sexual people. That was his flaw and I couldn't stand that about him—for obvious reasons. If Black ever found out that I was fucking 'round with a dude, I don't know what he would do. Black is very protective of my little sister and me, but I'm afraid of that things that could happen if my truth ever came out. That's one of the main reasons why I never really fucked around with dudes. I have too much to lose. Zach is the third dude that I've messed with and I hope for God that he will be the last. The first two dudes, including Raidon, was old news. When I got up with Zach too many people found out about me, but I knew that is something that will stay in Tallahassee. If Black ever found out—Jesus take the wheel.

"Are you ok?" Quinton asked, as he brought me back into reality.

"Umm," I said as I cleared my throat. "I'm good."

"Who was that?" he asked.

"That was just my brother being crazy as hell," I said. I didn't want Quinton to know how Black felt because I didn't feel like I could trust Quinton.

"You sure everything's ok?"

"I'm good," I said.

"Ight, breakfast is almost done."

"So, you're not doing the band thing this year?" I asked.

"No, I've served my time and I have left my mark. It's time to move on. I'm gonna miss it, but I gotta graduate and get the hell from up outta here."

"I feel you on that shit," I said. "I can't wait to get this damn piece of paper!"

"What are you gonna do after you graduate?" Quinton asked.

"Go to medical school," I said. "I'm trying to do big things."

"I feel you on that shit," he said. "My mom wants me to get involved in politics so I can be like her, but I don't know if I want to do that."

"Your mom is in politics?" I asked.

"Yeah," he said, as he handed me a plate and a glass of orange juice. "She is a congresswoman…umm… a representative from Ohio down on Capitol Hill in DC.

"Oh, shit, that's what's up!" I said.

"Yeah, she said she wanna run for a senate seat in the next election."

"Shit, that's hot," I said, as the door opened.

"WHAT'S THAT I SMELL IN HERE!" I heard Amir yell, as he entered the house.

"What's up, roommate," Quinton said, as he walked around the counter to give Amir some dap.

"What's been up, Eric?" Amir asked.

"Same ole, same ole. How was the summer?" I asked, looking at the tatted, dark-skinned, muscular roommate.

"It was cool, no complaints here. But let me get the rest of my stuff back in the house and I'll get back up with y'all boys."

"Ight," both Quinton and I said, as Amir went to his room.

"That boy is something else, I said, as I ate some bacon that Quinton fried.

"What time is it?" Quinton asked, as he looked around for his cell.

"A little after eleven."

"Oh, shit! Fuck! I gotta go! I'm gonna be late. I'ma get at you!" Quinton yelled, as he ran back to his room. A few seconds later he ran out the house.

"What's up with that?" I asked myself, as I got up to pour another glass of orange juice. I grabbed my plate and went to my room.

# Life of a College Bandsman 2: Is This Love

I turned on the TV and CNN was talking about a new study that was done. They were saying that the study found that African-Americans are leading the way in new cases of HIV.

*"I wonder what's up with Raidon?"* I asked myself. That segment really had me thinking about him. I hadn't talked to him in a few weeks. "I wonder how the test turned out."

# 22

## *Raidon*

*Norfolk, Virginia*

**M**y mom always knew how to get to me and being with her yesterday reconfirmed that. She really allowed me to open up and to be honest; it felt good to finally tell her the truth. I know she is in shock. Hell, I'm still in shock and to be honest, I don't know what to do.

I haven't talked to Phil since that night, so he doesn't know how my results came back. I have a lot of mixed emotions about him right now and I don't know what to do with them. I know I'm mad as hell and I've got to find a way to release these feelings! *Fuck the world! Hell, the world said fuck me!*

I got in my car and exhaled. I had to go to my mom's house to get something for my trip. I was leaving in a few days and she was determined that I take that gift with me. I knew that the house would be empty because mom, RJ and Michelle left this morning to go up to Richmond for a conference that the English department at Norfolk State wanted her to attend. My mom was trying to become the English Department Chair and this two-day trip would help her achieve that goal. My pops should be at work, so I shouldn't have to deal with anyone while I'm over there.

As soon as I pulled out of the driveway, my phone started to ring. I looked down at it and thought about not answering it, but I did.

"What's up, Raidon?" Eric said.

"Nothing much, just on the way over to my mom's place."

"Oh, ok," Eric said. He paused for a second.

"What's up?" I said.

"Umm," Eric said. "Umm."

He sounded a bit nervous. I knew what he wanted to ask, but I could hear the uncertainty in his voice.

"It's ok," I said.

"Well?" he said.

I didn't say anything, partly because I didn't know what to do. I shouldn't have told him in the first place as it wasn't his fucking business. Now, I didn't know whether to tell Eric the complete truth or not. I didn't need people talking about me, or knowing what was my personal business and I ain't even back in Tallahassee yet. I don't think Eric would talk like that, but you never know what a person would really do.

"Did the results come back?" he asked.

"Yeah, they came back."

"Well, how did it go?"

"What do you think?"

"Shit, I don't know," he said. "I hope it worked out for you."

I didn't say anything.

He said, "I'ma need you to tell me that you're negative."

"I'm negative," I lied, as I approached a red light.

"Really?" he said excited.

"Yep," I said, as I continued to lie.

"That's great, Raidon. Man, that was a close call."

"Yeah, it was," I said, as I pulled up at my childhood home. I was upset.

"I'm just so happy for you, Raidon," he said. "When are you coming up?"

"I should be in Tallahassee by the end of the week. But I'm at my mom's house, so I'll call you back."

"Ok, do that," Eric said, as he hung up the phone.

*"Why did I lie to him?"* I asked myself, as I turned off the car.

I really didn't have time to focus on that conversation, because I noticed that my dad was home. I really didn't want to face him, but it was no time better than the present.

When I walked in the house, I heard music coming from upstairs. I took my time in the kitchen because I was trying to figure out how I was gonna approach him. I needed to find out why he's hitting my mom, who he's sleeping with, and is that the reason why my mom insists on calling him a 'fucking faggot.'

I poured a glass of water and ate a banana before I started to go

# Life of a College Bandsman 2: Is This Love

upstairs.

"WHAT THE FUCK?" I said, as I started to walk upstairs. "What the fuck is he doing?"

The closer I got to the room, the more interested I became.

"HELL NAW!" I said, as I realized what was going on.

*I knew this man wasn't doing that shit in my mama's house.*

I stood by the door for a few minutes to listen to make sure I heard what I thought I heard.

"Damn," I heard a voice say over the music. "Do that shit, Daddy!"

I listened to other random sexual sayings, in-between grunts and moans.

"DAMN," I heard that voice yell again. "FUCK THIS SHIT, DADDY!"

The more I stood there, the more disgusted I became.

*I know this man ain't fucking no bitch in my mama's house.*

I turned the knob and walked in the room. I couldn't believe the scene in front of me. I yelled, "What the fuck are you doing?"

They both jumped and looked at me.

I stared at the person my dad was fucking and said, "What the fuck? What kinda fuck shit is this? What the fuck is this?"

"Son, calm down," my dad said, as he attempted to cover his body.

"HOW THE FUCK CAN I CALM DOWN? YOU'RE CHEATING ON MY MOTHER AND YOU'RE CHEATING WITH *HIM!* What the fuck is going on?"

They just stared at me.

"Y'all are some nasty bitches," I said in disgust, as I pointed at the dude that I knew. I turned to my dad and said, "Of all people— HIM! You and him?"

Upset, I walked out and closed the door. I couldn't look at that shit anymore.

"What the fuck is happening to me and my life?" I asked, as I went to the living room.

*I wanted answers and they weren't leaving this house until I got them!*

# 23

# *Raidon*

I was fucking heated as I made my way down to the living room. This man who is supposed to be my father is fucking around on my mom with *him*. What kinda shit is this?

My pops was everything to me. He was the person who made me into the man I was today. He was always there for me. He always gave advice and spoke the truth whether I wanted to hear it or not. Michael Harris was the king, the monarch, the emperor of this family. All of his kids looked up to this man like he was a God. Our father, our daddy, our pops could do no wrong.

Michael Harris was the oldest of seven kids. My pops was from a small town north of Atlanta, called Gainesville, Georgia. He went to school at Florida A&M University, where he earned his degree in pharmacy. My dad was also a member of the FAMU Marching '100' band during his tenure in Tallahassee.

My dad met my mom, Rachelle, while they were in school at FAMU. My dad was a junior and my mom was a freshman. My mom was the youngest of four kids. She was from Jacksonville, Florida, and she went to FAMU to fulfill a life-long dream of becoming a teacher.

Soon after my mom and dad met, they hit it off and they became really close. My mom had my brother, Ra'Jon, during her junior year of college. Ironically, because my dad was in the six-year pharmacy program, they graduated from FAMU together.

My dad was offered a job in Norfolk, Virginia, two days after he graduated from FAMU. My mom and dad packed up, with my brother RJ, and started a new life in Norfolk. A little while after they moved to Norfolk, they got married. I was the result of their first night as a married couple. Of course Morgan, Micah and Michelle followed me as a result of their union.

My dad was very a popular pharmacist and held high positions in Norfolk. He sat on many boards in the state and country. My parents worked hard to make sure that all of their kids were taken care of and successful and, so far it was not in vain. Until RJ's recent shit, he was an up and coming director in the FAMU band and a music professor. I was a visiting professor of education at Norfolk State University. I was just admitted into the educational leadership and administration doctoral program at Florida State University. This was one reason why I wanted to get a job at FAMU. I knew I was coming back to Tallahassee to get my Ph.D., and I really didn't want to go back to work in a secondary school setting. My brother, Morgan, will be graduating this year from FAMU with a degree in mathematics education. He stared off as an engineering major, but quickly changed. Micah is going into his second year of studying to be a pharmacist. Michelle was the only one left. This was her senior year of high school and if her high school progress is any indication of what's to come, she's gonna be very successful as well. My family was educated.

I had the perfect family. We were privileged kids. Both of my parents were together; this year would mark their twenty-fifth year of marriage. We've never seen our dad do anything wrong. He was always there and he was my mom's number one fan.

That's why this whole thing is such a shock to me. When my mom started telling me that things haven't been right, I just thought she was over-reacting. But as time went on, I started to see it for myself, as well as my other siblings. Even though I knew they were having problems, I never thought that my pops was cheating on my mom or worse, beating her.

I didn't think my dad was on a date that night I saw him at the Rib Shack. I thought that it might have been a dinner for his job or something, and to be honest, that makes sense because *he* wasn't the dude who joined my dad for dinner.

The more I think about things, I guess I can see that the apples don't fall too far from the tree. Even though I know it's a possibility that RJ isn't my brother from my dad, he is gay. I am gay. I know Morgan is gay, along with Micah. All my dad's boys like men. My dad is a cheater; so are his children.

# Life of a College Bandsman 2: Is This Love

When Morgan was in high school, he couldn't stay in a healthy relationship because he couldn't keep his dick in his pants. And if he is now with some dude, I know he is doing the same thing. Michelle told me that Micah and his high school boyfriend broke up because the dude caught Micah cheating on him. I can only imagine the things that RJ has done. And I'm no saint either. I've done my dirt when I was younger.

The only person I think that may have escaped all of this madness is Michelle, but that girl is too damn smart for her own good. And to be honest, that shit scares me.

The shit that I just caught my dad doing was disgusting, not because he was having sex with a man, but it was the man that he was having sex with. As I heard them coming down the stairs, I stood up and went to the door so they wouldn't get out.

My dad looked to me and said, "Son, it's not what you think."

I yelled, "The hell it's not! Y'all are some nasty ass motherfuckers!"

"Son, please let me explain," my dad said. "Everything isn't always what it seems."

"What the fuck is there to explain? You can't talk your way out of this one, dad!"

"Son, calm down," my father said. "And you can get from in front of the door. We're not leaving."

I looked at the dude and he had a look on his face, agreeing with my dad. I thought about it for a second, and then made my way over to the couch to have a seat.

"Everything isn't always what it seems," my pops repeated.

"What the fuck are you supposed to mean by that? It's looks pretty damn clear to me!" I said, frustrated.

My dad said, "I know you're upset, but I'm not going to sit here and allow you to continue to use profanity in front of me. I'm still your father."

As mad as I was, he was my father and I was being disrespectful. I sighed.

My dad continued, "Now, he isn't who you think he is."

"YOU'RE BROTHERS! Y'all are nasty!"

"Michael," the dude said.

"Uncle Alonzo, how can y'all do this?" I said, cutting him off.

"Son, it's not what it seems," my pops said.

"Why do you keep saying that? What is it then?" I asked.

My father took a deep breath and said, "Alonzo isn't your uncle."

"YES, HE IS," I yelled. "Y'all are half-brothers!"

"No, we're not," Alonzo stated.

"I'm confused. What is going on?" I asked.

"This is the truth, son," my dad stated.

"Do you want me to say it?" Alonzo asked my dad.

"No, I want to hear it from him," I yelled, as I stared at the older looking Morris Chestnut wannabe. Even though Alonzo was older, he was definitely attractive.

"Alonzo and I are both from Gainesville, Georgia," my dad stated. "We grew up together and people always said that we acted like brothers. But in reality, we are not related. We've always been close, and to be honest we have been seeing each other since before we left for college."

"WHAT?" I yelled. "YOU MET MOM IN COLLEGE!"

"Yes, I did," my dad confessed. "But I was in a relationship with Alonzo at the time as well."

"This is crazy," I said disgusted.

My dad said, "But you have to understand that this shit was taboo back then, Raidon. We couldn't be put out like that, so we kept it hidden under the covers. We had to live normal, straight lives. It just wasn't an option."

"We told your mom that we were brothers so she wouldn't think anything crazy," Alonzo added.

"Everybody said we were brothers, so when your mom came into the picture we just went along with the story," my dad said.

"So, y'all are not related?" I asked.

"No, son, we're not," my dad answered.

"Is Alonzo Jackson even your real name?" I asked.

"Yes, it is," he said.

"So, you have been cheating on my mom all these years with this dude?" I asked my father.

My dad said, "It's not like we met every day, but when we did see each other, we tended to do things. That's how I kept my balance. I am a gay man living in a straight world. And, Raidon, I'm at the point in my life where I want to be released."

"Why are you hitting my mom?"

"Oh, boy," my dad said. "Look, I don't mean to do those things, but she has just been pushing my buttons lately and I couldn't control myself. I really didn't mean to hit her."

# Life of a College Bandsman 2: Is This Love

"How long have you been hitting her?" I asked.

"It only happened a couple of times. I know it's not right and I'm really sorry that it went there. Every time she calls me a *fucking faggot*, that shit turns me into a different person. I don't know what has been happening to me as of late. Maybe I'm having a mid-life crisis. I don't know. I just know I feel better that this shit is out and in the open. I guess someway deep down, I wanted to get caught."

"Why does she call you a faggot?" I asked. "What did you do to make her call you that?"

"She caught me on the computer watching men having sex," he admitted.

"How long ago was that?" I asked.

"A few years back. She never said anything else about it after that. But she has brought it back up recently, and she keeps saying and doing shit that is really fucking with me. Raidon, I love my family and your mom is playing with my emotions."

"How?" I asked.

"I don't wanna talk about it," he said, as his tone of voice changed. I knew he was getting upset.

When I looked over at Alonzo, I thought about what my mom said some time back:

*"I really believe that your dad's half-brother is RJ's birth father," my mom confessed to me.*

*"Mama, stop playing!" I said.*

*"I'm not playing," she said. "I had an affair with Alonzo when I was in college. It didn't last long, but soon after I turned up pregnant. I had only slept with Alonzo a few times, but something deep inside of me tells me that Ra'Jon is his. I tried to convince myself that Michael is the father, but as the years passed and the more RJ came into himself, the more I saw Alonzo."*

*"Mama, is this your first time telling someone this?"*

*"Yes," she said. "I have kept this inside of me for twenty-eight years and it's tearing me to pieces."*

*"Does Alonzo know that he could be the father?"*

*"No," she said. "You are the only person that knows this."*

*"Dang, this is crazy."*

*"I know and I'm afraid of what your father would do to me if he ever found out."*

Alonzo brought me out of my trance by saying, "Why are you looking at me like that?"

"I guess this would explain why you were never around for family gatherings—because you're not blood. I always wondered why nobody ever really talked about you, but this all does make sense."

"Yeah," Alonzo said. "That would explain it."

"Are you married, too?" I asked him.

"No," he said.

"Oh, ok. So how long exactly have y'all been messing around?"

"Thirty-two years now," my dad interjected.

"Wow, this is crazy," I said, not sure how I should feel. I knew both of my parent's dark secrets and they both are centered around Alonzo Jackson.

"Raidon, life is crazy," my dad stated.

"Trust me, I know," I sighed, as I thought about my recent situation.

My dad begged, "Raidon, let me be the one to tell your mother. I promise I will tell her as soon as they get back in town. But please, she needs to hear this from me. You can be there, but I need to be the one to tell her."

"That's fine," I said. "But if she doesn't know by the end of the day tomorrow, I will tell her."

"Ok," he said.

"Do you have any more questions for me?" Alonzo asked.

"Do you have any kids?"

"Yes, I do," he said. "I have two sons. Both are currently students at FAMU."

"Oh, ok," I said as I got up to leave.

I couldn't take much more of this. I had my own issues to deal with. *This shit is crazy.*

# 24

## *Chaz*

Ian looked to me and asked, "Are you sure about this?"

"Yes, sir," I said, as I grabbed a bottled water and leaned against his kitchen counter. "There is no time better than the present."

"Wow," Ian said, as he sat at the breakfast bar. "I know I told you to get serious with her and this is a good way to start."

"Yeah, it is," I said.

I had been thinking for a while now about getting serious with Genevieve. Ian tells me a lot of things, and sometimes I don't wanna listen to what he has to say, but I know that he means good. Ian has been telling me for a while that I needed to get serious with Genevieve. Now, I think that's something I'll try to do. She is the mother of both of my children. I wasn't raised in a house with a father, and I want my kids to be raised in one.

"But in order for you to get serious with Genevieve, you're gonna have to drop this gay shit, Chaz," Ian sternly stated.

"I know," I said.

"Are you really ready to give this up?"

"I think so," I said. "I mean the dude that I want doesn't want shit to do with me."

"That is true," Ian said.

"You weren't supposed to agree with me," I rolled my eyes.

"Well, I was speaking the truth."

"Whatever, Ian," I took a sip of my water.

"So, have you really given up this thing with Zach?" he asked.

"Uhhh, yeah," I said.

"You're lying," Ian stared at me. "I know you like a book and I know when you're lying, and you're lying."

"No, I'm not," I lied.

"Don't bring that girl into your bullshit," Ian said.

"I'm done with Zach!" I stated.

"So, call Eric and straighten this shit out," Ian said.

"FOR WHAT!" I yelled. "FUCK THAT NIGGA!"

Ian sighed, "My point exactly. You ain't through with this shit."

"Yes, I am," I said, as I grabbed my keys.

"Where are you going?" he asked.

"To see Genevieve. I wanna see what she thinks about it."

"You're making a big mistake if you ain't done with that shit. Chaz, you're acting really stupid right now."

"IGHT, IAN!" I said, getting agitated. I was about fed up with his attacks.

Ian continued, "You don't wanna hear this shit because you know it's the fucking truth! I don't know what the fuck has gotten into you, but you need to get it together real fast, before you do some shit you can't fix!"

"BYE, IAN," I said, as I left his house.

I was getting upset with Ian because he was telling the truth. I wasn't done with the Zach thing. I wanted to get Eric back for betraying me and I would do anything to get with Zach again, even if it was on the side.

As I left Ian's complex, I made a call. Within seconds, Ra'Jon answered.

"Where you at?" I asked.

"In Richmond with my mom and sister," Ra'Jon replied.

"Oh, ok."

"Are you still trying to do this thing?" he asked.

"Yes," I said. "I was calling to make sure that you are still down."

"Of course I am," RJ said.

"Great, I'm working out all the details now, but I do want to put this thing into action sooner rather than later," I said.

"That's good with me. Will this require me to come down to Tallahassee?" RJ asked.

"Not exactly. You will be going somewhere, but as of now, Tallahassee isn't in the plans."

"Where the hell am I going?" he asked.

"In due time, Ra'Jon. It will be in Florida—that much I do know," I stated.

# Life of a College Bandsman 2: Is This Love

"Are you sure this thing of yours is gonna work?" he asked.

"Most definitely. I know people. I know how they'd react to certain situations. Trust me, this is going to work."

"Ok, Chaz," he said.

"Yep, but I will call you later once I finalize everything."

"Ok."

The one thing I knew how to do was fuck Eric up. With Ra'Jon stupid ass carrying out my dirty work, that shit would never come back to me.

Once I arrived at Genevieve's house, I took a moment to collect myself. I entered the house and said, "Hey, baby."

"What's going on, Chaz?" she hugged me.

"Nothing, really," I said, as I walked over and looked at both of my kids. I was a proud father and I would do anything for them. I turned back to her and said, "I've been thinking."

"Please don't wake them," she said. "It took a long ass time for me to get them to sleep."

"Ok," I started to smile. Genevieve had a natural beauty about her.

"So, what are you thinking about?" she asked.

"You know that we basically have a family together," I said, as we headed into the kitchen.

"Yeah, we do."

"And I think that we should take the next step," I admitted.

"What's the next step, Chaz?" she asked, with eyes wide.

"I think we should move in together."

"Really?" she said in a confused tone.

"Yeah, really," I said upset. "You don't seem excited."

"Is that really gonna work?" she asked.

"Yeah, if we make it work, Genevieve."

"So, are you really sure that you're done with your experimentation with men?" she asked.

I sighed, "Yes, I'm done. I thought we already had this discussion before."

"We have, but I have to be honest, Chaz, I still question it," she said.

"Well, let me prove it to you," I said. "Let's move in together."

"I don't know."

"You can keep your place here if it doesn't work out," I said.

"I don't know."

"The babies can sleep in the second room in my house," I said.

"I thought that was Eric's room?" she said.

"Not anymore," I said. "He doesn't live there anymore."

"Oh, ok."

"Let's just try it out and see how it goes," I said. "All we can do is try."

She didn't say anything.

I pleaded, "Like I said, if it doesn't work then you can move back in here to your place. How bad can that hurt?"

"I guess you've got a point," she said, as she started to smile.

"So what you say?"

She paused for a second then excitedly said, "Ok, let's do it!"

# 25

## *Dwight Taylor*

I really missed my boy and I couldn't wait for Big Z to get back in town. I know he doesn't like Kiki's ass, and to be honest, I don't really like her ass either. I've learned that sometimes you gotta give a little to get a lot.

I have decided to go about things a little differently this year and Kiki was part of that. When I really started to talk to her, I just wanted to fuck, but she's one of those bitches that wanna be in a fucking relationship before they give up the pussy. I hate that shit. *I wanna fuck, you wanna fuck, so let's just fuck.* Life would be a whole lot better if people would just be honest with their real feelings and say what they want from the start.

"Wait a minute," I told myself. *Did I just say that? Whoa, Dwight. Don't get carried away.*

Seriously, if I met you and I just wanted to fuck, we should just fuck. We shouldn't have to lie to get the pussy. That's why girls are so fucked up now—they want a relationship and in reality all we wanna do is fuck. If I want to be in a real relationship with you, then trust, you will know.

Zach is on that same shit. He needs to calm his lil ass down and breathe a little. Jumping from one dude to the next ain't cool. In the process of jumping from dude-to-dude, he really might miss out on a dude that is really feeling him. But for some reason he can't quite see that.

Nonetheless, that's my boy and I would do anything for him. I feel like I need to protect him from these nasty ass niggas up here in Tallahassee. I don't know why shawty has that effect on me, but he does. I really value our friendship and I wouldn't want to do anything that could possibly fuck it up. I've just got a feeling that this upcoming marching band season is gonna be a good one for Zach and myself.

My mom says that I shouldn't be so secretive. But I don't know about that. My mom says that I should tell people how I really feel about important things and I think I'm making good improvements in that area. I just don't like people to know my real intentions. I feel like I need to be one step above everyone at all times.

I think I can really trust shawty. When I told Zach about my incident with Mr. Alonzo Jackson, I really wanted to see if that shit was gonna come back to me. I mean you know how people talk when they get ahold to some juicy shit. They're gonna tell somebody and that person tells somebody, and before you know it the story has made a complete circle. Except when it gets back to you, it is a totally different story.

I took a chance and told Zach about my horrible experience with Mr. Jackson and I'm so happy that he didn't let me down. I have a higher respect for the dude because of that. Zach is a man of his word and that shit goes far with me.

Whatever that nigga need, if I got it, he got it. That's my boy and I take care of the people who I can trust and believe in.

His grandmother is a wise woman. Everything she told me that night still sticks in my head:

"I really like you Dwight," his grandma said. "Zachie talks about you a lot and after meeting you, I can see why."

"Thanks, Ms. Carrie," I stated.

She sighed, "Things are gonna get tough and it's gonna get very challenging. I can't put my finger on it, but there is something about the two of you. Well, I don't wanna hold your time, but can y'all do me one huge favor?"

"Yes, ma'am," Dwight said.

"What's up, Grandma?" Zach asked.

"Just make sure that y'all take care of each other. Y'all need to always look out for one another and don't let anything or anyone, come between y'all."

"Ok, Grandma," Zach said.

"I MEAN IT!" she stared at the both of us. "TAKE CARE OF EACH OTHER!"

"Yes, ma'am, Ms. Carrie," I said.

"Son, call me grandma."

I really liked his grandma and I'm glad that she liked me, too.

# Life of a College Bandsman 2: Is This Love

I'ma keep my promise and make sure that Zach is taken care of.

My thoughts were interrupted by my ringing phone. "Who the fuck is this?" I asked myself. I looked at the caller ID and the number wasn't saved in my phone. I normally don't answer unknown numbers, but I did anyway.

"DWIGHT! WHAT'S UP?"

"Oh, shit!" I said excited, hearing the voice. "What's going on? I ain't heard from you all summer."

"Ain't shit. This is my new number."

"Oh, ok," I said. "I'ma put that in my phone as soon as I get off the phone with you."

"Do that, but I was just hitting you up."

"That's what's up," I said. "When are you getting back in town?"

"I actually just got back in not too long ago."

"That's what's up," I said.

"Yep and we need to get up—like old times."

"Shit we can do that! I'm finished with my classes for today," I said.

"Bet that up. Let me clean myself up a bit and I'ma give you a call in about an hour."

"Ight, do that," I said.

"Yep, you know I'ma get yo' ass 'cause you got me the last time."

"Whatever, fool," I laughed. "Only experienced kats can do that and experience is something that you don't have."

"Oh, so you got jokes, nigga? I'll remember that when I'm handling that ass."

"Only in your dreams," I said laughing. "You know how shit goes and you know how I do. You must have gone home for the summer and lost your damn mind!"

"Laugh now, cry later."

"Whatever, fool. Hit me up when you're ready," I hung up.

As I headed for the shower, I thought, *"That fool done went and lost his damn mind thinking he's 'bout to get up in this shit. What da fuck is his problem?"*

# 26

# *Zach*

*Tallahassee, Florida*

My cousin followed me into my new apartment and said, "This place is nice, Zach."

"Thanks, man. My roommate picked it out."

"Well, he definitely has good taste."

"I wonder where he's at?" I asked, as I placed my things in my room. As I looked through the apartment, I could see that Micah had already moved in. I guess he was at work or something. When I got to my room, I really wasn't in the mood to be putting shit up, so we just took everything out of the car and sat it in the room.

"Yo, Zach, I'm a lil hungry," my cousin said.

"Me, too. Let's grab something," I said.

As we headed to the front of the apartment, my cousin said, "I wish I would have taken this route."

"What's that?" I asked my cousin.

"You know, went to school and stuff."

"Oh," I said.

"Yeah, man, don't stop," he said. "Finish this shit. The real world is hard. Money is tight. Having a college degree will definitely help move you up the financial ladder."

"Ight, cuzzo," I said.

"I'm serious, Zach. Don't lose focus of what you came here for," he said.

"I won't," I said.

"Ight, I'ma hold you to that," he said, as we left the house to get something to eat.

When we got in the car, I got a call from Eric. "What's going on?" I said, as I turned the volume down on my phone.

"Nothing, lil pimpin'. You in town?"

"Yeah, we just got in a few minutes ago."

"We?"

"Oh, my cousin had to drop me off," I stated, as I explained what happened to my car.

"Dang, that sucks," Eric said.

"Yeah, it does, so you're gonna have to come get me later," I said.

"Ight, I can do that. Just give me a call when you're ready."

"Ok, I'm probably gonna go with Dwight for a lil bit before I come over there."

"Ok, just hit me up," Eric said.

"Who was that?" my cousin asked, as I hung up the phone.

"One of my homeboy's."

As we ate a quick meal at Burger King, I asked, "Are you going back to my house or are you getting back on the road when we leave here?"

"I'm probably gonna get back on the road," he said. "Why, what's up?"

"I was wondering if you would drop me off at my homeboy's house. I can give you directions back to the interstate," I said.

"That ain't no problem," he said. "I can do that."

As we left the restaurant, I phoned Dwight. He answered, "What's up, Shawty?"

"Nigga, what are you doing?"

"About to get my ass in the shower," he said.

"Oh, ok."

"You in town?" he asked.

"Yeah. I'ma stop by your place in a little bit," I said.

"Ight, how long is it gonna take?" Dwight asked.

"Not too long," I said.

"Hit me up when you get here."

"Ight," I said, as I hung up the phone.

"Getting it all together, huh?" my cousin said.

"What do you mean by that?" I asked.

"Nothing, man," he started to laugh.

"What's funny?" I asked.

"Just forget about it," he said. "It went right over your head."

"I guess," I said, shrugging my shoulders.

# Life of a College Bandsman 2: Is This Love

But as I started to think about it, was my cousin trying to tell me that he knew what the deal was?

*****

# *Eric*

As I headed into the kitchen to wash out my dish, I said, "That nigga loves his Dwight."

I don't trust that Dwight nigga. He seems very sneaky to me.

"What you in here doing?" Amir asked, as he came out of his room.

"Nothing, really," I said.

"Oh, ok. I'm about to run to Walmart for a sec. You wanna ride?" he asked.

"Yeah, I don't have shit else to do." As we went outside, I said, "Damn, nigga!"

"What, fool?" Amir said, as he started smiling.

"Nigga, this shit is nice," I said.

"Thanks, man," he said.

"What made you get a new car?" I asked.

"My dad came down for my birthday and he took me to the car lot. Nigga told me to pick out anything I wanted as long as it was under $25,000."

"Damn, that shit must be nice."

"Yeah, man. He's been acting different lately, but I ain't complaining. I got me a new ride," Amir said.

"Shit, I feel you on that."

"So, what you been doing all summer?" Amir asked, as we headed for Walmart, that was a few minutes from the house.

"Nothing, really," I said. "Just school. I'm trying to get out this year."

"That's what's up. I wish I was that damn close to graduating," Amir said, as he turned into the Walmart shopping center.

"This is really nice," I said again, as we got out the car.

"Thanks, man," he said. "Let me see how many bitches I can pull with it."

"Nigga, you're crazy," I started laughing.

Amir was one of the cool roommates. He had his moments at times, but I didn't mind living with him. The nigga was very clean, didn't bother nobody or their shit, and for the most part, he was always in a happy spirit. That nigga was always full of life.

"Heyyyyy Amir," some girl said, as we walked in Walmart.

"What's up, Shawty," he said, as he walked over to give her a hug.

"Nothing," she said. "I missed you."

"I missed you, too, girl," he said.

"You should stop by the house," she said.

"When?" he asked.

"Whenever you want," she said. "You've got my number. Just give me a call."

"Ight," he said, as she walked away.

"I'M SERIOUS, AMIR!" she yelled.

"IGHT!"

He turned to me and said, "Can't keep 'em off my dick!"

I started laughing. "You're something else."

Amir was a nice catch. He had a nice chocolate skin completion. Amir was about 6'3" and sported a low cut. He had an earring in each ear. He had tattoos all over him. And if his dick print was any indication of the actual size, I felt sorry for the person the other end of the deal. He reminded me of a younger Morris Chestnut.

"You know what," he said.

"What's that?"

"That girl is a fucking freak. Hell, freak ain't even the word I need to describe her."

"Is that so?" I said.

"Yep," Amir said, as he grabbed a box of Special K Vanilla Almond cereal.

"So, what are you telling me for?" I asked.

"Because I know she would be down for anything," he said.

"Really?"

"Yep. I know she would let us run a train on her," he said, as he led me over to the deodorants section. "That's if you're down for it."

"I'm cool, man," I said.

"Man, her head game is stupid crazy and her pussy is tight as fuck," he said.

"I'm good, man," I said.

"If you say so," he said. "Why, who you fucking?"

# Life of a College Bandsman 2: Is This Love

"Damn, nigga," I said.

"Oh, it's like that?" he said, as he starting laughing.

"Like what?" I asked.

"Nothing, man," he said, as he continued to laugh.

As he picked out some deodorant, Amir got a phone call.

"What's going on," Amir answered. "Yeah, I'm here…ok…I got something to do first though… Ight…thanks for calling because I'm at the store now and I can get the stuff that I need… Ight… well, after I finish that I'ma hit you up… bet that."

*"I wonder what that was about?"* I said to myself, as I listened to Amir talk on the phone. I wish I could hear the other person.

"Let's go over here," Amir said, as he walked to another aisle.

"What you need that for?" I asked. Amir had just picked up a fleet.

"It ain't for me," he said. "My home girl asked me to get her one since I was going to the store."

"Oh, ok," I said.

"I guess I can pick some of these up though, cause I'ma need these," Amir said, as he grabbed a box of Magnums.

"It all just better fit," I said.

"Oh, trust, it fits."

When we returned home, Quinton was there.

"Where y'all been?" Quinton asked.

"Nigga, can't you see?" Amir said, as he placed the Walmart bags on the counter.

"Don't get slick," Quinton said.

Amir just started laughing. As he walked to his room, he said, "Quinton is telling *me* not to get slick."

"Y'all crazy," I said, as I went to my room.

A few minutes later I heard Amir's shower turn on.

# 27

## *Chaz*

Being that Genevieve was moving in the house with me, I had to be careful with the things I did. To be honest, I'm really not feeling any other dudes but Zach, and that's how I know I'm gonna be good to Genevieve. I should be ok as long as Zach isn't around.

I really do miss the lil nigga, but Eric can go to hell.

I still couldn't believe that he did that shit to me. That was my fucking cousin and I loved that nigga. That shit was foul.

"Oh well," I said, as I browsed the internet. "What goes around comes around."

Moments later, my doorbell started to ring. I headed to the door and saw a fellow drum major, Devin, standing there.

As I let him in the house, he took a deep breath and said, "Chaz."

"What's going on, Devin?" I asked.

"You know how I used to be," he said.

"What you mean used to be," I said, as I started laughing.

"Chaz, I'm serious," he said, as I motioned for him to sit down.

"Oh, what's wrong," I said, knowing something was up.

"I've changed a lot of my ways and I did it all because of Morgan. I am really feeling him," Devin confessed.

"So, what's the problem?" I asked.

"I've been nothing but faithful to him since we've been together, all because I'm really feeling him."

"So, what's the problem?" I asked again.

"That nigga is cheating on me," he said.

"What makes you think that?"

"He left his phone at home yesterday by mistake and it started to ring," Devin explained.

"Ok?"

"So, I went to see who it was. I wasn't trying to go through his phone," Devin said. "When I got to his phone, it was a text message that said, '*I'll be back in town tomorrow and you know what you gotta do*,'" Devin said.

"That could mean anything, Devin," I said.

"Yeah, but then it went off again."

"What did that one say?"

"It said, '*Damn, I can't wait to feel that dick.*'"

"Oh, wow."

"Yeah," Devin sighed.

"Did you say something to Morgan?" I asked.

"No, I wanted to but I really didn't know what to say," Devin said. "All I've been was good to him. I can't fucking believe this shit."

"I'm sorry, Devin," I said. "I wish there was something I could do."

"I know, Chaz. I just needed to get that shit off my chest. I can't believe this shit. Now if I go back to my old ways would I be wrong?" he asked.

"Well—"

"WOULD I BE WRONG?" Devin asked, as he cut me off.

"Not really, but why won't you just end it?"

"Because revenge is a bitch," Devin said, as he went to the door.

"That it is," I said, as I thought about Eric.

"Don't tell Morgan," he said.

"I won't," I said, as I watched him get inside his car.

Once he was gone, I exhaled and said, "Morgan is being Morgan."

I sat down on my couch and thought about what Devin said. I smiled a sinister smile and said, "Let me call this fool."

Within moments, he answered, "What's going on?"

"Ain't nothing. I was just calling to check on you. I haven't heard from you in a minute."

"That's what's up," my cousin, Blackwell said. "I'm good. Just living. How is everything up there?"

"Everything is good, Black. I'm about to get my master's degree, so I'm good."

# Life of a College Bandsman 2: Is This Love

"How are the kids?" Black asked.

"Xavier and Elijah are good," I said. "I'm so proud. I love my kids."

He said, "I can tell. Your mom talks about you and them all the time."

"That's what's up," I said. "You plan on leaving Orlando anytime soon?"

"Not really," he said. "I might come up there for a game or something, but I'll be here. What makes you ask that?"

"I was just wondering," I said. "Since I'm not marching in the band anymore, I just wanted to see if you were gonna be in Orlando when I come down."

"Oh, ok," he said. "I should be here."

"That's what's up," I said. "But I was just calling to holla at you for a sec."

"Oh, ok, it was nice to hear from you, Chaz," Black said.

"Likewise," I said, as I hung up the phone.

I smiled.

Everything is coming together.

*Revenge is a bitch!*

# 28

## *Zach*

After my cousin dropped me off, I made my way up to Dwight's room. I was really appreciative of what my cousin did for me today.

"Damn, it's hot," I said, as I walked up the stairs. I'm glad I put on my basketball shorts because it's too hot for anything else.

"Nigga, open the door," I said, as I called Dwight.

Dwight let me in the room and said, "What's going on, Shawty?"

"Ain't shit. Who you smelling all good for?" I asked.

"Nigga, I always smell good," he said.

"Whatever, Dwight," I said.

"Yep, so what's up with you?" he said, as I sat on his bed.

"Nothing, really. I just don't feel like putting all that shit up."

"You'll be alright," he said. "I saw Micah the other day."

"Really, what was he up to?"

"That nigga looks stressed out," Dwight said. "I don't know what it is, but something is going on with him."

"Oh," I said.

"Yeah, I hope everything is ok," Dwight stated.

"You got somewhere to be?" I asked because Dwight kept looking at his watch.

"No, but I am waiting on somebody."

"Oh, am I holding you up?" I asked.

"Not really," Dwight said.

"Whatever, man," I said. "If you got some pussy coming, just let me know."

"It ain't even like that," Dwight said.

"Umm, hmm. Cheating on Kiki?" I asked.

"It ain't like that," he said.

"Whatever, Dwight," I said, as I started laughing. "You can take me home; I get the hint."

"Where's your car?" he asked.

"It's a long story, but it's back in Orlando."

"Damn, Big Z," he said.

"Yeah, man, but you can take me home so you can have yo' lil date," I said.

"It ain't even like that," Dwight repeated.

"That's why you're dressed like that?"

"Nigga, it's hot outside," he said.

"Yeah, and it's gonna be hot in here in a sec. Baller shorts and a wife beater—EASY ACCESS!"

"Whatever, Shawty," he said as he grabbed his keys. "C'mon."

The ride to my house was pretty quiet. We just listened to music until Dwight phone started to ring.

"What's up?" Dwight said. He said, "I'm dropping my boy off at his crib, but I should be back there in about 10 minutes...Ok...whatever, nigga...you've lost your damn mind!" Dwight said, as he hung up the phone.

I looked at Dwight

"What, fool?" he asked.

"Nothing, man," I said.

I wasn't crazy. I have very good hearing and that was the sound of a man on the other side of that phone. I wonder if that's who Dwight was waiting for.

"Ight, Big Z," Dwight said, as he dapped me up. "Get at me."

"Yep," I said, as I got out of his car and headed inside of my new apartment.

*****

# Dwight

I drove away and said, "That nigga is too damn noisy."

A few moments later, my phone started to ring. It was my girlfriend. I answered, "What do you want, Kiki?"

"Where you at?" she asked.

"Minding my damn business," I said.

"Dwight, don't start with me," she said.

"Kiki, you called me."

"Damn, are you sure we're in a relationship?" she asked.

"You wanted it, not me," I said.

"You know what Dwight—"

"WHAT?" I cut her off.

"JUST FORGET IT," she said. "BYE!"

"Bye," I hung up the phone.

*That girl is really irking my nerves.*

When I got back to my house, my friend still hadn't arrived yet. I called him and asked, "Nigga, where you at?"

"I'm down the street," he said.

"You know what," I said.

"What's that?"

"Just meet me at the spot."

"Ight, I'll be there in a few," he said.

It didn't make any sense for him to come here because we were just gonna go to the spot anyway.

As I pulled up, I smiled and said, "Great. Nobody is here."

A few seconds later, a car pulled up next to mine. The windows came down and he said, "What's going on, man?"

"Shit, ready to get in that ass," I said.

"Whatever, fool," he said.

When we got out of our cars, we walked over to the place where it was to take place. He took off his shirt and said, "I'm glad ain't nobody here."

"Me, too. That way you won't have any excuses as to why I punished that ass the way I did," I said, as I slapped him on his ass.

"Ight, fool," he said. "You're talking a lot of shit."

"I wouldn't be me if I didn't talk shit," I said.

He stared at me and smiled.

"Are you ready or do you need to stretch or something, because you're about to get a total beat down," I said.

"Nigga, fuck you," he said. "You ain't gonna do shit!"

"Ight, keep on talking," I said.

"Whatever, man," he said. "What we going to?"

"Twenty-one, fool and I'ma give you ten points," I said, as I took the ball from him.

"Whatever, man," he said as he shot the ball.

"Ight, after I beat your ass in this game of basketball, I don't wanna hear shit."

"Gimmie the damn ball," Amir said. "I'm tired of talking. CHECK!"

I loved playing basketball with Amir. We've been doing this shit since high school and I've been whopping his ass since high school. Next to Zach, Amir was my next closest friend.

# 29

# *Zach*

After Dwight dropped me off, I spent the rest of the afternoon putting the rest of my belongings away. I really wanted to see Micah, but he still hadn't been around. "That nigga just better be that damn busy," I said, as I answered my phone. "Hello?"

"What's up, lil pimpin'," Eric said.

"Nothing much," I said. "I'm just putting up the rest of my stuff."

"Oh, ok. You done with Dwight for the day?"

"Yeah, what's up?"

"Just keep your evening free," Eric said.

"Why?" I asked.

"Just do it for me."

"Ok, Eric," I said.

"I'ma pick you up around nine."

"Why so late?"

"Don't ask so many questions," Eric said. "Be clean though, ok."

"I'm always clean, Eric," I stated, sitting down on the bed.

"I'm just saying because we might have to see somebody."

"Oh, ok," I said.

"Ight, I'ma call you when I'm on my way."

"Ight, Eric."

I got off the phone with Eric and sighed. *I wonder what he is up to.* The whole thing with Chaz and Eric still plays in my mind and I just want to put it to rest. I wish it would have never come to that.

I was a little tired and I figured that I would take a quick nap before Eric comes to get me. When I got in the room, I put on some music and got in the bed.

When I woke up a few hours later, I hopped in the shower. Once I was done, I checked to see if Micah had made it home yet, but that was to no avail.

"What is that fool doing?" I asked myself.

When I got in the car with Eric, he was all smiles. I asked, "What's going on, Eric?"

"Just be patient," he said. "I need to stop by my house for a little bit though."

Eric smiled the entire ride to his house.

*What is going on with this dude?* I asked myself. *Damn, he's so fucking cute.*

"Oh, my roommate is back home," Eric said, as we arrived at his house.

I immediately thought about my old section leader, Quinton.

I guess Eric saw the negative reaction on my face, chuckled and said, "I'm not talking about Quinton. This is a different roommate. It's crazy though that all the times you've been to my house in the spring semester, you've never met him."

"Yeah, that is strange," I said.

"Yeah, but we gotta keep it low, because I don't want him to know that we're together. I really think this particular roommate is straight."

"Ok, babe," I said, as I gave him a kiss and got out the car.

When we walked inside the house, his roommate was sitting in the living room talking on the phone.

"I'll be right back," Eric said, as he went to his room.

Dude only had on some basketball shorts. His chest and tatts game was sick! If I wasn't with Eric, it would be hard not to try something. The dude looked good. Whoever he was talking too had him on cloud nine.

He said, "Ight...that shit was hot though... round two later tonight... ight get at me."

"What's going on. I'm Amir," he said, as he got up to shake my hand. "ERIC OLD RUDE ASS COULDN'T EVEN INTRODUCE YOU!"

"Zach," I said, as I was mesmerized from the grip of his handshake.

"True. Nice to meet you. What y'all 'bout to do?" he asked, sitting

# Life of a College Bandsman 2: Is This Love

back down.

"Honestly, I don't know," I said. "I was going along with wherever Eric takes me. It's kinda boring at the house."

"Oh, I feel you on that tip," he said. "Where are you from?"

"Orlando and you."

"ATL Shawty," he said, as he started to laugh.

"Everybody is from Atlanta," I said.

"Yeah, man, we're deep up in this shit," he said, as Eric came out the room.

"I see you've met Zach," Eric said.

"Yep," Amir looked to me and smiled.

"Where you been all day, Amir?" Eric asked.

"Taking care of ole girl from Walmart," Amir said, as he started to smile. "I told you to come along man. That shit was HOT!"

"I'm cool," Eric said.

"Well, I may not be here tonight because I've got more plans," Amir said.

"Not even a full day back in town and you already hoeing around," Eric said, as he grabbed a bottle of water out the fridge. He looked to me and asked, "You want one?"

"Naw, I'm good," I said.

Eric motioned for me to come on. He said, "Ight, Amir," as we started to make our way to the door.

"Nice meeting you, Amir," I said.

"Same here."

"He's nice," I said to Eric as we got in the car.

"Yeah," Eric said. "He's one of the better ones in the house. We get along pretty well."

"So, where are we going?" I asked.

"Somewhere," he said.

"No shit, Sherlock," I said.

"You're just gonna have to wait and see," Eric said, as he starting laughing.

We were in the car for quite a minute and my curiosity was getting the best of me. *Where the fuck are we going?*

As Eric turned off to a side road, I asked, "Where the hell you taking me?" We weren't in Tallahassee anymore and, to be honest, I didn't like this shit.

"Oh, calm down," he said. "You will be ok."

After about ten more minutes of driving, he finally stopped the car. "Hold on one second, ok," he said, as he got out the car.

I sent Dwight a text that said, "If I don't get back to Tally safely...tell the police I was out with Eric!"

"Where the fuck y'all at?" Dwight sent.

I replied, "I don't know... this nigga got me out here in some woods."

"Well call me if some crazy shit goes down," he sent back.

"Ight...keep your phone on." I texted.

"I will... call me to let me know that you're safe," Dwight sent.

I was startled when Eric peeped in the window and said, "You can come on now. Just follow me."

I got out the car and I followed Eric up a hill. We walked for a few minutes and then I was given the shock of my life.

"You like it?" he asked, smiling.

"What did you do this for?" I asked.

"Because you're my nigga and I like to do shit for people that I care about," Eric said. "It may be a lil corny, but it's from my heart."

"It ain't corny," I said.

Eric had a small table with two chairs sitting on top of the hill. On the table was some food, nothing major, but something to get us through for the time. In the center of the table were two roses. It was dark outside, but the glow of the moon made it really nice.

"I just wanted to take you away for a while," he said, as we started to eat.

"How did you find this place?" I asked.

"One day a long time ago, I was mad and I just started driving. Before I knew it I ended up here. So I tend to come here to clear my mind or just to get away for a while. I don't think nobody even knows this place exists. This is my little spot, so I just wanted to let you see some of the things, some of the places that I like," Eric said.

"This is really nice."

We ate and we talked about everything under the moon. We really got to know each other a whole lot better. Eric was really a good, sincere dude and to be honest, I was happy that he was the man in my life.

"I've got something else for you," Eric said, as he reached for his bag.

"Ok."

Eric placed a big ass blanket down on the ground and motioned for me to come get on it with him.

# Life of a College Bandsman 2: Is This Love

"I hope this isn't corny," Eric said.

"I told you that it wasn't," I stated.

"I mean I'm really feeling you Zach, really feeling you. I want this shit to work. I'm serious. I want me and you to work."

"I feel that way, too," I said.

"Well, this is for you," he said, as he gave me a small wooden box.

"What's this?" I asked.

"Just open it," he said.

"Ok, Eric," I said, as I opened the box.

Nobody had ever done or given something like this to me. It was small, but it carried a lot of weight with me.

"Wow," I said, as I started to smile and cry. "Wow, Eric."

Inside of the box was an old fashioned key. But when I looked inside the top of the box, it was a small gold plate that had the words *The Key to My Heart* engraved inside.

"WOW," I said again as I reached over and our lips touched.

"I'm feeling you, Zach," he said.

"Me, too," I said.

"And I mean what that box said," Eric said.

"What's that?" I asked.

"You've got the key to my heart. You've got my heart."

# 30

## *Raidon*

I had my dad meet me at my house. He was there a few hours before my mom arrived. As she walked in the door, she said, "Raidon, what is this about?"

"He'll tell you," I said.

"Michael, what's going on?" my mom looked towards my father.

"Umm, Rachelle, there is something important that I have to say." my dad stated.

She stared at him. He motioned for her to have a seat. She nervously looked over to me. I said, "Yeah, mom, please sit down."

"I don't know what's going on, but I can tell you right now that I don't like it," she said, as she took a seat.

"And you ain't gonna like it," I mumbled to myself.

"Will someone please speak," she said.

"Dad," I motioned for him to speak.

"Well, Rachelle, I'm not gonna beat around the bush," he said. "First off let me apologize for any physical harm that I have caused to you over the past few weeks. I'm really sorry for that. I just don't know what has gotten into me."

"I don't know either, Michael, but I wish I could have my husband back," she stared at him.

"Well, that's the problem," he said, as she sighed.

"So, you *are* cheating on me," she said.

"Rachelle, let me finish," he said.

"Go ahead," she rolled her eyes, as I leaned against the wall.

He said, "I just have these urges—urges that you cannot satisfy."

"Michael, what are you saying?"

"I really do love you but I'm in love with someone else, too," he confessed.

My mom didn't say anything, so I asked, "Are you ok, mom?"

"Yes, I am," she said, wiping the tears.

He said, "I'm sorry, Rachelle. I never intended to hurt you."

I looked to my dad and said, "You're not finished."

"I know," he said. "I'm just gathering my thoughts."

"Well, who is it?" she asked.

My father took a deep breath and said, "I just want you to know that I didn't intentionally try to hurt you. But I was just put in a tough place, and to be honest, I didn't know how to get out. When I met you all those years ago at FAMU, I thought you were beautiful. You swept me off my feet. I didn't know what to do. I knew what the right thing was, but I was afraid of what could happen to me. Then I found out that you were pregnant with my first child and I knew that you were supposed to be the woman that I marry and have a life with," my dad explained.

"So, what happened?" she asked.

"I was in love with two people," he said.

"WAIT A MINUTE!" she said. "Are you telling me that you've been—LORD JESUS!"

"I have been in love with someone since before I met you," my dad explained.

"Who is it?" she demanded answers.

"Alonzo," he admitted.

"Excuse me?" she said. "Did you just say you're in love with your fucking brother?"

"Alonzo isn't my brother," my dad explained.

"The hell he's not. That is some nasty ass shit, Michael! What the hell has gotten into you?" my mother said upset. "This family is getting out of control!"

"Mama, they're not brothers," I said.

"How in the hell do you know?" she snapped at me.

"Because he caught us having sex yesterday," my dad added.

"EXCUSE ME?" she jumped up.

"It's true," I said. "They were having sex in the house."

"YOU'VE LOST YOUR DAMN MIND!" my mother yelled, as she rushed my father. "GET THE FUCK UP RIGHT NOW!"

He stood before her. My mother just looked at my father. She didn't say anything. The longer she looked, the more her anger built up and she started to cry.

"I CAN'T FUCKING BELIEVE THIS SHIT," she slapped him. "YOU'RE A NASTY ASS FAGGOT! I CAN'T BELIEVE I GAVE MY LIFE TO YOU!"

He stood there and listened to her as she continued to talk.

"EVERY MAN IN THIS FAMILY IS GAY! LOOK AT WHAT THE FUCK YOU'VE DONE, MICHAEL! ALL THE BOYS TAKE AFTER YOUR NASTY ASS!"

"Rachelle, please," he said. "Let me explain."

"THERE AIN'T SHIT TO EXPLAIN! YOU ARE A FUCKING FAGGOT!" she yelled. "I CAN'T BELIEVE THIS SHIT!"

She paused for a moment then said, "How are you not brothers?"

"People just said that we were because we were always so close, but we're not related," he said.

"So, you lied to me when you met me just so I could keep y'all's love affair a secret? This is disgusting. I married a fucking faggot," she said.

"Rachelle, you're going to stop calling me a fucking faggot!" my father said, as his voice got louder.

She stared him in the eyes and calmly said, "Well, guess what you fucking faggot—you aren't the only one with a damn secret!"

My father looked at her as if he wanted to kill her. He said, "What are you talking about, Rachelle?"

She smiled, backed away and said, "Hmmm, maybe I should have married his ass because his sex was a whole lot better than yours." She turned to me and said, "Raidon, I hope y'all boys don't fuck like your father because it sucks. All that damn dick and he doesn't know how to use it."

"That's enough, Rachelle! That's enough!" my father yelled, as he stepped in her face.

"I know you better not put your hands on her or it's gonna be a problem," I said looking at my dad. "So, if I were you, I would step the fuck back!"

My father looked at me.

I continued, "I'm serious, Pops. If you hit her, you're gonna wish you hadn't."

"No son of mine will talk to me like that!"

I stepped in closer and said, "Well, keep your damn hands off my mother. If you hit her again, it will be the last thing you do. Try me!"

"You're threatening me, Raidon? Boy, I brought your ass into the world and I will take you out!"

I looked him in the eyes and said, "Put your hands on her again and see who gets taken out first. Don't try me, man."

He looked at me like he wanted to hit me.

I moved my mother out of the way as I stepped in my dad's face. I said, "If you hit her I will fuck you up! I don't care if you are my father. If you hit my mom—"

"ALRIGHT, THAT'S ENOUGH!" my mom said, separating us. "AIN'T NOBODY HITTING NO ONE!"

"You better get your precious Raidon," my father said, walking away. "I never understood why you treated him so differently. RJ was our first child, not Raidon. You always put Raidon above all the other children and I know they can see it, too. Even to this day, Raidon sits on top of all the other kids. That shit ain't right, Rachelle."

I thought about what my dad said. He was right. My relationship with my mother was different. I was always the closest Harris to her. She loved all of her kids, but it was clear that I was her favorite. A mother will never say that she has a favorite, but everyone in the family knows that I am her favorite child. My mom would move mountains for me.

She said, "I treated Raidon so differently because he was different to me."

"What in the hell is that supposed to mean?" my father asked, taking his seat.

*Oh, God, here it goes.*

My mom said, "Raidon was the result of our first night of marriage. *We* conceived Raidon that night, and I knew he would bring nothing but joy and happiness to me. And he has. I love all of my children in a special way, but all of my children aren't all of your children."

"WHAT THE FUCK DID YOU JUST SAY?" my dad jumped up.

"YOUR FAGGOT ASS HEARD ME! ALL OF MY CHILDREN AREN'T ALL OF YOUR CHILDREN!"

"You better stop your mama from talking this foolishness," my dad said as he looked at me.

"It's not foolishness," I said.

"It's not," she said. "I've been holding this shit in for twenty-eight long, fucking, hard years. And it's time the truth be known."

"Twenty-eight years?" my dad said.

"Yes, twenty-eight fucking years!" she gloated.

"Are you trying to tell me that RJ isn't my son?" he asked.

"Oh, my, do you want a hero cookie for getting the answer correct?" my mom sarcastically stated.

"Stop playing games, Rachelle!" he said.

She stared him in the eyes and said, "This is not fucking game! I don't believe that Ra'Jon Harris is your child."

"Woman, you better stop your lying!" my dad said, as he started to cry.

"I am not lying," she said. "I had an affair when we were in college and I ended up pregnant. There is a possibility that he could be yours but *I know* he isn't. I've tried to convince myself that he was yours, but as the years passed, he reminded me more and more of his father. That's why Raidon was different to me. Raidon was our first child together."

My father didn't say anything.

She said, "How does it feel now that the shit has turned on your ass?"

"Who is the father?" he asked. "Who the fuck did you sleep with?"

"Oh," my mom giggled. "I guess lover boy didn't open his mouth on that one, huh? Was he too busy sucking your dick, or is it you who sucks the dick?"

"WHO THE FUCK IS IT, RACHELLE?" he demanded.

"WHO THE FUCK DO YOU THINK?" she said. "WHO IN THE HELL ARE YOU SLEEPING WITH?"

"Don't fucking play with me," my pops said, as he looked at my mother.

"Ain't nobody playing but your gay ass—and my boys—but that's a topic for another day. I guess what they say is true, what goes around comes around. You led me on while you already had someone. You and this man have been fucking for only God knows how many damn years, and it just so turns out that the man you're in love with is the father of my first born child. I guess that ain't quite a match made in heaven is it?"

"Are you telling me that Alonzo is Ra'Jon's father?" my dad asked in disbelief.

"Unfortunately, he is," my mom said, as she went into the

kitchen. She turned around and said, "Raidon, I would like it if you excused him from your house."

"WHAT?" my dad said. "THIS IS MY SON, TOO!"

"Yeah, but I'm asking you to leave," she said, as she came back in the living room. She said, "Michael, I will stay away tonight, but when I get home tomorrow, you and your shit needs to be out of my fucking house! I don't want shit else to do with you! Get the fuck out! GET THE FUCK OUT RIGHT FUCKING NOW!"

My dad didn't say another word. He slammed the door, accenting his exit. When he left, I could tell that she was trying to hold it together, but it wasn't working.

"You ok?" I asked.

She looked at me, busted out in tears and cried, "What am I gonna do? My marriage is over! What am I gonna do?"

# 31

## *Zach*

I still couldn't believe that Eric did that for me. I had spent the entire day thinking about that. I was really on cloud nine and it was all because of Eric. I think I finally made the right decision this time.

We ended up spending the entire night out there last night. It was risky, but it felt so right. We kissed and messed around for a while, but that's all we did. I felt that last night would have been perfect timing for Eric and me to finally have intercourse, but Eric still didn't take it there. After we finished messing around, we eventually fell asleep on the blanket that Eric had put out.

When I got home this morning, I was expecting to see Micah, but the nigga still wasn't here. I was starting to get worried, but then I remembered that Dwight said that he had seen him the other day. I wanted to call him, but I figured I would just wait until I saw him.

"Nigga, open up," I heard Jared say, as he pounded on the door.

"What the fuck is yo' problem?" I asked, as I let him and Omar inside.

"Damn, man, we're just fucking with you," Omar said.

"This is nice, Zach," Jared said, as he looked around. "I had thought about moving out here a while ago, but I settled on my place by campus."

"Where is your boyfriend?" Omar asked, as he looked in the refrigerator.

"In class," I said.

"Nigga, we ain't talking about that light skinned pretty boi," Jared said.

"Yep, we're talking about Dwight," Omar added.

"Dwight isn't my boyfriend," I said to them. "If that nigga says he ain't gay, then shit he ain't gay."

"Nigga, get real," Omar said. "You know what the deal is."

I started laughing and said, "I know, but I can't make the dude admit that he like dudes."

"But see that is where I'm having the problem," Jared said.

"What's that?" Omar interjected.

"What if Dwight doesn't like dudes," Jared said.

"But you just said that he was my boyfriend," I said.

"You're not following," Jared stated.

"Hell, I'm lost," Omar said.

"Think about it," Jared said. "What if he really doesn't like dudes, but, something about Zach is intriguing to him. What if he only likes Zach?"

"Damn, that would make a lot of sense," Omar agreed.

"That would explain a lot," I said, sitting at the breakfast bar.

"Yeah, it would," Jared added. "The nigga is probably really straight and hasn't ever messed with a dude before, but you do something for him and he doesn't know what to do about it."

"Damn, I think you're on to it," Omar said.

"I know I am," Jared said. "I have met and dealt with a lot of dudes like Dwight."

"Is that a good thing or bad thing?" Omar asked.

"It depends on the dude," Jared said. "Some dudes are more accepting of the fact and they wanna try something out, but other dudes will fuck you up because they don't know what to do with those strange feelings."

"I guess that would make sense," I added.

"Yeah, and I've been thinking about all the stuff that you said Dwight did to you last year. The more I think about it, the more I believe that he is one of those dudes," Jared said.

I rolled my eyes and asked Jared, "So, you think I should have tried something with him?"

"HELL, YEAH!" Omar interjected.

"HELL, NAW!" Jared said. "You did the right thing."

"Why is that?" Omar asked.

"Because for one it was the first trip. You don't wanna do anything that could have fucked up the season for you," Jared said. "But the real reason is that you need to let him come into that. Dudes like Dwight don't need to be rushed into doing something with another dude. If you try him he can turn the whole thing against you and then put you out there as a fag. But if you let him take the lead, that means that he's ready and you hold all the power. Don't ever give the other man the power. You have to keep that."

"Damn," I said, as I thought about what Jared was saying.

"Always remember, Zach, and you, too, Omar, that you keep the power, never give another person control. Especially a nigga. Because once they get it, it will be hard to get it back."

After some small talk, Jared said, "Are we still hitting the gym later? Pre-drill starts next week and we need to be on it."

"Yeah, man," I said. "I'm ready when you are."

"Ight, well we're about to go because I'm about to go get into some filth," Jared said, as he got up and went to the door.

"Y'all crazy," I said.

"No, I'm serious," Jared said. "I need some dick and my homeboy just hit me up, so I'm about to go and take care of that."

"Ight, y'all hit me up when y'all ready to go," I laughed as they left.

# 32

## *Dwight*

As I let Amir into my apartment, I said, "What's going on?"
"Ain't shit," he said. "Just wasting time."
"Umm, hmm," I said. "You must want that ass beat some more."

"Nigga, whatever," he said, as he started to laugh. "You won by one damn point."

"Nigga, I spotted you ten," I said, as I sat down in the living room.

"Whatever, man," Amir said, sitting down. "I'm gonna get yo' ass one of these days."

"How long have we been playing basketball and how long have I been beating that ass?"

"Whatever, man," Amir said, as he looked through his phone.

"So, when are you supposed to be graduating?" I asked.

"In two years," he replied. "I can't wait to get the fuck out of this shit."

"Nigga, it ain't that damn bad," I said.

"Yeah, but I'm ready to make some real money," Amir replied.

"So, when did you get that car?" I asked. "That shit is nice."

"I got it for my birthday a few weeks ago. My dad brought it for me," Amir said. "He's been acting really different lately, but I ain't complaining."

"I've never met your dad," I said.

"Yeah, because that nigga wasn't there," Amir stated. "I mean he would send money and stuff but that nigga had his own life."

"Is he in Atlanta?" I asked.

"No," Amir said. "He was for a minute, but then he moved to Alabama because he got a job down there."

"So, he broke up with your mom?" I asked.

"He was never with my mom," Amir stated. "I mean he knocked her up twice with me and my lil brother, but they weren't ever together."

"Oh, ok," I said.

"Yeah and I don't know what's gotten into him lately, but he's just been doing all kinds of strange shit."

"Like what?" I asked.

"Well, for one, he brought me a brand new fucking car. He told my brother that he would get him one next year."

"So, what happened to your car?"

"I gave it to my brother."

"So, what happened to his car?"

"He sold it and gave the money to my mom," Amir said.

"Oh, that was nice."

"Yeah, she needed it," he said.

"Your mom is real cool people," I said.

"Yeah, I love that woman to death," Amir said. "But he's been coming around a lot all summer."

"I take it he didn't used to do that."

"Naw, that nigga used to be ghost. My mom said she thinks that he'd stop in Atlanta on his way to go somewhere else. The nigga gave me and my brother some money for our rent for the semester. I mean he didn't pay for all of it, but he took care of a few months."

"Dang, where is he getting all this money from?" I asked.

"I don't know, but I know I'm enjoying it," Amir said.

"Shit, I would, too," I said, as Amir phone started to ring.

"Speaking of the devil," Amir said, as he looked at his phone.

"That's your dad?" I asked.

"Naw, my brother," he said, as he answered the phone.

"Hello?" Amir said, as he put the phone on speakerphone.

"Amir, what are you doing?" his brother asked.

"Chilling at Dwight's crib."

"Oh, tell him I said what's up."

I shook my head in acknowledgment of it.

"Dwight says 'what's up'," Amir said back to his brother.

His brother said, "Yeah, man, so I've got a problem."

"What's that?" Amir asked.

# Life of a College Bandsman 2: Is This Love

"I need some money."

"What the fuck you asking me for?" Amir asked.

"Because I know you got it and I don't wanna ask mom."

"What the fuck you need money for?" Amir said upset.

"I just do. I gotta go somewhere."

"Didn't dad just give you some?" Amir said.

"Yeah, but I spent that already," he said.

"Where the fuck you going?" Amir asked.

"To Jacksonville," he said.

"What the fuck is in Jacksonville?" Amir asked.

"Man, I've got something to do. Either you're gonna give me some or you're not."

"You're really pushing it, Dallis," Amir said, as he looked in his wallet. "Only because you're my fucking brother. How much you need?"

"Ummm, about $150," he said.

"WHAT THE FUCK YOU NEED ALL THAT FOR?" Amir said.

"DAMN, MAN," his brother said. "C'mon, Amir, PLEASE. I promise I will give it back as soon as I get my refund check from the school."

"Dallis, that ain't until September," Amir said.

"Please, Amir."

"When do you need it?" Amir asked.

"By tomorrow afternoon because we're leaving tomorrow afternoon."

"Who is we? I ain't giving you my money to take care of some fucking people," Amir said.

"It's just a few friends and they've got their own. We're going to Jacksonville for the weekend, just to get away for a lil bit before the season starts."

*"The season?"* I said to myself.

"Nigga, you're going back to the band?" Amir asked.

"Yeah, man," he said.

"I guess. Ight, I got you. I'll hit you up tomorrow," Amir said.

"Thanks, Amir," he said, as he hung up.

"Your brother is coming back to the band, huh?" I said.

"I guess, so," Amir said. "I thought that nigga said he was done with that shit."

"I thought so, too," I said.

"Can I ask you a question?" Amir said.

"What's up?"

"What happened to y'all?" Amir said.

"What do you mean?"

"I mean y'all were close, too, but he just stopped talking about you, and you stopped talking about him."

"Your brother be on that bullshit sometimes," I said.

"On what?" Amir asked.

"Don't worry about it. Just know that he's changed," I said.

"If we're talking about the same thing, I see that, too," Amir said. "But, hey, that's him."

"What exactly are you talking about?" I asked.

"Don't worry about it," Amir said, as he got another phone call.

"What's up," Amir said. He didn't put the phone on speakerphone this time.

"Umm, hmm," I said to myself.

"Yeah, I'm at my boy house…oh, he gone? That's what's up…how long is he gonna be gone?" He waited for a moment then said, "Oh, we can't go to my house…ight, I can do that… I'm leaving now… ight."

"Who was that?" I asked.

Amir started laughing, "Just some hoe I'm 'bout to go dig in. Her boyfriend gone, so she wants me to come over right quick."

"I guess," I said.

"Yeah, I'ma get at you."

"Ight," I said as he left.

*That nigga ain't fooling no damn body…*

# 33

## *Morgan*

*Tallahassee, Florida*

There was a knock on my door. *Damn, that was fast!* I looked out the peephole and saw my baby brother standing there. *What the hell is he doing here?* I let him in the house and he said, "Damn, you look shocked to see me."

"It ain't that. I just wasn't expecting you," I said.

"Well, I'm here now."

"What's up?" I said, leading him to the living room.

"It's so much shit going on right now," Micah said.

"Like what?"

"I know when you went home you had to see that shit between mama and pops," he said.

"Yeah, I saw it," I said. "I saw mama crying one day, too, but Raidon tried to pass it off as nothing."

"Raidon, huh?" Micah said. "You know she tells Raidon everything."

"Yeah, she does, but it's cool, as long as she has somebody she can talk to," I said.

"I've got a bad feeling about this," Micah said.

"About what?" I asked.

"The whole thing back at home," Micah said.

"Oh, it'll be alright. They're just going through some shit. It'll work itself out." I said.

"I hope so," he said.

"What else is bothering you?" I asked.

"I'm good," he said.

"Micah, you're lying. It's all on your damn face. And you haven't been around lately. That's not like you."

"I've just been busy with school and work," he said.

"Why are you working so damn much anyway?" I asked.

"Because I have to," he said.

"Why? Pops makes sure that we are taken care of."

"Because I just do," he said, as he looked at his phone.

"Ight, Micah. What's the real reason why you came over here?"

He didn't say anything for a second, then admitted, "Morgan, I fucked up!"

"What did you do?" I asked.

"I REALLY FUCKED UP!" he said again.

"Ok, what did you do?" I asked.

"You know I'm with Kris, right?" he said.

"Yeah," I said.

"Well, remember when I went with you on that trip up to Atlanta earlier this summer," he said.

"Yeah, I remember," I said, as I thought about the adventures I had on that trip.

"Well, when I dropped you off at the hotel so you could meet that dude, I caught up with one of my homeboys I had in one of my classes. We went to the club."

"Who saw you in the gay club?" I asked.

"I didn't go to a gay club," he said. "That dude doesn't know I like dudes. We went to a straight club."

"Oh, ok, so what's the problem?"

"When I got there, I met this girl," he said.

"Ok."

"So, we chilled and shit, nothing too bad."

"So, what's wrong with that?" I asked.

"Well, the next day she called me and we got up again. I learned a lot about her. She's from West Palm Beach, but goes to Spelman."

"Ight," I said.

"Yeah and we ended up fucking," he said.

"Ain't shit wrong with that," I said. "I'm about to fuck in a lil bit."

"Yeah, but I'm in a relationship," Micah said.

"And, I am, too. So, what's the problem?"

"WHAT'S THE PROBLEM? I CHEATED ON MY DUDE!" Micah said.

# Life of a College Bandsman 2: Is This Love

"As long as you didn't get the girl pregnant you're good. It ain't like you gonna see her again," I said.

Micah just looked at me.

I shook my head in disbelief and said, "Micah, please tell me you didn't."

"I did," he said. "She says that she is pregnant and I'm the father. I'm fucked! I'm so fucked!"

"DAMN, MICAH! I ALWAYS TOLD YO' DUMB ASS TO COVER YOUR FUCKING DICK AT ALL TIMES! DAMN, MICAH, YOU'RE FUCKING UP!" I said, as somebody knocked on my door.

"I fucked up!"

"We'll talk later," I said, as I went to the door. "I've got some shit to take care of now."

"Yeah, man," he said, following me. Micah looked at my friend and then said, "What's up, bruh?"

Once Micah was gone and my friend was in the house, he said, "Who was that? I've seen him somewhere before."

"Oh, that was my brother," I said. "Now, to what you came here for!"

"You ain't said nothing but a word," he said, as he reached down and started to play with my dick.

# 34

## Zach

*Wednesday, August 13, 2003*

For the first time in a long time, everything was good. My life was good. Chaz wasn't bothering me anymore and I hadn't heard from Tony since that last night I was with him. Eric was just pulling out all the stops for me and the more time I spent with him, I knew deep down that I had made the right decision.

My grandmother had been on better terms health wise and that is always a good thing for me to hear. My Uncle Alan was getting healthy again and that was even better news.

I'm extremely excited because we have just got underway with the new marching band season. This is my first year as an upperclassman and I'm looking forward to all the perks that comes with that.

The new band freshmen arrived last night and we've got our work cut out for us. On the flip side, Keli, the band camper that I met this summer is here and is ready to be part of the band. I have personally decided to take him under my wing and show him the ropes. He still looks a little nervous, but I guess that is to be expected. I mean I was in his shoes this time last year.

Dr. Hunter told us that we had to modify our pre-drill schedule this year because we have a performance in Charlotte, North Carolina next Saturday. He said that some other college bands such as North Carolina A&T, Johnson C. Smith and Howard would be in attendance. That somewhat made me excited because I've never seen Howard's band in person and I have not seen Johnson C. Smith since I was in the tenth grade. Seeing A&T is always a plus.

I finally saw Micah, but he is acting strange. I know something is going on with him, but he really isn't talking. I guess when he gets ready to talk, I will be here to listen.

Jared asked Kris and myself to come to help out with the freshmen pre-drill and to be honest, I felt that it was an honor. Most second year members in the band don't get that opportunity, and to me, that was a big plus. That means somebody see something in me.

"Yo, Zach, let me holla at you for a sec," Kris said, as I approached our designated music room for afternoon music sectionals.

"What's going on?"

"Be real with me for a sec," he said.

"I'm always real with you, freshman bruh," I stated, as looked at him.

When he was getting ready to talk, some people started to walk by. "Hold up for a sec, let me get Jared," he said.

"What's up?" Jared said, as he came out to where we were.

"Yo, man, I was just wondering if we could leave for a lil bit because I really need to holla at Zach for a second," Kris said to Jared.

"That's cool," he said. "I really don't need y'all right now anyway, but hurry back because you never know what can happen."

"Ight, man, thanks," Kris said, as Jared went back to deal with his freshmen.

"What's going on?" I asked again.

"I'll tell you when we get in the car," he said, as we got on the elevator.

I could tell that something was bothering him, and everything in my gut was telling me that it had something to do with Micah.

"Oh, great," I said to myself, as the elevator door opened. I really didn't feel like seeing him right now.

"What's going on?" Devin said, as he looked at us.

"Nothing much," Kris said.

"Oh, ok. Where is y'all freshman brother?" Devin asked.

"Who?" I said, knowing he was talking about Dwight.

"Umm, the tall one," he said.

"Most of us are tall," I said, as I looked at him. "Who are you talking about?"

"Umm, Dwight," he said.

"You knew his name from the start," I said. "I don't know why you're acting stupid."

He just looked at me for a second and asked with a little more authority, "Do you know where he is?"

"What do you need Dwight for?" Kris asked him. "That nigga doesn't like your ass."

"I know," he said. "That's why I wanna work on that you know—try and patch things up."

"For what?" I said. "What the fuck you trying to get out of it?"

"DO YOU KNOW WHERE THE FUCK HE'S AT?"

"Zach, he must have lost his damn mind," Kris said, as he looked at me. "We ain't no fucking freshmen anymore, talking to us like that. C'mon, let's go."

"Bet that up," I said, as we left Devin standing at the elevator.

"I don't like him," Kris said.

"I don't really care for him, either," I said. "Something about him just doesn't sit right with me."

"I totally feel you on that one, Zach," Kris said, as he led me to his car.

"So, what's really going on Kris?" I said once we were riding.

"Man, something is really up with Micah. He ain't himself," Kris stated.

"What'cha mean?"

"I mean everything about him is different. He doesn't even wanna have sex right now," Kris sadly stated.

"Dang."

"Yeah, man. His bodily actions are different and then he's always at that damn job. What the fuck he need to work so much for? I thought he said that his parents made sure that he was financially good," Kris said.

"I don't know, man," I said. "He really hasn't said much of anything to me either."

"Really?"

"Yeah, I was wondering what was up with him, too," I said.

"I really don't know what to think," Kris stated. "I mean I know I was away during the summer, but he was working that job so I really didn't think too much into it."

"So, how long has this been going on, Kris?"

"Like I said I really didn't think too much into it until now, but he has been acting different most of the summer," Kris said.

"Maybe the thing with his family is really getting to him."

"Maybe," Kris said. "Or what if it is something else?"

"Like what?" I asked.

"Hmmm, you tell me."

"You don't think he cheated on you, do you?" I asked.

"I don't know what to think. I just know this ain't the dude that I met last year."

"Man, Micah is good people and you know he wouldn't do that to you. Kris, you know how much he loves his family and maybe they are really just going through some tough stuff right now. You know everybody handles stress differently."

"Yeah, maybe you're right. I really hope so. You know how I felt about this gay shit and I gave myself to him. That would be really fucked up if—"

"Don't even say it," I said, as I cut him off. "Just think positive."

"If you say so, Zach."

"Yo, Kris?"

"Yeah, man?"

"Where the hell we going," I asked, as I started to laugh.

"Shit, I don't know; I was just driving."

# 35

# *Michelle Harris*

*Norfolk, Virginia*

I don't really like this shit. I know I'm the baby of the family, but everybody can't keep shit from me. I know some shit is going on with mom and dad and I know everyone knows what it is but me.

I'm so fucking sick of my brothers and shit, trying to "protect" me. I probably need to protect some of their gay asses.

I love all my brothers, but I just don't understand why all of them had to be gay. For the life of me, I just don't get it.

And nobody talks about it anymore, but I still believe, deep down in my gut that RJ had something to do with the robbery that happened in Micah's dorm room last year. I mean I love RJ, too, but that man has some serious issues that he needs to work out. Since he has been home from Tallahassee, I have really seen the real Ra'Jon, and I just don't understand how mom and dad can raise three other perfectly fine dudes and then there is him. Something ain't right with it.

Daddy hasn't been staying here and I really need to find out what's going on. Mom sits in her room and cries all night, every night, and when I ask her what's up, she always says, "Nothing is wrong." I'm not stupid…not by a long shot.

I'm getting ready to go into my senior year of high school and this ain't the shit I need on my plate.

"MICHELLE," I heard my brother, RJ, yell.

*"I should ignore him,"* I said to myself.

"MICHELLE!" he said again.

"WHAT?" I yelled back, as he knocked on the door. "What RJ?"

"Can I come in?"

"Yeah."

He walked in and said, "I'm gonna be going away for a days."

"Where are you going?"

"Down to Florida," he said.

"What's down there?"

"I just got some stuff that I need to take care of," he said.

"Stuff like what?"

"Just some unfinished business."

"Umm, hmm, yo' sneaky ass always up to something."

"I swear your damn mouth is too sassy for me," he said.

"And that's why you're you and I'm me. Either you like me or you don't. My mouth is part of me and if you don't like it, you can lick my pussy."

"Michelle, please."

"I'm just saying," I said. "SO?"

"So, what?" he said.

"Tell me the truth."

"About what?" he said.

"Did you have something to do with that shit that happened in Micah's dorm room?"

"What?" he said.

"WERE YOU BEHIND THAT ROBBERY THAT HAPPENED IN MICAH'S DORM ROOM LAST YEAR?"

"Where the hell you get that shit from?" he said.

"You just act funny. Who knows the things that you do. You know I just don't understand you. For you to be so handsome and so successful, I don't understand why you are the way you are."

"EXCUSE ME?"

"Nigga, you've got problems," I said, as I looked at him.

"Michelle, you're about to piss me off."

"I'm sure I wasn't the first and I won't be the last."

"You really pushing it," he said.

"What... you gonna get me back too for making you upset?"

"I'm just gonna go before I say something that I regret later. Tell mom I'll be back in a few days."

"Umm, hmm," I said, as he walked out.

*****

# Life of a College Bandsman 2: Is This Love

# *Eric*

Amir was walking a lil funny, so I asked, "You straight?"

"Yeah, I'm ok," he said. "I just hurt myself a little yesterday."

"How did you do that?" I asked.

"Oh, I was playing basketball and I fucked some shit up."

"Is that so?" I said.

"Yeah, what else could it be?" he said, as he looked at me.

"I don't know, I was just saying," I lied. But the truth of the matter was that it looked like somebody fucked the shit out of Amir and he was now paying the price for that. He was trying to walk straight, but I could see right through that.

"But what's going on with you today?" he asked.

"Nothing really, just at the house chilling."

"Who was the dude that you brought here the other day?" he asked.

"Who?" I asked. I knew who he was talking about, but I was just trying to play stupid.

"That dude that I was talking to in the living room that night. I forgot his name."

"Oh, you're talking about Zach," I stated.

"Yeah, that's him," he said. "What happened to him?"

"What'cha mean?"

"I mean he ain't came around no more since then. Why not?"

"I didn't know that you paid so much attention," I said.

"I see and hear everything," Amir said, as he looked at me with a big ass smile on his face.

"Is that so?" I said.

"Yeah, it is roommate—everything."

"I guess the same can be said about me, too," I said. "Just because I don't say anything doesn't mean that I don't know."

"Is that so?" he said.

"Yes, it is," I said. "I'm very observant. I see and hear everything, just like you do."

"Interesting," he said.

"Yes, indeed," I said, as I started to smile.

"Hmmmm, that's what's up," he said, as he put his hand down on his dick.

"But what you got going on today?" I asked.

"Shit, getting up on something later, but in the meantime, probably gonna hang out with my brother. I really haven't spent that much time with him lately."

"Oh, ok, that's cool. Y'all got a good relationship?"

"Yeah, man," I said. "I would do anything for that boy. I love my baby brother. I guess we've been through so much together, all we got is each other."

"Really?"

"Yeah, man," he said. "When we were younger, I took the protective role. We really didn't have a father figure in our house. I mean we know who our father is, but he wasn't really there. I just kind of became the man of the house. My mom went through a lot of shit while we were growing up, so all we had was each other. Shit, that's how I learned how to cook."

"How?" I asked

"Man, I had to feed the dude. I couldn't let my baby brother starve. There were times when my mom wasn't there and it wasn't shit in the house to eat, so I would find something and fix it up for him. I would go to bed at night hungry just so my brother would be ok. When I tell you I love that dude," Amir said, as his eyes started to get watery.

"Damn, man," I said. "I didn't know it was like that."

"Yeah, I ain't trying to sound like a charity case, but I look at where we came from and where we are today and I'm proud of that shit. My mom still has a way to go, but we are doing a whole lot better than what we were," Amir said. "My mom and my brother— man that's my fucking family and I would die for them."

"I feel you, bro," I said.

"Then when I met my best friend, things started to change," he said.

"How so?"

"I was about to get into that street life. Shit was getting hard and I didn't know what else to do. I knew that shit was wrong, but what else could I do," Amir said. "One of my boys was trying to get me to sell, but I knew that shit was wrong, but when I looked at how he was living and shit, that shit became tempting. But just when I was about to give in to that shit, my best friend came around."

"What did he do?"

"He doesn't know it, but he showed me that I just needed to keep on that right track, man. When I looked at him and his brother and how his brother looked up to him, it reminded me of my brother and I couldn't let my brother see me doing that shit. So, my best friend was like a pro at basketball and shit, so we started playing. I never really got into sports because I had to take care of my family. I mean I watched it and shit, but I never played it. I guess you can say that I really didn't have much a childhood."

"Wow, man, I never knew it was like this for you."

"It's a lot of shit that you don't know and it would take days to explain my life," Amir said. "But playing basketball with him started to take my mind off of the street life. I finally got to enjoy some of my childhood even though I was pushing sixteen. He was the first person that really showed a genuine interest in me and my lil brother. His mom took us in sometimes when my mom was going through. I really love that man, too, like he is my brother. I can honestly say that he played a big part in changing my life for the better. If it wasn't for him, I'm sure I wouldn't be here today. I was always a smart kid, but college and shit wasn't on my agenda. I just needed to make that money for my family. My dad sent money here and there, but between my mom and bills and shit, that money was gone like the wind. When I got up here, my best friend took my place and took after my lil brother, even though my brother was a year older than him. I mean my friend is really a true friend. That nigga never asked for anything, he just did shit out of the kindness of his heart. Anyone would be lucky to have someone like that in their life."

"Yeah, he seems like a good dude man," I said.

"Yeah, he is. But I'm about to get out of here, so get at me later, Eric," Amir said, as he got his things and left the house.

"Dang," I said to myself, as I picked up the phone to call my baby sister. "I didn't know it was like that."

Just talking to Amir, had me thinking of my relationship with my older brother, Blackwell, and my younger sister, Rozi. I really loved them and I would do anything for them, too. I hadn't talked to Rozi in a lil while and I just had the feeling that I needed to check in on her up there at Spelman College. *I hope everything is going well,* I thought as I phoned her.

"Hey, Eric," my baby sister answered.

"What's wrong with you? You don't sound too excited to hear from me," I said.

"No, it's not that. I've just so much shit going on right now,"

Rozi stated.

"What's wrong? You know I'm here for you," I said.

"Eric, this is big," she said.

"Ok," I stated. "What is it?"

"Eric, please—you know I kept your secret and you've got to keep mine," she said. "Just how Black can't find out that you like dudes, he can't find out about this."

"Ok," I said. "Rozi, what is it?"

"Eric, I'm pregnant."

"WHAT THE HELL, ROZI!" I yelled.

"C'mon, Eric, I don't need you to be tripping out, too. I've done enough of that shit myself."

"Ok, Rozi," I said. "But how can you do some shit like this?"

"Eric, I don't know! I swear it was a mistake. I don't want no damn kids!"

"So, when are you gonna tell mom?"

"I don't know, Eric," she said. "I don't know what to do."

"How many months are you?" I asked.

"I just made two and a half months," she said.

"Damn, Rozi," I stated. "Raising a kid and going to school is hard."

"I know," she said.

"Did you tell the dude yet?" I asked.

"See, that's the other problem," she said.

"You didn't tell him?"

"Yeah, I told him."

"Oh, he's one of those deadbeat ass niggas."

"No, Eric. This one is on me."

"What'cha mean, Rozi?"

"Ok, I met this dude during MLK weekend earlier this year. He's from Atlanta, but ironically, he goes to FAMU. We met at a party that some Kappa's at Morehouse were throwing. We kicked it off and before he left to go back to Tallahassee, I slept with him."

"Ok, but you said that you are two and a half months, January is a whole lot longer than two months ago," I said.

"Eric, let me finish," she said.

"Ok."

"Well, he turned out to be a good dude and we kept talking and he came back up another weekend, a few weeks later. We had sex again."

# Life of a College Bandsman 2: Is This Love

"Ok."

"Well, he kept coming up to Atlanta and we kept fucking. Then he told me that he wanted to make me his girl," Rozi stated. "I never told him that I would be his girl, but it's something that we could work on."

"Ok."

"So, then he came home for the summer. We were fucking a lot and then we had an argument over some bullshit. I think he started that damn argument so he could go and be with some of his friends. I knew somebody he knew from FAMU was coming into town that weekend and he wanted to chill with them instead of me. So, some of my girls was trying to take my mind off of him and they took me to this club," she said.

"What happened at the club, Rozi?" I asked.

"Well, I wasn't feeling the club because my mind was still on my friend, but then I saw this other dude who just blew me away," she said. "I went up to him and I introduced myself and he did the same and we got to know one another. He was a real gentleman. He was really polite and he was interested in me."

"That's good."

"So, we chilled out after the club let out, but we didn't do anything. I called him up the next day and we went out again. I learned that he goes to FAMU, too."

"What?" I said. "Now that's crazy, Rozi. Are you serious?"

"Yes, Eric, I promise," she said.

"Damn."

"Yeah, but we chilled out and shit and we eventually went back to his hotel and before you knew it, we had fucked, too."

"Damn, Rozi," I said. "You can't be giving out the goods to everyone."

"I'm not," she said. "I swear those are the only two dudes I fucked this year. But keep in mind that I had been fucking the first dude, too."

"Umm, hmm," I said.

"So, soon after I found out I was pregnant."

"And?"

"And I was too afraid to tell the first dude, so I told the second one that I was, but I told him that the kid was his. He went off on the deep end because he said that he was in a relationship and that was gonna fuck shit up. He asked me was I sure and I told him yeah.

But the problem is that the kid isn't his, it's the first dude," she said.

"How do you know? You were fucking both of them."

"Because the time doesn't add up," she stated. "The doctor said that I'm ten weeks pregnant, but I didn't have sex with the second dude until eight weeks ago. It ain't his."

"Oh, damn, why did you tell him that it was his?"

"Because at the time I thought it could have been. I didn't know how many months I was at the time. I found out after the fact. I just don't know how to tell him and then that means that I gotta tell the first dude."

"Rozi, you've got to tell him," I said.

"But I'm thinking about getting an abortion. I still have two weeks. Eric, I can't have any kids right now," she said.

"An abortion Rozi? You know that's against what we believe in."

"I DON'T KNOW WHAT ELSE TO DO!" she yelled.

"Well, who are the dudes?" I asked.

"I can't tell you," she said.

"Why not?" I asked.

"I told you that they both go to FAMU. You or Chaz might know them."

"You don't trust me, Rozi?" I asked. "Besides, I attend Florida State."

"I trust you, but you might wanna go and confront them and shit and I ain't ready for that yet," she said. "I know you go to FSU, but you or Chaz might know them."

"I guess, Rozi," I rolled my eyes.

"I gotta get off the phone, but please keep this one between us— like I kept your secret. Please—PLEASE—don't tell Black. Eric, please don't tell Black. You know how he gets."

"Ok, Rozi," I said. "This is between us."

"Ight, Eric, I'll call you and let you know what I decided."

"Ok."

When I got off the phone, one person immediately came in mind.

"Naw," I said, as I shook my head.

But, as I thought about it, he is from Atlanta. He did go up to Atlanta during MLK weekend because he asked me if I wanted to come. He was home the entire summer and he did make frequent trips up to Atlanta during the spring semester.

The more I thought about it, the more I told myself that I was just tripping. What's the chance that *he* was the dude that my sister

# Life of a College Bandsman 2: Is This Love

was talking about?

Now the second dude could be anyone, but if that first dude is who I think it is, it's gonna be a fucking problem!

"Matter fact—let me call his ass right now."

# 36

## *Dwight*

As Amir walked into my room, I noticed his strange walk. I laughed and said, "Damn, nigga who fucked you?"

"WHAT?" he snapped.

"Nigga, you heard me—who put their dick in your ass?"

"Man, you better watch that shit, dawg. I ain't gay," he said, upset.

"Yeah, man," I continued to laugh.

"Ain't shit funny, Dwight," Amir said.

"Ight, man, I'ma stop," I said, as I looked at him.

I've been wondering for years when was this fool was just gonna stop beating around the bush and just come out and say it. I mean I really can care less if he fucks with dudes or not. I figured that he would have figured that out by now, but to each his own.

"What bring you over today?" I asked.

"Just bored at the house. Just got finished having a heart-to-heart with one of my roommates," Amir said.

"Oh, ok," I said. "Roommates are things of the past and I can't wait to get into my one bed, one bath."

"Spoiled ass nigga," Amir said.

"Nigga it ain't being spoiled, it's called hard work."

"Whatever, nigga. Hard work with momma and daddy's help."

"Well, same difference," I chuckled.

"Take a trip with me," Amir said.

"Where?"

"To my brother's crib."

"Ight," I said, as I got my stuff.

On the ride over to his brother's apartment, Amir kept talking about these bitches that he was fucking.

"Man, this one bitch got a big ass, dawg. That's like the biggest shit I've ever seen."

"You know I thought I fucked a lot, but I think you got me beat," I said.

"Yeah, man, you know I fuck two, sometimes three times a day," he said.

"Nigga, yo' dick gonna fall off," I said.

"I've got enough of it to last for a long time," he said, as he looked over at me.

"Nigga, you're crazy," I said, as we got out of the car.

His brother, Dallis, let us in the apartment and said, "What's going on, y'all? It's good to see you again, Dwight."

"Same here," I said, as I looked at him. I immediately thought back to that night, and I couldn't believe that he did that shit. What the fuck got into his ass?

"You know I'm really sorry about that," he said.

"About what?" Amir asked.

"Just some stuff that happened a while ago," I said.

"Yeah, it was a long time ago," Dallis added.

"I guess. How was Jacksonville?" Amir asked.

"It was good, man," Dallis said. "I really appreciate it. I really needed that getaway."

"What y'all do down there?" I asked, as we sat down in the living room.

"Man, we had a lot of fun," he said. "We went out to a few clubs, partied, shopped, went to some more clubs, fucked a bit, you know," he said, as he started to laugh.

"Nigga, who you fucking?" Amir said, as he looked at his brother.

"Don't worry 'bout it," Dallis said. "Who you fucking?"

"Hell, who ain't he fucking needs to be the question," I laughed.

"It ain't even like that, Dwight," Amir chuckled.

"So, you're really going back to the band?" I asked.

"Yeah, man," Dallis said. "I know I said that it wasn't for me, but I really missed it last year, so I just told myself that I will give it another year. But if I ain't feeling that shit, then I'm out."

"I guess, man," I said.

"Yo, I've got to use the bathroom," Amir said, as he went to his brother's room.

"Yo, Dwight, I really meant that shit man," Dallis said. "I'm really sorry and I promise it won't happen again."

"I mean I kinda flipped out, too," I said. "And I said something's that I shouldn't have, but something happened in my past that called for that, and for that I'm sorry."

"You have no reason to apologize," he said. "I was in the wrong. I just don't know what came over me."

"So, how long have you been like that?" I asked.

"Since as far as I could remember, but I never did anything until I came up here. The band turned me out," he said, as he started to laugh.

"Yeah, I know of some people who have been turned out," I laughed.

"What y'all niggas in here laughing about, because I don't find shit funny!" Amir said, as he stood in the hallway.

"Nothing, man, we were just being stupid. What's wrong with you?" I said.

"WHAT THE FUCK IS THIS?" Amir said, as he tossed a DVD over to his brother.

When his brother got the DVD, he froze in place.

Amir yelled, "NIGGA, WHAT THE FUCK IS THAT? WHY THE FUCK YOU GOT PORNOS OF DUDES AND SHIT IN YOUR ROOM?"

"WHY YOU GOING THROUGH MY SHIT?" Dallis yelled back.

"NIGGA, IT WAS RIGHT THERE ON YOUR DAMN BED!" Amir said.

"YOU ALWAYS DO THIS SHIT!" his brother said. "YOU'RE TOO FUCKING NOSY!"

Amir took a deep breath and said, "Yo', I'ma ask you this shit and you better give me the fucking truth!"

His brother just looked at him. I could tell that he felt his world was crashing down.

Amir paused and said, "Hold up—is that why you went to Jacksonville, so you could go to *those* type of clubs?"

"I don't know what you're talking about," his brother said.

"Dallis, are you gay?" Amir asked, as he looked at his brother.

*"Oh, shit,"* I said to myself.

"WHAT?" Dallis yelled. "HOW THE FUCK CAN YOU ASK ME SOMETHING LIKE THAT?"

"I'm just saying, you've got a fucking gay porno and shit on your fucking bed. What the fuck am I supposed to think, Dallis Knight?" Amir said back to him.

"Amir Knight, why are you acting like this?" Dallis said, as tears started to flow from his eyes. "I thought you said that you loved me."

"I do love you and I will do anything for you. You're my fucking brother," Amir said.

"Why you tripping?" Dallis said. "If you love me then you will love everything that comes with me."

"So, are you admitting that you fuck with dudes?" Amir asked.

Dallis didn't say anything.

"Are you gay?" Amir asked.

"I'm what I am," Dallis said.

"What the fuck is that supposed to mean?" Amir asked.

"It means what it means," Dallis said, as he looked at Amir.

I personally didn't understand why Amir was tripping out like that especially since he fucks with dudes, too.

"Dwight, what the fuck does *I am what I am* supposed to mean?" Amir asked me.

"Dawg, this is between you and your brother," I said. I didn't want to get involved in this bullshit.

"YES, SHIT!" Dallis yelled. "IS THAT WHAT YOU WANTED TO HEAR?"

"I just want to hear the truth, baby bro," Amir said in a calm tone.

"Yes, I fuck around with dudes," Dallis finally stated. "Happy now?"

Amir looked at his brother for a second, and then he looked over at me. He said, "Dallis, let me explain something to you."

"What's that?" Dallis said.

"Being honest, I knew you were fucking around with dudes for a while now," Amir said.

"WHAT?" Dallis yelled.

"Yeah, bro, I'm not stupid by a long shot," Amir said. "I was just hoping that you would keep that shit on the low man, but this ain't the way to keep shit on the low."

"You knew I liked dudes?" Dallis said shocked.

"Yeah," Amir responded.

"And why didn't you say anything?" Dallis asked.

"Because it was your personal business," Amir stated. "That's yo' shit, bro."

"So, you don't care?" Dallis asked.

"I care. I care about everything that you do," Amir said. "But once again, that is your decision."

"Does it bother you?" Dallis asked his brother.

"Honestly?" Amir said.

"Yeah, honestly," Dallis said.

"No," Amir replied. "Everyman has to his life in the way that makes him happy."

"So, why were you tripping?" Dallis asked.

*I was a lil curious to that, too.*

"I really didn't mean to trip," Amir said. "But seeing that shit caught me off guard. But my main thing is if I saw it, then anyone else could have saw it. Dallis, you can't have everyone in your business. If you're gonna do that shit, just make sure you keep that shit on the low. You don't want everyone to know that you're going around fucking with dudes and shit. I'm not saying that anything is wrong with fucking with dudes, but I would hate if someone came up to me and told me some shit about you."

"Oh, ok," Dallis said. "So as long as I keep it on the low, it's ok? But if I decide to come out then it would be a problem?"

"All I'm saying is that I would prefer that this kind of shit be kept on the low," Amir stated.

"Well, you don't have to worry about that because I ain't trying to come out or nothing," Dallis said.

"Cool, bro," Amir stated.

"That's why I love you so much, you don't judge me," Dallis said, as he came over and gave his brother a hug.

"Ight, man, enough of this emotional shit," Amir said, as he started to laugh.

"I've got one more question," Dallis said, as he went back to his seat.

"What's that?" Amir stated.

"You're not gonna tell mom or dad are you?" Dallis asked.

"No, this is just between you, me and Dwight," Amir said, as he motioned for me to come on.

"Cool, thanks so much," Dallis said.

"Well, we're gonna be out," Amir said.

"Ight, y'all," Dallis said, as he walked us to the door.

"Be easy, man," I said as we left.

When we got in the car, Amir didn't say too much of nothing. I wanted to ask him about it, but I decided to wait until a later time. When we got back to my house, Amir still didn't say anything. I knew that this was my time and opportunity, so I just went for it.

"Is it really bothering you?" I asked.

"What's that?" Amir said, as he looked over at me. I could tell that I broke his train of thought.

"Is the situation with your brother really bothering you?" I asked.

"Man, it's just I really didn't want him to know that I knew," he said.

"Why is that?" I asked. "He should be a lil more free now."

"Yeah, but it's just hard to explain," Amir said.

"Why is it so hard?"

"I don't know," Amir said.

"Is it because you are one in the same?" I asked.

"What?" Amir said.

"Maybe it's so hard to explain because you and your brother are the same person," I said.

"What the hell is that supposed to mean?" he said, as he looked at me.

"It means that you are just like your brother—both of you like dudes," I said.

"DAWG, I AIN'T NO PUNK!" Amir yelled.

"I didn't call you a punk and it ain't no need to get upset. I don't care what y'all do and you don't have to keep lying to me. I know what the deal is and I know why you're walking like that," I said.

"Dawg, you just don't understand," Amir said, as his eyes started to tear up.

"Yes, I do," I said. "It's cool, and like you told your brother, every man has got to do what makes him happy."

"No, you don't understand," Amir stated.

"Well, help me to understand," I said.

"Man, it's hard," he said, as the tears started to flow. "I don't wanna be this way, but I can't help it."

"What's wrong?" I said.

"Dawg, this is hard for me to explain," he said.

"Ok, man," I said. "Just let it flow. Tell me what got you this way."

"Ok," he said, as he took a deep breath "This is my story…"

# 37

## *Dwight*

I stared at Amir and said, "So, what happened?"

"Like I said, this is big for me. I've never told anyone this before," Amir stated.

"Ok," I said, as Amir phone started to ring.

Amir looked at his phone and pushed the ignore button. He said, "When I was around twelve, my brother and I went to visit some family for the summer. When we got there, everything was cool, it wasn't any problems but then things started to change."

"What happened?"

"Well, my brother had found some friends to play with, but I really wasn't feeling the people there so I tended to stay in the house. That's when I started lifting weights. It gave me something to do."

"Ok."

"Well, *he* started talking to me and showing me shit."

"Shit like what?"

"Pornos and shit. That was my first time seeing something like that and I liked it. That went on for a few days and one day he told me to look up. When I looked up, he was naked with a hard dick. I asked him what was going on and he told me that it was natural, we were supposed to get like this. He told me to take off my clothes. I was a little nervous, but I did it."

Amir took a deep breath and continued, "He went down and started to suck my dick. That was the best feeling in the world at the time. He asked me if I like it and I told him yeah. He said I was supposed to like it."

"Ok, what happened next?"

"Well, that went on for a few days and then he asked me to do it to him," Amir stated. "I was a little nervous, but he did it to me, so I thought that it must have been ok, so I did it back. He then told me that this was the best part of it and he told me to lay on my back. He then put what I now know as lube on my ass and started to enter me. I was in pain, nervous and scared, but I knew that he wouldn't do anything to hurt me. The first few times I didn't like it, but the more we did it, the more I started to enjoy it. I knew it was wrong, but I couldn't help it. It was something that I looked forward too. This happened like two-to-three times a week. Then one day later in the summer I had enough of it and I told him that I couldn't do that shit no more. He tried to play a guilt trip on me and he started to say some shit about my brother. I didn't want my brother to experience this shit, so I continued to do it. I did it to protect my brother."

"Damn, Amir."

"Yeah, that went on until I was about sixteen. Every time I'd see him, we would do something. I knew it was wrong, but I couldn't allow it to happen to my brother. At this time, I was really feeling dudes and I couldn't help it. But when I was with other dudes, I felt different about it and I started to really get into it."

"Damn, this is crazy," I said.

"Yeah, it is. I knew that I was supposed to like females, but I had an attraction to dudes that I couldn't explain. Then I found out that one of my homeboy's that was deep in the street life was down with this shit and that changed everything for me. When I realized that dudes who look like me fucks with dudes, too—that shit put me in places that I've never been before. I was always low key about mine though, I couldn't let anyone know that I was fucking around with dudes. And to be honest, I've tried to change, but I can't. I fucks with females to remind myself that I'm still a man and, more importantly, so people won't think that I fuck with dudes. That's why I always keep females around."

"Damn, so what exactly is your role in the bedroom when you're with dudes?"

"I guess you can say that I'm versatile. I like to get fucked and I like to fuck, too," Amir stated.

"Damn."

"Yeah, right now, this dude is doing me in and I like that shit. But when I leave him, I go and return the favor to this other dude. You might know him, he's in the band."

# Life of a College Bandsman 2: Is This Love

"I probably do," I said. "Can I ask you a question?"

"Yeah."

"How come you never told someone in your family?"

"Because I didn't know how they would respond. I didn't know how *he* would respond. I didn't know what to do."

"You keep saying *he*. Who is *he*?" I asked.

"Damn, man," Amir said. "Please don't judge me or look at me any differently."

"I won't," I said.

"HE, the man who did this shit to me…HE the man who made me like dudes… HE…that man… is my father."

# 38

## Chaz

*Friday, August 15, 2003*

Genevieve came out of the bathroom and asked, "Baby, are you gonna be here all day?"

"Yeah, I think so," I said. "I don't really have anything planned. Why you ask?"

"Because I wanted to go out with my sister for a lil bit," she said.

"Oh, ok. I can watch Xavier and Elijah. It won't be a problem," I said.

"Oh, thanks so much," she said, as she walked over and kissed me. "I think moving in together was the best thing that we could have done."

"I think so, too," I said. "I really think this is working out for the best."

"Me, too," she said. "But look I'ma make you something to eat first and then I'ma head out."

"Ok, baby," I said, as I gave her a kiss.

A few moments later, she yelled from the kitchen, "Baby, Ian is outside!"

"He is?" I asked. He was supposed to be at practice.

"Hey, Ian," I heard her say, as I walked out to the living room with Elijah in my arms.

"What's going on, Genevieve?" he said.

"What are you doing here?" I asked. "Aren't you supposed to be at practice?"

"They're at lunch," Ian said. "You ain't been gone that long from the band not to know what's going on."

"Oh, yeah," I said. "I didn't realize what time it was. It was a long night and long morning."

"Y'all back at it again?" he said, as he started to laugh. "Baby number three is gonna be coming soon."

"NO, THE HELL IT AIN'T!" Genevieve yelled from the kitchen.

Ian chuckled.

I wouldn't mind having another kid. All was missing was marriage and a baby girl and everything would be complete.

Ian said, "Man, I don't know why you couldn't just come back and march another year. Dr. Hunter was tripping when he picked the two new drum majors. I have tried everything to get them up to par. One is getting it, but the other one sucks. I don't get it. He sucked at the audition and he still sucks. His concept sucks. His leadership skills suck and everyone in the band can see that he sucks. He's fucking up my lineup," Ian said frustrated.

"Well, Mr. Head Drum Major, you've gotta make him better," I said.

"But, Chaz I've been working with him since April. It's August and he still sucks. I don't know what else to do. I said that I wasn't gonna beat them, but he is really pushing me to that point," Ian stated.

"You know when we got selected for drum major, our head drum major wasn't having that shit and we got our ass tore out of the frame until we got everything perfect," I said.

"Yeah, I know, but I just didn't want to do that," Ian said.

"Sometimes you gotta do what you gotta do," I said. "The upperclassmen come back tomorrow and they are gonna tear his ass into pieces."

"Yeah, that is true," Ian stated.

"Plus, y'all have a performance next Saturday, and you know if some of the older drum majors hear that y'all fucking up, it's gonna be hell on the whole squad—especially you, Mr. Head Drum Major. So, you better fix it and fix it ASAP," I said.

"Baby," Genevieve said, as she came out of the kitchen.

"Yes."

"The food is done and my sister is outside, so I'll be back later," she said, as she came over and gave me kiss.

"Ok, have fun."

"See you later, Ian," she said, as she walked out the house.

# Life of a College Bandsman 2: Is This Love

"I'm so glad you came around," Ian said to me when Genevieve left.

"What do you mean?"

"I'm glad that you started a life with Genevieve and let that shit with Zach and Eric go," Ian said.

"Yeah, man," I said. "I realized that I couldn't keep dwelling on the past."

"That's good hear," Ian said. "I'm real proud of you, Chaz."

"Nigga, you better get your ass back to campus before they start calling you."

"Yeah, man, I guess I better go," he said, as he started to walk towards the door. "I'll get at you later."

"Ight, tell Quinton I said what's up."

"Ight, bro," Ian said as he left.

As soon as he left, my phone started to ring. "Hello?" I said.

"Chaz?"

"What's up, Ra'Jon?" I said.

"I just made it to Orlando."

*****

# Michelle

*Norfolk, Virginia*

I had finally caught my dad in the house and I was determined to get some answers. "Daddy, what's going on?"

"What do you mean, Princess?" he asked.

"Daddy, I'm not stupid," I said. "I may be the youngest in this family, but I'm no dummy."

"I know you're no dummy, Michelle. It's just I rather you not worry about some other stuff. You need to focus on finishing out your senior year in high school," he told me.

"But, Daddy, this is crazy! I deserve to know something!"

"Oh, Michelle, you're feisty just like your mother."

"Daddy!"

"Ok, Michelle," he sighed. "Your mother and I aren't seeing eye-to-eye right now."

"I can see that," I said. "What is the problem?"

187

"Just marriage pains," he said. "You know twenty-five years is a long time."

"Yeah, I know. But what is the real reason because that is a crazy answer."

He paused and said, "Michelle, I cheated on your mom."

"YOU DID WHAT?"

"I cheated," he said again, as he looked at me.

"But Daddy how can you do that to mommy? She's never done anything to you," I stated.

"Michelle, I'm gonna say this one last thing and I'm gonna leave this conversation alone."

"What is it?" I asked, leaning against the kitchen countertop.

"Everything isn't always what it seems," he said.

"What is that supposed to mean?"

"Ask your mom," he said, as he started to walk off.

"DADDY!" I said, as I ran after him.

"Yes?" he said, as he turned around.

"Where are you staying?"

"I'm staying at a hotel until I can find something."

"Find something? You're not coming back?"

"It doesn't seem that way, Princess. I think my marriage with your mom is over."

"BUT DADDY," I started to cry. "Why does it have to be like this? Why can't y'all work it out?"

"You know at some point in your life, you have to be real with yourself and stop lying. And I'm at one of those points right now. It is in the best interest of everyone in this family," he said.

"Daddy, this is ludicrous!"

"This is the way it has to be, Princess," he said, as he started to walk to the door.

"WHAT THE HELL ARE YOU DOING IN MY HOUSE!" my mother yelled, as she walked in.

"Rachelle, I don't have time for your antics and shit today," my dad said.

"You disgust me. Get the fuck out of my house!" she said.

"The last time I heard, the house was in both of our names, so technically it is still mine, too," he said.

"I don't give a fuck whose fucking name is on this house; you need to get the fuck out!" she yelled.

"Mommy, why are you talking to him like that?" I asked.

# Life of a College Bandsman 2: Is This Love

"Michelle, stay out of it," she said to me.

"SO, WHEN ARE YOU GONNA TELL THE BOY? HUH, RACHELLE? WHEN THE FUCK ARE YOU GONNA TELL HIS ASS THE FUCKING TRUTH? RUNNING AROUND HERE LIKE YOU'RE INNOCENT IN THIS WHOLE DAMN THING! WHEN THE FUCK ARE YOU GONNA TELL HIM?" my dad yelled.

"When are you gonna confront your fucking lover?" she asked him.

"What boy, what lover?" I asked.

"MICHELLE, GO TO YOUR ROOM RIGHT NOW!" my mom yelled at me.

"NO, BABY, YOU CAN STAY!" my father said. "AT SOME POINT SHE'S GOTTA KNOW THE TRUTH!"

"Do you really want that shit to come out, Michael?" my mom asked him.

"It's bound to come out at some point or another. But to be honest, I don't know what's worst, mine or yours. You ain't no damn saint in this shit, either," he said.

"Go to hell!" she said.

"I guess you'll join me there!" he said. "Running around here like your shit don't stink."

"Fuck you!" she said.

"You know if you would've told me the truth back then, maybe we wouldn't be in this damn situation now."

"Excuse me?" my mom said.

"WOMAN, YOU HEARD ME! IF YOU WOULD'VE TOLD ME THE TRUTH THEN, I PROBABLY WOULDN'T HAVE MARRIED YOUR ASS!"

My mom didn't say anything to him. She just looked at him. I could tell that the last statement really hurt her.

"GET … YOUR… FUCKING…FAGGOT… ASS… OUT … OF… MY … DAMN… HOUSE!" my mom yelled, as tears started to run from her eyes.

"Faggot?" I said. "Daddy?"

"Michelle," he said.

"Daddy, you're gay, too?" I asked.

"Michelle," he sighed.

"I guess it all makes sense now," I said, as I thought about all my brothers and their alternative life styles. I'm happy I got the straight gene. Dick is too damn good to be around here licking clits and shit.

He said, "You know, Rachelle, I'm gonna take the high road and leave this alone. I could tell your shit, but what good is that gonna do? You know what you need to do and it needs to happen ASAP, because I need to know the truth."

"GET OUT!" she said again.

With that, my dad left.

"Faggot?" I said again.

"Yes, Michelle, your dad is in love with a man," my mom coldly said, as she went upstairs.

*"What the fuck is happening to my family?"* I said to myself, as I took a seat at the dining room table.

RJ, Raidon, Morgan, Micah, and now my father all like dudes. What kind of shit is this?

# 39

# *Raidon*

I was back in Tallahassee and I feel like this is where I needed to be. I still couldn't believe that I was HIV-positive. How could someone like *me* be positive? I was the good dude, but they say that good dudes always finish last.

The man I was still in love with had moved on with someone else. Being here around Eric was going to be tough. I really wanted Eric, but I know that can't happen. On top of that, I lied and told him that I was negative. I know that was wrong, but I can't have people in my business like that.

*Why did I ask Eric to come over here today? What was I thinking?*

Hell, what the fuck am I supposed to do about sex? I'm in the fucking prime of my life and I need sex—it's not an option. I don't like to jack off, so something has got to give.

Just as I was getting settled into my new place, Phil called me. I answered, "What?"

"What's wrong with you?" he asked.

"I know you, of all people, is not asking me that shit. You just fucked my life over!"

He didn't say anything.

"What the fuck do you want, Phil?"

"Damn, I was just calling to check up on you and to see how everything was going."

"How the fuck do you think it's going?" I plopped down on the bed, trying to hold back the tears.

"I'm really sorry, Raidon. I didn't mean for this to happen. Shit, I'm positive, too!"

"And that's supposed to make me feel better? Phil, you're full of shit!"

"Raidon, don't be like that."

"Phil, if I were you, I would stay away from me right now because if I see you I might kill you."

"WHAT?"

"Phil, I'm serious. I fucking hate your ass right now and I would appreciate it if you didn't contact me again. If I need to talk to you, I will call you."

"Raidon, you don't mean that," he said.

"Phil, I'm not playing. Until I can get myself together, I don't want shit to do with you," I said, as I hung up the phone.

*What the fuck his problem? That fuck nigga just gave me the bug and he's acting like shit didn't happen. Fuck him!*

Just as I gathered my thoughts, there was a knock at my door. I was expecting Eric. When I looked out the peephole, he was standing there looking sexy as hell. I took a deep breath and then opened the door.

After we exchanged greetings, he looked around and said, "I like the place, Raidon."

"Thanks, I still have a lot of unpacking to do," I said, as I lead him into the living room. "Please, have a seat."

He looked at me for a moment then asked, "Are you ok, Raidon?"

"Yeah, I'm good. Why you ask?"

"You just look like someone killed your mom."

"Well, I am dealing with some family issues, but I'll be ok."

"You sure?" he asked.

"Yeah, I'm sure," I forced a smile.

"You know I'm really happy that those results came back negative. I know that had to have been a scary time for you," Eric said, as he looked at me.

"Man, I can't describe how that shit felt," I said.

"I can only imagine," he said. "But everything works out for the best, huh."

"Yeah, it does," I said. "So, how's the love life coming along?" I had to get the attention off of me.

He smiled and said, "It can't be better. We're really doing good right now."

"That's good to hear," I smiled.

# Life of a College Bandsman 2: Is This Love

He said, "You know when you up and left me and went back to Norfolk, I didn't know what I was gonna do, but I guess everything happens for a reason. This dude is the best thing that has happened to me."

"Is that so?" I said. Hearing him say that really hurt. The longer I sit here and talk about his new love life, the more I get frustrated.

"Yeah, man," he said. "If you ever meet him, you would understand why, too."

"Well, maybe we will cross paths one day," I said.

"I'm sure," Eric stood up and looked towards the front door.

"You're leaving already?" I asked.

"Yeah, I've gotta go pick him up from practice. I was just stopping by to see you and to check out the place," Eric said.

"Oh, ok," I said. I really didn't want him to leave. "Well, come see me again sometime."

"I will do," he said, as he gave me a hug. "It's nice to have you back in town."

"It's good to be back."

After he left, I exhaled.

*"Damn, I love his ass,"* I said to myself, as I went back to fixing up my new house.

# 40

## *Zach*

Eric was right on time. I smiled as I saw him pull up. Once I got in the car, I said, "Thanks, Eric." I wanted to kiss him but I was sweaty and stank.

"No problem, lil pimpin'," he said, as we drove off. "Why are you leaving so early?"

"They're at lunch. Jared said that Kris and I didn't have to come back until 7:30 when night practice resumes."

"Oh, ok."

"Yeah, so I just wanna go home, shower and catch up on some sleep," I said.

"Oh, ok," Eric said.

We listened to the radio in silence for a few moments, and then he blurted, "Raidon is back in town."

I looked over to Eric and said, "Really?"

"Yeah, I just came from visiting him."

"Oh," I said, as I turned back to face the passenger window. I really didn't like that shit, but I can't control who his friends are.

"He is good people, Zach. I promise you will like him once you meet him."

"If you say so," I said, as we arrived at my new place. *Who in the hell said I wanted to meet Raidon?*

As I opened the car door, Eric said, "Call me when you're ready to go back."

"Ok, baby," I said, getting out of the car, slamming the door.

When I walked inside my apartment, I went straight for my shower. I didn't turn the T.V. or the radio on because if I did, I knew

I wasn't gonna get any sleep. After my quick shower, I headed to my room and jumped on my bed. Just as I laid down, my phone started to ring. It was my grandma.

"Zachie, how are you doing?" she said.

"I'm ok," I said. "What's going on?"

"I just got the strangest feeling to call you. Something is telling me that you need to watch out," she said.

"Oh, grandma, are we back on this again? I thought that was over."

"Well, it was over, but now it's back," she said. "This feeling is strong. You and whoever that you're close too up there needs to be careful. Something bad is gonna happen."

"Grandma, no disrespect, but you sound crazy."

"You can call it what you like, but something or somebody is working hard against you and y'all need to be careful. I know what I'm talking about. Pay close attention to everything and don't trust anyone."

"Ok, Grandma."

"Watch yourself, Zachie," she said, as she hung up the phone.

She really irks my nerves with this *visionary* shit.

"Finally," I said, as I started to prepare myself to go to take a nap.

I didn't get too far into the sleep because a few minutes later, I heard Micah enter the house, talking on the phone.

"Yeah," he said. "Hold on...Ight."

"I don't know what to do," a female said.

*"Great, he put it on speakerphone, now I can hear the convo,"* I said to myself, as I quietly got out of my bed and took a seat on the floor by the door. Micah was in his room across the hall.

"Rozi, just get rid of it," Micah said.

"But that is against what I believe in," she said. "I wanna have an abortion, but I don't know if it is the right thing to do."

"I know I shouldn't have done that shit," he said. "What the fuck was I thinking?"

"Well, we can't go back to the past now," she said. "What's done is done."

"How the fuck am I supposed to know that the damn baby is mine?" Micah said. "I mean I slept with you the second day I met you. I don't know you. I don't know if you're fucking other niggas, too."

She yelled, "Micah, you are not going to call me a whore! I told you the baby is your child!"

"Yeah, whatever," he said. "This shit is really fucking up my life and my relationship."

"Well, you should've thought about that damn relationship before you put your damn dick in my pussy," she said.

"Rozi, just get rid of the damn baby and we can go back to our personal lives and shit," he said. "I have saved up enough money to get the fucking abortion. Time is running out!"

"Micah, I'ma call you back. My mom is calling," she hung up the phone.

"FUCK!" Micah yelled. "WHAT THE FUCK AM I GONNA DO!"

I quietly got back in my bed and exhaled.

Micah cheated on Kris and got somebody pregnant. Damn, that's why he's been acting like this. That is so fucked up. Kris is going to be devastated.

*****

# *Ra'Jon Harris*

Once I was situated, I phoned Chaz and said, "So, I'm in Orlando now."

"Where exactly are you?" he asked.

"I'm at the restaurant you said he goes to for lunch every day."

"Ok," Chaz said. "Do you see him?"

"I'm looking at the picture that you sent, but I don't see him yet," I said, looking around the establishment.

"Oh, maybe he's running a bit late. He eats there every day, so I know he's coming," Chaz said. "You remember what you gotta do, right?"

"Yes, Chaz," I said. "I remember."

"Good, because if this shit goes wrong then all of our asses gonna be fucked up," he said.

"I know," I said. "It won't go wrong though."

"You got all the documents and shit?"

"Yes, Chaz," I said. "I have everything."

"Ok."

"Oh, shit," I said a bit nervous.

"What?"

"He's coming in now," I said. "Damn, he's cute, Chaz."

"Ra'Jon, please. Umm, call me and let me know what happened."

"Ok," I said, as I hung up the phone. I took a deep breath and said, "*Here goes nothing*," as I walked over to him, sitting at the bar. I was a little nervous, but it had to be done. I took a seat next to him and said, "What's going on, man?"

"Ain't shit," he looked at me. "Just got off work a lil late."

"Oh, ok, that's what's up," I said, as the waiter came over to me. "Can I just have combo number two with a Coke?"

She said, "Ok." She looked to him and said, "The usual?"

"Yep," he smiled.

"Ok," she said, as she walked away.

"That number two combo is my favorite thing to eat here," he said to me.

"Yeah, it looked kinda good on the menu," I said.

"Trust me, it is," he said. "I've never seen you here before."

"Oh, I'm new to town," I said. "I'm just learning my way around."

"Oh, where are you coming from?" he asked.

"Virginia."

"Cool. What brings you down here?"

"Man, it's a long story," I said. "But I'm looking forward to the opportunities that await me here."

"That's what's up," he said.

"Man, you seem like good people," I said.

"I am," he said. "Just a hard working dude, trying to make it. It's rough out here in these streets, feel me."

"I feel you on that shit," I said.

"Yo, I can show you around town if you're up for that," he said.

"Yeah, that's cool," I said. "I was actually hoping I could get someone to do that shit. Orlando is a whole lot bigger than from where I'm from."

"Shit, that's a bet," he said. "I'm off for the next three days so maybe we can get up then."

"That's what's up. We can do that. Here's my number," I said, writing it down on a piece of paper.

He grabbed the paper, looked at it and said, "Cool, let me call it right now so I can put it in my phone."

# Life of a College Bandsman 2: Is This Love

After my phone rung, I said, "Ok, I got yours. My name is RJ. I didn't catch yours."

"Oh, my bad, RJ. My name is Blackwell, but everybody just calls me Black."

# 41

## *Chaz*

Now that Ra'Jon's dumb ass was taking care of my shit down in Orlando, it was time that I get my part on the road up here in Tallahassee. Nobody could know what I'm doing. I couldn't even tell Ian. This is strictly between Ra'Jon and myself, but he only knows certain parts of the plan. He must be a fool if he thinks I was to completely trust him with everything.

As much as I hated this part of it, I had to get it done. Ian was a part of this one. Well, not really, but I have to make it believable so nobody won't think no strange shit when everything finally goes down.

But being honest, I really do miss my cousin. I hate that it had to come to this, but I have come to the conclusion that I won't feel better until I get him back. Whether or not I get Zach back isn't important anymore. Being with Genevieve every day is kinda taking my mind off Zach. And once I get this shit over with, I believe that I can focus my total attention on being with and starting a life with her and my kids.

The upperclassmen came back today so I know that they are gonna be in practice for a lil minute, but I want Ian to be here when I do what I have to do. Genevieve and her sister took the kids for the weekend to go visit their parents, so I have the house to myself.

I phoned Ra'Jon and said, "How is everything down there going?"

"It's ok," he said. "I talked to Blackwell for a little bit today but he couldn't talk too long because he had to take a turn around trip down to West Palm Beach."

"Oh, ok, is everything ok?"

"Yeah, he said he had to take something to his mom."

"Oh, ok, well you still know what to do right?" I asked.

"Yes, Chaz, I know what to do. He's gonna take me to church tomorrow, so maybe I will get some time to talk with him then."

"Just let me know if you need anything."

"Ok, Chaz."

"Ight," I said, as I hung up the phone.

While I was waiting for Ian to get out of practice, I started to think about everything and realized how stupid I was. Ian was trying to tell me that Eric had something to do with my relationship with Zach, but because he was my cousin, I kept pushing it off. I really thought that Eric was straight. When he told me that he already knew about me and when he didn't want to tell me who he was talking to, I should have put two and two together. He got that one over on me, but I guarantee I will have the last laugh.

"What's going on, Chaz," Ian said, as he entered my house.

"How was practice?" I asked, leading him into the living room.

"It was cool. The band is gonna be about three hundred and thirty members strong this year. So, we've got a lot to work with," he sat down.

"Cool, but I think I'm ready." I sat down, too.

"Ready for what?" he asked.

"I think I'm ready to mend the fence with Eric," I said. I hated lying to Ian, but this was the only way.

"Really, Chaz?" he asked.

"Yeah, bro, I think I'm ready," I said.

"Shit, I saw him pick up Zach, so you still might be able to catch him before he gets home," Ian said.

"Oh, ok, but can you call him? I mean he might not answer my call," I said.

"Ight," Ian said, as he picked up the phone to call Eric. "What's going on Eric, this is Ian… yeah, but I have a question… can you meet me at Chaz's house ASAP…because there is something that he really wants to say to you…it ain't gonna be no bullshit…ight, see you soon."

"So, he's coming?" I asked.

"Yeah, man, he said he would be here in like fifteen minutes," Ian responded. "You sure about this?"

"Yeah, man," I said. "I'm as sure as I'm gonna be."

# Life of a College Bandsman 2: Is This Love

A few minutes later, I heard a car door close. I walked to the front door and saw Eric. I sighed and opened the door. He walked in the house and said, "What's up, Chaz?"

"What's up, man?" I responded, as I closed and locked the door.

"Ian," Eric said, as he took a seat on the couch.

"What's good?"

"So, what's up, Chaz?" Eric said.

"Where is Zach?" I asked.

"At his apartment. Why?" Eric asked.

"Because I just wanted you here."

He just stared at me.

I said, "But I know it's been a long time, and honestly, I feel that it's time that we squash this shit."

"Chaz, no disrespect, but you cut me off," Eric said.

"I know," I said. "That shit really hurt me, man. It's been about seven months now and I really just need to clear my mind of this shit and it starts with you."

Eric said, "You know to be honest, I was telling Zach about that and how I wish we could just go back to being how we were. I missed my relationship with you. You were like a brother to me."

"And you were to me, but when I found out, that shit killed me to my soul. I just felt like you said *fuck you* to me. You knew how much I loved that dude and you took him right from under me," I said.

"Yeah, I might have done some shit that was wrong, but I felt as if you let it happen. If you weren't going around cheating on him, then the opportunity wouldn't have ever presented itself. And to be clear, I didn't take Zach from you. We were friends. While I liked Zach, I respected your relationship with him. We never did anything sexual while y'all were together. It was just a friendship. I didn't want him to tell you because I didn't want you to find out about me. But when you told me about you, we were making plans to tell you that we knew each other. That's when Zach told me that he wanted to give it another shot with you. I never intended to hurt you."

"And I shouldn't have done what I did that night to you," I said.

"You know Chaz, that was really some foul shit and I really thought that we were better than that. That night changed everything."

"Yeah, it did," I said. "I don't know what got into me but I really want to apologize for my actions. I know that it's not gonna be

203

peaches and crème over night, but I want us to work on being close again."

"Me, too," Eric said, as he came over to give me a hug. "I'm really sorry for everything, too."

"Let's just squash this shit and start over fresh," I said.

"I can do that," he said, as he started to smile.

"Now this is what I'm talking about," Ian said. "This is what I miss."

"Ight, man," Eric said. "I gotta get going but I'ma get at you later, ok."

"Ight, cuzzo," I said as he left.

"See, that wasn't so bad, was it Chaz?" Ian said, as he started to smile.

"No, it wasn't," I said.

"I'm so happy that y'all worked that shit out," he said.

"Me, too," I said.

*But little does he know that this shit is far from over...*

# 42

# *Michael Harris*

*Norfolk, Virginia*

I was really getting fed up with Rachelle's bullshit. Every time I see her ass, she is throwing that shit up in my damn face. Her ass ain't perfect, but I guess she doesn't realize that I raised a kid that may not even be mine. That shit was hard for me to digest. That really hurt me to my soul. I loved all those kids and to hear that one of them may not be mine killed me. Part of that reason was why I hadn't talked to Alonzo. He had been calling me, but I would ignore his calls. I couldn't believe that he was behind this shit. They do say what's done in the dark will always come to the light.

I really hadn't thought of all the consequences that may come from revealing myself, but I did know that I'm ready to be real with myself and finally live my life as the gay man that I am. If I have family that wants to disown me, then to each his own. That simply means they never loved me from day one.

Life without Rachelle is gonna be hard. Honestly, I really did love her, but I feel bad because I involved her in my shit hole of a life.

Being in the hotel these last few weeks has allowed me to some time to really sit and think. I'm gonna take a much needed vacation and get myself together. I don't know where I'm gonna go, but I do know that no one will know where I am—not even Alonzo.

"Hello?" I said, as I finally answered his call.

"Damn, Mike, what the fuck has been going on?" Alonzo said. "I've been trying to call you forever."

"I'm just trying to get myself together," I said.

"So, I take it that you did tell Rachelle," he said.

"Yeah, I told her," I coldly replied.

"How did she take it?" he asked.

"How the fuck do you think she took it?"

"Damn, Mike," he said. "I didn't mean it like that."

"But you know I wasn't the only one who was holding a secret that day," I said.

"What do you mean?"

"I think you know quite clearly what I'm talking about," I stated.

"No, Mike, I don't," he said. "I don't have a clue as to what you're talking about."

"Alonzo, FUCK YOU!"

"Mike, what is the problem?" he said.

"You really don't get it, huh?"

"No, Mike, I swear I don't know what you're talking about," he said.

"Let's go back about twenty-eight, twenty-nine years," I said.

"Ok," he said. "We were in college then."

"Yes, we were," I said.

"Ok, I still don't get where you're coming from," Alonzo stated.

"Alonzo are you that fucking stupid!" I yelled. "How can I be in love with someone like you?"

"Mike, I really don't know what the fuck you're talking about. I honestly don't know."

"Why were you fucking Rachelle when we were in college?"

Alonzo didn't say anything.

"Why were you fucking her?" I yelled.

"Man," Alonzo finally stated. "It was a mistake, Mike."

"A FUCKING MISTAKE? IT DAMN SURE TURNED OUT TO BE A BIG ONE!"

"I swear, Mike, I was upset at you."

"Upset at me for what?" I asked.

"Because you were talking to her. I mean we were supposed to be together and I understand that we had to appear straight, but you were giving her more attention than you were giving me. I was the one you were supposed to be in love with. It was supposed to be me not her," Alonzo explained. "You just don't know how much that shit hurt me, so I was determined to get back at you."

"This is so fucked up, Alonzo."

"But it didn't last that long," Alonzo stated. "Both Rachelle and I decided that this wasn't the thing to do, so we stopped it."

# Life of a College Bandsman 2: Is This Love

"How long did it last?" I asked.

"About two weeks," he stated.

"And how many times, in that period, did y'all fuck?" I asked.

Alonzo didn't say anything.

"I'm waiting for a response," I stated.

"That was so long ago," he said.

"I need a fucking response!"

"Probably two or three times at most," he said.

"Interesting," I said. "Very interesting."

"Where is all this shit coming from?" he asked.

"Oh, just some shit Rachelle was telling me when I finally told her about you," I said.

"But what reasons would she have for telling you that?" he asked.

"Hmmm, let's see. If you just found out that your husband was in love with a dude for thirty-two years, how the fuck would you respond to it? She wanted me to hurt just like I hurt her."

"I guess that makes sense," he said.

"But you know what's funny," I said.

"What's that, Mike?"

"Her secret hurt me a whole lot worse than I hurt her," I said.

"I'm sorry, man. I really am. I didn't mean to, I was just mad at you," Alonzo stated.

"Oh, see what you fail to realize is that it's more than the deceiving and the fucking that is killing me," I said.

"I don't know how many ways to say I'm sorry, Mike," Alonzo pleaded.

"You can't really apologize for this one. See you can't take this one back. What's done has been done and we can't go back and change the past," I said.

"Mike, I don't see where you are going with this," Alonzo stated.

"How are your boys?" I asked.

"Amir and Dallis are fine," he stated. "What does Amir and Dallis have to do with this?"

"I asked how are your boys."

"And I told you," he said.

"Oh, but you're missing one," I stated.

"No, I'm not. I know how many children I have," Alonzo said.

"No, you don't," I said. "I thought I had five children, you know my four boys—Ra'Jon, Raidon, Morgan and Micah, and my Princess, Michelle."

"You do," he stated.

"No, sir. See that's where you're wrong, my friend."

"I'm not following," Alonzo stated.

"Between the two of us, we have seven kids."

"Ok."

"And I was supposed to have five of those seven, but actually I only have four of those seven."

"What?" Alonzo stated.

"See, during that time when you and my wife were messing around, she got pregnant."

"Mike, what are you saying?" he asked.

"I'm saying that my first born son's name is Raidon, not Ra'Jon. And that, my friend, means that, you, sir, Alonzo Jackson, is the father of Ra'Jon Harris."

"Ok, that game was cute Mike, but really is the problem?"

"IT'S NOT A FUCKING GAME! YOU COULD HAVE FATHERED RA'JON NOT ME. YOU COULD HAVE THREE SONS, NOT TWO!"

"You have to be kidding, right," Alonzo stated.

"DO I SOUND LIKE I'M KIDDING," I said.

"OH, FUCK!" Alonzo yelled. "MIKE, I DIDN'T KNOW! OH, MY GOD! I'M SO SORRY!"

"It's too late for apologies now," I said.

"Mike, I'm sorry. Oh, my God."

"Right now I need some time to myself, so don't call me. If and when I want to talk to you, I will call you," I said, as I hung up the phone.

# 43

## *Devin Morrison*

I was getting ready to head out. I walked into his room and asked, "Baby, do you want something from the store?"

"What store are you going to?"

"Walmart."

"Oh, no, I'm good," he said, as his phone started to ring.

"Who's that?" I asked.

"Nobody, just a friend," he said.

"At one in the morning, Morgan?"

"Yeah. I can't have friends that call at one in the morning?" he stared at me.

"Whatever, man. I'll be sleeping at my house tonight," I stormed out of his house.

I still couldn't believe that Morgan was cheating on me. I finally met a dude that I actually liked and this is what he does to me. I finally stopped hoeing around because I wanted to be faithful to him, but he can't be faithful to me. I really didn't want to go back to my old ways, but like I told Chaz the other day, revenge is sweet. Two can play that game. I only wish I knew who he was fucking.

I really wanted to get up with Dwight. Something about his swag turns me the fuck on, but that damn Zach keeps getting in the fucking way.

"Damn," I said to myself, as I walked in Walmart. It was like *trade heaven* up in this bitch. All these damn niggas walking 'round with these fucking basketball shorts and beaters was turning me the fuck on. As I continued to get everything I needed, one dude really caught my eye. I looked at his tall, muscular, chocolate frame. *Fuck.* He was perfect.

I went a few aisles down and when I looked back, he was on the same aisle with me.

"Let me do this again," I said to myself. "If he goes to the next aisle, then I know what's up."

I took my time and went a few more aisles down and when I turned around, he was coming onto that aisle, too.

"Ight, Devin, do what you do best," I said, as I turned around and headed in his direction. He stopped at the canned fruits and I stopped a few feet next to him. I could see him looking out of the corner of his eye, as I fumbled with a can of peaches.

"Excuse me, bruh," I said, as I walked past him.

"Oh, my bad, Shawty," he said back to me. "What you doing out here so late?"

"Just picking up a lil something to last me for a few days," I said.

"Why so late?" he asked.

"I be busy all day and all night, so this is the only time I have to take care of stuff," I said.

"Oh, ok, I feel you," he said.

"Where yo' lady at?" I asked.

"Oh, I'm doing me right now," he responded.

"Is that so?"

"Yep, it is," he said back to me. "Where yo' old lady, Shawty?"

"I'm doing me right now, too," I said.

"Shit, it be like that sometimes," he said.

"I know, man. A nigga like me need to go find me a bitch so I can take care of this nut," I said.

"Damn, I know the feeling," he said. "It's been a lil minute for me, too. I mean some head or something would be like great right now and shit."

"Hell, yeah," I said. "I understand that shit."

"I just can't find a bitch that can suck a nigga dick like how I need it to be sucked. These bitches see my shit and they get scared of it. I need someone that knows how to work a dick like mine, that can embrace this shit," he grabbing his package.

"Shittttt, I know of somebody who can get the job done," I said, as I looked down at the outline of his growing dick.

"Is that so, Shawty?" he said, gripping his dick a bit harder.

"Yeah, it is," I said, as I looked up at him while I licked my lips.

"So, when you gonna hook a nigga like me up on that, Shawty,"

# Life of a College Bandsman 2: Is This Love

he asked, looking around to make sure no one was eavesdropping on our conversation.

"Shit, when you free?" I asked.

"Let me go pay for this stuff and take it home, then I can get at you."

"Ight," I said. "Let me do the same."

"True. Let me get yo' number so I can get at you," he said.

"Ight," I said, as I gave him my number. "Devin."

"Ight, Devin, I'm Amir," he said. "This my number. I'ma hit you up in like forty-five, ok."

"Ight, man," I said, walking away.

I smiled.

*Fuck Morgan. The real Devin is back in business...*

# 44

## Zach

It felt really good to be around all my freshmen brothers again. We had a lot of work to do, but I just knew this edition of the Marching '100' band was going be unstoppable.

I wished it would stop raining. It started raining last night and it hasn't let up at all. We have practice later today and we really need to get this first show together. Our first performance is in a week!

Personally, I'm sexually frustrated. I really need for Eric to get with the program and give me the dick! *Shit!* Foreplay and oral sex is good, but I need to be penetrated. Hell, I can fuck him if that's what he wants. I do have a dick and I'm not afraid to use it.

The last dick I had was Chaz's and that was in December of 2002. It's August of 2003. I know relationships ain't supposed to be based off sex, and that's one of the reasons why Eric didn't want us to have sex like that, but, damn, it's been eight months for me. I think the relationship is pretty fucking strong.

But something really bothers me about this whole thing—why doesn't he want to have sexual intercourse? Eric is twenty-one, soon to be twenty-two years old. Dudes at that age usually have very high sex drives. What is the real reason he doesn't want to have sex? I don't wanna think anything crazy but I don't know what else to think.

My phone started to vibrate, but I didn't recognize the number. I answered it anyway. It was Tony. He said, "What's going on, Z?"

"Oh, what's up," I said.

"This is my new number, so save it," he said.

"Ight. How is everything?" I asked.

"Everything is good," he said. "Coach is really working us hard, but I think I got a good shot at some serious playing time."

"Well, that's good," I said, realizing that Tony was actually in Tallahassee, too. "How is the baby?"

"TJ is good," he said.

"TJ?"

"He's a junior," Tony said. "I don't wanna be walking around here calling him Tony Jr. all the time, so I just say TJ."

"Oh. Is the mother still moving up here?"

"Yeah," he said. "April is coming up in September."

"Oh, ok."

"Yo, Zach?"

"What's up, Tony?"

"I'm really sorry about trying to force you to do something that you didn't want to do," he said.

"Are you really?" I asked.

"Yeah, I am," he said. "I know that shit was wrong and I know you got a dude, but it's just hard for me. I was really feeling you, Z."

"Was?" I said taken aback.

"Yeah, you know you've been telling me for a long time that it's time that we move on. I think that it's time I finally listen to what you've been telling me," Tony explained.

"What brought this on?" I asked somewhat disappointed.

"Just a lot of thinking."

"Nigga, who you fucking?" I asked.

"I ain't fucking nobody," he said.

"All those fine ass dudes on the Florida State football team and you ain't messing with any of 'em?"

"No, man. Not yet anyway," he chuckled. "Seriously though, do you remember that night before you came up to FAMU last year?"

"Yeah, that's when you cooked for me and shit," I said.

"Yeah and then we had sex," Tony said.

"Yeah, I remember," I said, remembering it was unprotected.

"Well, I was thinking about that night and it made me realize a lot of things."

"Things like what?" I asked.

"Us," he said. "I can't keep wasting time on you, trying to get with you. Since you've made it clear that we're not going to happen, I guess that it's best that I just let go of this thing that I want to have with you."

# Life of a College Bandsman 2: Is This Love

"Oh," I said shocked. I really didn't know how to take what he just told me. It really was a slap in my face. I guess I liked the cat and mouse games we played with each other. Not really sure what to say, I replied, "Well, maybe you'll find someone that compliments you."

"I hope so."

"Tony, you'll always be my friend. I'll always be here for you, and you for me, I hope."

"Of course," he said. "But coach wants us to go to church this morning, so I'ma hit you later. I was just checking in on you."

"Ight, Tony," I said. "Get at me later."

"Yep," he said as he hung up the phone.

*Ouch...that shit hurt.*

# 45

## *Raidon*

I hate this shit. I'm sitting here all alone on a Sunday morning and it's raining stupid outside. I'm slowly dying inside and no one knows.

It felt good to be in Tallahassee, but I was trying to avoid facing the truth. This shit really hurts and I don't know what to do. I feel as if I'm locked in a small room with no windows. I just want to escape this hell that I've been put in.

I have HIV. I HAVE HIV!

I know I'm not supposed to feel sorry for myself, but I don't know what else to do. I wanna just sit and cry, but I think I'm all cried out.

Eric doesn't see me like that anymore. If I would have just stayed my ass in Tallahassee, then none of this shit would have ever happened in the first damn place.

"Maybe I should take my ass to church," I told myself, as my phone started to ring.

"Hello?" I answered the phone.

"Hey, baby," my mom said.

"Hey, Mom," I stated. "What's up?"

"I'm calling to see if you're ok," she said.

"I'm ok," I replied.

"Boy, stop lying to me," she said.

"Everything is ok," I said.

"Whatever, Raidon. Are you taking care of yourself?"

"Yes, I'm taking my medications and stuff."

"Good. That's the only way you can live a normal life," she

stated.

"My life isn't normal anymore," I replied.

"It's as normal as you want it to be. You can't sit around here and feel sorry for yourself. Yes, you got it, but now you have to face the facts and live with it. It isn't going anywhere, so you need to make the proper adjustments and continue to live your life. Stop feeling sorry for yourself. This isn't the man I raised!"

I didn't say anything.

"I know you hear me, Raidon," she stated.

"I hear you," I rolled my eyes.

"Good."

"You seem to be in a good mood," I stated.

"I am," she said. "I got up this morning and I went to the early morning church service."

"Yeah, I think I'm gonna go to church, too," I said.

"That's good, Raidon. I went to the alter and released all my worries. I feel so much better. You should do the same. I feel like I can go on with my life."

"Wow, you sound serious," I said.

"I am serious," she said. "I have come to face the facts. I still love your father, but it's time that I move on from that period in my life. But I need you to do me a favor, ok."

"What's that?"

"Go and check on your baby brother," she stated. "I don't want to, but I might need to make a guest appearance down there."

"Why? What's wrong with Micah?" I asked.

"Baby, I don't know," she said. "I call him and he's not himself. I asked Morgan what was going on with Micah and he played stupid with me. I know when something is up with my children and something is wrong with Micah. You know what, don't go over there. Don't tell anyone that I'm coming. I'm gonna book the next flight out. I'll call you when I get everything together so you can pick me up from the airport."

"Is it really this serious, Mom?"

"Raidon, I don't play when it comes to my children. I need to see for myself what's wrong with my baby. I don't care how old you all get, my love and affection for ALL of you will never change."

"Ok, Mom," I said.

"Well, I'm gonna do that right now. So you go ahead and get ready for church and I'll call you back later," she stated.

# Life of a College Bandsman 2: Is This Love

"Ight," I hung up the phone.

After I showered and dressed, I headed to the church on the south side of Tallahassee that I used to attend when was in undergrad at FAMU.

"Nothing has changed," I said to myself, as I looked at all the cars parked at the church. "This place is packed."

I hurried out of car and into the church; it was still raining outside. I was stopped in the lobby because they were praying inside of the sanctuary. Once the prayer was over, the usher opened the door. I immediately noticed a gang of dudes sitting in one section.

"They must play ball or something," I said to myself, as I finally found a seat.

As the service went on, I found out that they did play ball. They were football players for the Florida State Seminoles.

In the midst of the service, one dude caught my attention. He seemed fairly young, but he was a nice catch. The more I looked at him, the more I realized that something was bothering him.

*I wonder what it is?*

I tried to focus my attention on the service, something was really bothering that young man, and I really wanted to help him. I guess that is the teacher in me. It bothers me to see young people in trouble, especially young African-American men. I think that's one of the main reasons why I got into the field of education. Even though I have my own problems, they don't compare to helping others.

I've been teaching for some years now, but I refuse to go to *other* schools. I only get jobs in low income, poverty stricken areas. That's where I feel as if I can really make a difference. Our young black brothers need guidance and that's why I joined this field.

When service was over, the young man quickly left the building. I saw a few friends that I knew from my days at FAMU and spoke to them, but I was ready to get to my car and head home. I had to get my place ready for my mom.

The rain had briefly stopped once I got outside. The sky looked as if it were going to open at any moment, so I quickly headed for my car. Once I reached my car I saw the young man from the service standing next to an SUV that was parked next to mine.

"What's going on?" I said, as I approached the young man.

He stared at me and said, "I'm ready to go, but the person I'm riding with hasn't come out of the church yet."

"Oh," I said. "Is everything ok with you?"

"Yeah, I'm fine," he said.

*Yes, you are fine!* He was definitely attractive.

I gathered myself, cleared my throat and said, "What's your name?"

"Tony and you?"

"Raidon."

"Nice to meet you, Raidon," he said.

"Same here. But look, I ain't trying to be funny or anything, or come off crazy, but I can see that something is bothering you. I saw it once I walked into the church. I'm a new professor at FAMU and if you just want somebody to talk to, man-to-man, I'll be glad to do that with you," I said.

"Thanks," he said. "But, I'm ok."

"You sure?" I said, as I reached for my wallet.

"Yeah, man," he said.

"Ight, well, take my business card. Don't feel ashamed to give me a call if you change your mind. You can call me anytime, day or night."

"Ight, man," Tony said, as he looked at the card.

"Call me," I said, as I got in my car and left the church.

# 46

## *Zach*

Even though the sky was looking as if it was threatening to rain again, we were out here on the field getting as much practice in as we could. It had stopped raining just in time for practice to start. Once we were dismissed for a water break, Dwight ran over to me and asked, "What's bothering you?"

"You don't even want to know," I said, as I continued my journey over to my bag to get my bottled water.

"Stop beating around the damn bush and tell me what's on your fucking mind," Dwight said.

"I'M HORNY!"

Dwight started to laugh, then said, "Why? Old boy ain't throwing the D the right way?"

I didn't find the situation to be funny. I took a sip of water and said, "It ain't even like that."

"So, what's the problem?" he asked.

"We've never done it," I stated.

"Y'all still ain't had yet?" Dwight asked, surprised.

"No," I responded.

"Is the nigga scared or something?"

"I don't know what to say," I stated.

"Man, y'all boys crazy," he said, as Kris, Peanut and Omar walked over.

"What's going on?" Kris asked.

"Ain't shit," Dwight stated.

"Man, these freshmen suck!" Peanut added.

"You ain't ever lied," Omar interjected.

"Hell, look who trained them," Dwight said, as he started to laugh.

"FUCK YOU!" Kris yelled at Dwight, as we all started to laugh.

As we continued to talk, I noticed the freshman, Keli, walking by us. He still looked a little nervous. I wish he would just loosen up a bit.

"Come here," I called him over.

"Yes?" he said, when he approached us.

"Are you ok?" I asked.

"Yes," he shyly stated.

"Are you grasping everything?" I asked. "I know it's a lot to process in a short amount of time."

"I'm still trying to get it, but I'll be ok," he said.

"Where are you from again?" Peanut asked.

"A small town north of Atlanta," Keli stated.

"WHAT THE FUCK IS A SMALL TOWN NORTH OF ATLANTA? BITCH, I WANT A FUCKING NAME!" Peanut yelled.

*"Damn,"* I thought to myself. *"He's fitting right into the upperclassman role."*

"Ummm, Gainesville, Georgia," Keli responded. "I'm sorry, I just didn't know any better."

"BITCH, GET THE FUCK FROM OUT OF MY FACE!" Peanut stated.

"Ight, Quinton #2," Kris said to Peanut.

"Man, fuck these fuck ass freshmen," Peanut responded. "I don't know why y'all getting so close to their ass. Nobody was close to our asses like that."

"It ain't that serious, man," I added.

"Man, fuck that! I need some ass to beat ASAP," Peanut said, as Ian blew the whistle to resume practice.

*****

# Ra'Jon

I smiled when I saw his name pop up on the screen of my phone. I immediately answered. He said, "What's going on man, this is Black."

"Oh, shit, what's up," I said.

"My bad about church. My mom wanted me to stay down in Palm Beach and go with her to the early morning service. I just got on the road and I'm headed back to Orlando now," Blackwell stated.

"Oh, man, it's cool," I said.

"You sure?" he asked.

"Yeah, it's no problem," I said. "I needed to catch up on some sleep anyway."

"True. Do you still want me to show you around?" Black asked.

"Yeah," I said.

"Ight, when I get back and get settled, I'll call you."

"Ok, do that," I hung up the phone.

A few hours later, Black called and asked me to meet him at the same diner where I first saw him. Once inside, I went to his table and asked, "So, where are we going?"

"Shit, I was hoping that we could get something to eat first," he said. "I'm starved."

"That's what's up," I said, as the waitress came over to take our order.

"I'll be right back," Black said, as his phone started to ring.

While he was gone, I started to realize that Black was a good dude. I wasn't too sure if he was on the down low, but I liked his company. If he was on the down low, he was the kind of dude that I wouldn't mind getting to know on a different kind of level.

"Perfect timing," Black said, as he came back to the table. The waitress was bringing out our food.

"Everything ok?" I asked, as I took a sip of my soda.

"Yeah, I was just talking to my baby sister," he said. "I'm so proud of her."

"What does she do?" I asked.

"Oh, she's in college. Spelman College," he said proudly.

"Wow, that's what's up!"

"Yeah, but why did you really move down to Orlando?" he asked.

"A lot of personal reasons," I said.

"I see," Black stated.

"Yeah, man, I was going through a lot of stuff with my family and some things at my previous job. I just needed a break away," I explained.

"Oh, what do you do for a living?" Black asked, as he ate more of his food.

"I'm an educator," I said.

"Oh, you teach bad ass kids," he laughed.

"Something like that," I smiled. "It runs in my family."

"And you're from Virginia, right?"

"Yep," I said. "So, tell me something about you."

"Well, I'm the oldest of three kids," he said. "I love my brother and sister to death."

"I do, too," I said, as I made reference to my siblings.

"I grew up in West Palm Beach, Florida," Black stated.

"How did you end up in Orlando?" I asked.

"My dad's sister moved up Orlando when we were younger and we used to come up here a lot. I fell in love with the city of Orlando and I told myself that I was gonna move here when I grew up. When I left home, I came to Orlando," Black stated.

"Oh, so what do you do?" I asked.

"I'm a C.O.," he said.

"Do you like being a corrections officer?" I asked.

"It's cool," he said. "I've worked my way up the ladder, so I can't complain."

"That's what's up," I said. "So, what is the thing you hate worst in the world?"

"Hmmm," Black said as he thought about my question. "That's tough."

"Why do you say that?" I asked.

"Because it's a lot of things that I don't really care for," he said.

"Of all of those things that you're thinking about, what is the one thing that just irks the fuck out of you?"

Black thought about my question for a little bit, looked at me and answered, "I guess it would be gay people. Especially black, gay, down low men."

"Really?"

"Yeah, I don't like gay dudes. There are too many women out there for that shit."

# Life of a College Bandsman 2: Is This Love

"What about women who like women?" I asked.

"I don't like that shit, either," Black said. "I wasn't raised like that and I just don't see what two dudes or two girls can see in each other."

"Well, let me ask you this," I said.

"What's up?"

"Since you say that you hate gay people, and you say that you love your brother and sister to death, but hypothetically, what if your brother was fucking 'round with dudes, what would you do?"

"If my brother knows what's good for him, he better keep his ass on the straight and narrow! RJ, I would fuck his ass up! He knows I don't play that shit." He smiled and said, "But we don't have to worry about that because my brother isn't gay." He took a sip of his drink and said, "That was random. Why you ask me that anyway?"

"I was just asking, just trying to get inside your head," I said.

"Umm, hmm," Black said, as he stood up.

"You ready?" I asked.

"Yeah, let's get this tour on the road," Black said, as we left the restaurant.

I smiled and laughed to myself and thought about Zach, Chaz and Eric.

*Oh, I'm gonna have a good time fucking some shit up. Those fuck niggas gonna learn not to fuck with me. Their bitch asses are gonna learn!*

# 47

## Antonio "Tony" Shaw

Since I've been in Tallahassee, I have only talked to Zach once and that was the other day. He may think I am about games, but it really isn't like that. I'm really feeling that dude. But one thing I know for sure is that I am a fucking man. I'm not gonna keep hurting my pride chasing some dude that doesn't want me.

It really killed me inside to tell Zach that I was moving on. I really didn't want to do that, but there is no need in trying to force the issue with him. There are a lot of dudes here in Tally, and I'm sure one day I will meet one that's for me.

I'm tripping out about the dude that I met at church the other day. That shit was so random. What made him come up to me of all people? I've been thinking about calling the man. He seems like cool people, and I can use a mentor, but I don't know.

My thoughts were interrupted by a knock on my door. I figured it was my cousin since he just called asking if he could stop over for a second. I walked to the door and let Eric inside my dorm room. "What's going on, man," I said.

"Nothing much, just checking on my lil cousin," he said, as he looked around the dorm.

"That's nice of you," I said, as I took a seat on my bed.

"Where's your roommate?" he asked me.

"Oh, he's probably in the gym or something," I replied.

"He's on the football team, too?" Eric asked.

"Yea," I said. "He's a wide receiver. His name is Kameron, but he just goes by Killa."

"Oh, ok," Eric said.

"This whole dorm building is for athletes."

"I know that, Tony. I am a student at Florida State, too."

"Yeah, what was I thinking?" I said, as I walked over to my mini fridge. "You want something?"

"No, I'm good," Eric said, as he started to type a text message.

"Who you talking to?" I asked.

"Just one of my homeboy's," he replied.

"How is Rozi?" I asked. "I hadn't heard from her since I saw her down in Palm Beach a lil while ago."

"I talked to her the other day. She's doing the best she can under the circumstances," Eric said.

"What's wrong with her?" I asked.

"Nothing major," Eric said. "She's just trying to figure out some stuff."

"I guess, Eric."

"Yeah, so Black told me that you had him get some liquor for you," Eric said.

"Yeah, I did," I said, as I thought back to that night I had Zach meet Black. I really wish that things would have gone down my way, but there's no need to dwell in the past.

"So, what you need liq for?" Eric asked.

"Nigga, I wanted to drink," I said, as I looked at him.

"Umm, hmmm. Who were you trying to get fucked up?" Eric chuckled.

"Man, me and my homeboy was just chilling. But we went out and got some hoes and took care of business," I lied to Eric. I was starting to wonder why he was questioning me on this shit. I know Black is anti-gay, but I know he didn't send Eric over here to see if me and Zach were fucking.

"Nigga, you're always fucking. That dick gonna get yo' ass in trouble," Eric said.

"Shit, it already did," I said, as I thought about my kid.

"How is the baby?" Eric asked.

"TJ is doing good," I said.

"TJ?" Eric asked.

"Tony Jr.," I said.

"Damn, the baby ain't even a month old yet and y'all giving the boy nicknames and shit," Eric laughed.

"Whatever, man," I said. "What made you come by here today?"

"Like I said earlier, I was just checking in on you, just seeing how the football thing is coming along," Eric stated.

"We've got practice later tonight and I really don't wanna go," I said.

"Nigga, you can't start that shit already," Eric said. "The season just started."

"Shit, I know," I said, as I thought about the long road ahead of me.

"You know you can come to my place whenever you feel the need to get away from everything. I mean I got roommates and shit, but you can chill out in my room or whatever," Eric said.

"Thanks, cuz," I said. "You know I'ma take you up on that shit at some point."

"No, doubt," Eric said, as he stood up.

"You're leaving already?"

"Yeah, I gotta go pick-up one of my homeboy's," Eric said, walking towards the door.

As soon as Eric left, I stretched out across my bed. I started to think of the good times that Zach and I shared. Zach was really a sincere dude and he was the first dude that I really felt *like that*.

"Ight, Tony," I said to myself, as I gathered my composure and walked over to the mirror. I couldn't let myself fall back into that trap.

"You look to damn good to be stressing 'bout some damn dude," I said to myself, as I looked at my nicely sculptured body. "I mean who wouldn't want this?"

For some reason, I started to think about that man that I met after church on Sunday.

"Raidon Harris," I said to myself, as looked at the card that he gave me. *Maybe I should give him a call. How bad can it hurt?*

I thought about it for a second.

"Oh, what the hell," I said, as I picked up the phone and dialed the number. He answered and I nervously said, May I speak to Raidon?"

"May I ask who this is?"

"This is Tony, the dude you met at church the other day."

"Ohhhh, ok. I'm so glad that you called," Raidon said. "What's up with you?"

# 48

# *Amir Knight*

I needed to stop this shit. Sometimes I feel like a man whore. Since I met Devin the other night at Walmart, I'm now fucking with three regular dudes in Tally and Rozi back up in Atlanta. I can't forget the random one-night stands I have with dudes.

Every night seems like a new adventure. Some days are hard because I gotta go to Morgan, take his dick, turn around and go to my other dude and dish out the dick. Now I gotta see Devin and let him suck me up.

I don't know where I got this high ass sex drive from, but I just can't get enough of it. Fucking is gonna be the death of me if I don't stop.

I laid down on my bed and started to play with my dick. I thought about putting in a porn, but that thought didn't get very far as my phone started to ring. I looked at the name and sighed. *What the fuck does she want?*

I took a deep breath and answered. She yelled, "AMIR!"

"What Rozi?"

"What the fuck is your problem?" she barked.

"I don't have time for your shit today," I said.

"AMIR!"

"WHAT?"

"Why do you treat me like this?" she asked.

"Like what?"

"You know what, just forget it. Just fucking forget it!"

"What is the problem?" I asked.

"You're full of shit!" she said. "Just forget it. You just made my decision for me."

"What decision?" I asked, sitting up in the bed. "Rozi, what is going on?"

"I'm not gonna subject him to this shit. I can already see how this shit would be years from now, so I just need to do the right thing," she said.

"What the fuck are you talking about?" I asked. "Who are you subjecting and what are you subjecting him to? Who is him?"

"Just forget it. Bye, Amir!" she hung up.

"Ok, that was strange," I said, as I thought about what just happened. "What the fuck is her problem?"

# 49

## *Ra'Jon*

I really enjoyed spending time with Blackwell. He was so different than both Chaz and Eric. I mean Eric was ok, too, but that nigga isn't everything that he portrays to be.

I kinda feel bad about doing this, but I will be as secretive about this as possible. God forbids that Black finds out about what I'm planning on doing.

I know Chaz thinks that he's got me, but that nigga is stupid as hell. I'm using his money for a mini-vacation in Orlando, and in the process, I plan on fucking his shit up, too.

That fuck nigga must have thought that I was just gonna forget about that nigga forcing me to resign from a position that I worked so hard to achieve. People may call me things, but Chaz is stupid as fuck! After that shit went down, all the feelings I had for Chaz went out the window with his ass. I play that *I'm still in love with you* role so that the nigga won't think anything crazy. He thinks I'm working with him to fuck up Eric for taking Zach away from him. Fuck that. I'm working for myself on Chaz's expense to get that nigga back for fucking up my professional life. That shit was higher than any fucking relationship that I may have wanted. I had goals and aspirations. Being on the FAMU band staff was one of those goals.

Don't get it twisted. I'm still gonna get Zach and Eric back for this shit. There is no secret that I despise Zachariah Finley, but this Eric dude is another question.

I've had a run in or two with Eric before, but that's something Chaz doesn't know about. All that shit happened when Eric was fucking with my brother, Raidon. I was trying to be a good dude to

Eric to let him know that my precious brother wasn't the angel that he thought he was. I know the ways of my brother, but no one would listen to little old me.

Eric tried to fight me because I told him that I knew he was fucking around with dudes. I knew because he was fucking with my brother. Eric did get a few good hits on me, but he had the audacity to threaten me off all people. Eric did lil slick shit on the side to try to fuck up my relationship with Chaz, but thankfully Chaz never picked up on the things that Eric was doing. It took everything in me not to out Eric, but I knew how much Chaz loved that dude, so I let that shit go—until now.

Payback is a bitch!

I understand that Eric didn't want his business to get out there because he was on the down low, but I was just trying to look out for the young man. Like I said earlier, I knew the ways of my brother.

I've never told anyone this, but I always wanted to be Raidon. I wanted that love and affection that my mom showed him. I never understood why she treated him so differently than me. I was the first born, but Raidon was God's gift to her. I just wanted the love that she showed Raidon. With that in mind, I could never do anything to Raidon because it would kill my mom. I loved my mom with all my heart, and despite how I feel about some shit, I could never see her hurt.

That is the reason and the only reason why I didn't out Raidon. See, Raidon has a nasty past, too. He isn't the perfect son that everyone makes him out to be. Raidon is a good person, but everyone has a past. His bitch ass ain't no better than me.

I guess being honest with myself, I've always been a little afraid of Raidon. Something about his presence scares me a little.

When I think about how everything went down last year with Chaz forcing me to leave Tallahassee, I get upset. Luckily for me, I had most of my special videotapes locked up in storage. The ones that I had in my house were the most recent ones. Something told me to leave that camera on before I left to go to Chicago. If I did, I would know who was in my house. I mean I know that Chaz and Micah was in on this shit together, but I couldn't prove it, so I just left it alone.

I had cameras all across my house. When Raidon was living in Tallahassee, he stayed with me for a year, and unknowing to him, I know everything and everyone he did in that house. I'm surprised that my dear brother isn't sick—the gay man's sick. With all those dudes that he fucked, with he has had to caught some type of STD or something. I ain't wishing that shit on anyone, but as much fucking as Raidon did, with different dudes, the numbers just don't look good in his favor.

I tried to warn Eric—warn him without directly telling him that he needed to be careful. He didn't want to listen to what I had to say. I guess it worked out that Raidon moved back to Norfolk because had he stayed, eventually, all hell would have broken loose.

I guess I can't blame Chaz for this one because he didn't know about Raidon and Eric. But Raidon knew and he knew about Chaz and Eric's relationship. Chaz and Raidon used to fuck and they fucked a lot! And they didn't always use protection. *The tapes don't lie.*

That's the good shit I have locked up in storage. Along with Chaz and Raidon, I have Raidon and Eric, and Raidon and a few *other* people. Like I said, Raidon has a past. He isn't exempt from that Harris blood. Raidon was quite a player back in his day. As he got older, he matured and stopped a lot of his shit. But your past is the one thing that never leaves you. It's with you until the day you die, and, hell, it sometimes lives on after you die.

Originally, the cameras weren't installed to secretly tape dudes, they were put in for security reasons. As time went on, they changed from security cameras to my personal cameras.

That's the thing Chaz doesn't know. He doesn't know that I know about him and Raidon. He doesn't know that I have my own evidence against him. How in the hell are you gonna try to fuck up my life and then expect me to just forget about it and join your team? NO FUCKING MA'AM! It doesn't work like that.

But I'm no dummy. I have purchased some professional editing equipment so I can block out my brother's face. I plan to edit the tape so no one would recognize that it is my house. I'm making sure that I cover all my tracks.

When I set this thing into action, we'll see who has the last laugh. Ra'Jon Harris ain't the one to be fucked with—and you can take that to the grave.

# 50

# *Zach*

Jared turned his attention to the section and said, "Y'all are really pissing me the fuck off! How many fucking times do I have to go over this shit? I'm getting sick of Dr. Burton calling out my damn section!"

Jared was right. We were getting called out a lot and to be honest, I was getting sick of it, too.

He looked at Keli and said, "Get that shit together! Toughen the fuck up!"

I looked at Keli and sighed.

Jared yelled, "WE LEAVE FOR CHARLOTTE TOMORROW! THIS SECTION LOOKS AND SOUNDS A FUCKING MESS! I KNOW ONE FUCKING THING, BEFORE NIGHT PRACTICE TONIGHT, THIS SHIT BETTER BE RIGHT OR ELSE!"

After Jared made that statement, he turned around and walked away. I hated to see Jared upset because he became a completely different person.

"Yo," Kris said, as he called everyone over to him. "Listen up. We need to meet back here at six."

"Who is we?" Randy asked.

"LOOK, FUCK NIGGA!" Dwight stated, as I thought about their fight last year in Cincinnati. "WE'RE NOT GONNA GO THROUGH THIS BULLSHIT WITH YOU AGAIN THIS YEAR!"

"*We* includes everyone," Kris stated. "I am the assistant section leader of this section and everyone under the sound of my voice needs to be at this sectional at six sharp."

I really didn't want to come back this early, but I guess I didn't have too much of a choice.

Kris looked at Randy and said, "And if you are not here at SIX O'CLOCK, just don't come back because you won't march a game this year."

"You trying to be funny?" Randy asked Kris.

"I'm just stating the facts!" Kris said, as he turned and walked away.

"Man, I don't know what's wrong," Omar said.

"I don't either, freshman bruh," I said, as we walked to his car.

"What was Kris talking about?" Jared asked, when we got to the car.

"Nothing, really," Omar said. "He just wants us back here at six."

"Oh, I see," Jared said, as he looked down at his watch. "We'll, it's a little after five."

"I know," Omar said. "We're just gonna go get something to eat. You can drop us back off and you can take the car to the crib."

"That's cool," Jared said.

Jared and Omar moved in together this summer and they seemed to be happy roommates. They both had cars, but they took turns driving when it came time for practice.

"You ok back there, Zach?" Omar asked, as we arrived at Burger King. "Yeah, I'm good, just thinking about a lot of things."

"I don't know what's wrong," Jared interjected. "I'm trying my best to get this section right, but it's not working. I don't wanna use the tactics that Quinton used, but I'm starting to think that is the only way."

"You might have a point," I stated.

"Yeah some people only do what they're supposed to do when they are threatened," Omar added.

"I see that shit now," Jared said. "I just didn't want to go down that path, but it is what it is."

"Just give them a lil time," I said. "I mean their pre-drill was cut short because of this performance on Saturday."

"That's true," Jared said. "But the people ain't gonna care about excuses, they're only they gonna say is that the Hundred ain't up to par. We've got too much history and legacy to let our name go down like that. This shit gotta get right, quick and in a hurry."

He was right.

# Life of a College Bandsman 2: Is This Love

"I need to relieve some stress," Jared said, as he started to look through his phone.

"Just don't fuck on my bed," Omar said, as he started to laugh.

"Y'all boys wild," I stated, as I started to place my order.

*****

# *Raidon*

I smiled as I picked up my mom from the airport. I turned to her and said, "I'm glad you finally came."

"I know, baby," she said, as she gave me a kiss. "I wanted to leave on Sunday, but I had to take care of some stuff at the office and then things just got bad."

"What happened?"

"Oh, don't worry about it, baby," she said. "All that matters is that I'm here now."

As we drove around Tallahassee, she said, "I miss this place. I grew so much as a woman during my time here."

"Is that so?"

"Yes, it is," she stated. "They say that college is the best time of your life and I couldn't disagree with that statement."

I nodded my head. I damn sure had the time of my life in college.

"So, you still haven't figured out what's wrong with Micah?" she asked, as she changed the subject.

"No, I haven't," I said. The truth of the matter was that I really hadn't been to check on Micah. I wasn't trying to be selfish, but I have my own issues to deal with right now. I'm getting sick of my family's problems.

"I know Morgan knows what it is and I'm upset that he is lying to me," she said, as she looked out the window.

"He's just protecting his brother," I said. "You know how close they are."

"I know," she said. "But—"

"No buts mom," I cut her off. "Just let it be."

"You didn't tell them I was coming did you?"

"No, I didn't tell anyone."

"Good," she said, as we arrived at my apartment. Once inside, she looked around and said, "I can say that you have good taste. You did get that gene from me."

"You're crazy," I smiled, as she sat down in the living room. I placed her things in the guest room.

When I was back in the living room, she asked, "Have you talked to your father?"

"No, I haven't. Why you ask? I thought you wasn't worried about him anymore."

"I'm asking because Michelle is worried. She hadn't talked to him in about a week and no one has seen him either," my mom stated.

"Oh," I said.

"I mean I'm sure that he is ok. I know your dad. He's probably just somewhere clearing his mind, but he needs to call Michelle," my mom said.

"I'll call him later and see if he answers," I said.

"Ok, baby."

"So, what are you gonna do about RJ?" I asked.

"What do you mean?" she said.

"You've gotta tell him," I said.

"I know but I just don't know how."

"Well, you need to tell him before he finds out from Pops or Alonzo," I stated.

"Yeah, I thought about that," she said. "Have you talked to Ra'Jon?"

"No."

"Michelle said that he was coming down to Florida to get away for a little while," my mom said. "I thought that he might have been here or something."

"Well, I haven't seen or heard from him," I stated.

"I've been trying to figure out who he knows in Florida, but I guess he could know a lot of people from college, huh."

"Yeah," I said. "You should be happy that he went away for a while."

"Oh, don't get it wrong, Raidon," she said. "I'm enjoying the peace and quiet of the house since it's only been Michelle and me. I was just wondering, that's all."

"Well, I'm gonna go and fix something to eat," I said, as I made my way into the kitchen. "Make yourself at home, Ma. Relax. Get comfortable."

"Thanks, baby," she said, as she turned on the TV.

# 51

## Eric

I still wasn't for certain, but I had a feeling, deep in my gut, that Amir was the dude my sister was talking about. I looked around the kitchen and exhaled.

Everything just adds up. Amir was from Atlanta. He did go up to Atlanta during MLK weekend because he clearly asked me if I wanted to come with him. Amir was home in Atlanta the entire summer, and Amir did make frequent trips up to Atlanta during the spring semester.

*"But, of all people, what are the chances that Amir was fucking my sister?"* I said to myself as reality struck in. *"Get real, Eric. There are hundreds of dudes from Atlanta that attend FAMU."*

The thing that really made me upset about the whole incident wasn't the fact that my sister was fucking, it was that she could be possibly fucking Amir. He fucked with dudes. I don't need my sister involved in none of that drama and bullshit.

"What's up, Eric?" Amir said, as he walked into the kitchen.

"Nothing, really," I said, as I looked at him with suspicion.

"What?" he said. "Why are you looking at me like that?"

"I'm just thinking about some shit," I said. "Don't pay me any attention."

"What's going on with you?" Amir asked, as he learned on the counter.

"Just dealing with some family shit," I said.

"Oh, ok, Eric. If you need to talk, you know you can holla at me," he said.

"Bet that up," I said, as Amir phone started to ring. He answered,

"What's up… Oh, you heading to the crib… where yo' roommate… bet that up… let me hop in the shower right quick and I'll head over that way… ight."

"Another fuck session, huh?" I said, as I looked at him.

"You know how it be, Eric," Amir said, as he gently punched me in the arm.

"Naw, I don't know it like that," I said.

"WHATEVER, SHAWTY!" Amir yelled, as he went into his room.

"What's up with you?" Quinton asked, as he walked into the apartment.

"Nothing, really," I said. "Where you been? I haven't seen you in a few days."

"I had to go up north. My mom was tripping about some shit," Quinton said, as he got a bottled water out of the fridge.

"Yo, they say that we're gonna get a new roommate because the other dude ain't coming back," I said.

"Oh, really," Quinton said disappointed.

"Yeah, man," I said. "I'm just happy that he ain't coming back. That nigga irked the fucked out of me."

"When is the new dude supposed to come?" Quinton asked.

"I'm not sure. I guess sometime this weekend because classes start on Monday."

"I just hope that he's clean," Quinton said. "I'ma get at you later. I need to get some rest."

I did wonder what this roommate was gonna be like. We had been in this place for a few years now, and despite how I felt about Quinton irking my nerves, I just got used to living with him and Amir. That other dude was really the problem though. That nigga was just nasty as fuck. Quinton's ass was inconsiderate of others personal space, but he has gotten a lot better since he caught me and Zach in the room that night last year. I just hope this roommate is cool because I don't have time for roommate drama again.

I headed to the living room to watch some TV. A few moments later Amir walked in. I said, "You out?" Amir had on a black tank top, a black du-rag, some black basketball shorts that clearly showed his hanging dick, and some black ankle socks with some Michael Jordan flip-flops. I could tell that he dressed to undress—easy access. I guess it ain't no need in putting on a lot of clothes when all you gonna do is take them right back off.

# Life of a College Bandsman 2: Is This Love

"Yeah, I'm out," he said. "Gotta go take care of this shit."

"Nigga, you fuck all day, every day," I said.

"Is something wrong with that?" he asked.

"I guess not," I said. "Be careful."

"I'm always careful," he said, as he walked out the house.

*I hope so.*

*****

# *Amir*

Here I go again—can't stop thinking with my damn dick. I like this dude though, real talk. He was the kind of dude that I could get to know. The only problem was that he was close to a few people that I knew. I knew that he wasn't gonna give us up like that, but I don't want people thinking crazy things, either.

"What's up?" I answered my phone.

"Nigga, where you at?" Dwight asked.

"On my way to fuck," I said.

"Nigga, I thought I fucked a lot, but you got me beat," Dwight said.

"I gotta keep lil big man happy," I said, making reference to my dick.

"Whatever."

"Where you at?" I asked.

"About to go back to practice," Dwight said.

"That's right—y'all got a trip this weekend," I stated.

"Yeah, we're leaving for North Carolina tomorrow," Dwight said.

"Is my brother still out there?" I asked.

"Yeah, Dallis is still here," Dwight stated.

"I really didn't think that he would go back to the band."

"Me, either," Dwight said. "You should come through tonight and chill out for a second when we get out of practice."

"I think I'll do that," I said. "But let me hit you back up, ok."

"Ight, bruh."

As soon as I got to the house, he opened the door.

"We don't have much time because I gotta get back," he said, as he looked at me.

"Ight," I followed him to his room.

I kinda felt bad because Morgan fucked me last night. This dude wanted to fuck me, but I just couldn't let him. His ass felt too good. Besides, I had to redeem myself after Morgan fucked me, by fucking him. I wanted to fuck that dude, Devin, that I met at Walmart, but I didn't push the issue. I'm content with him sucking my dick for the moment.

"Why is your roommate's car here? I thought you said he was gone," I said, as I looked out the window.

"He is. He's at practice. Now, c'mon so I can get my ass back to practice on time," Jared said, as he took off my pants exposing my throbbing dick.

"You ain't said nothing but a word," I said, as I started to play with his ass.

*****

# *Eric*

Once Amir left, I went in my room to think about things. I had so much on my mind, but the thing that just stuck out above everything else was my sister's situation.

"Let me call her ass and see what's up," I said, as I picked up the phone.

"ERIC!" she answered the phone.

"What's up, Rozi?"

"I was just about to call you," she said.

"You sound happy," I said.

"I am happy," she said.

"Why? What happened?"

"Well, I talked to the real father a few nights ago, and after I talked to him, he made me realize some stuff," Rozi explained.

"Stuff like what?" I asked.

"I don't think that he is the type of man I want to be a father to my child," she said.

"What makes you think that?"

"Just his actions—you know they speak a whole lot more than

his words," she stated.

"So, what exactly are you saying? Did you tell him about the baby?"

"No," she said. "Not yet anyway."

"So, the other dude still thinks that the baby is his?"

"Yeah," she sighed.

"So, what exactly are you gonna do?" I asked.

"Well, after talking to him, I know that I have to get the abortion," she said.

"Wow, Rozi," I said, shocked.

"Don't be mad at me Eric. I feel that this is in the best interest for everyone involved," she said.

"I'm not mad at you. Baby sis, you are a grown woman and you have to live by the choices that you make," I said. "Do you have the money to get the abortion?"

"I have a way to get it," she said.

"You sure?" I asked.

"Yes."

"Ok, let me know when you get it done."

"Ok, Eric. You still promise not to tell Black, right?"

"I'm not gonna tell Black," I said.

"Ok, thank you, Eric. I'll call you. I love you."

"I love you, too," I said, as I hung up the phone.

When I got off the phone with her I turned on the TV to CNN. I hadn't caught the news in a few days and I needed to catch up on that.

*"This is Don Lemon and welcome to the CNN Newsroom. We have breaking news from Durham, North Carolina. Soledad O'Brien is on the scene with more details. Soledad."*

*"Yes, Don, I'm here in Durham and the Durham police are reporting that they have the body of an African-American man. He was found murdered on Tuesday, but the police haven't received any leads as of yet, so they wanted to bring it to the national stage. They are hoping that someone may have some information on this case. The man is a big mystery because he didn't have any identification and his face is dismembered. No one knows who this man is. They would like to contact the family of the deceased, but that is kind of impossible right now."*

*"How old do authorities believe the man is?" Don Lemon asked.*

*"They suspect that he is in his mid-forties to early-fifties."*

*"They don't have any witnesses?"*

*"They don't have anything, Don. This is a big mystery. If you have any information that may help in this case, please call the Durham Police. The number is at the bottom of your screen."*

*"Thanks, Soledad. We will come back to you in a little bit,"* Don said. *"In other news, Hurricane Gordon is now a Category 4 storm and is making his way—"*

"Damn," I said, as I turned off the TV. "That shit is fucked up."

# Part Three:

## Is This Love?

# 52

## *Devin*

Thankfully, things had finally died down on the bus and I was able to get some time to think. I really was feeling Morgan and the more that I mess with Amir, the worse off I feel about the whole situation. After our altercation last night, I know Morgan is gonna go out and do some shit with only God knows who. I knew that I needed to let go of this thing with Morgan, but I just can't build up the courage to do it.

Despite the fact I knew Morgan was cheating on me, I loved the way he made he feel. I loved the way he touched me. I loved the way he kissed me; his lips were so damn soft. I loved his masculinity. I loved his raging pecks and his defining abs. I loved the color of his skin. I loved the tattoos on his arms. I loved the way he looked at me. I even loved the rubber band that he always sported on his right wrist. Morgan had an effect on me like no other man.

Maybe this is why I was changing my ways. Maybe Morgan was the reason I was becoming a better person.

With Morgan it wasn't always about sex. Don't get me wrong, the sex was the best, but Morgan took the time to listen to me. He listened to me blab on and on about the band. Morgan listened to my never ending stories of my crazy life. Morgan was there for me when times were hard. He was the dude that I could see myself really spending some serious time with.

That's why I don't understand why he's doing this to me. I thought that we shared something deeper than just a fuck, but I guess I was wrong. One of my close friends always told me to never trust a nigga because he would always fuck you over in the end.

I guess what they say about karma is true—what goes around, comes around.

I once was "that nigga." I was the dude that niggas couldn't trust. I can admit that I was a male whore. I got around. That's just how it was, point blank. There is no need to sugarcoat it.

I told myself that I wasn't gonna go back to the *old Devin*, but when I realized that Morgan was cheating on me, especially after I've only been faithful to him, it caused me to go on the defense and protect myself and my interests.

Now that I have messed with Amir, I don't feel good about it. Amir is hot, but my heart is with Morgan. It doesn't feel the same. I'm not that *old Devin* anymore.

As I sat at the front of the charter bus, I realized how much I have grown as a person, as a man, since I've been with Morgan.

I looked up at the monitor and the credits to *Save the Last Dance* were going off. I thought about getting up to take out the DVD, but I really didn't want to move out of my seat. After a few more minutes of pondering about the DVD, I stood up and removed the DVD from the DVD player in the overhead bin on the charter bus. When I turned around to face the rest of the bus, everyone was asleep. The freshmen on my bus finally looked like they were at peace, as we took this trip to North Carolina. This drive to Charlotte wasn't as long as some of our other bus rides, but when you calculate all the driver stops and breaks we were gonna be on the bus for about eleven hours.

Before I sat back down, I reached into the bin above my seat and grabbed my pillow and blanket. It was raining outside and I knew this was the perfect opportunity to join my fellow band mates on some much needed sleep.

"Excuse me," I said, as I spoke to the bus driver.

"Yes?"

"Can you turn the air down a little. It's a little cold on here."

"Ok," he said, as he reached for a button.

When I sat down, I placed the pillow against the window, stretched my left leg out on the other seat, placed my right leg on the floor and threw the blanket over my body. It was still cold, but I'm sure that I would be ok.

As I listened to the sound of the rain drops falling, I started to think back to last night. For the last couple of days, every time I'd see Morgan, I would catch an attitude and I guess he finally got fed

# Life of a College Bandsman 2: Is This Love

up with it.

"What the fuck is your problem?" Morgan said, as he approached me.

"YOU'RE MY FUCKING PROBLEM!" I yelled back.

"What the fuck I do to you?" he said as we were now face-to-face.

Everything inside of me just wanted to punch the fuck of Morgan for making me feel the way that I do, but I wasn't one for violence. Instead, I asked, "Morgan, why are you doing this?"

"Doing what?"

"Must I really spell it out?"

"Yeah, because I don't have a clue as to what you're referring to," Morgan said, as he walked away and took a seat on the couch.

"WHY ARE YOU CHEATING ON ME?" I yelled.

Morgan didn't say anything for a second. He just looked at me. I wanted to see what kind of lie he was gonna come up with.

He said, "What the fuck makes you think some crazy shit like that?"

"It's not crazy, now answer the question."

"I'm not cheating on you."

"Why are you such a fucking liar?" I said. "I don't understand how I fell for you."

"I don't see what got you bugging out. I'm your nigga and you have to trust me with shit like this. How are we gonna be in a relationship if you don't trust me?"

"I don't trust you because I know what the fuck you're doing," I said.

The entire time we argued, Morgan didn't seem bothered by it one bit. He raised his voice a few times, but other than that, he had an emotionless facial expression.

"I changed everything for you and you know how much I've changed. WHY MORGAN?" I said, as I let the tears of anger, frustration and confusion fall from my eyes. I tried my hardest not to cry, but it was to no avail.

"I ain't did shit wrong. I don't know why the fuck you bugging out. You gotta trust me Devin," Morgan said, as his phone started to ring.

"WHO THE FUCK IS THAT MORGAN?" I said, as I looked at my phone. "IT'S ALMOST MIDNIGHT!"

He answered, "Yo, let me call you back. I'm in the middle of something." He hung up his phone.

"WHO THE FUCK WAS THAT? WAS THAT HIM?" I yelled.

"That was my fucking brother!" he replied

"THAT'S THE BEST YOU CAN COME UP WITH?" I said, as I stormed into his bedroom. "FUCK YOU, MORGAN!"

"Whooooah, what you doing?" Morgan said, as he followed me into his room.

"What the fuck does it look like?" I said, as I started to throw the clothes that I had at his house on the bed.

"I know you ain't leaving," he said.

"Move!" I said, as I left the room and went to the kitchen to get a garbage bag.

"Baby, what the fuck?" he said, he followed me to the kitchen.

"Morgan, you're full of shit!" I said, as tears continued to fall, as I made my way back to his room. "I did everything I was supposed to do and I still got fucked over!"

As I started to place my belongings in the bag, he said, "Baby, stop! STOP!" He had authority in his voice. I stopped and looked over to him. The tears only fell harder.

He walked over to me and said, "Please don't do this, Devin."

"FUCK YOU!" I said, as I turned around to finish putting my things in the bag.

"I'll do whatever it takes to make this right," Morgan whispered in my ear, as he brushed up against me with his hands wrapped around waist.

As much as I hated this, I couldn't resist his touch. Amongst all the anger I felt, I melted when he touched me.

"Whatever it takes," he whispered again in my ear.

I sighed.

"I'm sorry, baby," he said, as he placed a kiss on my neck. "Let… me… make… this… right." He placed a kiss on my body between every word.

"Morgan," I struggled to get out.

"Shhhh," he said, as he turned me around and kissed me on my lips.

While he kissed me, he placed his hands on my chest and they started to explore my body. The way he moved his hands across my body just took me places. A few seconds later, I felt his dick starting to stiffen in his pants. As much as I wanted to say fuck it and let Morgan take me to ecstasy, I couldn't forget what I was mad about. I couldn't forget about his infidelity, or mines in retaliation of him cheating on me.

"No," I said, as I tried to push him off of me. "NO, MORGAN, STOP!" I said, as he backed off of me.

He looked at me. I could tell that he felt sorry for his actions.

"So, you gonna leave me? You gonna let our relationship go?" he said, as he sat on the bed.

I thought about everything, but I wasn't really sure if I really wanted to end things with Morgan. I just wanted him to be honest with me.

"I need to go so I can pack for our trip. We leave in a few hours," I said, as I walked to the door. I didn't grab the clothes that I put in the bag; I left them

# Life of a College Bandsman 2: Is This Love

*on the bed.*

*"Call me, ok, baby," he said. "Please call just to let me know that y'all made it safely or something, ok."*

*"We'll be back Sunday night," I said, as I left his place.*

"Are you ok, Devin?" asked Keli, one of the freshmen that sat directly behind me.

"Huh?" I said, as I realized that I had been crying on the bus.

"Everything ok? You're crying," Keli said.

"I'm good, just thinking about some stuff," I said.

"Ok," he said, as he sat back in his seat.

*"What am I gonna do?"* I asked myself, as I prepared to finally get some rest. *"What am I gonna do?"*

# 53

## *Zach*

For some strange reason, I couldn't sleep. Everyone on the bus was knocked out but me. I don't know if it was Dwight resting his head on my shoulder or just thinking about what my grandmother told me about this *evil presence,* but I could not get any sleep.

We couldn't be that far from Charlotte because we had been on the bus for a while now. It seemed like it took forever, but we finally got in an area where it stopped raining. I looked down at Dwight sleeping on my shoulder and I just can't get these feelings that I have for him out of my system.

I feel like I always put myself in stupid situations and here I am once again. I finally got a good dude in Eric, a man that will do any and everything for me, but the person I really want is my best friend, Dwight.

I can sense some hesitation in Eric whenever I talk about Dwight. I know Eric isn't stupid and I can tell that he knows that something is brewing between Dwight and I. On top of everything else, Dwight and Eric don't like each other. I guess I could understand their positions if I were in their shoes—well maybe not. I mean I can understand Eric's position, but I can't quite understand Dwight's position. Dwight is supposed to be *straight* so why does he care who I talk to. Eric isn't anything like Chaz, so it shouldn't be a problem, should it?

The thing with Dwight is beyond the physical. It's past the lust. I love that dude. I want to tell him how I really feel, but inside, I don't know if that's the right thing to do. I have been thinking about what Jared told me about letting Dwight come into himself first and allow him to come to me, but I don't know if I have that kind of patience—and I'm still with Eric.

Maybe I am moving too fast with dudes. Maybe I need to take some time to myself and see what's really going on inside of me. It's just that I really like Eric, as well as Dwight. But I think I like Dwight more than Eric.

Sometimes I feel like I'm cheating on Eric because I constantly think about what life would be like if I was with Dwight. I know that shit is wrong to do because I have a man, but I can't help it. I want to be with Dwight.

I do know I won't do anything that will fuck up my relationship with Eric. He is too good to me for me to do some crazy shit to him. While it may be wrong for me to think like this, but it did feel good as fuck to feel Dwight resting on me like that.

I looked out the window as we drove on Interstate 77. Seeing the green trees made me think of my grandmother. That woman was in love with the beauty of nature. She took pride in her flowers and her garden. I remember the days when we would just sit on the porch, take in the great scenery and talk about absolutely nothing. I just loved the presence of my grandmother; she was so wise beyond her years. I really loved her and as much as I didn't want to think about her leaving me one day, I knew that it was indeed a reality.

She always told me that she was never afraid of death. She said she looked forward to the day when God called her name.

As I continued to look out the window, I was reminded of a day when the unthinkable happened:

*The day was Thursday, February 1, 1996. I was twelve. As long as I have breath in my body I would never forget that day. It was my little cousin's ninth birthday. My grandma had been sick most of that week, but as the days went by, her situation became worse.*

*I was in the sixth grade and I didn't want to go to school that day, but my mom told me that it would be ok. She said she would call and check on my grandma throughout the day.*

*Despite how I felt about the situation, I walked to the nearby neighborhood school. I couldn't focus my attention in class because I was worried about my grandmother.*

*When school was dismissed at 3:45, I ran the entire way home; I had to get back to her. She was still in the bed, but she was soaking wet. The night grown that she wore, was drenched in sweat.*

# Life of a College Bandsman 2: Is This Love

*"Are you ok, Grandma?" I asked.*

*She just shook her head in the "yes" notion. "Bring me some water," she quietly stated. Like an obedient child, I did as I was told.*

*About thirty minutes later, my mom stopped by once she got off work. She dried my grandma off and changed her gown. My mom wanted to bathe her, but my grandma didn't have the energy.*

*I fixed a peanut butter and jelly sandwich. Once I finished that, I made my way back to my bedroom. A few minutes later, my mom came back in my room and told me that I needed to keep a close eye on my grandma. Every so often I would go and check on her to make sure that she was ok.*

*At about 7:30 that night, I turned on the TV because I wanted to catch the Orlando Magic basketball game. They were up in New York going against Patrick Ewing and the New York Knicks. A little while later, I heard my grandma call my name.*

*"Ma'am?" I said, when I got to her room.*

*"Turn on my oxygen tank," she softly said.*

*"Yes, ma'am," I said, as I went to the living room to flip the switch on the oxygen tank. My grandmother used the tank as a way to assist her in her breathing. The cord was long enough to where it could travel around the house three times.*

*"You need anything else?" I said, as I got back to her room. She shook her head "no."*

*When I got back to my room, I closed my door and turned on my music. I never understood why I did this, but I had a bad habit of watching TV and listening to music at the same time. A few minutes later, my grandmother came to my room and told me to turn my music down. Being obedient, I did. She closed the door, as she walked back to her room.*

*I watched more of the basketball game until she came back to my room. She didn't say anything this time, she just opened my door and left.*

*"Ok?" I said to myself, as I wondered why she would just open the door and leave. I couldn't get into the game because it was starting to bother me. Something inside of me told me to go and see what was up.*

*When I walked out my room, I knew she made her way to the living room because that's the direction the oxygen cord was facing.*

*"OH, MY GOD!" I yelled, when I saw my grandmother. She couldn't breathe; she was gasping for air. I could tell that her lungs were closing up with each breath that she took.*

*"HOLD ON, GRANDMA!" I said, as I started to cry, as I ran for the phone. "DON'T DIE ON ME, GRANDMA!"*

*"911, what's your emergency?"*

*"My grandma is dying. She can't breathe! She can't breathe," I frantically said over and over. "PLEASE HURRY UP! PLEASE, MY GRANDMA CAN'T DIE. PLEASE HURRY!" I begged the 911 operator, as I looked at my grandma. Each time she took a breath, it became shorter and shorter.*

*"DON'T DIE ON ME, GRANDMA!" I said again, as I called my mother to let her know what happened. "PLEASE DON'T DIE, GRANDMA. HOLD ON, GRANDMA, THEY'RE COMING. DON'T DIE!"*

*What normally takes about a fifteen-minute ride from my mom's house to my grandma house, only took about seven. My mom, step-dad and the EMT all arrived at the same time.*

*We spent quite a bit of time at the hospital that night. It turned out that my grandma had a severe case of pneumonia. The doctor came and told me that If I hadn't called when I did, she would have died.*

*"He saved her life," he said to my family, as he walked out of the hospital room.*

I didn't realize that Dwight had removed his head from my shoulder and had been looking at me the entire time, I replayed that night in my head.

"Big Z, you cool?" he asked.

"I'm good," I said. "Just thankful."

"Thankful for what?" he asked.

"For everything—for my life, health and strength. For my grandmother, for my mom, for this band, for *you*," I said with the emphasis on the word, you.

"For me?" he asked confused.

"Yes, for you," I said, as I looked at him. "You just don't know how much you mean to me. Life is short and I'm now convinced that God placed you specifically in my life for a reason and I'm thankful for it."

"What's the reason?" he asked.

"Only time will tell, Dwight," I said, as I looked out the window. "Only time will tell."

# 54

## *Morgan*

Last night was a reality check for my ass. Devin scared the fuck out of me when he threatened to leave me. I don't know why I do the things that I do. It is as if I can't help it. It's not that I like cheating on Devin; it's just the thrill about it that drives me crazy. I've always lived life on the edge and cheating on Devin was like playing with fire.

I don't know how he figured out that I was cheating on him but he did. I tried my best to deny it, but my dude ain't that stupid. I never came out and admitted it, but I said it, without saying it.

Devin was right. He has changed. Everything about him has changed since we have been together. I want to do right by him, but it's just hard. I get bored easily and I need constant excitement in my life.

As hard as I may act, I really loved this dude. Damn, it has been over a year since I met Devin. Time moves fast. When we first met in the club on Memorial Day weekend in Atlanta, we were just chilling. When I found out that he went to FAMU that made things even better. We chilled for a few months, but the more we chilled the more we started to fall for each other. During this time, I was still doing me and he was still doing him.

But after I caught Chaz, Ian and Micah at Ra'Jon's house last year, things started to change. Once I came back in contact with Chaz, I tried to sleep with him, but Chaz wasn't gonna do his dude like that. I think it's so funny that Chaz's dude turned out to be Micah's roommate, Zach. I even tried to put myself on Zach a few times, but he wasn't gonna cheat on Chaz. After all this shit happened, Chaz and I got close as friends, and Devin and I started to really get serious. We were in a relationship soon after.

I remember Chaz telling me that Zach thought Chaz was cheating on him with me. That shit never happened. Chaz and I just became really good friends; he kinda helped me to really see the good in Devin.

After a few months of being faithful to Devin, I started to get bored with the relationship and my dick started to talk for me. In mid-November of 2002, I went with Chaz to his cousin's Eric crib to get something, and while I was there, I met Eric's roommate, Amir.

*"What's up, man?" I said, as I saw Amir. His face was very familiar.*

*"Yo, ain't you in Dr. Nkansah's calculus-II class?" he asked.*

*"Yeah, I am. That's where I know you from," I said. "How are you doing in there?"*

*"Man, it's a struggle, but I'm managing a C," he said. "What's your name?"*

*"Morgan and you?"*

*"Amir."*

*"Maybe we should study sometime," I said. "Two brains are better than one."*

*Amir said, "Yeah, we need to do that. This my number, call me so we can get up."*

*"Ight," I said, as I gave him my number.*

Ironically, the next week, our professor, Dr. Nkansah split the class into groups of two to work on a group question. We had a week to answer the question that was presented to us and present our findings to the class. Amir and I were in the same group.

As time went on, Amir and I got close and we starting fucking around. At first it happened twice before Christmas break, and once before MLK weekend in January. We would hook up here and there during the spring semester, but when spring break hit in March, things changed.

Amir and I started to fuck on a regular basis. I would never go to his house because I didn't want his roommates to think that something was going down, especially since I knew Eric. When he went home during the summer, I had stopped fucking around on Devin, but Amir had me come up to Atlanta one weekend. He said that this girl he was fucking was irking his last nerve and he needed some dick to take his mind off of her.

# Life of a College Bandsman 2: Is This Love

Micah joined me on that trip and I had Micah drop me off at a hotel that Amir got for us. Micah went out and had some fun in Atlanta and I had my fun with Amir in that room.

I made a few other trips up to Atlanta to fuck with Amir after that. I even took Devin on one of those trips, talking about playing with fire...

I still don't understand how Devin knows that I'm cheating on him. Everything I do, I do it carefully. The only thing I can come up with is that he went through my phone when I wasn't around. But however he found it, he knows it and I'm fucked. I don't want Devin to end things with me. I want to make this shit work.

We've learned a lot from each other. The main thing I learned since I've been with Devin is that people can change. If I put forward my best effort, I know I can do it, too.

On the other side, since I've been kicking it with Amir, I have started to develop some feelings for him. I mean we have been fucking for damn near eight months. I know he has his side action, too, but I got feelings for that dude. It's not the same feelings that I have for Devin, but I like Amir. I just don't want to hurt him when I end this thing with him. Amir and I were supposed to get up tonight because I told him that my dude was gonna be out of town.

"Devin should be in Charlotte by now," I said to myself, as I realized that he hadn't called me. "Hopefully he answers," I said, as I called his phone. "C'mon, Devin," I said, as I let his phone ring.

I called his phone a few times, but each time I called, he didn't answer.

"I will try again tomorrow," I said, as I went to my room and got on the bed.

"GREAT," I said, as my phone started to ring. I just knew it was Devin. But when I looked at the caller ID, it wasn't Devin, it was Amir.

"Hello?" I said, as I didn't want to have this conversation. I had to end this tonight. I wanted and needed Devin in my life.

"What's wrong?" Amir said. "You sound down."

"I was just thinking," I said.

"You don't want me to come through?" Amir asked.

"See, that's what I'm thinking about," I said.

"What's going on?" Amir asked. "What's up, Morgan? Be honest."

"Look, it's like this..."

# 55

## Micah Harris

I finally had a night off from work and I wanted to take this time to just do me. I didn't want to be bothered with Rozi and her shit. I really wish she would just have the damn abortion so we can end this shit. Zach was gone for the weekend and I wanted to take advantage of having the house to myself.

I walked over to the mirror in my bathroom and looked at myself. *"What the fuck have you done, Micah?"*

I turned to my left, reached down and turned on the shower. I walked back to my room and took off the gray boxer briefs that I was sporting. I looked at my body in the nude and realized that all the Harris men had crazy bodies. Our father did, too.

Right as I got ready to step into the shower my phone started to ring.

"WHO DA FUCK?" I said out loud, as I ran to my bed with my dick flopping up and down against my naked body.

"Oh, it's just him," I said, as I pushed the ignore button. "I'll call Raidon when I get back out."

I stepped in the shower and turned my back to the water. I let the sizzling water hit my shoulder and serve as a form of medicine. As I stood there under the water, I started to feel better, as the water started to release some of the stress and tension that had built up around my neck and shoulders. The longer I stood there, the better I felt.

After about five minutes of standing under the water, I turned around retrieved my wash cloth and soap. As I started to lather up my body, I couldn't get Kris out of my mind and how devastated he would be when he found out that I cheated on him and is fathering a child.

The longer I stood in the shower, the more I realized how bad I had fucked up. I wasn't ready to take care of a child and I was now stuck to this girl forever. My mom and pops was gonna be so disappointed in me; Raidon was gonna kill me. The last thing my mom told me before I came up to school last year was not to make any babies.

I turned the water off and stepped out on the towel that I had lying on the floor. I took the other towel that was hanging on the nearby rack and proceeded to dry myself off. After I put some lotion on my body, I turned around and turned on the water in the sink so I could brush my teeth. After I brushed my teeth, I took a rubber band and wrapped it around my hair. My home girl was going to braid up my hair tomorrow. I loved the crazy designs she put in my head.

There wasn't any need to put on any clothes since Zach wasn't here. I walked my naked ass to the kitchen to fix myself a cup of water. I still couldn't get Rozi and the baby off my mind. The time period was almost up and she needed to get this abortion.

As I walked back to my room, my phone started to ring again. I looked at it and sighed. I just didn't feel like talking to Raidon right now. Hell, I didn't feel like talking to anyone, so I pushed the ignore button again.

I turned on the TV and the people in the news were talking about a man who was murdered in Durham, North Carolina.

For some reason that made me think of my pops, and despite how I felt about talking to anyone, I had the urgent need to call him.

"Answer the phone," I said, as I let the phone ring.

"You have reached the personal voice mailbox of Dr. Michael Harris…"

"Let me try again," I said, as I hung up the phone and called him again.

After about five or six rings, he answered, "Hello?"

"Hey, Pops," I said.

"What's going on, Micah?" he asked.

"Just checking in on you. I hadn't heard from you in a little bit," I said.

"I'm just doing me right now," he said.

"What's going on?"

# Life of a College Bandsman 2: Is This Love

"It's just some crazy things between your mom and me," he said. "But I don't really want to get into that right now."

"Where is mom?" I asked.

"I don't know, I'm not in Norfolk," he said.

"Where are you?" I asked.

"I was in Richmond, but now I'm in Texas," my pops stated.

"What's down there?" I asked.

"I just took a vacation," he said. "I wasn't gonna answer the call because I didn't want to be bothered, but I have been watching the news, and I didn't want anyone to think that the man that was murdered was me. So, you can tell everyone that I'm ok."

"Ok, Pops."

"Ight, Micah, I will talk to you later."

"Ok, Pops. Take care of yourself."

"I will and I love you."

"I love you, too, Pops," I said, as I hung up the phone. A few seconds later, I was startled by someone beating on my door.

"MICAH, OPEN THIS DAMN DOOR RIGHT NOW!" I heard Raidon yell.

I sighed, as I struggled to put on some basketball shorts.

He continued to beat on the door. As I made my way to the front of the house, I said, "I'm coming."

I opened the door and said, "Why are you beating on my door like that?"

"Why didn't you answer the phone?" he asked.

"I was in the shower," I replied.

"Nigga, you sent me to voicemail two times," Raidon said.

"I was in the shower," I said, as I walked back in the house.

"Whatever," he said, as I heard him walk in the house. When I turned around, my mother was with him.

"WHAT ARE YOU DOING HERE?" I asked when I saw my mom.

"You don't want me here?" she asked me.

"I didn't mean it like that," I said, as I walked over and gave her a hug.

"Umm, hmm," she said, as she looked around my apartment. "This is nice, Micah."

"Thanks, Ma," I said.

She said, "You need to put on some clothes."

"I'll be right back," I said, as I ran to my room. I had to remove the picture that I had of Kris and myself on my desk. If I knew my mom, I knew she was gonna make her way to my room and I couldn't let her find out that I was gay like this.

"You had to go hide something you didn't want me to see," she said, when I came back in the living room putting on a black wife beater.

"It ain't even like that, Ma," I said, as I took a seat.

"Whatever, boy. I was once your age," she looked at me.

"Raidon, get me something to drink." She looked at me and asked, "Do you have anything to drink?"

"Yes, it's some water, tea and Coke in the fridge," I said.

"Tea would be good, Raidon," my mom said, as Raidon made his way to the kitchen.

"Now to you," she said, as she sternly looked at me. "What's going on, Micah?"

"Everything is good, Mom," I said.

"DON'T LIE TO ME!" she commanded. "You even got Morgan lying for you."

"It's nothing major," I said.

"Here you are," Raidon said, as he handed her a glass of iced tea.

"Thanks, baby," she said, as she took a sip.

I looked at my mom and I loved her natural authority, her natural beauty. My mom aged so gracefully. My mom was a fairly petite woman, but she was something to die for. Her long black hair accented with her smooth buttermilk skin, high cheek bones and piercing eyes was a sight to see.

"MICAH!" she stated. "I'm waiting for an answer."

"No disrespect, but I don't have to tell you everything little thing that goes wrong in my life," I stated, as I stood up and walked to the window.

"Excuse me?" she said, as she stood and looked up to me. "What did you just say to me?"

"Mom, I don't think he meant it to be nasty," Raidon interjected.

When my mom looked at Raidon, he just knew that he needed to shut up. She turned to me and said, "I don't care how old you get, you are still MY son and no child of mine will talk to me in that tone. Do you understand me?"

"Yes, ma'am," I said. I didn't mean for it to come out the way it did, but I guess my tone of voice was a bit over the top.

"Now, what's going on with you?" she asked again.

# Life of a College Bandsman 2: Is This Love

"I got it under control," I said. "Mom, you don't have to worry."

"A parent always worries about their children," she said.

"By the way, I talked to Pops earlier and he told me to tell y'all hello," I added.

"We are not talking about your father; we're talking about you! Now, what is wrong, Micah? You are really starting to worry me."

I sighed.

She said, "I call you and you don't wanna talk on the phone, you brush me off. You're not talking to your sister. Raidon said he hasn't talked to you. I guess you talk to Morgan because y'all scheme together. I have thought about everything and I just wanna know what is wrong," she said.

I looked over at Raidon and I could tell that he was interested in seeing what the problem was, too. I looked back at my mom and I knew she was getting frustrated with me. I know that I had to tell her at some point, but I didn't want to say anything until I found out if Rozi had the abortion or not. If she had the abortion, there wasn't a need for me to open my mouth. But my mom wasn't gonna drop the subject and I was a horrible liar.

"I'm waiting, Micah," she said again.

*Why won't she just stop pressing the issue?* I took a deep breath and just let the words flow from my mouth. I stared my mother in the eyes and said, "I met this girl in Atlanta this summer, and I slept with her. And now she is almost three months pregnant with my child."

"YOU WHAT?" she yelled, as she looked at me.

"I have a kid on the way," I stated.

"I TOLD YOU NOT TO HAVE ANY BASTARD BABIES UNTIL IT WAS THE RIGHT TIME WITH THE RIGHT WOMAN," my mom yelled, as she slapped me. "YOU'RE JUST LIKE YOUR DAMN FATHER—JUST LIKE YOUR FUCKING FATHER!"

# 56

## *Micah*

I stood in disbelief because I couldn't believe that my mom just slapped the fuck out of me.

"Ma," Raidon said, as he got off the chair and came over to her. "Calm down."

"How can I?" she said, as she started to cry. "It's happening all over again."

"What's happening all over again," he asked, as he led her to the couch.

"Micah," my mom said as she looked at me, as she wiped the tears from her eyes. "I'm sorry."

"It's ok," I said, as I walked over to her. Raidon was sitting on the left of her and I took my seat on the right.

"Are you sure that the baby is your kid?" she asked.

"I mean I don't know," I said. "I slept with her and everything adds up, but I don't know. I can only go by what she tells me."

"Well, once she has the baby a paternity test needs to be done. And if the kid is yours, then we will gladly accept the baby into our family," my mom said, as she gave me a hug.

"Why are you crying, Mom?" I asked.

"Yeah," Raidon added. "You never answered my question."

"What question?" she said.

"What's happening all over again?" Raidon stated.

"Before I get into that, I need to catch Micah up on what's been happening," my mom stated, as my phone started to ring.

"Hold on," I said, as I answered the phone.

"You at home?" he asked.

"Yeah," I said. "You coming over?"

"Yeah, I'm down the street. I should be there in like three minutes."

"Ok," I said as I hung up.

"Who is coming over here?" my mom asked.

"Morgan," I replied.

"Well, that's even better," she said. "I can say this one time and one time only."

"Are you sure that you're ready for that, Mom?" Raidon asked.

"Yeah," she said. "It's gotta come out some day and in order for me to tell why I tripped out like that, I need to let Morgan and Micah in on what's been happening."

"I know that something happened between you and pops, but I'm a little afraid to find out what exactly it is," I said.

"There is nothing to be afraid of. It's life. Shit happens," she said, as she looked at Raidon. "Can you get me another glass of tea?"

"Ok," Raidon said, as he went into the kitchen.

"I'm really sorry, Micah," my mom said. "I just let my anger get the best of me."

"It's ok," I said.

"Are you sure? I don't want my boys mad at me. Y'all and your sister is all I got in this world," she confessed.

"Mama, I'm not mad," I said, as I heard a door close. I walked to the front door to let Morgan inside.

As I opened the door, Morgan said, "Why is Raidon's car here?"

"Because," I said, as I moved out the way and let Morgan in the house.

"MAMA?" Morgan said shocked, as he rushed over to her and gave her a hug. "What are you doing here?"

"I can't visit my boys?" she asked.

"You can do whatever you like," Morgan said, as he had a seat across from her. "It's so good to see you, Mom."

"It's good to see you, too, baby," my mom stated.

"Where is Michelle?" Morgan asked, as Raidon came out of the kitchen.

"She's at the house in Norfolk," my mom said.

"Oh, how's pops?" he asked.

"I'm happy that you asked," my mom said, as she took a sip of the tea. "I have a lot to say."

"I take it Raidon already knows," Morgan interjected.

# Life of a College Bandsman 2: Is This Love

"Raidon knows *some* of it," my mom said. "But I want to tell y'all *all* of it."

"Oh, boy," I said to myself, as I prepared to take in what my mom was getting ready to say.

I just knew this was gonna get messy…very messy.

# 57

# *Zach*

We finally had some time to go out and view the city. We had been in Charlotte for a few hours now, but as soon as we got here, we went straight to practice. God knows we needed it.

It felt good not to be on the freshmen buses anymore. I was now on the fourth bus, Bus D. Our wait time to eat and go get into the hotel wasn't as long as it was last year.

Since we weren't freshmen anymore and we weren't forced to be together, George wasn't placed in our room this year. The Fab Four—Dwight, Kris, Peanut and I, were back together once again, sharing the hotel room. I could only imagine what kind of adventures we would embark on this band season.

When we showered and changed out of our band sweat suits, we headed downstairs to get something to eat. All of the allocations that we got were all ours! We didn't have to give our money up anymore. That shit felt great. The more I thought about things, the more I realized that I am not a freshman anymore. When we walked outside, another band was arriving at the hotel across the street.

"I wonder who that is," Dwight asked, as the five charter buses came to a complete stop.

Peanut said, "I don't know, but it feels good to be back in this environment."

When I looked down the street, there were a few places to choose from. There was a McDonald's, Burger King, Waffle House, IHOP, Denny's, Ponderosa, a Chinese place. We were definitely in a good location.

"HOLD UP, Y'ALL!" Omar said, as he rushed out the door. "I wanna go."

"What y'all want to eat?" Dwight asked, as he looked at the places to choose from.

"Since we don't have one in Tally, I can do IHOP," I said, as I looked at the group. My mouth was watering for one of those buttermilk pancakes.

"Shit, that sounds good to me," Kris said.

"That's cool with y'all?" Dwight asked.

"Yeah," we all said.

Once we settled in IHOP and ordered our food, it became clear whose band that was across from us at the hotel. One-by-one, a sea of blue and gold entered the restaurant.

"That's North Carolina A&T," Omar stated.

"It sure is," I said, as I looked at one of the shirts that their band members sported.

"Didn't you have a friend in that band?" Dwight asked, as he looked at me.

"Yeah, I did," I said, as I thought back to Phil. He was the small dick dude who I met in his hotel last year, after our football game against North Carolina A&T. When I saw his small ass dick, I almost vomited. Thankfully, nothing happened between us because Quinton called a meeting with the freshmen leaders of the section. That was the night Dwight, Kris and me got our asses beat for the first time.

"Aye, Zach," Dwight said, as he brought my attention back to the table.

"What's up?" I said, as I looked at him.

"Your phone is ringing," he said.

When I looked down, Dwight had sent me a text.

"Ain't that yo' friend right there over there."

When I looked up at Dwight, he moved his head in the direction of the dude. Once I focused my attention on the dude, it was Phil, in all of his chocolate glory. I immediately thought back to his extremely small dick and started to laugh.

"What's funny?" Kris asked me.

"Nothing, man," I said. "Just an inside joke."

When I looked back over at him, he was looking and had a smile on his face.

"I hope he don't think we're gonna finish what was started," I said to myself, as the waitress brought out our food.

*****

# *Chaz*

Things with Genevieve were getting better by the day. The more time I spend with her, the more I know this is the woman for me. Ra'Jon had been in Orlando for a cute minute now and I needed him to get this thing popping.

"Yes, Chaz?" RJ said, as he answered the phone.

"What are you doing down there?" I asked.

"I've already done my part," he said. "Black should be getting a package either tomorrow or Monday. I sent it off the other day."

"You mailed it to him?" I asked.

"Yes, I didn't put a return address on it, though," he said.

"And you put the pictures and shit in there?" I asked.

"Yes," he said.

"This is not the way I told you to do it," I said. "You might fuck this shit up."

"I couldn't do it your way because I didn't want Black to know that I was behind this shit," Ra'Jon said.

"You bitching up now?" I said. "I know I couldn't have trusted yo' ass with this shit."

"It's gonna get done," Ra'Jon said. "Stop worrying, Chaz. DAMN. If I said I was gonna do it, I'm gonna do it and everything will be fine. SHIT. You're about to piss me off."

"IGHT, MAN," I said cutting him off. "This shit just better turn out right."

"Oh, it will, for everyone involved," Ra'Jon said.

"Whatever, man, we'll see," I said, as I hung up the phone.

*****

# *Amir*

Eric walked into the kitchen and asked, "Are you alright?"

"Yeah," I said, as I grabbed a shot glass. I needed some liquor to ease some of the pain I was feeling. "You want some?"

"No, I'm good," Eric said, as went back into the living room to finish watching Law and Order: SVU.

I poured some Patron into the shot glass. "SHIT," I said, as the liquor rushed down my throat.

I headed into the living room. Eric looked at me and asked, "Have you met the new roommate yet?"

"No," I said. "I didn't know someone moved in."

"Yeah, when I got home, the door was open and some stuff was in the room. I haven't met him, though," Eric said. "You sure you're ok?"

"Yeah, man," I said.

"What—no date for the evening?" Eric said, as he started to laugh.

I didn't find anything funny. Morgan broke it off with me. That nigga was talking about he wanted to be faithful to his nigga and shit. I mean that's good for him, but he just left me out there like that. I ain't pressed because its only dick, and I can find that shit anywhere. But I wanted *his* dick. Oh, well, it's just time to move on to something else.

"I think I hear yo' phone ringing," Eric said, as I ran to my room to get it.

"Hello?" I said, as I answered the phone.

"Hi, Son."

"Hi, Dad," I said. "How are you?"

"I'm ok," he said.

"Are you back in Alabama?" I asked.

"Yes, I am. School started last week," he said.

"Oh, how are your students?" I asked.

"They're ok," he said. "I just talked to your brother and I just wanted to tell you that I'm gonna put some money in your account on Monday."

"Ok," I said. "Dad?"

"Yes, Amir?"

# Life of a College Bandsman 2: Is This Love

"Why are you doing this?" I asked.

"Doing what?"

"Giving all of this. I mean you brought me a new car and you are paying for some of my rent, as well as just giving me money. Why?"

"Never question it, just take it," he said.

"I need a real answer," I said.

"Well, something is about to happen. I don't want it to happen, but sometimes you gotta face facts. In the meantime, it just makes me feel better knowing that I can provide for you right now because I may not have the chance to do it in the future," he said.

"What are you supposed to mean by that?" I asked.

"Well, hopefully it doesn't happen, but if and when it does, you will know. Trust me."

"You're talking in circles right now, but ok, Dad," I said. "Thanks for the cash. Call me when you deposit it."

"Ok, I'll talk to you later. I love you."

"Yep," I said, as I hung up the phone.

I hate it when he says that he loves me. If you love someone, then he wouldn't have done the things that he did to me. When I walked back out to the living room, Eric was still on the couch watching TV.

"Who was that?" he asked, as I took a seat.

"My dad," I said as I heard someone unlocking the door.

"YASSSS, I LIVE HONEY... IGHT, GIRL. NO TEA, NO SHADE, BITCH! WHATEVER, GIRL. Let me call you back. Girl, I'm about to walk in this house," I heard *him* say as he walked in the house.

Eric immediately looked at me and shook his head. I just know we don't have no damn queen as our fourth roommate.

"What's the tea?" he said, as he approached us.

"Excuse me?" I said.

"Pardon my manners," he said, as he came over to me. "I'm Dezmond and you are?"

"Amir."

"Eric."

"Nice to meet you, boys," he said in his girly voice, as he strutted across the floor and went to his room.

Dezmond was about 5'7 and was very petite and very feminine. He had on some tight, tight jeans with an extra small t-shirt. He sported a low, sharp cut. He just looked and dressed like the "stereotypical fag." God knows I don't like fems.

"I can't believe this shit," I said.

"We got a fucking fag for a roommate," Eric said.

"A fag that's out!" I added.

"THE HEAD FAG!" Dezmond shouted from his room.

I just looked at Eric and shook my head. It was gonna be a long year with this *thing* living in the house.

# 58

## *Micah*

My mom stared each of us in the eyes and said, "I'm gonna try to make a long story short. Your father and I aren't together anymore."

"WHAT?" both Morgan and I said simultaneously.

"We are going to get a divorce," my mom said.

"What happened?" I asked.

"Is this what you were crying about that day in the kitchen when you were talking to Raidon?" Morgan asked.

"Well, it's something related to it," she said.

"What caused this?" Morgan asked.

"Your father and I have been having some problems for some time now," she said.

"We know that," I added.

"Ok, but we are both to blame for something's that has happened," she stated.

"Like what?" Morgan asked.

"Well, for one, your father is gay," she said.

"Stop lying," I said to my mom.

"I'm not lying," she said.

"No, she isn't," Raidon added. "I caught him with another dude a few weeks ago."

"You can't be serious," Morgan interjected.

"I'm serious," she said. "I have known for some time that your father liked men."

"How?" I asked.

"I caught him looking at men on the computer some years ago," she said.

"This is too much," Morgan said.

"I'm not done," she said.

I took a deep breath and prepared for the rest of it.

"The dude that your dad was sleeping with is your Uncle Alonzo."

"WHAT THE HELL?" Morgan yelled. "THAT'S NASTY AS F—"

"WATCH YOUR MOUTH!" my mom said, as she cut Morgan off.

"Sorry, mom," he said. "But that's incest."

"Not quite," Raidon said. "He isn't our real uncle."

"I'm lost," I said. "I know we don't know the man like that, but we know he is dad's half-brother."

"That was a lie," my mom said. "It turns out that people said that they acted like brothers, so they just kept the title when they met me."

"Y'all met up here at FAMU, right?" Morgan asked.

"Yes, we did," my mom said. "I fell in love with your father during that time but I did something that wasn't right, either."

"What was that?" I asked.

"I slept with Alonzo," she said.

"Ok," Morgan nonchalantly said.

"It didn't happen but a few times, but we knew it was wrong so we ended it and it never happened again," my mom said.

"Ok," I said.

"This was around the same time that I got pregnant with your brother, Ra'Jon," she said.

"I KNEW IT, I KNEW IT!" Morgan yelled. "THAT'S WHY HE ACTS LIKE THAT!"

"RJ isn't your father's child, he's Alonzo's," my mom confessed.

"It all makes sense," Morgan said. "I knew something was different about him."

"So RJ is our half-brother?" I said.

"Yes, he is," my mom said.

"Does he know this?" I asked.

She said, "No, but please let me be the one to tell him."

"Ok," I said.

"You got that Morgan?" she said.

"Yes, ma'am."

# Life of a College Bandsman 2: Is This Love

"How come you never said anything to us about that?" I asked.

"Because I wanted to keep that a secret. No one knew that but me, but as the years passed, I was killing myself inside because of that secret. As things heated up between your father and I, and he confessed the truth about Alonzo, I told him the truth about RJ," she said.

"So all this just came out?" I said.

"Yes."

"Wait a minute!" Morgan said. "The dude who is sleeping with dad, is RJ's real father?"

"Yes," my mom stated.

"WOW," I said in disbelief. What was happening to my family?

"Pops *is* gay?" Morgan said.

"Yes, he is," my mom said.

*"I guess we got that gene from him,"* I thought to myself as I looked at Morgan. I could tell that Morgan was thinking the same thing because he looked over at me with the same look I gave him.

"So, now that's out of the way, back to what happened earlier," Raidon said.

"What happened earlier?" Morgan asked.

"I don't like the way that you two scheme together," my mom said, as she looked at Morgan.

"Mom, what are you talking about?" Morgan asked.

"You and Micah. Y'all have always been like that, taking up and lying for each other."

"What are you talking about?" Morgan said again.

"She knows," I said, as I looked at Morgan.

"She does?" he asked, confused.

"Yes, I do," she said. "I'm not too excited about the baby, but this is life and we have to adjust accordingly."

"Ok. Enough of Micah and the baby," Raidon said. "Why did you make that statement that Micah was just like pops?"

"Yeah," I said. "What's happening all over again?"

"Well," my mom said, as she took a deep breath.

"Well, what?" Morgan said.

"Do you remember when your father had to go out of town for some work that he had to do a long time ago," she asked. "Morgan and Micah you must have been about twelve and nine. Raidon you were fifteen because RJ was eighteen and getting ready to come up to FAMU. Michelle was seven."

"Is that when he was gone for a few weeks and went to Texas?" Raidon asked.

"Yes, it was," she said.

"I think I remember that because Michelle was always asking for pops," I said.

"Yeah, I do, too," Morgan said.

"Well, he really didn't have to go for his job," she said. "He actually was right in Richmond."

"Richmond? Why did y'all lie to us?" Raidon asked.

"Because we had split up."

"Why?" I asked.

"Your father had cheated on me," she said.

"So, he does this a lot?" Raidon asked. You could hear the frustration in his voice.

"He's your father and all of you take after him," my mom said.

"No, we don't," I said.

"Yes, you do. I know each and every last one of you inside and out," my mom said. "And all of you take after Michael. That's why I tell you not to do this and not to do that. I say it because I don't want you to end up like your father has ended up. Just because things look good on the outside, doesn't mean that it's always good on the inside. I love you father, don't get me wrong, I really do, but we have had our share of problems. We just didn't want to bring y'all into our problems. Y'all don't know the half of things that went down between your father and myself." My mom looked at me and said, "Micah, when I slapped you, I did it out of anger. Your confession brought back up years of frustration that I kept hidden for about twelve years now. When I tell you not to go to school and have babies, I say it for a reason. I got pregnant with RJ when I was in college. When I say don't have any kids unless it is with the right person, I mean that. You don't wanna meet the perfect woman, and then have to bring all your damn kids into her life. It's not fair to either you or her. Just put a damn rubber on your dick."

"What are you trying to say?" Raidon asked.

"Like I said, your father and I split because he cheated on me. He met this woman who used to live in Norfolk. She was an accountant. They became good friends and they got intimate," my mom said.

"Is she still in Norfolk?" Morgan asked.

"No, she lives in Texas now," my mom stated.

# Life of a College Bandsman 2: Is This Love

*"My dad is in Texas,"* I said to myself, as I thought about our conversation from earlier. *"Is he with her?"*

"She got pregnant and had a little boy," my mom said.

"WHOA!" Raidon yelled. "DAD HAS ANOTHER KID FROM ANOTHER WOMAN AND WE DIDN'T KNOW ABOUT IT!"

"We have another brother?" Morgan asked, confused.

"This is too much," I said.

"That's why I tripped out on you, Micah. It brought back horrible memories," my mom said.

"Where is our brother?" Raidon asked.

"If I'm adding correctly that means that he is about eleven or twelve years old now. What's his name?" Morgan asked.

"You are right, Morgan," my mom said. "Travis would be about twelve now."

"What do you mean would?" I asked.

"Yeah, where is he?" Raidon asked.

"Well, Travis didn't make it," my mom said. "He died of an enlarged heart when he was two months old."

"This is crazy," I said to myself, as I got up and left the room.

*What the hell happened to my family?*

# 59

## *Zach*

That was a long ass ride back to Tallahassee and I wasn't happy. No one in the band was happy.

When Eric arrived at my house, he gave me a kiss and asked, "How was the trip?"

"I don't wanna talk about it," I said, as I continued to put away my things.

"Why, what happened?"

"We got fucked over!"

"How?" he asked.

"That shit was rigged," I said. "First off, this was a competition. Dr. Hunter said that we don't compete in things like this. We were here to do an exhibition show; we weren't supposed to be in the competition. But somehow, our name got included in the competition and we were judged like everyone else."

"So, what happened?" Eric asked.

"We came in third! How the fuck does The Hundred come in third? We were the best damn band at that stupid ass battle of the bands!" I said upset.

"Wow, who was first?"

"See, that's why this shit was rigged. Ironically, North Carolina A&T came in first. Sounds suspicious doesn't it, especially with that whack ass show they had. First place for the home band."

"Damn, that is fucked," Eric said. "Who came in second?"

"Howard. Now if somebody should have come in first other than us, it should have been Howard. I can't even lie; those boys were on point. Dr. Hunter said Charlotte will never again be graced by the presence of The Hundred as long as he's the director."

"Wow, it is really that serious?" Eric asked.

"Hell, yeah, it's that serious…to us anyway," I said, as I went to the kitchen to get a bottled water.

"So, are you ready for the test?" I said, when I walked back in the room.

"I've been studying all weekend. I'd take a break and watch TV here and there, but I guess I'm as ready as I'm gonna be," Eric said.

"I know you're gonna do fine," I said.

"I'm a lil nervous," he said.

"Why?"

"Because my future rides on this test," Eric said. "I need to get into a good medical school and that all depends on how I do on this exam. I know I'll kill the interviews."

"You will be fine," I said. "With those grades that you have anyone will gladly take you."

"I hope so," Eric said, as he came over and gave me a kiss.

"I don't feel like going to school tomorrow," I said.

"I don't either, but this is my last year so I'm excited to get this shit over with," Eric said.

"Well, you've got something to look forward to," I said.

"Hell, you do, too," he said.

"And what is that?" I asked as I sat up and looked at him.

"Look at it this way—this is one less year that you have to go," Eric said.

"I guess, Eric."

"YO, ZACH!" Micah said, as he knocked on the door.

"IT'S OPEN!"

"What's up, Eric?" Micah said, as he walked in the room.

"Ain't shit, bruh," Eric replied.

"Yo, I brought some food home. If y'all want some, y'all are free to get some," Micah said.

"Thanks, bruh," I said. "But I already grabbed something before I came home."

"Ight, well if y'all get hungry, it's out there," he said. "I'm about to go get Kris."

"You seem a little at ease," I said. "You don't seem stressed anymore."

"My mom came down here this weekend and we got a lot off our chests. Things are a little bit better, but I still have a long way to go," he said.

"What's wrong? You never told me what happened," I said as I thought back to when I overheard him talking on the phone the other day. *I can't believe Micah cheated on Kris and got some girl pregnant.*

"It's just some crazy shit. I'll holla at you and let you know what's up later. Kris is waiting on me," he said.

"Ight, bruh," I said.

"Take care, Micah," Eric stated.

"Ight, y'all," Micah said, as he closed the door and left the apartment.

"Eric, I'm a lil confused," I said.

"What's up?"

"I know what's bothering Micah."

"What is it?" he asked.

"Out of respect for his privacy, I'm not gonna say it," I said. "But he didn't know I was home one day and I overheard him talking on the phone. Micah is my roommate and my friend and it's got some stuff to do with some other people that I know. Those people are my friends, too. I don't want my friends to get hurt, but I don't wanna tell on Micah because it ain't my business."

"Well, I think you should go to Micah and let him know that you know what it is and figure out something together, because he's putting you in a tough situation as well," Eric said.

"Yeah, I think that's what I will do," I said, as I placed my body directly on top of Eric's body.

"What are you doing?" he said, as he started to smile.

"What do you think?" I said, as I reached down and kissed my baby.

I felt his manhood starting to rise and as I result, I started to rise, too. *Maybe this is the time.*

While I was on top of Eric's body, I started to place kisses around his neck. He pulled me back over to him and forced his tongue inside of my mouth. I loved the way Eric made me feel.

We kissed for about five minutes. He flipped me over. I was on the bottom and he was on top. Eric seductively pulled off my shirt and started to lick around my chest. A few seconds later, he started to suck on my nipples.

"Damn, baby," I said, as pleasure started to take over my body. My dick was begging to be released from my shorts.

Eric worked his way back up, licking and kissing on my body

until he got back to my lips. We started to kiss again and in the process, he started to feel on my dick.

A few seconds later, he rose up and quickly took off his shirt. He came up and placed another kiss on my lips then he went down to my pants. Eric felt my dick once again and then he pulled my shorts down leaving me in my boxers.

"Damn, I love yo' ass," Eric said, as he kissed me.

"I love you, too," I replied.

Eric then pulled down my plaid boxers, releasing my now throbbing manhood. Eric started to lick around the shaft of my dick. I was so ready for my dick to be inside of his cavity. Like the pro that he was, Eric immediately took me inside of his mouth.

"OH, SHIT," I yelled from the intense pleasure that Eric showed me.

Eric made love to my dick. The way he looked as he went up and down on my dick turned me the fuck on. That shit was hot. The slurping noises combined with the wetness of his mouth just took me places.

The next thing I knew, Eric slowly came off of my dick and slowly went back down, going further than he's ever gone before.

"OH, FUCK," I said in pleasure, as my dick now rested in the back of his throat. I wanted to release myself right then and there, but I wanted to make this last. Once he came off of my dick, I got up and he placed himself on the bed. I pulled down his pants and boxers and immediately took him inside my mouth.

I showed no mercy on his dick, as I wanted him to feel the same pleasure that he made me feel. The way he moved around in the bed, and the way he kept trying to pull his dick out of my mouth let me know that I was doing the job.

This was good and all, but I wanted to take it to the next level. I wanted to finally make love to my baby.

I when I came off of his dick, I sat down on top of him. His dick was at my entrance. I reached down and kissed my baby.

While I was on top of Eric, I reached over into the nightstand and grabbed my bag of condoms and lube. I removed myself from his body, to put the condom on his dick. As I was putting the condom on, I could feel Eric's hesitation. I took the lube and put some on his dick and did the same for my ass.

When I sat back down on him, I kissed him but he didn't kiss me the same way he had been kissing me all night.

# Life of a College Bandsman 2: Is This Love

I reached behind me, grabbed his dick and placed it at my awaiting hole. As I got ready to go down and sit on his dick, he pulled me off of him.

"WHAT THE FUCK ERIC?" I yelled.

"I can't do this man," he said. "I'm sorry."

"I'M GETTING SICK OF THIS SHIT," I said. "WHAT IS THE FUCKING PROBLEM? WHY DON'T YOU WANNA HAVE SEX WITH ME?"

"It's not you, it's me," he said.

"Well, what is it?" I asked. "This shit is getting frustrating! We've been together since February and we haven't made love one damn time. It's almost September! At the beginning, I brought the story that you said that you wanted to build this relationship off real shit other than just sex, but Eric we have a strong relationship. I want to feel you inside of me. Eric, it's past due. Why won't you make love to me?"

"Baby, I swear it's not you, it's me. I don't wanna hurt you like this. I wanna make love to you. I wanna feel all of you. I wanna do those things to you, but I can't. It's hard for me to do that," he explained.

"What's so hard about it?" I said as I looked at him. "It doesn't seem that hard to me. What are you, a bottom or something?"

"No, I'm not a bottom," he said, as he pulled the condom off of his softening dick.

"Well, what is it? I have sat and thought about every damn thing in the book and I can't come up with anything. All that shit you talked when we met about you being a freak and shit was just talk when we were driving back to Tallahassee last October," I said.

"No, I'm a freak and I love sex. I really do," Eric said.

"Do you have HIV or something? Are you sick?"

"No! We can go take that test together. I ain't sick," he said. "It's just I had a bad experience."

"What kind of experience?" I asked.

"I told you that I messed with two dudes. You know of Raidon, and then there's the other dude. Well, I met the other dude after Raidon left," Eric explained.

"Ok," I said.

"We kicked it for a while and we used to mess around. It wasn't no big deal," Eric said.

"Ight."

"Well, one night we actually got into it—I mean it was hot," Eric said. "And I wanted to go all the way. Well, when I went in all the way, the nigga shitted on me."

"What?" I said.

"That nigga shitted on my dick," Eric said. "It wasn't no lil shit—he SHITTED on my dick! That was the nastiest thing ever and I can't get that image out of my head."

"Damn."

"I want to have sex with you," Eric said. "I'm not saying that you're gonna do that crap to me, but I can't get that shit of out my head. Every single time I think about making love to you, I think about what happened and it turns me off."

"Oh," I said, as I listen to Eric's confession.

"I'm sorry," he said, as he put on his boxers.

"It's cool," I said, as I put on mine and got back in the bed.

"I really want us to do this," he said, as he pulled me in close to him.

"Well, you've got to trust me," I said. "I'm not gonna do that to you. I know how to properly clean my ass."

"I know, baby," he said, as he kissed me on the back of my head. "I know."

# 60

## Zach

I woke up early Monday morning so I could get this new school year under my belt.

"Eric," I said, as pushed him so he could get up.

"Hmm?"

"What time is your class?"

"Hmm?"

"ERIC, GET UP!"

He slowly turned over and looked at me.

"What time is your first class?" I asked again.

"10:10," he said, "What time is it?"

"A little after eight," I replied.

"What time you gotta be to school?" he asked.

"My class starts at 9:05," I said, as I headed to the bathroom to take care of my morning duties.

"Ok," he said, as he looked at his phone.

A few minutes later, Eric brushed his teeth and joined me in the shower. I wanted to mess around a little bit, but after I thought about what he said last night about the dude shitting on his dick and thinking about being to class on time, I just left it alone.

Once I got out of the shower and put on my clothes, I went in the kitchen and fixed a bowl of cereal. A few minutes later, Kris came out.

"What's up, freshman bruh," he said, as he opened the fridge.

"Ain't shit," I said. "Just don't feel like going to class."

"You can't start this shit already," he said.

"I know," I said, as Eric walked out.

"Sup, Kris. I'm ready when you are, baby," Eric said, as he took a seat in the living room.

"Ight," I said, as I quickly finished my breakfast and washed out my bowl.

"I'll see you at practice, freshman bruh," Kris said, as he went back into Micah's room.

"Ight, Eric," I said, as I grabbed my book bag and went to his car.

The ride to campus was silent for the most part, as we listen to the Tom Joyner Morning Show.

"Call me later, ok," Eric said as we arrived at the back of Coleman Library on FAMU's campus.

"Ok," I said, as I reached over and gave him a kiss.

When I got out the car, I realized that I had forgotten my class schedule on my desk in my room. I had about ten minutes until class started, so I rushed into the library and found a computer so I could print out my schedule again.

"Teaching Diverse Populations," I said, as I read the name of my first class for the day. I heard that Dr. Erving was a good professor and everybody passed his class. People said that you were gonna do some serious work, but if you didn't get at least a 'B' then something was wrong with you.

I wanted to keep my high GPA, so that's why I took his class. I was lazy when it came to doing school work, but I will do the damn work if I'm guaranteed good grade in the class.

When I walked over to the College of Education building, I passed some people that I had in previous classes last semester.

"This is it," I said, as I walked into the room.

"What's up, Zach," said Raheim Tyms, one of my freshman brothers that played saxophone, when he saw me walk in the room.

"What's up, bruh," I said, as I made my way over to him and sat down. "I'm so tired."

"Tell me about it," he said. "Practice is killing me."

We engaged in small talk about the band for a few minutes. I checked my phone and it was now 9:05. Dr. Erving wasn't here.

A few minutes later, a few more people rushed in the class with a sigh of relief when they realized that Dr. Erving was late.

"I wish he would hurry up," one girl said.

I wished he would, too. It was now 9:10.

While waiting for Dr. Erving to arrive, I started to think back to

# Life of a College Bandsman 2: Is This Love

the first time Eric and I almost did the do. That was the night we got caught by Quinton last year. I still can't believe he just burst into Eric's room like that.

*"Boy, how times have changed,"* I said, as I looked at my phone. It was now 9:20 and Dr. Erving still hadn't arrived.

"Excuse me," a woman said, as she walked in the class. "The professor wanted me to stop by and tell you all that he is on his way. He will be down in a few minutes. Something important just came up and he had to take care of the situation immediately."

We had been in the class for fifteen minutes without a teacher. I could have stayed in the bed a little bit longer.

About ten minutes later, a man walked in the room. He had on a nice blue suit with a yellow shirt. He had a striped blue and yellow tie to accent the suit. He wore some brown shoes. His hair cut was very sharp. The man looked good. But the more I looked at him the more I realized he looked like someone that I knew.

He walked in the class and didn't say anything. He put his briefcase on the desk in the front of the class and opened it up. He took out the class syllabus and started to pass it out. Once that was done, he finally spoke.

He said, "You may look up for inspiration, down in desperation but never to the side for information, for if you do, you will have just failed this course. Greetings, I am Raidon M. Harris, and I will be your professor in this course for the semester."

# 61

## *Zach*

As I realized who the fuck he was, I sighed. *This has to be fucking joke!*

"Dr. Erving was supposed to teach this class, but he was appointed as the chairman of the Educational Leadership Department, so he won't be teaching anymore undergraduate classes. My name isn't in the system yet, that's why his name is still listed as the professor for the course," he said.

*"What kind of sick game are you playing on me?"* I asked God, as I looked up to the ceiling.

"I am originally from Norfolk, Virginia," he stated. "I am the second of five children. Both my parents are Rattlers and all my siblings, including myself, have followed in their footsteps. My baby sister will be a FAMU Rattler next year. Once I earned my bachelors, I continued on for my master's degree in education. I moved back to Norfolk a few years ago and taught at Norfolk State University. I returned to Tallahassee a few weeks ago and later today, I will officially start my Ph.D. program over at Florida State University. Now that I have introduced myself, I would like to get to know you."

As each person introduced themselves, I was trying to figure out a way to get out of this class, but I couldn't. This class was a pre-requisite for some classes that I needed to take in the spring semester. The last time I checked, all the classes under this course was closed.

After Raheim finished his introduction, Mr. Harris looked to me and said, "Sir," as motioned for me to stand up.

"I am Zachariah Finley, a second year English education major from Orlando, Florida. I am a member of the Marching '100'."

"What did you say your name was again?" he asked, me as he looked at me strangely.

"Zachariah, Zach for short," I replied, as I stared him in his eyes.

"I see," he said, as he stared at me for a second. "All right, thank you."

As he went through the class, he kept looking over at me. I know that he knows I am Eric's dude.

I really didn't know what to do. Being that he was a professional, I wouldn't think that he would treat me any differently. But he was human. I was with his ex.

"FUCK," I said to myself, as I looked at his course syllabus. This is not the way I wanted to start off my semester.

"We will adjourn until 9:05 on Wednesday. Until that time, please be safe," he said, as he dismissed the class.

"Umm, Zach," he said, as I attempted to walk past him.

"Yes?" I said, as I looked back at him.

"Can I see you for second?"

He waited until everyone was out of the class before he started to talk.

"Do you know someone named Eric McDaniel?"

"Yes," I quickly replied.

"Oh, ok," he said, as he stared at me a little longer.

"Why?" I asked.

"I just wanted to see if you were that person," he said.

"I am *that person*," I replied.

"So, I guess you know who I am?" he said.

"I do."

"I see," he said, as he looked at me. "That's all I wanted to know. See you on Wednesday."

"Umm, hmm," I said, as I grabbed my book-bag and exited the room.

# 62

## *Ra'Jon*

Today was the day. I knew Black didn't get the package on Saturday because nothing happened. I was a little excited to see how exactly this thing was gonna turn out.

On the flipside, I was starting to fall in love. Not with Black, but with the city of Orlando. I do like Black, but the city was growing on me. The more time I spend down here, the more I think I want to settle here.

Everything about this city was nice. It was just a beautiful place to be.

I really didn't want to have to go back to teaching in a secondary school setting, but I needed a job. I was living off of my savings for the past year and that money is staring to run short.

I told myself that I was gonna look into finding a job down here. If I can find a decent job, then I was gonna make that move from Norfolk to Orlando for good.

"Hello," I said, as I answered the phone.

"What's up, RJ?" Black stated.

"Nothing," I said. "I'm about to go job hunting in a second."

"Oh, ok," he said. "I was wondering when you were gonna go and do that."

"Yeah, I was being lazy, but I'm ready to go out now."

"Well, you shouldn't have a problem getting a job," he said.

"I hope not," I replied. "Where are you?"

"I'm on my break," he said. "I'm getting off around two this afternoon. We should get up and catch lunch or something."

"Yeah, we can do that," I said. "You wanna meet at your spot?"

"Of course," he replied.

"Ight, Black. I'll see you then," I said, as I hung up the phone.

*"Hopefully, the mail will be at his house when he gets home,"* I told myself, as I got in my car and headed down to the Orange County Public School's county office.

When I got in the building, I got information leading me to the floor for employment opportunities. Inside the room, there were about ten computers. When I sat at my computer, the job listings popped up. As I scrolled down the list, I didn't see anything for music teachers.

"Damn," I said to myself, as nothing was going my way. I wanted to give up, but something told me to keep scrolling down.

"Yes," I said, as I got to the bottom of the list.

*"Open position until filled: Band Director at Westridge Middle School."*

I smiled, clicking on the link to find out more information.

"That's all they pay down here?" I asked myself, as I looked at the $35,000 starting salary.

"Well, I've been teaching for five years and I have a master's degree, so that would put me at $44,500," I said, as I continued to examine their salary schedule.

Something told me to visit the University of Central Florida's (UCF) website to see if they had any positions.

I looked through their stuff, but I didn't find anything. I really didn't want to go work with lil bad ass middle school kids, but this would have to do until I found something better.

I went back to the service desk to find out more information about how to get a job here. The lady told me that I needed to do a background check as well as bring proof of my degrees. Once I had that done, I was free to interview for the position, if selected.

I went ahead and started my application and paid the $75 fee for the background check. She said that it would take about two days for it to come back, and once it clears and I bring proof of my degrees, I was good to go. She went ahead and contacted the principal at Westridge Middle School and I have an interview scheduled for Thursday, pending the results of my background check. I called my mom and she will overnight my official transcripts so I can get it to the lady tomorrow. If everything goes as planned, I will be back at work next week.

*****

# Life of a College Bandsman 2: Is This Love

# *Eric*

I was done with my classes for today and all I wanted to do was go home to my peaceful house and get some last minute studying done before I take that medical school entrance exam later today. On the way home, I grabbed a two-piece chicken dinner from Popeye's.

I knew this not having sex thing was bothering Zach, but I don't know what to do. I lose all interest when it comes time to fuck because I can still see that nigga's shit.

Zach was the first person I told that story to, and hopefully, I can get past my issues to do this thing for the both of us. I know I'm playing with fire because if I don't give my baby what he wants, he is gonna go get it somewhere else.

"What the fuck?" I said when I got in the house. All I heard was Beyoncé and Jay Z's song *Crazy in Love* blaring from out of Dezmond's room.

"God, give me strength," I said, as I went to my room. Once I ate my food, I tried to ignore the music, but it was too loud for me to concentrate. I took a deep breath, walked out my room, headed down the hall and knocked on Desmond's door.

"WHAT'S THE TEA?" he said, as he opened the door. The music got louder.

I looked at him and said, "I'm trying to study and I can't concentrate."

"No tea, no shade," he said, as he turned down the music. "Anything else?"

"No," I said, as I turned around and walked away. When I got to my room I turned back around and Dezmond was still looking at me smiling. He licked his lips.

"WHAT THE FUCK YOU LOOKING AT?" I yelled at Dezmond.

"YOU!" he said as he went inside his room.

I just shook my head and closed my door.

*It's gonna be a long year...*

# 63

## *Micah*

I was still in shock after my mom confessed everything to us about my pops, but I have just come to accept things for what they were. There wasn't a need for me to go off the deep end, besides I had my own issues to deal with. I still couldn't believe that my pops was gay. But I guess you can say that it runs in the family.

After I told my mom the truth about the baby, it made things so much easier for me. I was at some sort of ease within myself. I still had to figure out a way to tell Kris. Regardless of whether Rozi keeps the baby or not, I have the support of my family and that's all that matters. I do want her to get rid of the baby for everyone involved, but if she keeps the baby, I can't wait to be a father to my lil man.

Last night with Kris was great. I missed spending time with my baby like that. I still can't believe that we have been seeing each other for nearly a year now. Time files when you're having fun. I could tell that he was happy to have me back. I know that I've been under some crazy stress lately, but all that is over now. I'm thankful that he has stuck by me while I was bugging out.

"Damn," I said to myself, as I grabbed my dick and thought about the way he rode my dick last night. That nigga was a beast in the bedroom. When we first started having sex, he was always trying to give out the dick, and it was good. But I wanted to get in some ass, too. After a long time of convincing him that it would be ok, he finally gave in and let me hit that shit. Oh, my God, that was the greatest shit on earth! I think that is part of what keeps our sex life interesting. One night I can give the dick and he takes it, then the next he can give the dick and I take it.

I don't know why I cheated on Kris in the first place. He never deserved that. I don't know what made me sleep with Rozi.

As I looked at my schedule, I realized that I had a class that Dwight took over the summer.

"Yo, Dwight," I said, when he answered the phone.

"What's up, fool," he said.

"Yo, didn't you take Organic Chemistry II this summer?" I asked.

"Yeah, what's up?" he stated.

"Do you still have that book?" I asked.

"Yeah, I got it," he said.

"Can I use it for the semester, if you don't mind."

"It's cool," he said. "I'll give it to Big Z at practice today."

"Thanks, man."

"No problem," he said, as he hung up the phone.

After I got off the phone with Dwight, I looked at my clock and realized that I had a few hours before my class started.

"Great," I said, as I looked at my bed. Kris kept me up last night and I needed to catch up on some sleep. When I got in the bed, I grabbed my phone and set the alarm for 12:30 so I wouldn't be late for my class.

I laid in the bed for about ten minutes and I couldn't fall asleep. I wanted to go to sleep, but I guess my body wasn't that tired.

I reached over to the nightstand and grabbed the remote. I flipped through the TV looking for something to watch, but I didn't find anything that sparked my interest. I ended up settling on CNN.

*"This is just in—the Durham Police have identified the body of a man that was murdered last week. His name was Joel Clarke and he was trucker. The police still aren't sure of how Mr. Clarke was murdered. We will bring you more details as they arrive in the CNN Newsroom."*

"Hello," I said, as I turned down the volume on the TV.

"What are you doing, Micah?" Rozi asked.

"Watching television," I said.

"Oh, well I've made up my mind," she said.

"So, what are you gonna do?" I asked.

"I'm gonna have the abortion."

"You sure?" I asked.

"Yes. I've thought long and hard about it and it's the right thing to do for everyone," she said.

"Ok, when are you gonna get it done?" I asked.

# Life of a College Bandsman 2: Is This Love

"I wanna do it today, but if not today, then tomorrow," she said. "I need you to wire the money up here so I can do it though."

"Ok, I'ma go do it right now. I'll call you when I send it," I said, as I got off the phone.

I smiled.

I wasn't happy that we were killing an innocent baby. But I was happy that Kris didn't have to learn about my infidelity and my life could go back to normal.

I will never make that mistake again!

# 64

# *Blackwell McDaniel*

I hated traffic. I just wanted to get where I wanted to go in peace. As I sat in the bumper-to-bumper traffic, I thought about my brother. I knew he had that important medical school entrance exam coming up. I picked up my phone and called him. Once answered, I said, "Where you at?"

"At home laying down," Eric answered.

"Isn't your test coming up?" I asked.

"Yeah, it's later today," he sighed.

"Oh, damn. You ready?"

"As ready as I'm gonna be. I'm a lil nervous, but it's cool."

"You'll be fine," I smiled. I had all the confidence in the world in my little brother. Eric has never disappointed me. Everyone in the family is proud of him. He was destined to do big things.

"Thanks, Black. Where you at?" he asked.

"Stuck in traffic, but I'm heading to meet one of my homeboy's for lunch."

"Oh, ok. That's what's up. But let me try to calm my nerves before this exam."

"Ight, Eric. Good luck."

"Thanks, Black. I'll call you tomorrow."

I reached the diner about twenty minutes later, but I didn't see RJ. I sat down at the counter. I thought I would have been late, being stuck in traffic. A few minutes later, he came and took a seat next to me.

He smiled and said, "Sorry 'bout that. I got caught up in some stuff. I hope you didn't wait too long."

"It's cool," I said, sipping on my Dr. Pepper. "How did the job search turn out?"

"I found an open position at a middle school, so I'm just waiting on my background check to come back in and I should be good to go," he said.

"That's what's up," I said, as we ordered our food.

"So, what's going on with you?" RJ asked once the waitress was gone.

"Nothing, really. I just finished talking to my brother. He's getting ready to take the MCAT."

"Oh, really?" RJ said.

"Yeah, he's a lil nervous, but I know he will do fine," I said. "I need to call my sister and see what's going on with her."

"She goes to Spelman, right?"

"Yes," I sighed. "I wish I would have gone to school. I think that's why I'm so proud of them. I mean I'm doing well for myself down here, but if I had the education that they are getting my life could be so much better."

"So go back to school and get it," RJ stated.

"It ain't that easy," I said.

"Yes, it is. You're just making excuses."

"That's easy for you to say. You have two degrees."

RJ stared at me, "So, what is that supposed to mean? It's only a piece of paper. You can do it but you've gotta believe in yourself."

I just stared at him.

He replied, "We're gonna get you back in school."

"How will it work with my work schedule?" I asked.

"Don't you work in the morning?" he asked.

"Yeah."

"Well, they have night classes. Take one or two classes in the beginning to get back in the groove of it, but once you can find a balance between school and work, you will be fine. I did that for two years while I got my master's degree. It's possible," he said, as he took a bite of his chicken.

"I guess I'll look into it," I said, as I looked over at the door. I was disgusted as I saw two extremely feminine dudes walk into the diner. I said, "I can't stand faggots!"

"They ain't bothering you," RJ said.

"That's not the point," I said. "I just don't understand why people gotta be gay and shit. There is too much pussy out there for that shit. And even if you are gay why do you have to wear it on your chest?"

"Some people are proud of who they are," RJ said.

"I just don't get that shit. That shit is crazy."

"Let those people live their lives," he said.

"What are you about to do?" I asked as we finished our meal.

"Nothing really," he said.

"Follow me to the house," I said. "I can call some of my boys over and we can play spades or something."

"Ight," he said, as he went to his car and I went to mine.

I don't know what it was about RJ, but he was turning out to be a good friend. He never asked for anything and he's been very supportive of me. My mom always said that you need people like RJ in your life and I'm starting to see why. All my *friends* are wanna be thugs, in and out of jail and deep into that street life. That's how I grew up. That's the environment I came from. That's why I'm so proud of Eric and Rozi. They have a chance to do big things. I've never really been around *successful* people but I think that's who I need to position myself around. I've never been in trouble with the law, but I've come close a few times. I find it ironic that I'm working for the law now, but everything happens for a reason.

When I got to my house, RJ followed me in. "Make yourself at home," I said, as I went to change out of my work clothes. When I came back out, RJ was on the couch watching Judge Judy. "That lady is crazy," I said.

"Yeah, she's something else," RJ stated.

"Do you want something to drink?" I yelled from the kitchen.

"No, I'm good," he replied.

When I got back in the living room, my doorbell started to ring. I looked out the peephole and opened the door. The postman said, "This is a package for Blackwell McDaniel. Can you sign here?"

"Ok," I said, as I signed the slip.

"Thanks and have a good day," the postman said, as he handed me my mail and my package. I stared at the envelope as I made my way back to the living room. *What is this?*

"Somebody send you something?" RJ asked.

"Yeah, but it doesn't have a return address," I said, as I opened the package. I was a little suspicious to see what was in it.

"What is it?" he asked.

"A DVD," I said, as I took the DVD out of the plastic case.

"Ok, that's strange," RJ said.

"I know right," I said, as I walked to the DVD player. I wanted to see what was on the disc. I flipped on the DVD player and sat down on the couch. I flipped the TV from Judge Judy to the auxiliary channel.

There was a blank screen. I fast-forwarded the DVD until I saw an image on the screen.

"What is that?" RJ asked.

"Nigga, I don't know," I said, as I looked at the grainy screen. "It looks like a bed."

The picture soon became very clear. "WHAT THE FUCK?" I yelled, as I looked at the TV. "OH, FUCK NO. THIS HAS GOTTA BE A FUCKING GAME!"

"Is that two dudes?" RJ said.

"HELL, FUCK NAW!" I said, as I watched these two men have sex.

"Why is someone sending you this? Why is the other dudes face blocked out? Do you know them?" RJ asked.

"THAT'S MY FUCKING BROTHER!" I yelled, as I jumped up from my seat. "WHAT KINDA FUCKSHIT IS THIS? I KNOW MY BROTHER AIN'T NO FUCKING FAGGOT!"

"Oh, damn," RJ said.

"GET THE FUCK OUT! GET OUT!" I said, ejecting the DVD.

"Black, are you ok?" he asked, as he stood up.

"GET THE FUCK OUT!" I said again, as I grabbed the DVD, my phone and my keys and forced him to the door.

"Where are you going?" he asked, as he stumbled out the house.

"TO TAKE CARE OF THIS SHIT!"

"Don't do anything stupid," he said.

"I JUST FOUND OUT THAT MY BROTHER IS A FUCKING FAGGOT AND I'M JUST SUPPOSED TO CHILL? GET THE FUCK OUT MY WAY!" I said, as I went to my car.

"Where are you going?" he asked again.

"To take care of this," I repeated.

"Where, Black? Where are you going?"

I stared RJ in the eyes and said, "I'm going to Tallahassee!"

# 65

## Ra' Jon

I felt bad about doing this, but it had to be done. Black is on his way up to Tallahassee to take care of his brother and hopefully, Zach is there with him. Even if Zach isn't there, I'm sure he'll feel the aftermath of Blackwell McDaniel.

I wanted to put the shit I had on Chaz in that package too, but I have to let Chaz believe that I did that right thing. I want him to be happy and feel like he has succeeded. As soon as he gets comfortable and feels like he came out on top—*BAM*—here come's his dirty laundry. My mom always said that patience is key, and it really is key in this situation.

I smiled a sinister smile as I phoned Chaz. Once he answered, I said, "It's done."

"Are you serious?" he asked.

"Yes, I am. Black is on his way up to Tallahassee right now," I said. "He's pissed."

"Wow, it worked," he said, shocked. "This is great, now Eric's ass can feel some of the shit that I felt."

"I guess, Chaz," I rolled my eyes.

"This is great," he said again. "Thanks so much!"

"Just doing my job," I said.

"Now that that's done, when are you going back to Norfolk?" he asked.

"I'm not," I said.

"You're not what?" he asked in a serious tone.

"I'm not going back to Norfolk," I said. "I like it here and if I get this job, I will be making the move to Orlando."

"You fell for Black didn't you?" Chaz asked.

"What?"

"You like my cousin, don't you?"

"I have feelings for him, but I'm not moving to Orlando for him. This move is for me."

"Well, please save yourself the embarrassment. Black is *not* gay," Chaz stated.

"I can see that," I said.

"Well, I'm just saying," Chaz said.

"Ight, Chaz. I'm 'bout to get off the phone. I was just letting you know that I did my part."

"Thanks, RJ. You've been a big help. If there is anything you need, just hit me up," Chaz said.

"I will do."

"Until later, take care," he said.

"You do the same," I said, as I hung up the phone.

I chuckled, as I thought how stupid Chaz was. He must be really crazy to think this shit is gonna end here.

*Dumb bitch!*

*****

# Zach

I smiled once I saw his name pop up on my phone. I eagerly answered, "Are you done?"

"Yes," Eric said.

"Well, how do think you did?"

"I think I did ok," he said. "But I will find out in a few weeks."

"I know you did a good job, Eric," I said, as I made my way into the kitchen to fix a bowl of buttered pecan ice cream.

"I'm gonna stop by the house for a second to change clothes, then I'ma come over your way, ok," Eric said.

"Ight, baby," I stated, as Micah walked in the house. "Just hit me up when you're outside."

"Ight," Eric said, as he hung up the phone.

"What's up, Zach?" Micah said, placing the mail down on the dining table.

# Life of a College Bandsman 2: Is This Love

"Ain't shit, man," I said, as I walked over to the dinner table with my bowl of ice cream.

"Yo, I need to holla at you," he said.

"What's up, Micah?"

"Promise me whatever I tell you will stay between you and me, ok," he said, as he looked at me.

"Ok."

"I did some foul shit," Micah explained, as he sat down across from me.

"Like what?" I asked, wondering if Micah was gonna tell the truth about cheating on Kris and getting that Rozi girl pregnant.

He sighed, placed his head down in shame and said, "I cheated on Kris."

"You did what?" I said acting shocked.

"I cheated on him over the summer. I didn't mean to do it. It just happened and the girl ended up pregnant with my child," Micah confessed.

"Damn, Micah."

"Yeah, man, that's why I've been bugging out lately. But when my mom came, I told her the truth and that helped out a lot," Micah said.

"Well, that's good," I said. "But what's gonna happen with the baby?"

"The girl called me today and told me that she was gonna get an abortion," Micah said.

"She is?" I asked.

"Yeah. I'm a lil upset that the baby is gonna die, but I'm not ready to be a father, either," Micah said.

"Are you gonna tell Kris?" I asked.

"That's the problem I'm having now," he said. "I don't really know what to do. I want to tell Kris, but I'm afraid that he will leave me. And since she is gonna have the abortion, it ain't really a need to open my mouth like that. I'm never gonna cheat on Kris again, so there isn't a need for him to know this. All it's gonna do is cause problems."

"Nothing stays in the dark, Micah. Everything has a way of coming out. Would you rather Kris find out by you or by some other strange event?"

"I would rather he not know at all," he said.

"Well, my lips are sealed but that's the choice that you're gonna have to live with," I said as my phone started to ring. "This is my grandma," I said, as I grabbed my ice cream and went back to my room. I answered and she said, "Hey, Zachie, how are you?"

"I'm ok," I said.

"How was school?" she asked.

"It was ok. I've got a teacher that I really didn't want, but I'm stuck with him now, so it ain't even a need to complain about it," I said.

"Yeah because you know I hate people that complain," she said.

"I know, Grandma. How is Uncle Alan?"

"He's doing much better," she said. "I think he is out of the danger zone for the moment."

"That's great," I said. "I hope he lives another twenty years."

"I hope so, too, baby," she said, as her tone of voice changed.

"What's wrong, Grandma?" I asked.

"Something is about to go down," she said.

"What are you talking about?" I asked.

"You listen to me," she said. "LISTEN TO ME!"

"I'm listening, Grandma."

"Something or someone is about to cause trouble for someone that you know. I need you to stay put in your house, you hear me," she said.

"Yes, ma'am," I replied.

"I mean it," she said. "You stay put in your house tonight. Don't go anywhere. That's the only way you will be ok."

"Ok, Grandma," I said. "I will stay at my house tonight."

"AND STAY BY YOURSELF," she added. "NO OVERNIGHT GUESTS!"

"Ok, Grandma."

"Call me first thing in the morning, ok," she said.

"Ok, Grandma," I said sounding like a broken record.

"I love you. Be safe."

"I love you, too," I said, as I hung up the phone.

When I got off the phone with her, I sat and thought about what she was saying. I usually brush off her visions, but for some reason I could tell that she was serious today. I wasn't gonna go against the will of my grandma.

I finished my ice cream and washed out my bowl. Micah was in his room listening to gospel artist Smokie Norful's hit song I Need You Now. *Niggas only get religious when their asses are in trouble.*

# Life of a College Bandsman 2: Is This Love

Micah sang along with Smokie, "Not a second or another minute, not an hour of another day. But at this moment with my arms outstretched, I need you to make a way as you have done so many times before, through a window or an open door. I stretch my hands to thee, come rescue me, I need you right away. I need you now. I need you now. Not another second or another minute. Not an hour of another day, but Lord, I need you right away."

I stood next to Micah's door and shook my head. I hope he gets it together.

I headed back to my room to see my phone ringing. It was Eric. He was outside. We kissed as soon as he walked in the house. He heard the gospel music blaring from Micah's room and said, "What's up with him?"

"Just leave it alone," I sighed, as we headed to my room. "It's the situation I was telling you about."

"Oh," he said, as we entered my room. He sat down on the bed and said, "It's so good to see you again."

"You just saw me earlier today," I smiled.

"Yeah, but that was too long ago," he said, as he gave me another kiss.

"Whatever, Eric."

"How was your day?" he asked.

"Guess who I have for a professor," I said, sitting on the bed next to him, Indian style.

"I don't have a clue."

"You should," I said, as I looked at him.

"I don't know... Chaz?"

"No," I said. "Someone really close to you."

"Chaz is close to me," he said.

"It's not Chaz," I replied.

He thought about it for a second and then he looked at me and started to shake his head as if it was starting to click.

"Umm, hmm," I said.

"No, he's not," Eric said in disbelief.

"Yes, he is," I said. "What a way to meet your ex."

"Raidon is not your teacher," Eric said, shocked.

"Yes, he is. He's the first thing I get to see every Monday, Wednesday and Friday," I said. "He knew who I was once I introduced myself to the class."

"Wow," Eric said, as he stared at his phone.

"Yeah, and to be honest, I don't know about this Eric. I mean he was your ex and now he is my professor. I don't know."

"Raidon isn't that type of dude."

"I hope not," I said.

"You wanna go to my house for a lil bit since Micah is in a mood," Eric asked, as Micah's music got louder.

"Naw, I'm ok," I said, as I thought back to what my grandma said. "I need to get an early start on some of my homework."

"You sure?"

"Yeah. I don't want to start off the semester the wrong way."

"I feel you. Well, I'm gonna head on home. I'll get at you sometime later tonight," Eric said, as he gave me a kiss.

"Ight, Eric," I said, as I walked him to the door.

# 66

## *Eric*

I couldn't believe that Raidon was Zach's professor. This is a small fucking world! How in the hell did that shit happen? I know Raidon told me he got a teaching job at FAMU, but I would have never thought that he would be teaching my baby. I had to phone him. Once Raidon answered, I asked, "Where are you?"

"Leaving my first Ph.D. class," Raidon said, excited. "It's good to hear from you."

"Good to hear from you, too," I said. "So, how did you manage this one?"

"You're talking about your lil boyfriend?" Raidon asked.

"Yes," I replied. "How did he end up in your class?"

"I don't know," Raidon said. "He's cute though, Eric."

"I guess, Raidon," I said. "Don't treat my boy any differently than anyone else."

"Now why would I do that?"

"I'm just saying," I said, as I headed home.

"I ain't even like that," Raidon said. "If he does what he is supposed to do, then he will be fine."

"Ight, Raidon, I'm just checking."

"Yeah, man," he said, as he hung up the phone.

"Great," I said to myself when I got to my house. I didn't see any of my roommate cars and that meant that I had the house to myself. I liked it when it was quiet, but ever since Dezmond moved in, this house has been anything but quiet. As soon as I got in my room, my phone started to ring. I answered, "What's up, Rozi?"

"Hey, Eric," she said, as if she were crying.

"What's wrong? Are you ok?"

"I just had the abortion," she said. "I feel bad about it."

"Well, it's done now," I said. "No need to dwell in the past."

"I'm a little relieved," she said.

"I'm sure you are."

"I want to call Black, but I'm scared that he's gonna sense something is wrong with me. You know how he trips out over lil shit," Rozi stated.

"Yeah, I know," I said. "Just give it a few days so you can get yourself together first and then call him."

"I think that's what I'm gonna do," she said.

"I love you Rozi and I'm always proud of you, no matter what," I said.

"I love you, too, Eric. I really do. I don't know what I'll do if it wasn't for you. Just promise me that you will be around for a long time."

"Rozi, why wouldn't I be here? I'm only twenty-two. I've got a long life to live."

"I'm just saying, you know how bad things always happen to good people. I'm just saying I need you here."

"I will be here, Rozi. Just get some rest and I will call you tomorrow."

"Ok, Eric. I love you."

"I love you, too," I said, as I hung up the phone.

Quinton peeped his head in my door and spoke.

"What's up," I replied back.

"Just came in to grab something. I'm about to head out. I'll catch up with you later."

"Where are you going?" I asked.

"I'ma click it with Ian tonight," Quinton smiled.

"Oh, that's what's up."

He said, "I don't know where Amir is, but Dezmond had to leave town for a family emergency. I don't know when he's gonna be back."

"What happened?"

"I don't know," Quinton stated. "He just rushed out this afternoon with a suitcase and said that he had to get home ASAP."

"I hope everything is ok."

"Yeah, me, too. But I'ma get at you."

"Ight, Q," I said, as he left the house.

# Life of a College Bandsman 2: Is This Love

Like clockwork, as soon as Quinton left, Amir arrived. He stopped in my room and said, "It's awfully quiet in here. Where is everybody?"

"Dezmond had to go home and Quinton just left."

"I thought that was him I just passed," Amir said.

"What you up to?" I asked.

"You know me," he said.

"Another date, huh?"

"Yep, 'bout to go get in the shower and then go take care of that shit," he said, as he left the room.

I turned on the TV and caught a rerun of The Fresh Prince of Bel-Air. About twenty minutes later, Amir came back to my door and said, "Ight, Eric. I'll be back later."

"Ight, man. Be safe."

"Always," he said, as he left the house.

I smiled. I finally had the house to myself. I continued to watch TV and before I knew it I had feel asleep on the bed. I woke up to someone beating on the front door. I looked at the phone to check the time.

"OPEN THIS DAMN DOOR, ERIC!" I heard someone yell, as they continued to beat on the door.

I didn't say anything as I approached the door.

"OPEN THE FUCKING DOOR!" I heard. The voice was as clear as day and it was confirmed when I looked out the peephole.

I opened the door and let the angry man into the house. I said, "What are you doing here, Black?"

"WHAT THE FUCK IS WRONG WITH YOU?" he said, as he slammed my door, knocking a painting off the wall.

"WHAT THE FUCK IS WRONG WITH YOU?" I said back to him, upset that he barged into my house like this without explanation.

"YOU SHUT THE FUCK UP AND I TALK!" he said, as he stepped in my face, backing me against the wall. I stared my brother in the eyes, not sure what to make of this. We just spoke earlier today and he was saying how proud he was of me. What the fuck is going on?

He yelled, "SO, YOU'RE A FUCKING FAGGOT NOW? YOU A FAGGOT?"

"What?" I said frightened.

"NIGGA, DON'T PLAY STUPID!" Black said, as he punched

me in the chest.

"Man, what the hell is wrong with you," I said, grabbing my chest.

"DIDN'T I SAY SHUT THE FUCK UP AND I TALK!" Black said, as he punched me a few more times in the chest. "I DON'T HAVE FAGGOTS FOR BROTHERS!" he said, as he punched me again. I tried to punch him back, but I didn't have the power. He was knocking the wind of out me.

"THE ONLY THING I SAID NOT TO BE IS WHAT THE FUCK YOU BECAME—A FUCKING FAGGOT," Black said, as he continued his assault on me, knocking me to the ground.

"GET THE FUCK UP!" Black commanded, as he forced me off the ground.

"Man, I ain't no faggot!" I said, as I stood up, catching my breath.

"DIDN'T I TELL YOU TO SHUT UP!" he said, as he bitch-slapped me.

Tears had started to fall from my eyes. I didn't know how the hell this happened, but I was fucked. I wanted to fight back, but I knew better. When Black gets in one of these rages, everyone needs to leave him alone because it will only end up worse for you. I know from personal experience.

I ain't no lil bitch, but Black just always overpowered me. We used to fight all the time growing up. The older he got, the stronger he got. After taking some serious beat-downs from Black over the years, I've learned just to let him have his way.

"I TOLD YO' BITCH ASS MEN DON'T CRY!" Black said, as he punched me in the jaw. "MAN THE FUCK UP!" he commanded.

I was breathing so hard, I felt as if my heart was about to beat out of my chest. I collected myself and stared my brother in the eyes. He stopped yelling and calmly said, "So, you wanna be a fag, huh? You wanna suck dick and get fucked in the ass? Huh? I can't believe my fucking brother is a faggot!" He sighed and yelled, "WELL, I DON'T HAVE FAGGOTS AS FAMILY MEMBERS."

Black reached his hand behind his body. I started to shake uncontrollably, as I saw what he pulled out. I felt like I was about to shit on myself.

Black placed the gun on my bottom lip and said, "Yeah, nigga, you see this shit, huh. This is what happen to faggots in the real world! They get killed!"

My breathing only intensified as I stared down the barrel of my brother's gun.

He said, "Yeah, nigga. Say some shit now. Say something! All I ever wanted to do was protect your ass from shit like this, but faggots can't be protected. Faggots deserve to die!"

He pulled the trigger and said, "But since you're my brother, you get a chance to redeem yourself."

I couldn't take my eyes off the gun.

He said, "Tell me your faggot ways are over. Tell me it was just an experiment and it would never happen again. Then we can just squash this shit!"

I couldn't say anything. I couldn't take my tear filled eyes off that gun. My brother had taken this shit too damn far. I wanted to say something. I would say anything he wanted to hear just to get that damn gun from out of my face.

"I'M WAITING, ERIC!" he yelled, as I heard a door slam outside. "TELL ME YOUR FAGGOT WAYS ARE OVER!"

"WHAT THE FUCK?" I heard Quinton yell, as he rushed over to Black and me. "WHAT THE FUCK?"

Quinton hit Black in the back as he went for the gun that Black still had placed at my mouth. Black was too strong for Quinton, but Quinton kept fighting. Black never lost control of the gun as he hit Quinton back.

"WHAT THE FUCK IS YOUR PROBLEM?" I heard Black yell, as they continued their struggle. I couldn't move. I was stuck in that position.

The three of us were now in a circle with Black and Quinton facing each other as they went at it.

"GIMMIE THIS SHIT!" Quinton yelled, as he tried to take control of the gun from Black.

"FUCK YOU!" Black stated as the unthinkable happened—the gun went off.

I looked at the floor and yelled, "OH, SHIT! WHAT THE FUCK DID YOU DO? WHAT THE FUCK DID YOU DO?"

# 67

## *Eric*

I finally found the courage to move. I kneeled down to the ground, looked up to him and repeated for the third time, "WHAT THE FUCK DID YOU DO?"

"He's alright," Quinton said, as he walked away.

"MAN, THE FUCK IS WRONG WITH YOU?" Black stated, as he looked at Quinton.

"WHO THE FUCK ARE YOU?" Quinton asked.

"That's my brother!" I said, as Black stood up.

Black yelled, "THAT NIGGA ALMOST KILLED ME!"

"WHY THE FUCK YOU GOT A DAMN GUN IN OUR HOUSE?" Quinton replied.

"You better get yo' boy," Black said, as he looked at me.

"Quinton," I said, as I looked at him.

"FUCK THAT," Quinton said, as he emptied the bullets out of the gun and held it in his hand.

"THIS IS BETWEEN ME AND MY BROTHER!" Black stated, as he walked over to Quinton. "NOW GIMMIE MY SHIT!"

"Whatever," Quinton said, as he handed Black the empty gun. "Y'all crazy as hell! I'm out this bitch!"

As Quinton left, I walked out and looked at the couch. The bullet shot right through the couch. I turned to Black and said, "What the hell is wrong with you? You trying to kill me?"

"No," he said. "It wasn't supposed to go that far. I was trying to prove a point."

"BY PUTTING A LOADED GUN IN MY FUCKING FACE!" I yelled.

Black sat down on the love seat and said, "If your ass wasn't a fucking faggot then we wouldn't be having this problem right now!"

"I'm not a faggot," I said. *Where was he getting this from?*

"The hell you're not," he said. "And you gonna sit here and lie to me about it, when I saw you sucking some dude's dick!"

"I don't know what the hell you're talking about," I said.

"Well, somebody wanted me to see you because they sent me a tape of you with this dude," Black said.

"Let me see it," I said.

"No," he said.

"Then you're lying," I said. I had only had sex with two, well three, dudes if you count my thing with Zach, so I don't know where this *tape* could come from.

"Oh, nigga, I got the shit!"

"Whatever, Black. I don't know why you came up here with this crazy ass foolishness," I said, as I went to the kitchen.

"DAMN, ERIC," he said disappointed, as he followed me into the kitchen. "WHY YOU GOTTA BE GAY?"

"I ain't gay!" I turned and looked at him.

"STOP FUCKING LYING TO ME!" he yelled, as he grabbed me by the throat and jacked me up against the wall.

"LET ME GO!"

"TELL ME THE DAMN TRUTH!" he said.

"I AIN'T GAY!"

"STOP LYING TO ME, ERIC!" Black said, as his grip got a lil tighter.

The more Blackwell talked, the more I realized that he was serious and he knew that I was fucking with dudes. I don't know if I bought that damn tape story, but I know he found out. This situation wasn't gonna get better until I spoke the truth. I said, "Let me go and I will tell you the truth."

He released me.

I took a deep breath and said, "I'm not gay, I'm bisexual."

"WHAT THE FUCK EVER, IT'S THE SAME DAMN THING," he said.

"Well, I am who I am, Black."

He looked at me; I could see the rage in his eyes. He said, "You need to give this shit up. No member of this family will be a faggot!"

"I'm not a faggot!"

He stared at me and said, "Well, this is the plan."

# Life of a College Bandsman 2: Is This Love

"What plan?" I asked.

"Like I said earlier before that dude came and fucked shit up, since you are my brother, you get a chance to redeem yourself. Tell me right here, right now that your faggot ways are over. Tell me that it was just an experiment and that it will never happen again and this shit will be squashed. This will be the end of it," Black said.

"Why are you—"

"WHAT THE HELL IS GOING ON?" Chaz busted in the house, cutting me off mid-sentence.

"Ask your faggot ass cousin," Black said, as he sat down at the dining table.

"Why did you have a gun at his face?" Chaz asked in a concerned tone.

"How the fuck you know?" Black said, as he looked at Chaz.

"Quinton is one of his friends," I said.

Chaz said, "I don't know what's going on, but whatever the problem is, it's going too damn far!"

"Did you know he fucks with dudes?" Black asked Chaz.

"What?" Chaz said, confused. Thankfully, Chaz was playing stupid.

"Eric is a faggot!" Black stated with hatred in his voice.

"I'm not a faggot," I said.

"Stop lying, Black," Chaz said.

"I'm not lying. The nigga is gay," Black said.

"Is that why you're tripping and shit?" Chaz asked.

"Uhhhhh, YEAH," Black said, looking at Chaz as if he were stupid.

"Damn, Black. You didn't have to pull a gun out on the man," Chaz said.

"You ok with this gay shit?" Black asked Chaz.

"The nigga can do whatever he wants," Chaz said. "Eric has to live his own life."

"You sound like you're part of that gay shit, too. ARE YOU GAY?" Black asked Chaz.

"HELL, NAW! DA HELL WRONG WITH YOU?" Chaz said to Black, as he looked at me.

I thought back to the other day when Chaz and I worked out our differences. If Chaz hadn't called me and worked that shit out, I would have put his ass out there, too. But since we had squashed our beef, it wasn't a need to do him like that.

"I'm just saying," Black said as he looked at Chaz. "You're taking up for that shit, made me think you were down with that shit."

Chaz said, "Living up here has opened up my eyes to a lot of things. You learn to accept the different factors in life."

"Well, I ain't gonna accept my brother being gay," Black said. He looked to me and said, "If you want to remain my brother, say what the fuck I told you to say!"

I looked at Black and I looked at Chaz. I didn't know what to do. It seemed simple just to say what he wanted to hear, but what about Zach. How could I just drop him like that? Even if I tell Black what he wants to hear, he isn't gonna drop this shit. He's gonna become an investigator into my life and see if I'm living up to my end of the bargain.

"Well, what's it gonna be, Eric?" Black said.

"IGHT, SHIT!" I yelled. "I'm done with dudes!"

"Do you mean it?" Black asked, as Chaz looked at me.

"YES," I said.

"Then that's that. It's over. This shit is squashed," Black said, as he started to head to the door.

"You're leaving?" Chaz asked.

"Yeah, I gotta get back down to Orlando for work in the morning," Black said.

"Ight, drive safe," Chaz said, as Black left my apartment. Chaz walked to window to make sure Black was gone. He locked the door and came back into the kitchen. He looked at me and asked, "Are you ok?"

"Yeah, I guess," I shrugged my shoulders.

"I didn't know Black was gonna trip out like that," Chaz said.

"What?"

"I meant, I didn't think Black had it in him to act like that. That shit was a little crazy," Chaz said, as he went in the living room.

I followed behind him.

"Damn," Chaz said, as he looked at the couch. "This could have been fatal."

"You think," I sarcastically stated.

"Man, I'm 'bout to go back to the crib," Chaz said, as he walked over and gave me a hug.

"Ight, man," I said.

"Get some rest, cuzzo," he said, as he walked to the door.

"I'll try," I said.

# Life of a College Bandsman 2: Is This Love

"I love you," he said.

"I love you, too. Tell Genevieve hey."

"Ight," he said, as he left the apartment.

When everyone was gone, I went back to my room. I couldn't believe the things that just happened.

Black had done some crazy things in the past, but this shit took the cake. I sat on my bed and had a plethora of emotions. I didn't know what to do with them. I wanted to cry, but I couldn't. I wanted to yell, but I couldn't.

I sat in the dark for a few minutes until I saw the light from my phone. Zach was calling. When I answered, he said, "What's up, Eric?"

"Hey," I replied, dryly.

"Are you ok, Eric?" he asked.

"Yes, I'm ok."

"You sure? You sound a lil upset," he said.

"I'm ok," I replied.

"Well, I got a call from my grandmother tonight and she told me a lot of shit. She always tells me stuff and I just kinda brush it off, but tonight she seemed a bit serious about it. I really didn't think too much of what she said until after you left. I thought about the things that she said and I just want to tell you to be careful," Zach said.

"Why you say that?" I asked.

"My grandma said that something is gonna happen to someone that I'm close to and I didn't really think about you, but it all makes sense now. I'm just telling you to be careful and watch yourself ok."

"Ight, Zach," I said.

"Ok, well I will talk to you tomorrow, ok."

"Ight," I said, as I hung up the phone.

I was stuck. I didn't know what the hell to do. My brother said that I have to give up my homosexual lifestyle if I wanted to remain in his life. I love my brother. I love my family. I couldn't allow them to find out that I was fucking around with dudes. I know Black is gonna keep this to himself because he doesn't want to hurt my mom, but if he finds out that I'm still fucking with dudes, he will tell everyone. I value the relationship that I have with my family and I don't want to lose it over my homosexuality. The only person who knows about this is my sister, but what about everyone else? My family is against homosexuality. FUCK! I don't wanna have to do this to Zach, but I don't know what else to do.

# Jaxon Grant

I love that man, but I love my family. Things weren't supposed to be this way. I don't wanna hurt Zach, but when it all comes down to it, I guess I don't really have much of a choice...

# Part Four:
## I Love You, Too

# 68

## Zach

*Thursday, August 28, 2003*
*Tallahassee, Florida*

Our first football game of the season was finally here! I was beyond excited because we were getting ready to go to Detroit to play Alabama State in the Ford Football Classic. I just knew this was gonna be a great weekend. The only downside to this whole thing was the twenty-two hours that we had to spend on the damn bus.

"What three did you bring?" Peanut asked, as I made my way to my seat.

"Boyz in the Hood, Kings of Comedy and Set It Off," I said.

When we went to Charlotte last weekend, the drum major on our bus told everyone to bring three movies a piece so that we would have more than enough movies to choose from to watch while we embarked on this long ass ride to Michigan.

I smiled as Dwight walked on the bus. The only positive about being on the bus for twenty-two hours is sitting next to him.

When we left Tallahassee, everyone was pretty hyped. It was the middle of a Thursday afternoon and we wouldn't be back until around two Monday morning. Thankfully, Monday was Labor Day and we didn't have school. This was gonna be a sweet five-day weekend for us band members.

"You straight?" Dwight asked me, as the drum major put on the movie, Coming to America.

"I'm ok," I said.

"You seem a lil distant lately," Dwight said.

"I've just been thinking about something my grandma told me," I said.

"What's that?" Dwight inquired.

"She always tells me to watch out for this and watch out for that, but she called me and told me that again on Monday night. She told me that I needed to be careful and she stressed that I shouldn't leave my house. She went on to say that I didn't need any overnight guests and I should just watch everything around me. She said that something or someone was out to cause trouble."

"You need to listen to the words of your grandma," Dwight said. "Ms. Carrie is a very wise woman. You know she wouldn't lead you in the wrong direction."

"I know, it's just some of the stuff she says be off the wall. She has a lot of these visions and shit. I listen to her, but some of the stuff just sounds crazy."

"Take heed to what your grandma tells you," Dwight said.

"But, listen, Eric came to my house Monday night after he took the MCAT. He ended up going to his house that night and I stayed at mine. I really didn't think too much of what my grandma said until later that night. I was doing some of my school work and it came to me that she could have been talking about Eric."

"What did you do?" Dwight asked.

"I called him as soon as I realized it," I said. "He answered the phone and he sounded a lil different."

"What you mean by different?" Dwight asked.

"He didn't quite sound like himself."

"So, what did you do?" Dwight inquired.

"I told him what my grandma said and he insisted that he was fine, but he didn't sound fine."

"You think something happened?" Dwight asked.

"I don't know. He hasn't been himself since he left my house that night. He hasn't slept over the house, either. It seems like there is something that he wants to say, but he's afraid to say it. It's comes across as if someone is watching him or something."

"Damn, that's fucked up," Dwight said. "I don't like the dude, but I don't wish anything bad on him."

"How is the thing with Kiki?" I asked Dwight, trying to change the subject.

"Man, I'm so sick of her ass," he said. "She really irks the fuck out of me."

# Life of a College Bandsman 2: Is This Love

"So, why are you still with her?"

"Because her pussy good and she knows how to suck *all* of my dick," Dwight said.

"Nigga, anyone can suck a dick," I stated.

"Yeah, but she knows how to handle *all* of my dick. Everybody can't do that shit," he said. "It gets frustrating because bitches wanna run from me when they see my shit. But she was gangster and she embraces that shit. I need somebody in my life like her, you know what I mean?"

"Why is everything always about sex with you?" I asked.

"I'm a growing young man. I need to release myself on continual basis," Dwight said.

"Whatever, fool."

"I'm serious," he said. "She's been on that bullshit lately. If she doesn't give up the pussy on this trip, then I'ma have to find someone else that's gonna take care of my needs, know what I mean."

"You mean you're gonna cheat on Kiki," I said.

"Shit, it ain't no real relationship anyway," Dwight said. "We're only fucking. She's the one that wants that bitch ass title. I don't have time for that shit. If all I wanna do is fuck and all you wanna do is fuck, why we gotta have titles and shit to fuck? You know what you want and I know what I want, so shit, let's just fuck."

"You sound a lil angry," I said.

"Man, whatever. I'm just expressing my feelings," he stated.

"So, you got feelings now?" I said.

"Fuck you, Zach," Dwight said.

"Awwww, I love you, too," I said, as I started smiling.

Dwight just looked at me and started to shake his head.

*"Damn, I loved this dude,"* I told myself, as I sat back and prepared to enjoy the rest of the movie.

\*\*\*\*\*

# Ra'Jon

This is exactly the start I needed!

"Thank you, God," I said, as I left the office.

Ever since Black made that impromptu trip up to Tallahassee on Monday, I haven't seen or heard from him. I wanted to see and find out what's up with him. He left in such as rage on Monday. I know Chaz said that he had anger problems, but I didn't think he was gonna get that upset. I kinda felt a lil bad once I thought about everything, but I couldn't dwell on it. I had shit that I needed to get done.

Once I turned in my documents to the school board on Tuesday morning, I caught an afternoon flight and headed back up to Norfolk, Virginia. I knew I was gonna get that job, so I wanted to pack some more of my personal belongings and clothes until I would be able to come back up and get the rest of my things. I was excited about this move to Orlando. Maybe this is the change that I needed in my life.

The secretary from the school board called me on Wednesday and told me that my background check was cleared and I was able to do the interview today. I caught an overnight flight back to Orlando and I had spent most of the day preparing for the interview. I needed to make a good impression.

Luckily for me, it worked out and the principal offered me the job right on the spot. I told him I was moving from Norfolk and he told me to take care of my personal things and I wouldn't have to report to work until the following Monday. I was gonna take advantage of this time—find somewhere permanent to stay, and move the rest of my stuff down from Norfolk to Orlando. If I would have known that he was gonna give me a week to get myself together, I would not have wasted my damn money buying a plane ticket to Norfolk this week.

I guess I'm starting to realize a lot of shit about myself and the main thing was that I'm too old to be playing childish games. I needed to act my age and do the things that people my age do.

I was torn because I know what I need to do, but on the other side, I just wanna get Chaz's ass back. I just want him to feel what I felt when he forced me out of Tallahassee. I know the things that I

# Life of a College Bandsman 2: Is This Love

did was bad, but I guess I just have mixed feelings on a lot of shit.

My brothers always treated me differently and I want to correct that. I want to be respectable like them, and that's why I'm moving to Orlando. Nobody knows me here. I can start over fresh, maybe even find a dude just for me. I would like for that dude to be Black, but I know that's not possible cause Black ain't gay—*or is he?*

I wonder if he's on to me. He's really friendly with me. He doesn't talk about women like that, nor have I seen him with one. He always talks about how much he hates faggots, but a faggot is staring him right in his eyes. Maybe he doesn't know that I'm gay. Everybody doesn't have gaydar. So unless it was blatantly put right in front of his face, he probably wouldn't know.

I just know that I'm feeling this dude. But for once in my life, I'm scared of what the results would be if I approached him with that bullshit.

On second thought, I guess I'll leave that alone.

# 69

# *Zach*

*Friday, August 29, 2003*
*Detroit, Michigan*

I looked out at the neighborhood in fear. This couldn't be real.
"They want us to practice in this shit?" Kris asked, as it
approached 8:30 at night.

Everyone in the band was looking out the window, a little afraid
for our lives.

We were on the way to practice. I didn't know the name of the
school, but that shit was right in the middle of the damn hood, not
that make believe shit they show you on TV. This shit was real. That
place looked like bullet could start falling out of thin air at any
moment. The closer we got to the high school stadium, the scarier it
became.

"Doc done lost this damn mind!" Omar yelled. "What the fuck
is his problem? Got us out here in this shit!"

"I came to college to make a better life for myself, not get killed
in a shootout on a band trip in Detroit," Kris added.

When we got to the stadium, there were like a thousand people
there.

"Are we at a performance or are we going to practice?" Dwight
asked.

"Looks like we're about to put on a show, buddy," I said, as the
bus came to a complete stop.

"You know band, you gotta give the people what they want,"
Peanut said in his best Dr. Hunter impression, as everyone started
to laugh. "The people don't care if you don't eat. They don't care if

a hurricane is directly over us and tears the city apart. The people don't care if you don't have your financial aid and you can't go to class. They don't care if you sleep outside in the cold at night. The people don't care if the entire band gets shot and killed at practice in Detroit! THE PEOPLE WANNA SEE A SHOW! GIVE THE PEOPLE A SHOWWWWWWWW!"

"Man, you're crazy," I said, as we departed the bus.

"Nigga, I ain't crazy. Dr. Hunter is crazy for putting us out here in this shit," Peanut said, as the band took our starting positions.

Once practice was over, the drum majors passed out KFC chicken boxes and that was our dinner for the evening.

The mayor of Detroit, Kwame Kilpatrick, was a former FAMU football player as well as a former president of the FAMU Student Government Association. As a result, he made sure the band was well taken care of.

We were placed in a hotel right across the water from Canada. We wanted to go over there, but the staff wouldn't allow us to do it.

The hotel was really nice, and for the first time ever, we were put two in a room, compared to the normal four to a room. When the hotel list was passed out, I was hoping that I got the room with Dwight, but I was put in the room with Kris. Peanut and Dwight were roomed together.

After we got settled in our rooms and showered, Kris left and went to join some of our freshmen brothers and sisters that played saxophone. I chilled out in our freshmen room, messing with Keli for a second until I got a call from Dwight.

"Where you at, Shawty?"

"Down in Keli and them room," I said.

"Oh, what they doing?" he asked.

"Nothing. Jared and Omar just messing with 'em, being stupid and shit," I replied.

"Oh, ok, that's what's up. You should come through," he said.

"Where you at?"

"2024."

"Ight, I'll be up there in a second," I said, as I left the freshmen room.

"What's up, Zach," Ian said, as I caught him and Devin waiting on the elevator.

"Nothing much, man," I said.

"How have you been?" Ian asked.

# Life of a College Bandsman 2: Is This Love

"I'm good, you know, same ole, same ole," I replied.

"That's what's up. You know Eric and Chaz finally squashed that shit," he said.

"I know, Eric told me," I said. "I'm happy that they are on good terms again."

"Me, too," Ian said, as the three of us got on the elevator.

"What floor?" Devin asked me as he pushed the button for the twenty-second floor.

"Twentieth," I said.

"Yeah, but I don't know what to do," Devin said, as he put his attention back on Ian.

"Just tell the man how you really feel," Ian said.

"That shit is easier said than done," Devin stated.

"Yeah but that's the only way y'all are gonna see eye-to-eye," Ian said, as I got to my floor. "Ight, Zach."

"Ight Ian, Devin," I said, as I left the elevator. *I hope he was talking about Morgan and not trying to get up with Dwight,"* I said to myself, as I knocked on Dwight's door.

Once Dwight let me in, I said, "Why are you sitting in here by yourself?"

"Because I'm horny as hell," Dwight said.

"So, call Kiki," I said, as I took a seat. "Her ass ain't doing nothing."

"Man, fuck Kiki!" Dwight said, as he went to the bathroom.

When I looked over at the nightstand between the two beds, there was a Magnum XL condom sitting there.

"Ight," Dwight said, as he came out of the bathroom. "So back to what you were telling me earlier."

"And that was?" I asked.

"About them being gay," Dwight said.

"Oh," I said, as I thought about where to pick back up at. Dwight had an interest in knowing who in the band was gay and he counted on me to give him the tea. Hanging around Jared and Omar provided me with a crazy list of people in the band that were gay and who were messing with whom. Dwight found great interest in this and he was always curious to see if I had any new *tea*.

"But, yeah, James and David use to fuck around, too," I said.

"Nigga, you're lying," Dwight said, as he grabbed his dick.

"No, I'm serious. David fucked James when James was freshman," I said.

"Not the drum major, David," Dwight said as he stood up. I could see the outline of his heavy dick print through his shorts.

"Yes, the drum major, David. Jared said that they were a couple back in '99."

"James *is* Jared and Quinton's freshman brother, huh," Dwight said, as he walked to the door.

"Yeah," I said, as I stood up and got on the bed.

"Have you seen Peanut?" Dwight asked, as he walked back over and had a seat on the chair.

"Nigga, that's yo' roommate," I said, as I turned on my stomach and put my face in Dwight's direction. "You should know where he's at."

"He came in, took his shower and then he bounced. I tried to call him to see where he was at, but he didn't answer his phone," Dwight said, as he got up again.

"Maybe that nigga fucking," I said. "He gotta get him some, too."

"Shit, that's what I need to be doing. I'm so fucking horny right now. FUCK!" Dwight stated.

"Nigga, you will be alright," I said, as I thought back to Eric. Damn, I wanted to feel Eric inside of me. I needed to figure out a way to get him over that problem that he is having.

"Shit, everybody ain't able to go eight months like yo' ass," Dwight said, as he walked to the door again.

"Whatever, fool," I yelled back, as I thought about what it would be like with Eric.

"Damn, where that nigga at?" Dwight yelled, as he stood at the door. I assumed he was looking out the peephole.

"Let that nigga be," I said, as I continued to lay on my stomach.

"NIGGA, SHUT UP!" Dwight said, as he ran and jumped on me. Things in the room kinda stopped for a few seconds. I had to process what just happened.

My best friend had just jumped on me. His hard dick laid perfectly on my ass. I felt every inch of Dwight's dick on my ass. It was unreal.

"Nigga, get off me," I said, as I pushed Dwight off me and I got off the bed. I didn't know what to do. I didn't know how to take the situation. I had a bunch of emotions rush through my body and I didn't know how to react to the situation.

"I was just fucking with you, damn," Dwight said, as the door tried to open.

# Life of a College Bandsman 2: Is This Love

"Open the door, Dwight!" Peanut said, as he tried to push the door open.

Dwight looked at me while he readjusted his dick. He hurried over to the door to let Peanut in.

Peanut said, "Nigga, why you had that lock on the door? Who you in here fucking?" When Peanut saw me standing in the corner, he paused for a second and then he looked back at Dwight.

"What nigga?" Dwight said to Peanut.

"What's up, Zach," Peanut said, as he ignored Dwight's last statement.

"Ain't shit," I said, as I started to make my way to the door.

"You out, Zach?" Dwight asked.

"Yeah, man, I need to get some sleep. We've got a long day tomorrow."

"Ight, Zach," Peanut smiled.

"Ight, get at me," Dwight said, as I walked out the room.

As I waited for the elevator, I paused and sighed.

*Damn, what the fuck was that about and why was Peanut looking at me like that?*

As I thought about everything that happened in that short period of time, I said, "Fuck, this is crazy."

Once I was on the elevator, some band member said, "This is gonna be one hell of a season."

By the way things were already turning out, I couldn't agree with him more.

# 70

# *Zach*

*Wednesday, September 3, 2003*
*Tallahassee, Florida*

I don't normally answer unknown numbers, but something about this number was familiar. I took a chance on faith and answered it anyway. He said, "May I speak to Zach?"

"Who is this?" I answered.

"This is Jordan!"

"Jordan? THE JORDAN?" I said excited.

"THE JORDAN," he said.

"OH, SHIT! What's up boy?" I said to my former high school classmate and fuck buddy. "I haven't heard from you since we graduated."

"Yeah, man, I'm just out here doing the damn thing," Jordan responded.

"You in school?" I asked.

"I am now," he said. "You know I went to the military after we graduated, but I had to get out. That wasn't for me."

"Oh, ok, that's what's up. How did you get my number?"

"I had it in one of my old cell phones that I came across today. I just wanted to see if this was still your number."

"Yeah, man, this is me," I said.

"Shit, that's what's up. I don't mean to hold you up, but save my number and give me a call sometime," Jordan stated.

"Ight, bruh, where are you now?" I asked.

"I live in Atlanta now," Jordan replied.

"Oh, ok, that's what's up," I said, as Eric walked in my room.

"Yeah, man, but get at me," he said.

"Ight," I said, as I hung up.

"Hey, who was that?" Eric asked, as he took a seat at my desk.

"Just a friend from high school that I hadn't talked to since we graduated," I said, as I went over and kissed him. "What's going on with you?"

"Just checking in on you before I head out," he said.

"Where are you going?" I asked, confused.

"You forgot?" he asked, sitting on my bed.

I just stared at him.

"I'm driving up to Atlanta to see my sister and then I'm flying to D.C. for my med school interview tomorrow. After the interview I'm flying back to Atlanta to finish spending time with my sister."

"That's right. That completely slipped my mind. It's been a crazy week. When are you coming back to Tallahassee?"

"I'll be back on Sunday. I wish you could come but I know y'all got a game this weekend," Eric said.

"Yeah, I would like to meet your sister," I said.

"She is something else," Eric said.

"You seem a little at ease," I said.

"What do you mean?" Eric asked.

"You haven't been yourself the last week or so," I said.

"Oh, it's just been the stress of everything—school and life and shit."

"Is that it?"

"Yeah. What else is it supposed to be?"

"I honestly don't know, Eric. I'm just a lil concerned about you," I said.

"I'm ok. I promise," Eric said, as he kissed me.

"When are you leaving?" I asked.

"In the morning," he said.

"So, you're not gonna spend the night?" I asked.

"No, I really gotta prepare for the interview," Eric said. "And I have some work to do."

"Oh, ok," I stated. "I just miss you sleeping here and stuff."

"I promise when I get back in town, we can get back to how things were."

"If you say so Eric," I stated, as I got up and went to the bathroom.

Something was still definitely up with Eric and to be honest, I didn't like it. I've got to find out what happened that night he left here. He hasn't been the same since.

"Come here," Eric said, as I stepped out of the bathroom.

"Yes?" I went over to him.

"Stop stressing about me," he said, as he gave me a kiss. "I'm fine!"

"If you say so, Eric," I said, as I attempted to walk away.

"I said I am," Eric stated, as he pulled me back to him and threw me on the bed. "Now give me something to remember you by while I'm gone," he said, as he started to lick and kiss all over my body.

"You can have whatever you like," I said, as we started to please each other.

*****

# *Raidon*

Things were starting to work out in my favor. I was teaching at my alma mater and I am a doctoral candidate. I was taking my medication and trying my best to stay healthy even though I was HIV-positive. I have a lot of built of anger inside of me, but keeping busy has allowed me to keep my mind off of the truth.

Today was a long day. I dreaded Wednesday's. I had to teach class at FAMU at 8:00 in the morning and I taught classes all day long. When I left FAMU at five, I had to drive over to Florida State to sit in my class there for another three hours. Once this class was over, all I wanted to do was go home, get something to eat, jack my dick and go to sleep. I was leaving my night class over at Florida State University, when I was startled.

"RAIDON!" I heard someone yell.

*"Who the fuck knows me over here?"* I said to myself, as I turned around to see who it was.

"HOLD UP!" he said, as he made his over to me.

"Oh, what's going on, man," I said, when I realized who it was.

"Ain't shit," Tony said. "I was just coming from the library."

"I just got out of class myself," I said.

"It's good to see you again," Tony said, as we started to walk.

"Same here," I said.

"Where are you about to go?" he asked.

"Just to my house," I said. "It's been a long day."

"Oh, ok," he said.

"Why—what are you about to do?" I asked.

"Nothing, really. We got out of practice earlier, so it really ain't shit for me to do," Tony said, as he looked over at me.

"Oh, you can come by my place if you like," I said. "I can cook something and we can chill out."

"Shit, that's what's up," Tony said. "Let me go put my shit up in my room and grab my charger."

"Ok, meet me in front of the parking garage by the library," I said.

"Ight," Tony said, as he ran off to his dorm room.

Ever since that day I met Tony at church, we have started to become good friends. I was surprised that he called me, but it's been a good ride since then. I haven't seen him since that day at church, but we have been talking on the phone quite often. I really don't say too much; I just listen to him as he gets things off his chest. Something is really bothering him but he won't let me inside of him to see what it is. I think it is past petty shit such as relationships, I think something is really wrong with him. He is traumatized by something. I am going to get to the bottom of it before it's all over.

"Ight," he said, as he got in the car.

"What's all that?" I asked.

"Oh, it's just my overnight bag," he said. "I don't want you do have to drive me back to campus tonight if you don't want to. I don't have class until eleven in the morning. You can just drop me back off on your way to FAMU."

"Oh, ok," I said, as we left campus. *Did this fool just invite himself to sleep at my house?*

"So, what you are cooking tonight?" Tony asked.

"I don't know," I said. "I've gotta see what's in the freezer."

"I can cook if you want me to," Tony stated.

"You don't know how to cook," I laughed.

"Please don't let my good looks fool you," Tony said, as he looked in the mirror.

"Whatever, boy," I chuckled, as we reached my apartment.

Tony stepped inside and said, "Yo, Raidon this is nice."

"Thanks, man. My mom said that same thing."

"Shit, it is," Tony said, as he made his way into the kitchen. "So, what do you want me to cook?"

"Whatever you want to," I said, as I looked in the freezer. "There are some chicken, ribs, shrimp in here."

"Is that diced chicken?" Tony asked, as he walked up behind me. "Yeah," I said.

"Umm," he said, as he looked in the cabinet. "Great, I can do this."

"What?"

"Since you got some Alfredo sauce and the pasta, I can just make some chicken Alfredo," Tony stated.

"Sounds good to me," I said.

"You got some frozen broccoli in freezer?" he asked.

"Yeah," I said, as I passed it to him.

"Good. I can add some broccoli and cheese to that," Tony said. "It won't take long at all."

"Alright, Mr. Chef. It just better be good," I stated.

"Everything I do is good," Tony said.

"Whatever!"

"Yeah, so you can go relax or something. I got this," Tony said.

"Well, I'm gonna go take a shower."

When I went in the room, I couldn't believe that he was taking the initiative like this. He was really turning out to be something else.

I thought about a lot of the things that he told me on the phone. I wish I knew who the dude was that broke his heart. Even though Tony had an arrogance about him, it was kinda cute. He was very confident in himself and that was a good thing to me.

Tony was still kinda young. He would be nineteen in October; I would be twenty-six in December. Well, I guess it ain't that bad, but it does seem a little odd though.

I spent quite a bit of time in the shower than what I normally do. I really needed that. The water felt really good beating against my skin.

*"Damn, that shit smells good,"* I said to myself, as I stepped out my shower.

Before I headed back out Tony, I wanted to check my messages. I signed on to Black Gay Chat to see who was on. I had a friend that I've been talking to on there since I moved here, but we never met or anything or talked on the phone. We just chat online. I would like to meet him.

When I walked in the kitchen, Tony was sitting at the table in a daze.

"You ok?" I asked, as I headed over to him.

"Yeah, man, I was just thinking," he said.

"Thinking about what?"

"Something that happened back in high school. I did something crazy. I mean I always did crazy shit because I could, but this was crazy as hell. And as a result, some more crazy things happened. I guess I kinda feel bad about the whole situation. If I wouldn't have done what I did, then who know—"

"How long ago was this?" I asked.

"A couple of years ago. It just pops in my mind from time-to-time," Tony said.

"Oh, what did you do?" I asked.

"I don't feel like talking about that right now," Tony said, as he stood up.

"Is it that bad?" I asked.

"Just leave it alone, man," Tony said, as he grabbed some plates from the cabinet. "The food is done."

"Good, because I'm starved!"

# 71

## *Dwight*

I was fucking miserable. I couldn't sleep. I've spent the past few hours tossing and turning in bed, but I just can't sleep. Bored out of my mind, I picked up my phone and called my other best friend. Amir answered, "Nigga, why you up so damn late calling me and shit? It's three in the morning."

"I can't sleep."

"So force yo' ass to go to sleep," Amir said, clearing his throat.

"I tried."

"Call Kiki's ole stank ass," Amir stated. "I'm sure she'd keep you company."

"Man, I broke up with her bitch ass," I said.

"Oh—when you do that?" Amir asked.

"A few days ago. She wasn't giving up the pussy so it wasn't a need for me to stay attached to her ass," I stated.

"You're something else," Amir said.

"I mean we didn't have a real relationship anyway. The whole damn thing was based off fucking," I explained.

"I guess, Dwight. But look, nigga, I ain't trying to be rude, but I'm trying to sleep. Get at me tomorrow, bruh."

"Ight, Amir," I said, as I hung up the phone.

I sighed. I know why I can't sleep. When I haven't released in a while, my body won't allow me to go to sleep. I refuse to do what every other dude in the world does—masturbate—so that's out of the question. I've never done it and I don't plan on doing it now.

"Ight, Dwight," I said to myself, as I laid back down in the bed. "Just go to sleep."

I laid in the bed for another five minutes but still couldn't sleep. I yelled, "FUCK!" in frustration, as I grabbed my dick.

"I need some pussy *right now*," I said, as I picked up my phone. Within a few rings he sluggishly answered, "Heello?"

"FUCK YOU!" I said.

"I love you, too, Dwight," Zach said.

"What you doing?" I asked.

"Ummm...sleeping," he sarcastically said.

"I'm horny."

"Ok," Zach said.

"Nigga, I'M HORNY! I need to fuck!" I said.

"So call one of those bitches that you fuck with," Zach said.

"They ain't answering," I said, knowing I hadn't called anyone.

"Oh, must suck to be you. I'm going back to sleep," Zach said, as he hung up the phone.

"FUCK!" I yelled, as I listened to the dial tone. I sighed and said, "Oh, well, fuck it," as I dialed another number. After a few rings, I heard, "Hello?"

"What's up?" I said.

"What's up, Dwight?"

"I wanna fuck," I said.

"Damn, you don't waste no time saying what you want, do you?"

"Look, are you game or what? I don't have time to hold conversations and shit," I said.

"Yeah, come through."

"Ight, I'll be over there in about twenty minutes," I said.

"Ight, call me when you're outside."

"Bet that up," I said, as I hung up.

I smiled and hopped in the shower.

*I can finally catch this nut!*

# 72

## *Chaz*

I wanted to get Eric back for taking Zach from me, but I didn't want to get the man killed. I didn't know Black was gonna trip out like that. I knew he was gonna get mad, but not *that* mad.

I guess I feel a lil at ease though. Thankfully, nothing tragic happened. I don't think I could live with myself had someone died, all at my expense of playing a game to get revenge on Eric.

That was a few weeks ago; things have calmed down now. I'm really starting to feel for Eric again; we're starting to really get close. I love Zach and I miss Zach, but it's time to let that shit go. I've got two kids at home and I need to focus my attention on them.

Besides, I don't have the time to be running behind Zach. I'm graduating with my master's degree in December and I need to really focus on finishing these classes strong.

I really am falling for Genevieve. She is the best! Even though she knows that I had dealings with dudes on a sexual level, she doesn't even talk about it anymore. I think that is a thing of the past with her and I can really appreciate that. No one is perfect. Everybody has things in their past that they aren't proud of and she isn't excluded from that list. She knows that I'm with her now and I'm committed to her and our boys, Xavier and Elijah. Moving in together was really the best thing that we could have done. My lil man Xavier is a year old. Damn, time flies.

I parked my car and headed upstairs. When I reached his door, I knocked on it and said, "Open the door!"

Within a few moments Ian opened the door and said, "Damn, you got here fast!"

I walked in the apartment and headed for the living room. I saw Quinton and said, "What's up?" as I sat down.

"Chilling, Chaz," he said, as he looked at me and shook his head. I know he was still bothered by Black having that gun in his apartment.

"How is everything going for you?" I asked.

"It's ok," Quinton said. "I'm doing my internship now, so come December I'm out this bitch!"

"Damn, all of us will be out," I said.

"That's true," Ian said. "We'll have our master's and my baby is getting his bachelor's."

"There is nothing like an educated black man," Quinton said, as he stood up.

"You 'bout to leave, baby?" Ian asked.

"Yeah, I gotta go finish my lesson plans for next week," he said, as he walked over and kissed Ian. "I'm sure I'll be back with that damn roommate we got living there now."

"Yeah, Eric was telling me about him," I added.

"I hate dudes like him, but it is what it is," Quinton said, as he walked to the door. "I'll be back."

"Ight, baby," Ian said. Once Quinton was gone, Ian looked to me and said, "So, what's going on?"

"Man, it's good to see you again. You've been so damn busy with the band and shit," I said.

"Yeah, we're starting to get into the meat of the season now, so things are starting to pop off," Ian said.

"I didn't realize that we were busy like that. It's really different to see things from the outside," I said.

"Yeah, we've got a trip tomorrow," Ian added.

"Where y'all going?"

"A battle of the bands in Jackson, Mississippi," Ian said. "So much for having an off weekend."

"You know how that shit goes," I said, as we started to laugh.

"But what's really up, Chaz?" Ian said, as he looked at me. "I can tell that there's something you wanna say."

I didn't say anything.

"What did you do now?" Ian asked.

"I was responsible for that shit," I said.

"For what?"

"The thing with Black," I said.

# Life of a College Bandsman 2: Is This Love

"You're talking about what Quinton told me about that nigga having a gun pulled out on Eric?" Ian asked.

"Yeah, but I didn't know he was gonna bring a gun and shit into the pic. I just wanted to mess with Eric," I tried to explain.

"WHAT THE FUCK IS WRONG WITH YOU, CHAZ?" Ian yelled. "NIGGA, YOU COULD HAVE HAD THAT DAMN BOY KILLED!"

"I know. I didn't mean for it to be like that."

"Chaz, you've done some foul shit before but this takes the cake. What the fuck is wrong with you?"

"I was mad when I set it up."

"SET IT UP?" Ian said. "WHAT THE FUCK DID YOU DO?"

"I had Ra'Jon—"

"RA'JON?" Ian yelled, cutting me off. "CHAZ, WHAT THE FUCK ARE YOU TALKING TO THAT NIGGA FOR?"

"Shit, it's done now," I said getting upset. I don't know why I opened my damn mouth.

"YOU TRUSTED THAT NIGGA?" Ian said.

"Not really, but he was game because he wanted to get Zach back," I said.

"How does he get Zach back for fucking with Eric?" Ian asked, confused.

"Well, Eric is gonna have to give up his thing with Zach so he can keep his relationship with his brother," I said. "Zach is gonna lose Eric—that's how he gets Zach back. I originally wanted this to happen so I could get Zach back, but I don't want him anymore. I mean I love the lil nigga, but I wanna do the right thing with Genevieve."

"Chaz, this is crazy. So, that whole makeup thing with Eric was fake too?"

"In the beginning it was," I said. "But we're on good terms—for real now."

"Let's see how much of good terms y'all would be on if he knew what the fuck you did!"

"Well, he won't," I said, staring at Ian.

"That nigga ain't done with yo' ass," Ian stated.

"Who?"

"Ra'Jon," Ian said. "You're a fucking fool for doing this shit. He's gonna fuck yo' ass up, too!"

"No, he's not," I said.

"Chaz, you forced that man to lose his job. Mark my words—he's gonna get your ass back!"

"Man, whatever."

"Ight, Chaz. The only way, and I mean the only way, he doesn't get you back is if he magically grows the fuck up, and I seriously doubt that. I know he has thought about it. You better watch it, Chaz. You're so fucking stupid," Ian said, as he left me sitting in the living room.

I sighed.

He walked back in and said, "What the hell is wrong with you? You're so damn stupid! STUPID!"

\*\*\*\*\*

# *Morgan*

My boyfriend, Devin, walked in my house and said, "What do you want, Morgan? We've got a trip in the morning and I need to get some sleep."

"Devin, please just hear me out."

He stared at me, as he sat down.

I said, "You've made your point. This shit has gone on too damn long."

"Morgan, you're full of shit!"

"Devin, don't be like that. I'm trying to do right and I'm doing it because I want you. I get it now!"

"No, you don't get it," he said to me. "I got it when I gave up my ways to be with you. Nigga, you don't get it."

"Devin, I promise that I've learned. I ain't gonna do that shit no more," I confessed. "I fucked up. Yeah, I cheated on you on numerous occasions. I did it because I could. I did it because I knew that you were gonna be here anyway. I took advantage of you, but I get it now. Devin, that shit ain't worth it. Just come back! I need you. Please, just come back! I don't know how many times I've gotta beg! I get it! I'M SORRY!"

"We've got a trip in the morning and I need to get home," Devin said, as he got up.

"You didn't hear what I just said?"

# Life of a College Bandsman 2: Is This Love

"I heard you, Morgan," he said, as he walked to the door. "I hear everything you say."

"So, you're not gonna come back home?"

"HOME?" he said. "Don't even take it there, Morgan, especially when you were fucking those niggas in our *home*. But see it ain't my home, it's yours. This is your place. I was just an invited guest along with everybody else you fucked."

As I looked at Devin run his mouth, I realized that he was as sexually frustrated as I was. Since that day, three weeks ago when Devin *left* me, I haven't done anything with another dude. I want to make this shit work and I'm committed to it. I can tell that he wants to make it work, too, but he's just being an ass about it. That's why I keep begging him. This is what he wants to hear. If this was another nigga, I wouldn't be stressed about this shit. But Devin—I want that nigga. Our shit was real. I fucked up, but I just wanna make it right.

"Devin," I said, as I walked over to him.

"What?"

"Come home," I said, as I invaded his personal space. I was now face-to-face with the man that I fell for.

"Fuck you!" he said.

"Come home," I said, as I started to kiss him on his neck. "Come home—where you belong."

"No," he said.

"Yes," I said, as I started to kiss on his spot. I felt his dick get hard, so I put my hands on it.

"Stop, Morgan," he lustfully stated.

"Ok," I said, as I continued to work my baby.

"Stop."

"Do you really want me to?" I asked, as I pulled his pants down. He didn't say anything.

"Do you really want me to stop?" I asked, as I licked on his neck and massaged his dick. "Huh? You want me to stop?"

"No," Devin said, as lust and pleasure took over his body. "Don't stop."

# 73

# Zach

*Sunday, September 14, 2003*
*Jackson, Mississippi*

It was a little after one in the afternoon and we had just arrived in Jackson, leaving Tallahassee a little over eight hours ago. We had about five hours before the battle of the bands were to start, so the promoters of the event booked the band a hotel so we could chill out and relax.

Like usual, it takes forever to get off the bus, but since we didn't have luggage with us, the process was a little quicker. We traveled in our band trousers on this trip.

We didn't get any allocations on this trip because the event promoters paid the hotel to provide lunch. They also paid for the band to eat at Golden Corral once the performance was over.

I was starving and standing in a long ass line, waiting to eat, didn't help. When I finally got my plate, I found an empty table in the hotel conference room. Dwight quickly joined me at the table. I took a bite of my food and was disgusted. Dwight ate some of his and spit it back out. We looked at each other and shook our heads. We knew this wasn't gonna cut it. We had to find us something to eat.

We headed back to the hotel room we shared with Kris and Peanut. On the elevator, Dwight looked at me and said, "Fuck you!"

"I love you, too, Dwight," I smiled.

Recently, I've noticed that Dwight could be very cold and he is very emotionless. He isn't very affectionate, either. He's been saying *fuck you* quite a lot lately and it comes out of thin air. When he used to say it, I just to ask myself why does he just blurt out *fuck you* to me. But then something told me that maybe that was his way of saying *I love you* without directly saying it. This way, he can keep his *masculinity* and no one will never know what it really means—at least this is the theory I've come to believe.

When I started saying *I love you, too, Dwight,* he would leave it alone. It's as if that's what he was waiting on me to say. And to be honest, I actually kinda like the game. It's cute. Maybe he's now coming around, on his terms, like Jared said.

I really didn't know what to do, or how to take it, that night he called me talking about he was horny. I mean this dude, who I call my best friend, who is supposed to be straight, and by every indication, he is straight, throws me for loops at times.

He really caught me off guard with that phone call. I thought about pushing it with him, but then thought about our relationship. What if I was taking the call the wrong way? He could have been talking in general terms. If I would have pressed the issue, and he was talking in general terms, then my ass is out on the line and I don't know if I really want to risk that. Hell, Dwight does random shit because he's a random dude. But I just don't get it. Dwight stays horny, but I just don't get it.

I told Jared what happened in the hotel with Dwight and how he called me. I told him about how Peanut looked me kinda strange. Jared said that I needed to keep my eyes on Peanut because he would be the person that comes and takes Dwight right from under me. Jared also said that Dwight maybe hinting at me, but is scared to come out and say it, so he hopes that I would be bold and push it to that limit. But I don't know. Besides, I still have Eric. *This shit sucks.*

"You got some money?" Dwight asked once we got back to the room.

"Yeah, I've got a couple dollars," I said.

"Shawty, we've gotta go find something to eat."

"Shit, let's go."

As we headed out of the hotel, other band members stared at us. I know we were the center of conversation, but I just took it in stride as I moved a lil bit closer to him.

*"Let me give them something to talk about,"* I said to myself.

That's been a constant thing recently. Based on the way some people talk and look at us, I know they think we're fucking. Hell, we're always together. I ride with him to practice. I leave with him. We're always together on trips. We're at the mall together. We're on campus together. That passenger seat in his car has my name on it and everyone knows it. Some people have even made lil smart comments such as, "When you ride with Dwight, you better get yo' ass in the back because that front seat is for Zach."

I remember last week, we were leaving practice and one of our freshmen brothers, Raheim, that plays saxophone, wanted to catch a ride with Dwight. Raheim was already at Dwight's car when we got there and he was standing by the passenger door. I was prepared to get in the back, as it wasn't a big deal to me.

"Naw, Shawty," Dwight said, as he opened the door. "That's Zach's seat. You can hop back there."

"It's cool," I said to Dwight. "He can ride up there."

"Naw, he can ride in the back," Dwight aggressively stated, as he got in the car and closed the door. "Let's go!"

To be honest, it really made me feel like it was something more between us, but I know it was just my imagination running wild.

We still had on our uniform trousers as we navigated thought the streets of Jackson.

"We're crazy as hell," Dwight said, as we continued to walk trying to find somewhere to eat, but nothing was in sight.

"Why you say that?" I asked.

"Because we have on our uniform pants and all this shit is home to Jackson State. That's disrespect, Zach. I hear people down here are crazy. I don't wanna have to fight nobody over no band shit," he said.

"Nigga, you scared?" I asked.

"I ain't scared of shit," he said, as he looked at me.

"I know one thing that you're scared of," I said.

"And what's that?" he said.

"Don't worry about it," I said, as I started to laugh.

We made lil small talk until we finally found a string of fast food restaurants. We had been walking for about forty minutes.

We ate at the McDonald's, because about time we got back to the hotel, the food would have been cold. We walked back to the hotel in silence. Food will do that to you. Besides, I was trying to get my mind mentally prepared for the twenty-five-minute show that we were about to put on.

"You know what my mom told me," Dwight said out of nowhere.

"What's that?" I asked.

"She said that if I was gay, just tell her, but don't lead no secret life like my daddy."

"Where is that coming from? Wait—your dad is gay?"

"My momma believes he's gay," Dwight stated.

"Why would she think that? Aren't they still married?" I asked.

"Yeah, they're married, but my momma knows that he's gay, but she really doesn't care. But, yeah, she told me just to tell her if I was gay because leading a secret life ain't good," Dwight said.

"Dwight, where is this coming from?" I asked.

"I don't know, I was just talking," he said, as we got back at the hotel.

I was still puzzled by what he said. Was he trying to tell me that he was gay? When we got back to the room, no one was in there, so he continued to talk about his dad.

He said, "She says my dad got all these gay acting friends and he does gay shit. She said she knows that he's fucking one of those dudes."

"So, why is she still with him if she knows that he's gay?" I asked, as Peanut walked in the room.

When he walked in, everything got quiet. It was very obvious that something in the room wasn't right and Peanut picked right up on it as he looked at Dwight. Then Peanut looked at me.

I guess it didn't help that we both were sitting on the bed and Dwight only had on the basketball shorts that he wears under his uniform.

"What y'all doing in here?" Peanut suspiciously asked.

"Nothing," Dwight said.

"Hmm," Peanut said, as he looked at me. "I forgot what I came in here for."

He left.

"That nigga is thinking something crazy," I said to Dwight.

"Yeah I—" is all Dwight could say because Peanut came right back in the room.

Peanut looked at me, then over to Dwight and asked, "Why does it get silent every time I come in the room?"

"Because we don't want you to hear what we're talking about," Dwight said.

"Umm, hmm," Peanut said, as he went to his book bag. "That's cool freshman bruh. Be secretive—it's best that way."

Peanut smiled and left the room.

# 74

# *Zach*

I was sitting in the living room, in some basketball shorts and a beater, thinking about the recent events in my life while listening to the R&B group, 112. Dwight has really been throwing me for loops over the last week or so. I don't know what's up with him and I don't really know how to take it.

I am secretly in love with my best friend. I know that I'm with Eric, but my heart is really with Dwight. I can't lie or deny it anymore. I have to be real with myself. I love Eric, but if Dwight were to tell me, right now, that he wants to get with me, then the relationship with Eric would be a thing of the past. It's past the physical attraction with Dwight; this thing is serious!

I try to play hard or act like nothing Dwight does bothers me, but they actually do. I don't want him to feel like I'm coming on to him, so that's one of the reasons why I tend to keep a certain distance on some issues.

Eric has kept his word with me and has been coming around more since returning from his med school interview and visiting his sister. However, I know Eric can sense something between brewing Dwight and me. Every time I talk about Dwight, he gets upset. He doesn't express it verbally, but it's all in his body language.

Being inside of Raidon's class hasn't been as bad as I thought it would be. I can actually see why Eric fell for him. The man is kinda cool. Raidon seems to be down to earth and he has a natural confidence about himself. Since the initial day we met in class, he hasn't said anything about my relationship with Eric. I really respect that Mr. Harris is very professional. He is nothing like his brother,

Ra'Jon.

Peanut has really acting differently around me and giving me these strange looks at practice. I'm really starting to believe Jared when he said Peanut would be the dude to take Dwight right from under me. I don't wanna think that my freshman brother gets down with dudes, but you can't put it past anyone nowadays. Peanut has never given me reason to believe that he fucks around with dudes, but either he is after Dwight or he thinks Dwight and I are fucking.

I don't know if it's me being jealous, but I'm starting to get sick of Kris and Micah. They be at it all night, every night. They fuck like rabbits. They fuck when they go to bed and they fuck when they wake up in the morning. If we didn't have class during the day, they'd probably fuck then, too. I know Eric can hear their asses because I can hear them. I just wish I was having sex like that. Nonetheless, I'm happy Kris and Micah are back on good terms.

I was brought out of my trance when I heard my phone ringing. I answered because my favorite uncle was calling.

"Hey, Nephew," my Uncle Alan said.

"What's up, Unc," I said. Hearing his voice immediately made me excited. I hadn't heard from him in a while.

"Nothing much, Nephew. I was just calling to see how you were doing."

"I'm doing really good, really good."

"That's good. So, your birthday is coming up next week."

"Yes, sir," I smiled. "I'll be twenty. Just one more year and then I'm legal!"

He laughed, "Don't be such in a rush to grow up because once those real bills start, they don't stop."

"I hear you, Unc," I chuckled. "How are things with you?"

"I can't complain; I'm still living. But my health has gotten a lil better over the last few weeks. The doctors still say that my time is getting close. My T-Cell counts are getting lower. But it is what it is. I'm just gonna leave that in the hands of the Lord. There is nothing I can do about it now."

"Wow," I said, as the thought of losing my uncle bothered me. He had been living with HIV since I was seven. He now has full blown AIDS.

"Yeah, don't get down, though, because only one thing is promised to every living being," he said.

"What's that?" I asked.

# Life of a College Bandsman 2: Is This Love

"Someday, we all must leave this earth."

"Yeah, but it ain't your time, yet. You are too young," I said, realizing that he'd only be forty in October.

"God determines when it is time. All I can do is be ready," he said.

"Well, I'm happy you have a positive outlook on this."

"There is no need to be negative. I messed up years ago, thinking I was invisible having sex with this dude and that dude. I was young and living a carefree life because I knew nothing was going to happen to me. But it did. And now I've gotta live with the consequences of my actions. Even though HIV and AIDS wasn't talked about in the early nineties how it is now, I knew better. I did what I did because I chose to do it. HIV isn't a gay disease, Zach; it's everybody's disease. Just make sure you put Mr. Trojan around your dick whenever you're having sex."

"I know," I said, as I thought back to the times Tony and I had sex and never used a condom.

"Zach, I'm serious! This shit is nothing to play with for a few minutes of pleasure. I'm telling you what I know from personal experience. Yes, you can take some pills but it's the constant doctor visits. It's the constant bloodwork. It's the money out of your pocket. Man, just protect yourself, Zach. I know it's tempting up there at FAMU, but just remember what's more important—those few minutes of pleasure or your life."

"Ok, Unc."

"Well, I didn't call to lecture you, but I just look at my experiences and I know what you're doing."

*Know what I'm doing?*

"And just be cautious, that's all nephew. I just want you to live a healthy life. I caught this disease in my mid-twenties. I've basically lived my entire adult life trying to fight this. It's not worth it."

I sighed.

"Well, let me get off this phone. It was good to hear your voice," he said.

"It was good to hear your voice, too, Uncle Alan. I will try to call you when we get some time."

"Ok," he said, as he hung up the phone.

When I got off the phone with him, I realized that I had never taken a HIV test, partly because I was always afraid of what the results could be. But I know I've got to get it done. I have too.

I thought back to a previous conversation with Eric when he didn't want to have sex with me. I said, *"Do you have HIV or something? Are you sick?"*

*"No! We can go take that test together. I ain't sick,"* he said.

Maybe we should go get that test done together—yep, that's exactly what we're gonna do.

I picked up my phone and called Eric. When he answered I said, "I wanna take you up on that proposal."

"What proposal?" he asked.

"The one about the HIV test. Let's get it together."

"Shit, I'm ready when you are."

"Ight, come scoop me up."

# 75

## *Amir*

My little brother called and woke me up. He was on his way over to my apartment. I was happy that he was coming because I was starving! I asked him to stop by Popeye's and grab me some spicy chicken.

Once I got out of bed, I realized that it was the middle of the afternoon and I missed my 2:30pm class. *Oh, well. Fuck it.* I needed the rest.

I didn't hear Dezmond's music and that was first. I really can't stand living with him. He's so fucking gay and I hate that shit.

I really missed fucking around with Morgan, but I guess he's gotta do what's best for his relationship. I don't believe in gay relationships. They never last.

I've been calling Devin, the boy I met in Walmart, but he has been ignoring my calls. All he gotta say is that he ain't interested, but it's cool because I get the picture. Jared, on the other hand, is really servicing my dick. That nigga is wild! But I gotta find something else. One dude just doesn't do it for me.

I headed to the door once my brother called and said that he was parked. Dallis walked in the house and handed me the food.

"Thanks, man," I said, as I took the chicken box and made my way over to the dining table.

"No problem, bruh," Dallis said, as he sat down across from me.

"So, what's going on?" I said, as I took a bite of the chicken breast.

"Nothing, really. Oh, here you are," Dallis said, as he reached in his pocket and handed me some money.

"What's this?" I asked.

"The money that I borrowed from you back in August when I went to Jacksonville."

"Oh, ok. I had forgot all about that shit," I said, as I took another bite.

"So, Amir, be honest with me," Dallis said.

"What's up?" I said, as I looked at him.

"I don't want you to be mad or anything, but I was just wondering—"

"What's up?" I asked. I wanted to know what was bothering my kid brother.

"That night."

"What night?"

"The night when you saw my DVD."

"Oh, what about it?" I asked, realizing where this conversation was heading.

"When you asked me was I fucking with dudes, I told you the truth. Well, I wanna know if you are fucking with dudes, too."

"What makes you ask that?" I asked, placing the chicken back in the box.

"Because I pay attention to a lot of things," Dallis said. "And I just wanna know."

"What are you paying attention to?"

"I see the things that you do. And I saw you with Devin one day."

"How do you know Devin?" I asked, confused.

"He is one of our drum majors," Dallis said.

"HE IS?" I asked, shocked.

"Yeah."

"And where exactly did you see us?" I asked.

"I saw you go inside his house a few weeks ago—at two in the morning," Dallis answered.

"You're watching me now?" I asked, as I picked up the chicken and took another bite. "No. I was leaving a friend's crib and I saw your car pull up. So I asked myself, 'why is my brother going to Devin's house?' Everybody in the band knows what Devin is about."

"And what is that?"

"What dude hasn't Devin sucked or fucked with?" Dallis said.

"Oh."

"So, are you?"

"You seem to already know that answer," I said, as I took a sip of the Pepsi that he got with the meal.

"Really?" he said excited. "You get down, too?"

"Yeah, man," I said. "BUT YOU BETTER NOT TELL A FUCKING SOUL!"

"I won't, I promise. But if you're down, too, why did you trip out like that when you saw the DVD?" Dallis asked.

"Dallis, I've known about you for some time now, but I was hoping that you would stay on the low with it. That's why I never said anything. I tripped out because anybody could have saw that shit. You don't want your name ruined. Shit, do what you do, but be discreet with it."

"I see," Dallis said, as Dezmond walked in the house.

Dezmond stepped in the dining room and said, "Good afternoon, gentlemen." He looked at my brother, smiled and said, "Dallis, it's been a long time." He walked away.

I looked at my brother and said in disgust, "You know him?"

"Yeah," he softly said, hanging his head in shame.

"How?" I asked, trying to figure out how their paths would cross. I know my brother ain't interested in the punk ass gays.

"I used to suck your brother's dick a lot," Dezmond interrupted, as he stepped back in the dining room.

"YOU'RE SO FUCKING MESSY!" I said to Dezmond, as I got up and made my way in the kitchen.

"Well, I will take my messy ass and be out of y'all way," Dezmond stated, as he walked into the kitchen. "Y'all ain't fooling nobody anyway—you, Quinton and Eric. All y'all fucking with dudes!"

"BITCH NIGGA, YOU DON'T KNOW SHIT!" I said, as I got in his face.

"Look, I ain't the girl for violence, so you can step back. I said was I gonna be out y'all fucking way, so y'all can go back to living y'all undercover lives," Dezmond stated.

"Where are you going?" Dallis asked, walking into the kitchen.

"I got to go back home for good. I had some family shit that I've got to take care of and right now my family is more important than this school. I can go to school at home," Dezmond stated.

"When are you leaving?" I asked.

"I will be out y'all way in the morning," Dezmond said, as he looked at Dallis. "But?"

"But what?" Dallis asked.

"You should let me take care of you really quick. I'm sure Amir won't mind," Dezmond said to my brother.

Dallis looked over at me. I guess he was waiting for my approval. I didn't see what he saw in that feminine thing, but if that's what floats his boat, then so be it.

"Do what you do," I said with a disgusted look on my face.

"It's only head," Dallis said to me.

"Whatever," I said, as I walked away.

*At least that thing is leaving my damn house...for good.*

# 76

## Zach

I smiled when I saw Dwight's name pop up on my phone. When I answered, he said, "What are you doing, Big Z?"

"Nothing, really, just looking at TV," I replied.

"Let's get up," Dwight said.

"What are we gonna do?" I asked.

"Shit, I don't know. Let's hit the mall or something," Dwight said.

"That's what's up."

"Ight, I'm on my way."

"Yep," I said. I hung up and headed into the kitchen to grab something to drink. As I poured some Kool-Aid that Kris made, Micah walked in the house.

"What's good," Micah said.

"Shit, 'bout to get up with Dwight," I said.

"That's what's up."

Kris walked in the house and said, "Hey, freshman bruh!"

I said, "I knew you couldn't have been too far behind."

"You got jokes?" Micah said.

"Shit, I'm just telling the truth. Y'all niggas be stuck to each other all day and all night."

"Hell, we're about to go get stuck again," Kris said, as Micah started smiling.

"Just wait till I leave," I said, as I finished the cup of Kool-Aid.

Dwight called a few minutes later and said he was out front. When I got in the car, he smiled and said, "Fuck you!"

"I love you, too."

"Whatever," Dwight said, as he pulled off.

A few moments later, my phone started to ring.

"Who's that?" Dwight asked, as he looked over at me.

"Eric," I said, as I answered the phone. "What's up?"

"Baby, where you at?" Eric asked.

"I just went out with Dwight," I said.

"OH."

"You straight?" I asked.

"Yeah, I'm good. Call me when you get in."

"Ight, Eric," I said, as I hung up.

"That nigga got a problem?" Dwight asked, as he looked over at me.

"Naw, he cool," I said.

"Don't be lying for his ass," Dwight said. "If he got a problem with us chilling and shit, then that punk nigga can step to me."

"Dwight, it ain't that serious."

"Why the fuck are you still with that bitch ass nigga?" Dwight asked in an upset tone.

"Because."

"Because what, Zach? What the fuck does that nigga do for you? He obviously ain't putting the dick down."

"I just like him," I said.

"WHAT THE FUCK DOES THAT NIGGA DO FOR YOU?" Dwight asked, again, raising his voice.

"WHY THE FUCK DO YOU CARE?" I yelled back.

"Man, whatever. Just forget I asked," Dwight said. "How is your grandma."

"She's cool. Her birthday is tomorrow. She'll be sixty-two."

"That's what's up! I'ma give her a call tomorrow," Dwight said.

"She'd appreciate that," I said, as we got to the mall.

"Damn, y'all birthdates are close," Dwight stated.

"Yeah, just one week a part."

As we walked through the mall, I couldn't help but be happy. It just felt right. Being with Dwight felt right. He made a good point about Eric. What does Eric do for me?

"Yo, Big Z, let's check out a movie," Dwight said.

"That's what's up," I said.

"Yo, I got you, so you don't have to pay for nothing," Dwight said, as we walked over to the box office.

"Thanks, bruh."

# Life of a College Bandsman 2: Is This Love

"What you wanna see?" he asked.

"Shit, it doesn't matter. Freddy vs Jason is cool, but it doesn't start for another hour and some change."

"That's cool. I was hoping you said that because that's what I wanted to see," Dwight said, as he went to purchase the tickets. When he came back, he asked, "You want something to eat?"

"Yeah, I can eat," I said.

"Shit, since we got some time, let's go cop something. About time we finish with, the movie should be getting ready to start."

"That's what's up," I said.

"I got a taste for Red Lobster," Dwight said, as we got to his car.

"I don't have no Red Lobster money," I said.

"Nigga, I said I got you," Dwight said.

*Did this boy just fool me into going on a 'date' with his ass, without directly asking me?*

It only took a couple of minutes to get to the Red Lobster. As we waited for our food, Dwight said, "Yeah, man, so I'm like really excited about the band this year."

"Yeah, this band is a fucking beast!" I said. "I can't wait until we get down to Atlanta next weekend."

"Shit, I can't either," Dwight said. "I miss my brother."

"Your brother is funny," I said. "His name is Ced, right?"

"Yeah, that fool is crazy. He's coming up here next year."

"That's what's up," I said. "I'm sure you can teach him the ropes."

"Hell, that nigga gonna teach me the ropes. Ced be on more pussy than I do," Dwight said, as he took a sip of the drink.

"Both of y'all crazy as hell," I smiled.

"But real talk, check this out."

"What's up, Dwight?"

"I know what people are saying and shit," he said.

"What are they saying?" I asked.

"Nigga, you ain't stupid. You know they're talking 'bout our asses," he said.

"Oh."

"Yeah. I know they think we're fucking and shit," he said.

"Does that bother you?" I asked.

"Not really," he said. "Let they asses talk. They're just mad that they don't have the kind of relationship that we have."

"We got a relationship?" I asked.

"Nigga, you know what I mean," Dwight said.

"Umm, hmm. But if they think we're fucking, then that means that you're *gay*, too," I said.

"I know what I am and I know what I'm not, so let they asses talk," Dwight said. "I just was wondering if it was bothering you."

"I hear it and shit, but it's whatever, man. I ain't gonna stress out 'bout that shit. I mean it's cool if you don't wanna hang around me like that in public."

"Hell naw!" he said upset. "Fuck them! You're my best friend and they aren't about to fuck up what we got! Niggas gonna talk regardless. Fuck them! Nigga, you're my best friend. Fuck those pussy ass niggas! Don't let those rumors and shit fuck us up."

"Shit, I'm cool with it if you are," I said.

"Then that's that," Dwight said, as the food came out. "Let 'em talk."

Once the waiter left, he looked at his food and said a quick prayer. I said one, too. When I looked up, he was staring at me smiling.

He said, "Fuck you!"

I smiled, "I love you, too, Dwight."

# 77

## *Zach*

*Tuesday, September 23, 2003*

As I got out of the bed, I heard, "HAPPY BIRTHDAY!"
I smiled and said, "Thanks, Eric."
"So, how does it feel to be twenty?" he asked, standing the doorway in nothing but some plaid boxers.

"You make it seem like I'm still a kid," I said, as I went to the bathroom.

"Naw, it ain't like that," he said, as he followed me into bathroom.

"Does my age bother you, Eric?"

"No, I'm only twenty-two," he replied, staring at me as if I were crazy.

"I'm just saying," I replied.

"What are you doing today?" he asked.

"The usual—class and practice."

"Do y'all have night practice tonight?" he asked.

"I don't think so."

"Good, keep the night open," he said.

"Ok, baby," I said, as I got in the shower.

"HOLD UP!" he yelled, as he walked back into the bedroom.

"WHAT?" I yelled.

"I WANNA GET IN, TOO," he said, as he ran back in the bathroom.

"You're so stupid," I said, as I started smiling.

I loved looking at Eric's body. It was so perfect. His sickening six pack, outlined by the happy trail that led to his love area was stupid. Everything about Eric's body was perfect, but one could never tell under all the damn clothes that he wears.

"What are you thinking about, birthday boy?" Eric said, as he took the rag and started to lather me up.

"You," I said.

"What about me?"

"Just how you turn me the fuck on!"

"Shitttttt, I can tell," he said, as he looked down at my dick. "And you do the same thing for me."

"I see," I said, as I reached back and grabbed his dick.

"Come here," he said, as I turned around to face him.

"Yes?"

"I love you! Don't ever forget that, ok, baby," Eric said, as he started to kiss me.

"Ok, Eric. I love you, too," I said, as we kissed some more.

"Let me give you an early b-day present," Eric said, as he kneeled down and took my member into his mouth.

"Damn, baby," I said, as I was taken aback by the pleasure he was giving to my dick. It was something about dudes—hard, straight acting dudes—who had a dick in their mouth. That turned me the fuck on. That shit is hot. And as I looked at my baby suck the fuck out of my dick, I couldn't help but to be taken places beyond the control of my imagination.

"SHIT, ERIC!" I managed to get out.

I guess hearing my cries and moans made him work harder at getting my nut, because the more I moaned, the more he got into it.

"I'm cumming," I said, as I pulled my dick out his mouth. "OH, SHIT!" I yelled, as my seed burst out my dick, all while my body jerked. It took a few minutes to gather my composure.

"You ok?" Eric asked, as I looked over at him. He was all smiles.

"Yeah, I'm good," I said, as I took the rag to finish my shower.

"I got you," he said, as he took the rag from me and started to bathe me again. "This is your day. I got you."

Maybe I was wrong to think like this, but I need some dick and I need some *right now!* If I don't get what I want soon—then who knows...

Luckily today was Tuesday and that meant that I didn't have class until twelve-thirty. I really didn't feel like doing too much of anything today. I just wanted to sit at the house and enjoy being lazy, watching TV and shit. I wanted to enjoy my day.

# Life of a College Bandsman 2: Is This Love

"Baby, I'ma run to class right quick then I'll be back so we can go to the place to get the tests back," Eric said, as he came out the bathroom.

"Ok, I'll be here," I said, as I kissed him.

"Ok," he said as he left.

"Happy Birthday," Micah said, as he came in the room.

"Thanks, man," I said.

"Yeah, bruh, I'm 'bout to be out, too. I'll get at you later," he said.

"Where is Kris?" I asked.

"He had to leave early this morning," Micah said.

"Oh, ight."

"Yep, I'll get at you," Micah said as he left.

Moments later, my phone started to ring. When I answered, Dwight said, "It's my dawg birthday! It's my dawg birthday! Happy birthday, my nigga!"

"Thanks, man," I smiled, laying on the bed.

"So, are we gonna get up tonight?" he asked.

"Oh, I don't know. Eric told me to keep my night open."

"Oh, that nigga gonna finally give up the dick?" Dwight sarcastically replied.

"We will see," I sighed.

"I don't see why you're still with that punk ass nigga," Dwight said.

"Dwight, I don't wanna hear that shit today," I said.

"Alright, Shawty," he said. "I was just calling to tell you happy birthday."

"Thanks, bruh," I stated.

"I'll see you at practice."

"Ight, man," I said, as we hung up the phone.

When I got off the phone with Dwight, I was a little hungry, so I got out the bed and made my way to the kitchen. I didn't know what I had a taste for, so I just kept it simple and poured a bowl of Cinnamon Toasted Crunch. That was one of my favorite cereals. I walked over to the living room, with my cereal in tow, and turned on the TV. I flipped through the channels until I got to Family Feud. I loved that show. A few minutes later, I heard my phone.

"Who is this?" I said, as I put my cereal down on the coffee table and ran to my room to get my phone. "Oh," I said as I looked at the name. "Hello?"

"Happy Birthday, Zachie!" my grandma said.

"Thanks, Grandma."

"How are you doing today?" she asked.

"Doing really good," I said.

"Did you thank God for another year?" she asked.

"Yes, ma'am. That was the first thing I did before I went to bed last night."

"Oh, you had a long night, huh?" she said.

"It was nothing like that," I said.

"Whatever, boy," she chuckled. "Y'all youngins tell us old folks anything."

"You're so crazy, Grandma."

"You know they had your high school band on TV yesterday," she said.

"Why were they on TV?" I asked.

"Your high school band director, Mr. Simpson, was trying to raise money because the band was invited to perform at the Sugar Bowl in New Orleans in January."

"Oh, wow, that's good." I said.

"Yeah, you know I always liked Mr. Simpson. What was his first name again?" she asked.

"Kevin," I said.

"That's right, Kevin. He was very influential in helping you get a lot of money to go to FAMU. He is a good man," my grandma stated.

"Yes, he is," I said. "I talked to Uncle Alan the other day."

"Yeah, he told me," she said. "He's really proud of you, Zach. We all are, especially your mother."

"Why did you have to bring her name up?" I said.

"Because y'all need to develop a better relationship than what it is now. I ain't always gonna be here, Zach. Regardless of how you view me, that is still your mother. She gave life to you twenty years ago today."

"Well, she's the one who acted like she didn't want me," I said. "She knows my number."

"Somebody needs to be the adult in this relationship and step up to the plate," my grandma said.

"If you say so, Grandma," I replied, rolling my eyes.

"But on another note," she said.

"What's up?"

# Life of a College Bandsman 2: Is This Love

"You still need to keep your guard up," my grandma said.

"What you talking about now?"

"I can still sense that presence and it ain't a good one," my grandma stated. "Just keep your guard up. Watch everyone and be careful."

"Ok, Grandma."

"Well, I don't mean to keep you too long because I know you've got a busy day. Oh, yeah, how is the Dwight fella? You know he has been on my mind," she said.

"He was on your mind?"

"Yeah, I don't know why, but I have been thinking about him ever since he called me for my birthday. I'm not quite sure what exactly that means yet. Just tell him I was thinking about him," she said.

"Ok, Grandma, I will do."

"Ight, Zachie, I love you and I will talk to you later."

"I love you, too, Grandma," I said, as I hung up the phone.

*Why is she thinking about Dwight of all people?* I asked myself, as I dumped that bowl of cereal and poured another one.

Eric returned to the house a few hours later and said, "You ready?"

"I guess," I sighed. I don't know why I was going to get my HIV results on my birthday of all days, but it had to be done.

"You're gonna be straight," he said, as we got in the car.

"If you say so, Eric," I replied.

"When I took my first test I was scared as shit, but everything was cool. I know the feeling that you have, but I also know that you're gonna be straight," he said.

"Umm, hmm," I said. But I was scared and I had good reason to be. I've had unprotected sex before, on numerous occasions with Tony, and some other dudes back in high school.

"Stop stressing," Eric said, as he turned up the radio.

As we walked into the clinic, I had to convince myself that it was going to be ok. After waiting for about ten minutes, a clinic worker called Eric back to the room. A few minutes later, another worker called me back.

"Mr. Finley," she said, as she took out my file. "Everything is fine with you. You have nothing to worry about."

"So, I'm negative, right?" I asked, trying to get a second confirmation.

"Yes, sir, you are HIV-negative," she said, as she filled out a card and gave it to me.

"THANKS SO MUCH!" I said, as I left the room with a bag full of condoms.

"I guess I know what that smile means," Eric said, as we walked to the car. "See, I told you not to worry."

"So, how did your results come back?" I asked.

"Here you are," Eric said, as he gave me his card.

"HIV-negative," I said, as I read his card.

"I told you so," he said. "Don't you feel better that you took the test."

"Yep, much better," I said, as Eric took me to campus.

"Don't forget to keep the night open," Eric said.

"Ok, baby," I said, as I kissed him and got out the car.

# 78

## *Ra'Jon*

Everything was starting to fall in place. I was getting my life back on track, the way it needed to be. While I did miss my job at FAMU, it was time to move on and let that shit go. I had been without a job for a year now and even though I was now teaching at a middle school, it felt good.

Being in Orlando felt good; this city was full of life. Outside of the connection I had with FAMU, nobody knew me and that's how I liked it.

I loved my new students. They were a handful, but I was looking forward to starting their musical careers out on the right path, all while brainwashing them to go to FAMU and be part of the band.

I've learned that in a lot of black schools, the program that your band director graduated from has a lot of influence on the type of band that high school band will be. And as a result, a lot of those kids follow their director and attend the college that they attended.

Being that I was teaching at a black middle school that feeds directly into W.P. Foster High School, whose director was also a FAMU graduate, means if I start preaching FAMU to them now at six, seventh and eighth grades, about time they get to eleventh and twelfth grade, FAMU is where they are gonna want to be.

"This is Mr. Harris," I said, as I answered my office phone. School had been out for about twenty minutes and I was getting ready to head home.

"Ra'Jon, why didn't you tell me that you were teaching here?" a familiar voice said.

"Kevin, is that you?"

"Yep and now I'm pissed at your ass," he said.

"Kevin, I was gonna get around to it, but I had to get myself situated first," I said.

"Umm, hmm," he said. "You don't know it yet, but you just joined my band staff."

"I did?" I asked.

"Yep, you know I can use you over here at the school," Kevin said. "All the help I can get would be wonderful. After all the damn yeas I've been at this school, they still haven't given me an assistant band director. It's hard to do this shit by myself. Some faculty from the school helps out, as well as another middle school director, but he went to Bethune-Cookman. And you know our philosophies don't always match."

"Yeah, I know how that goes."

"I mean, I love the help they give, but I need someone from FAMU who's been in the 100," he said.

"I feel you, Kevin," I said.

"So you're gonna come, right?" he asked. "Practice just stared a few minutes ago. I would love to have you over today."

"Ight, let me finish up here and I'll make my way over there," I said, as I hung up the phone.

Kevin was the band director at W. P. Foster High School. When I was a freshman at FAMU, Kevin was a junior and had just made drum major. I always thought Kevin Simpson was one of the better drum majors the band had. I don't know what Kevin saw in me, but he really helped me out when I got to FAMU. I will always look up to that man and I could never say no to anything he asked. Kevin marched his last two years in undergrad as a drum major and he marched the two years he spent in grad school as a drum major. He was the head drum major in the 1995-96 school year, his last year of grad school. Kevin left FAMU with two degrees and immediately got a job as assistant band director at W. P. Foster High in Orlando for the 1996-97 school year. He took over as head director two years later and has been in charge ever since. Ironically, he was Zach's band director. Kevin married Sasha, a former piccolo section leader in the FAMU band during our time there. She was now an elementary school teacher in Orlando. Together, they had two little girls.

W.P. Foster wasn't too far from my school, only about ten minutes or so. When I walked in the building, Kevin jumped up and smiled. He said, "What's going on, Ra'Jon?"

"Man, you know. Just trying to get it straight," I said, as I followed him into the office.

"What happened? Why did you leave FAMU? That's my goal to get on the staff," he stated.

"It's a long story; a lot of personal stuff," I said.

"Oh, ok, I see," he said, as my phone started to ring.

"What's up, Black?" I said, as I stepped out the building.

"I need to holla at you," he said. "Can I meet you somewhere?"

"I'm kinda busy at the school right now," I said.

"Well, can you talk on the phone for a lil bit?" he asked.

"Yeah, I've got a few minutes."

"Look, this shit is bothering me!" he said

"What's that?" I asked.

"When I left to go to Tally, I pulled out a gun on my brother," Black confessed.

"YOU DID WHAT?" I said.

"I know, it was dumb, but I wasn't thinking," Black said.

"It wasn't loaded was it?" I asked.

"Yes, it was," he said. "And it went off. I could have killed my brother."

"WHOA, BLACK!" I said, as I listened to what he was telling me. "How did that happen?"

"It's a long story. I'll tell you about it when I see you. But Eric could be dead and it would be my fault," Black said. "I didn't mean for it to go down like that. All I wanted to do was scare him and make him straight again."

"You can't make someone be what they don't wanna be," I said.

"I know, but he promised me that he was gonna drop that shit," Black said.

"Ok."

"But I know he's not going to do it. I don't wanna lose my brother, but I can't have no gay brothers, man. I know Eric is still fucking 'round with dudes," Black said.

"How do you know that?" I asked.

"I don't need to get into all of that right now, but I just know. I don't like that shit, RJ. It needs to stop," he said.

"Wow," I said, as I thought about what happened. If Eric would have died, it would have been my fault. I didn't want the dude to die, I just wanted to play a game. I know I need to leave this shit alone.

"Yeah, but I'll let you get back to what you were doing. Call me when you get finished and I will explain everything to you."

"Ok, Black," I said, as I hung up the phone.

"Everything ok?" Kevin said, as I walked back into the office.

"Yeah, my homeboy just told me some disturbing news, but it's good though," I said.

We talked a bit more, before Kevin took me to the rehearsal hall to introduce me to the band. After he introduced me, we listened to the band for a few minutes while the drum majors took them through the show music for this week.

As we headed back into the office, he said, "I really do have a good group."

"They sound good, Kevin," I added. "Really good."

"We're trying to raise money to get to New Orleans for the Sugar Bowl," he said.

"Really?"

"Yeah, man. These kids come from poor neighborhoods and poor families. Their parents don't have the money to pay for them to go on the trip," he said. "I really want them to go so they can be exposed to life outside of Orlando. Many of these kids have never left Florida."

"How much is it gonna cost?"

"Well, we've got about half of it raised, but it's getting the rest that's gonna be the problem," Kevin said.

"How much more are you talking?" I asked.

"We're looking at another twenty-five thousand," he said.

"That's it?"

"That's it? What the hell you talking about. These kids can't afford that," he said.

"I didn't mean it like that," I said, as I started laughing. "I mean I think I know how y'all can get the money."

"How?" he asked.

"I'ma talk to my dad. He's one of the top pharmacists in Virginia. I know he can use his power and influence to get the people who run those big companies to get that done for you. I may be able to get the entire trip paid for and y'all can use the money that you have already raised for something else," I said.

"DON'T PLAY WITH ME!" Kevin said.

"I'm not playing," I said. "I'ma call my dad when I get home and see what's happens."

# Life of a College Bandsman 2: Is This Love

"WOW. That would be great if you can get that done," Kevin said, as another dude walked into the office.

"What's going on, Kevin," he said. He turned to me and said, "What's up?

"DAMN," I said to myself. His voice was deep and he was beautiful. He had a nice cinnamon brown skin tone. He was very sharp in his appearance. He had a nice clean cut. He looked damn good.

"Ra'Jon, this is Damien Duvel. He teaches American History at the school and he works with the percussion section. Damien, this is Ra'Jon. We were in the band together at FAMU. He is the new band director at Westridge and he is gonna be helping us out."

"Nice to meet you," Damien said, as he took a seat.

"Same here," I said, as I looked at him.

Shit, I had a reason to come to the damn school now. This fool was fine as fuck.

*****

# *Zach*

Eric walked in the house and said, "C'mon, baby!"

"Where are we going?" I asked.

"We're just going out to eat. I just wanted to spend some time with you," he said.

"Oh, ok," I said, as I thought back to Dwight. *I could spend time with Eric later. I wanted to spend time with Dwight right now.*

"What do you have a taste for?" he asked.

"It doesn't really matter," I said. "I guess Olive Garden is cool."

"Then Olive Garden it is."

I really wasn't feeling this and I don't know why. *Stop lying, Zach. You do know.* I wanted to chill out with Dwight, but I told Eric that I would keep my night free.

"Are you ok?" Eric asked as we ate.

"Yeah, I'm good," I said. "Just thinking about a lot of things."

"You know what," he said.

"What's that?"

"I met you on your birthday last year."

"You surely did," I said. "We met in the post office on campus."

"Yep, I was talking to my home girl, but when I saw you, I had to get to know you," he said.

"Shit, when I saw you, I almost died. You looked good as fuck," I said.

"LOOKED?"

"You know what I mean," I said, as I started laughing.

"Yeah, I know, but who would have imagined that we would be together one year later," he said.

"I know I didn't," I said. "I didn't even think you got down with dudes."

"That's how I like it," Eric said, as the waitress brought us the check.

Micah and Kris wasn't at the house when we got in.

"I gotta use the bathroom," I said.

"Ok, baby."

I went in the bathroom and cleaned myself out. It was my birthday and I wanted to be ready just in case it happened tonight. Besides, I knew he had to have something else planned besides dinner. It was my fucking birthday!

After I did all the things I needed to clean myself out, I hopped in the shower. When I got out, Eric got in.

All I wanted was some dick and I felt that Eric finally giving me what I wanted would put an ending to a great day.

I guess he could sense that I wanted something, because when he got out the shower, he came right over to the bed and started kissing me.

We played with each other—kissing, licking and sucking—for about twenty minutes. I didn't want to get my dick sucked anymore. I didn't want to suck his dick anymore. I wanted to feel his dick inside of my body.

So, I stopped the foreplay that we were doing and I went into my nightstand and grabbed the condoms and lube.

I could still see Eric's hesitation when I got back over to the bed. That shit pissed me off!

I stared at him and said, "You're still not ready?"

"I want to please you in all the ways that you desire, but—"

"But you can't do it," I said, frustrated.

"I'm sorry, baby. I can't."

"I'M SICK OF THIS SHIT, ERIC! ALL I WANT IS TO

# Life of a College Bandsman 2: Is This Love

HAVE AN INTIMATE NIGHT WITH MY FUCKING BOYFRIEND! IS THAT SHIT TOO MUCH TO ASK?"

"No, but I just can't do it. Not yet anyway."

"That's fine," I said, as I put the condom and lube back down on nightstand.

"You sure?"

"Yeah—how about you just go home tonight."

"What?" he sat up in the bed.

"Yeah, you can go home. I'm straight."

"You're kicking me out?" he said in disbelief.

"You can call it what you like, but I just wanna be by myself," I said.

"Are you serious? So, you're about to cheat on me now?" Eric said standing up.

"Why are you still here? I told you to leave!" I said, as I put on my shorts and walked to my door.

"IT'S LIKE THAT, ZACH?"

"Goodnight, Eric," I said, opening the door.

"Don't go and do no crazy shit!" he put on his clothes.

"Goodnight, Eric," I said, as he exited my room and made his way to the front door.

"Don't forget that I love you! Don't forget that, Zach. Don't do anything that's gonna fuck that up."

"GOODNIGHT, ERIC!" I sternly stated.

"I'll call you in the morning," he said, as he walked out.

"Whatever," I said, as I slammed the door in his face.

I went back in my room and thought about what just happened. I do love Eric, but I need some dick.

I started to think about all the things that happened with Dwight, and the way I feel right now—*oh, God, be with me.*

I thought about calling Dwight to see *what's up,* but I couldn't get the courage to do it.

"Ok," I told myself.

If Dwight calls me with some crazy shit tonight, then I'm gonna put it out there and get the dick that supposed to be mines.

*Yep…that's exactly what I'm gonna do.*

# 79

## Zach

*Friday, September 26, 2003*

I saw Dwight heading for the charter bus, but he didn't have any luggage with him. When he stepped on the bus and reached our seat, he asked, "How did you get to campus?"

"I rode with Kris. He spent the night with Micah."

"Oh, ok."

"Where's your stuff?" I asked, checking the time. It was a little after six in the morning.

"It's in my car," he replied.

"You're gonna drive up there?" I asked.

"Yeah, Shawty. My mom called last night and told me that they were going out of town today. My brother is going on a band trip to South Carolina and I'ma have the house to myself. So, I'ma drive so I can get around town since nobody is there to pick me up," he stated.

"Shit, that's what's up," I said.

"Soooo, get your shit so you can ride with me," Dwight commanded.

"You ain't gotta tell me twice," I smiled, as I got off the bus.

"I think I'ma follow the band so we can get inside the Georgia Dome for practice," Dwight said.

"That's fine," I said. "But can we go get something to eat first because I'm hungry."

"Ight," Dwight said, as we got in his car and left campus.

I was tired and once we actually got rolling, I was knocked out. When we stopped at one of the rest stations, Dwight woke me up so we could get our allocations for the weekend. They gave us forty-four dollars this trip. When we got back in the car, I went back to sleep. The next thing I knew we were in Atlanta at the Georgia Dome.

I wasn't a big fan of out of town practices, but it was something that we did on every trip. I did, however, like practice at the Georgia Dome because we were limited to only one hour. Once that hour was up, we were free to do whatever we wanted.

When practice was over, the band went to the CNN Center for lunch; I rode with Dwight to his house. I hadn't been here since last year's Atlanta Classic when they threw the BBQ for him.

"What are you thinking about?" Dwight asked when we got inside the house.

"When we came here last year," I said.

"Oh, my family is crazy," he said, as he started laughing.

"Yeah, they are, but you had us laughing, too," I said.

"I did?"

"Yeah, you did."

"What did I do?"

"Oh, so you acting dumb now?" I said. "You don't remember Shayla?"

"Oh, whatever, nigga," he said.

"Umm, hmm," I said, as I thought back to when we met Shayla. That was one ugly girl, but he fucked the shit out of her. I'll never forget standing at the door with my freshmen brothers listening to Dwight lay the dick. We were so dumb last year, listening to that.

My attention was brought to my phone. My friend from high school was calling. I answered and he said, "What's up, Zach?"

"What's good, Jordan?" I replied.

"Aye, are you in Atlanta? I know the classic is this weekend."

"Yeah, I'm up here at my homeboy house," I said.

"Shit, see if he wanna come out and eat or something. I would love to get up with you again. I haven't seen you since we graduated," Jordan said.

"Hold on," I said, as I called Dwight's name.

"Sup?" Dwight said.

"Are we 'bout to do something?" I asked.

"No, not really," he said. "Why?"

"One of my friends from high school lives in Atlanta and I wanna get up with him for lunch."

# Life of a College Bandsman 2: Is This Love

"That's what's up. Is it room for me?" he asked.

"Yeah, nigga," I said.

"Ight, just see where he wants to meet and what time and we can head over there," Dwight said.

"Yo, Jordan, he says it's cool," I said, as I came back to the phone.

*****

# *Eric*

Ever since that night Zach kicked me out, a lot of shit has been going through my mind. I know he didn't cheat on me because I stayed at his house, in my car, until about five the next morning. I didn't know what else to do. It's just I can't keep an eye on him all the time and I can't give him what he wants. I think I can, but I just get disgusted at the thought of it. I have been trying, in my mind, to get it straight, but I guess I need to put it into action to see if I can really do it.

That happened about three days ago. Zach still doesn't want me to stay at the house. So, despite how I feel about it, I respect his wishes. That shit was a slap in my fucking face when he told me to leave. Hopefully, he comes around and lets me back in. I miss him.

I checked the time and exhaled. I was ready to go. I walked in Amir's room and asked, "Are you ready?"

"Yeah, man, I'm coming right now," Amir stated.

Once we were in his car, I said, "You shouldn't have had that ass out so late last night."

"I had to catch this nut," he said.

"Umm, hmm."

"You just take yo' ass to sleep," Amir said. "I know that's what you're gonna do anyway."

"Whatever," I chuckled. "You just make sure that you get us to Atlanta safely."

"I got this, man!" Amir said as we left the apartment, headed for Atlanta.

*****

# *Morgan*

My little brother and I had been on the road for about an hour, headed to Atlanta for the FAMU/Tennessee State football game. We still had another three hours to go. We had spent majority of the hour talking about his situation with Kris and that girl, Rozi. Micah changed the subject and said, "So, is everything ok now with you and Devin?"

"Yeah, Devin and me are getting back on good terms," I replied, keeping my focus on the road.

"That's good," Micah stated. "You even seem different."

"How is that?" I asked.

"Your presence is different. You just seem like a better man," Micah said.

"I've been trying my hardest to do the right things," I said. "Ever since that night Devin left, I haven't done anything wrong. I've been faithful to him. I love that man, Micah."

"Just how I love Kris," he stated.

"Yeah. I like Kris," I said. "He seems like a good dude, bruh."

"He really is," Micah said. "That's why I was tripping out when I found out that ole girl was pregnant. I mean it was bad enough that I cheated on him, but the girl came up pregnant, too."

"I've done a lot of shit—and I mean a lot—but I ain't made no babies and I've had my fair share of pussy."

"Not to dwell back on it, but I'm just happy that I don't have to worry about that anymore," Micah stated.

"Have you talked to Raidon lately?" I asked.

"Not really," Micah said. "He be too busy with that school shit."

"Well, he ain't that damn busy," I said, glancing at my brother.

"Why you say that?" Micah asked.

"I've been trying to get in contact with him to chill or whatever. Every single time I call I either get voicemail or he tells me that he's busy and he will call me back," I explained.

"Same thing with me," Micah said.

"Yeah, but I decided to take a trip to his house one night to surprise him. But when I got there he wasn't there. I didn't drive my car; I drove Devin's car. As I was getting ready to leave, I saw him getting ready to turn down the street, so I drove in the opposite direction to make a U-turn. When I got back to his house, some younger boy was with him. He looks like he can play football or something," I said.

"Really?"

"Yeah, man, so I called him to see what he was gonna say and he told me again that he was busy with work. I wanted to knock on the door and expose his ass. Raidon ass fucks with dudes just like me, you and RJ," I said.

"Damn, I guess we all got that damn gene from pops," Micah said.

"It sure seems that way," I sighed, as I turned up the music.

# 80

## *Zach*

*Atlanta, Georgia*

I turned to Dwight and said, "See, this is why I couldn't live in Atlanta."

"Why is that?" Dwight asked.

"It takes too damn long to get into the city."

"That's because nobody really lives in Atlanta, everybody lives on the outskirts," Dwight said, as his phone started to ring. "Hello? What's up, Amir?"

*"Amir?"* I said to myself. *Where the fuck do I know that name from?*

"Yeah, man we're here," Dwight said.

*"OH, SHIT!"* I said to myself, as I realized I met Amir as Eric's roommate.

"Ight, then, get at me, Amir," Dwight said, as he hung up the phone.

I turned to Dwight and asked, "Who is Amir?"

"That's my other best friend," Dwight said.

"He goes to FAMU?" I asked.

"Yeah," Dwight stated.

"Is he tall and dark skinned?" I asked.

"Yeah," Dwight said, as he looked at me with suspicion.

"And he's from Atlanta?" I asked.

"Yeah. We went to high school together. Dallis, that plays trumpet, is his brother," Dwight said.

"The same Dallis that tried to suck your dick?" I asked.

"Yeah, the same Dallis," Dwight sighed. "Why are you asking me all these questions about Amir? You know him?"

"I met him once. If we're talking about the same person, he's Eric's roommate," I said.

"Wow, I've been to Amir house a few times and I've never met any of his roommates. He usually comes over to my crib though. So, that means that Quinton is his roommate, too?" Dwight asked.

"Yep," I said. "All three of them are roommates."

"Damn," Dwight said, as we arrived at the restaurant on time, at three o'clock. "It is really a small fucking world."

"Yeah, it is," I sighed.

"So, about this friend of yours," Dwight said, as we got out of the car.

"Jordan."

"Yeah, Jordan. Did y'all fuck around, too?" Dwight asked.

"JORDAN WASHINGTON!" I said, as I saw him come around the corner. I ignored Dwight's statement.

"What's going on, Zach," he said, as he walked over to me. He was still sexy as hell. Tall, brown, athletic. He definitely gained a lot of muscle mass working out in the military.

"What's good?" Jordan said, as he shook Dwight's hand.

"Jordan, this is my best friend, Dwight. Dwight, this is my boy, Jordan," I said.

"Nice to meet you," Jordan said.

"Same here," Dwight said, as he stared at Jordan.

"Damn, fool," I said, as we walked in the restaurant. "You've put on some muscle."

"Shit, that's what the military does to your ass," he said. "But you have, too."

"I told Zach he put on some muscle weight," Dwight chimed in.

"Shit, you have," Jordan said.

"So, how has everything been?" I asked.

"Everything is cool," Jordan said. "Since I left the military, I've started going to school, trying to get back on the right track. You know I was fucked up after everything happened."

"Yeah, we all were," I said.

"What happened?" Dwight asked.

"I'll explain it to you later. It's too much right now," I said.

"Yeah, not now," Jordan pleaded.

"So, what else has been new?" I asked.

"Shit, I just need to get back down to Orlando. You know Christian's brother, Cordell, and my sister, Jamie, is graduating this year," Jordan added.

"Damn, they're seniors already," I said in disbelief.

"Yeah, time is moving. Have you seen Christian's twin sister, Cat, up in Tally? She lives there. She looks just like him," Jordan said.

"Naw, I haven't seen her, but I'm sure our paths will cross one day. Tally ain't but so big," I said.

"Yeah, ain't that the truth," Jordan said, as he looked at the menu.

The entire time we were at the restaurant, Dwight didn't say much; he was very observant. I know he was gonna have some questions at a later point. That's just how he was.

*****

# *Micah*

As we reached the hotel, I asked Morgan, "So, are you gonna stay at the hotel with the band?"

"Yeah, I'm gonna chill out with Devin. He says that the drum majors sleep two-to-a room compared to the four-to-a-room that the regular band members have. He said that Ian is in his room, so it would be ok for me to chill with him," Morgan said.

"Oh, are you gonna come to our hotel at all?" I asked.

"Probably not," Morgan said. "You can take Kris and spend that time with him."

"That's what's up," I said, as Morgan got out the car.

I got out and moved over to the driver's seat and called Kris.

"What's up, baby?" Kris answered.

"Yo, do you wanna stay with me in our hotel?" I asked.

"What about your brother?"

"He's gonna stay in the hotel with Devin and Ian," I said.

"Oh, shit. Hell yeah I wanna stay with you! Where you at?" Kris asked.

"Outside. I just dropped Morgan off," I said.

"Ok, let me get my shit. We've gotta be at the parade site at nine in the morning though," Kris stated.

"That's cool, baby. Just come on," I said.

"Ok."

When he got to the car, I gave him as kiss and we took off. I said,

"I wanna go to the mall for a second."

"Ight," Kris said.

When we got to the mall, it was a lot of people there. We walked around and went from store-to-store. I brought Kris some new shoes and I picked myself up a new outfit.

"I've gotta use the bathroom," Kris said, as we approached a rest area.

"Ight," I said, as I took a seat.

*"Damn, it's a lot of people in here,"* I said to myself, as I waited for Kris to come out.

"MICAH! MICAH HARRIS!"

*"Oh, shit,"* I said to myself, as I recognized that voice even before I turned around to see who it was.

"I KNOW YOU HEAR ME!" Rozi said, as she walked in front of me.

"What's up, Rozi?" I said, looking around for Kris. *This is not what I needed. She had to go before Kris showed back up. There's no telling what might come out of her mouth. Oh, boy. I'm so fucked.*

"What are you doing here?" she asked.

"I'm here for the classic," I said.

"Oh, ok. I guess, Micah," she said.

"Ight, ba--," Kris said, as he walked out the bathroom. He stopped in mid-sentence when he saw Rozi.

My heart was beating profusely fast.

"Oh, what's up," he said to her. I know she knew he was gonna say *baby* because I heard it coming out his mouth.

"How are you?" she said. She turned to me and replied, "Micah, who is this?"

"Oh… umm… this is Kris," I said.

"Kris, umm, hmm," she said, as she looked at him.

Kris looked over at me with a curious look on his face.

I forced a fake smile.

*Oh, God. Please don't let this girl get my ass in trouble…*

# 81

## *Amir*

As I paid for my new shoes, Eric said, "When we leave here, I wanna go see my sister."

"Ight, we can go see your sister," I said, as we left Foot Locker.

"You hungry?" Eric asked.

"Yeah, let's stop by the food court on the way out," I said.

"It's a lot of damn people in here," Eric said, as we navigated through the mall.

"Yeah, it is," I said. "A lot more than usual, but I guess the game has something to do with that."

"So, how far you stay from here?" Eric asked.

"About twenty-five minutes," I added. "My mom is looking forward to meeting you."

"Yeah, I am, too," Eric said, as he looked at his phone.

*That is not who I think it is,* I said to myself, as I saw Rozi off in a distance talking to a dude.

"Yo, let's go back this way," I said to Eric, as I tried to get him to turn around.

Eric said, "Why? The food court is this way. Nigga I'm hungry."

I didn't say anything as we continued our journey. The closer we got to Rozi, the more I wanted to turn around. I didn't feel like seeing her right now.

"ROZI?" Eric said, startling me.

"How do you know Rozi?" I asked, confused.

"Nigga, that's my sister! How the fuck you know her?" Eric asked, as he looked at me.

"ERIC!" Rozi yelled, as she ran over and hugged him. She looked at me and said, "Amir?" She stared at us then looked at me and said, "How do you know my brother?"

"He's my roommate," I said.

"Oh, wow," she said.

Eric looked at the rest of the group and said, "Kris and Micah, how do y'all know my sister?"

Kris said, "I'm just here with Micah. Micah is one of her friends."

"Isn't Morgan your brother?" I asked Micah, thinking back to the night I passed him walking out of Morgan's house as I walked in.

"Yeah, he is," Micah said, as he looked at me strangely. He quickly turned his attention to Eric and said in disbelief, "Rozi is your sister?"

"Yes," Eric replied.

"How do y'all know each other?" Rozi asked Eric.

"He's Zach's roommate," Eric replied.

"HE is Zach's roommate—HE is as in MICAH?" Rozi stated, as she pointed to Micah.

"Yeah," Eric said.

*This is fucking crazy. Just one big ass circle.*

"How do you know Amir?" Eric asked Rozi.

"I met him a long time ago at some event," Rozi said to Eric, brushing him off.

"Oh, ok," Eric said, as he looked at me. I know he's thinking something else. I can tell by the look on his face.

*"I was fucking Eric's sister,"* I said to myself in shock.

"Are you ok?" Rozi asked me.

"Yeah, I'm fine," I said. "Just processing everything."

"Hell, that makes two of us," she said.

"Ight, y'all, I'm hungry, so I'll get up with y'all later," Eric said, as he hugged Rozi.

"Call me so we can get up, Eric," she said.

"Ight, Sis."

"Ight, y'all," I said, as I left with Eric.

I sighed as we headed for the food court.

Damn, that shit was close—too close. Micah could have put my ass out there, as well as Rozi. Thank God nothing happened.

*Whew.*

\*\*\*\*\*

# Life of a College Bandsman 2: Is This Love

# Rozi McDaniel

As I joined my girlfriend at the table, she said, "Damn girl, what took you so long? Your food is probably cold now."

"They must think I'm crazy," I said.

"Who, girl?"

"Girl, I just saw my brother and he was with Amir," I said.

"Amir? The boy who got you pregnant?"

"Yes, girl. Amir and my brother are roommates."

"GET OUTTA HERE!"

"I'm serious. And how about this—the boy who I had sex with who I told was the baby father, the one who sent the money up for the abortion—"

"What about him?" my friend said.

"Girl, he's in here, too. We were all just together. They all know each other."

"Bitch, stop lying!"

"Girl, do I look like I'm lying," I said, exhaling.

"Damn, you are serious."

"Bitch, it gets worse. Micah is Zach's roommate."

"Who is Zach?" she asked. "I don't remember that name."

"Zach is my brother's boyfriend," I said.

"HOLD UP—didn't you say your brother said that Zach's roommate be fucking all night long and shit?"

"Yeah," I replied, sipping on my sweet tea.

"But I thought you said that your brother said that Zach's roommate was gay."

"That's what Eric said," I stated.

"So, you're telling me Micah is gay?"

"Yes, girl. But wait, it gets better!"

"There's more?" she said in disbelief.

"Micah's boyfriend was there with him. Initially, Micah was waiting on his boyfriend to come out of the bathroom. That's when I saw Micah by himself. When the boyfriend came out the bathroom, he started to say *'Ight, baby'* or something to that level, but when he saw me standing there, he stopped mid-sentence. His boyfriend looked familiar though. I think I know him from back home."

"You know him from Florida?"

"I think so," I sighed. "I know that face from somewhere."

"Girl, this is just too much tea for me," my friend said, as she got up from the table. "My cup has overfloweth!"

"Bitch, tell me about it!"

# 82

## *Zach*

Dwight stepped in the room, fresh out of the shower and said, "You straight?"

"Yeah. I'm just thinking about a lot of shit."

"Something that Jordan said earlier?" Dwight asked.

"Yeah, that and some other stuff," I said.

"Oh, so tell me this," Dwight said, as he sat down on the bed in a black beater and some red basketball shorts.

"What's that?"

"What happened back in high school?" Dwight said.

"Oh," I said as I took a deep breath and prepared to tell Dwight what happened with my classmate, Christian Goodley, who was Jordan's best friend. That situation was truly *Crimes of the Heart*.

"Wow," Dwight said, as I finished my story. "That shit is fucked up."

"Yeah, tell me about it," I sighed.

"Dang, man," Dwight said. "I don't know what I would have done."

"Yeah, but enough of that. Let me go take a shower," I said.

The entire time in the shower, I couldn't help but think about what could happen. Finally, all the elements were in our favor. Eric was with Amir at Amir's house. Dwight's parents were out of town. Dwight's little brother was on a band trip to South Carolina and Peanut wasn't here to fuck it up. We had this house to ourselves and if something was to happen, it would be tonight.

"Damn," I said, as I grabbed my hard dick. "You can't get scared now, Zach. It's time to man up."

I turned the shower on cold as I stepped out the shower and went into my bag. I pulled out my cleaning materials and prepared to clean out my insides. If tonight was gonna be the night Dwight and I get together, I needed to be ready. Once I did that, I turned the water back to hot and I got back in the shower to wash off again.

"YOU ALRIGHT IN THERE?" Dwight yelled through the door.

"YEAH," I said, as I turned the water off. I had been in there for a lil minute.

As I put lotion on my body, I thought about everything and the consequences of my actions if this were to happen.

"If Eric would just give me what I want, then this wouldn't even be an option," I tried to convince myself.

After I thought about things more, I put my boxers and my shirt back into my bag. I only slipped on my basketball shorts. I wanted Dwight to see my body; I wanted him to have easy access.

"Ight, Zach," I said to myself, as I prepared to step out the bathroom. "There's no turning back now."

"Bout time, nigga," Dwight said, as he looked at me as I came out the shower.

*"Ight, Zach, control it,"* I said to myself. I felt my dick getting hard and being that I didn't have anything on my body but my basketball shorts, it was easy to see. Especially being that my dick isn't small.

Dwight was walking around in his tank-top and boxer briefs. While I was in the shower, he managed to take off his basketball shorts. I remembered Dwight saying last year when we were freshmen, on the Miami trip, that he couldn't sleep in anything but his boxers.

This time was different though, much different. Everything about Dwight was different. The mood was different. This was a different Zach and well as a different Dwight, and it was obvious.

*"Control it, Zach,"* I said to myself, as I looked at the print of his dick when he stood up.

"You straight, man?" Dwight asked, as he walked past me.

"Yeah, I'm good," I said, as I put my bag down. When I turned back around, he was sitting on the bed looking at me.

He grabbed his phone and I said in reference to his brother, "So, both of y'all sleep in here?"

"Yeah, that's his bed right there," Dwight pointed to it, as he placed his phone back down.

# Life of a College Bandsman 2: Is This Love

"Oh, ok," I said.

"I don't mean to be mean, but he told me not to put anyone on his bed. Ced is real picky about his shit," Dwight said. "So, either you can sleep in my bed with me or you can sleep on the floor. You can't sleep on the couch; my momma would have a fit."

"I'm not sleeping on the floor," I said. "I guess the bed it is."

"That's what's up," Dwight said, as he stood up and walked out the room.

A few moments later, he yelled from the other room, "YO, BIG Z!"

"What's up?" I said, making my way into the other room.

"Play this with me," he said, as he threw me the joystick.

"Ight," I said, as I took it and had a seat and prepared to play NBA LIVE 2002. 2003 hadn't come out yet."

We played that game for a few hours and I won most of the games.

"We need to get in the bed," Dwight said, as he turned the TV off. "We've got a long day tomorrow."

"Yeah, I know," I said, as I walked back into his room.

Dwight stayed out in the common area for a second. I guess he was making sure that all the doors were locked.

"You ok, Shawty?" Dwight asked, when he walked back into the room.

"Yeah, what side you want?" I asked.

"I always sleep on this side," Dwight said, as he went to the side of the bed closest to the window.

Dwight walked back around, closed and locked the door to his room. He shut off the ceiling light, leaving on only his lamp light.

"Goodnight, freshman bruh," Dwight said, as he shut off the lamp and got in the bed.

"Goodnight," I said, as I turned on my side with my back facing him.

A few minutes later, I felt Dwight moving under the cover.

"You straight?" I asked.

"Yeah, just getting comfortable," he said. He had turned on his side. Now we were both back-to-back.

I was nervous as shit. I couldn't sleep as that shit was the last thing on my mind.

A few minutes later, Dwight turned back around. I could tell that he was on his side still, but my back was now to his chest, my ass to his dick.

"You sleep?" he quietly asked.

"Naw."

"What you thinking about?" he asked.

"A lot of everything," I said.

"Oh," he said.

"Yeah, what you thinking about?" I asked.

He didn't say anything.

"Did you hear me?" I asked.

"Yeah, I heard you," he said.

"So?"

"I'm thinking about a lot of shit. A lot of shit is going through my mind."

"Shit like what?" I asked.

"How I'm falling for somebody, but they're to engaged in other shit to see it," Dwight said.

"Oh," I said.

"Yeah," he replied.

It got quiet for a few minutes.

"You sleep?" he said again.

"No," I replied.

"Can I stretch my arm out? It's hurting like this," he said.

"Yeah, it's your bed," I said.

"Ight, lift your head up," he said.

"Yeah," I said, lifting my head.

"Ight, you're cool," Dwight said, as I put my head back down, resting inside of Dwight arms. I was even more nervous than before.

After a long time of just lying there, my body finally fell asleep.

When I woke up, Dwight was right on me, with his arms wrapped around me. His head laid on my head.

"You ok?" he said. I guess he felt that I was awake.

"Yeah," I said, as I had to take in the moment for what it was. I felt his dick on my ass and it wasn't soft. I immediately got hard. "Are you ok?" I softly asked.

"Yeah, I'm good," he said, as he kissed me on the neck.

*DID HE JUST KISS ME?*

"You ok?" he asked.

"Yeah."

"Ok," he said, as he kissed me again on my neck. He held me a lil tighter this time around.

# Life of a College Bandsman 2: Is This Love

I couldn't believe this was happening.

"Yo, Shawty," he softly said.

"Yeah?"

"Why we playing with each other?" he said, as he took his fingers and gently ran them up and down my arm.

"I don't know."

"How long has this shit been going on?" he asked.

"Too long," I replied.

"I love yo' ass and I know you love me," Dwight said. "I know you were feeling me that day we met at band camp before we came to FAMU."

"Yeah, I was," I said.

"So, why *are* we playing with each other, huh?"

"I don't know."

"Look, I've never felt this way about no other dude before, but this shit just feels right. Being with you just feels right and I can't hide that shit no more," Dwight said. "I love your ass, Zach."

"I love you, too."

"Turn around," Dwight said.

We were looking each other dead in the eyes.

He said, "I'm scared, Zach."

"I'm scared, too, Dwight, but this is where we belong."

"I know," he said, as he leaned down and started to French kiss me.

We kissed for what seemed like an eternity; I ended up on top of him.

I pulled his tank top off, licking and touching his rock hard body. When I got to his love area. I took my time. I wanted to enjoy every single second of this.

I pulled his boxer briefs down, exposing his hard dick.

"Damn," I said, as I finally saw Dwight's dick in the flesh.

"I take it you like it," he said.

"Hell, yeah," I said, as I touched it. That shit was big. It had to be about ten inches, and it was thick as fuck! His shit stood straight up. It was just perfect with that damn mushroom head.

I slowly licked the head of his penis causing him to exhale. Once I got it wet enough and took the courage to take all of Dwight into my mouth, I went for the kill. I took a deep breath, and put his dick in my mouth.

"Shit, Shawty, do that shit," he said passionately.

I opened wider, allowing inch-by-inch of his dick to enter my mouth. I let my oral skills please him. Every time I took his dick to the back of my throat, Dwight said, "FUCK, SHAWTY!" Listening to him caused me to work even harder on pleasing him. I wanted this experience, his first time with a man, to be something that he would never forget.

"DAMN, SHAWTY," Dwight stated.

I knew this is where I was supposed to be.

"Hold up," Dwight said, as he got off the bed. "Take off your shorts."

"Ight," I said, as I slid out of them.

"Damn, that ass is bigger than I imagined," Dwight said, as he slapped me on my ass. "Get on the bed," he commanded. "On all fours."

I did as I was told.

"SHIT," Dwight said, pulling my ass cheeks a part. "Damn, Shawty. This shit is phat!"

He leaned down and started to place kisses on my ass. Soon after, he started to lick around my hole.

"FUCK!" I screamed in intense pleasure.

For about ten minutes, he continued to please me by eating my hole, causing me to moan in ecstasy. If I didn't know any better, I would think that he has done this before.

He turned me around and started to play with my dick. He leaned down and start to suck on my dick. I could tell that was his first time doing that.

"Ight, baby," I said, as I pulled him off my dick.

He walked over to his brother's dresser and pulled out a Magnum XL condom and some lube. I turned back over on all fours. I felt something cold and wet drip down my ass. He took his finger and ran the lube around my hole. Once he felt that it was lubed up enough, he took is finger and inserted it in me.

I hissed at his entry. He took his finger out, put some lube at the tip of his right index finger and re-entered my body.

"Relax. I got you," he said.

He inserted another, his middle finger. Soon, he pulled both of them out.

A few seconds later, I heard the condom rip open. I turned my head to the side and he was putting the condom on his dick.

"Damn, I know this shit gonna feel good," Dwight said, as he put some lube on the condom and placed his dick at my entrance.

*"TGHT, ZACH,"* I said to myself, as I prepared to take Dwight. *"RELAX."*

He started to slowly enter his dick inside, but my hole wasn't ready. He started to finger me some more trying to open it up. A few minutes later, he tried again. It still didn't work.

"Get on the bed," I commanded.

When he got on the bed, I got on top of him. I faced him. I wanted to see his facial expression as my body pleased his body.

I lined his dick up at my hole and prepared to sit on it. I went slow, letting my body get used to his size.

"DAMN, YOU TIGHT AS FUCK!" he yelled, as his eyes closed.

I went up and down on his dick, each time going a little deeper. I liked it this way because I could control how the dick was being entered and I could stop if the pain was becoming too much.

After a few minutes, Dwight was fully inside of me and I started to really ride his dick.

"OH, SHIT!" he yelled, as I caught a rhythm on his dick. "Do that shit, man. Do that shit."

Words couldn't describe how I felt at this moment in time.

Soon, I started to let my sexual appetite consume by body and my pain turned into pleasure. Once Dwight realized that I was fully ready and relaxed, told me to get up and get back on all fours. When I did that, he inserted his dick back inside and he started to really work his love muscle. I felt every inch of him as he thrusted inside of me.

"Shit...shit...shit," I said, as he worked on me. That shit felt so fucking good. Dwight worked this position for about ten minutes. He flipped me over and prepared to enter me in the missionary position.

"Fuckkk," I lustfully said, as he started to work me again. "Damn, this shit feels so good!" Looking at Dwight get pleasure out of fucking me took me places.

Dwight went for broke as he fucked the shit out of me. His sweat was dripping down from his body. I looked up at him. He was biting his bottom lip while he was looking back at me, all while continuing to work my ass.

He flipped me back over to the doggy-style position and let my ass have it. In this position, his dick found my prostate and started to please it. Minutes later, I felt my balls tighten up.

"I'm cumin!" I screamed.

"Umm, hmm, catch that nut, Shawty," he said.

"Shhitttttttttt, aw fuck!" I yelled, as my dick erupted and I came all on his sheets.

Simultaneously, he yelled, "I'm cumin," as he released his seed deep in his condom, deep inside of my bowels.

"Damn, I love yo' ass," he said, as he pulled out.

"I love you, too," I said.

"So, that thing with Eric is done, right? You're with me now, right?"

"Yeah, I'm with you now," I said.

"Good," he said as he reached down as kissed me. "Let's go shower."

# Part Five:
## Love Hurts

# 83

## *Zach*

I turned over and said, "Good morning, Baby."

"Good morning. It's nice to see you in a good mood," he said to me.

"I'm always in a good mood," I replied.

"Whatever," he said, as he starting laughing and got out of the bed.

When he went into the bathroom, I thought about things. I thought about the things that I needed to do—we needed to do—to make this work.

"You ok?" he asked, when he came back out.

"Yeah, I'm just thinking," I said.

"Thinking about last night?"

"Yeah, thinking about last night," I replied.

"YO, ZACH YOU UP?" I heard Micah say, as he came to my room.

"Yeah, I'm up," I said, as I walked over and opened the door.

"Yo, I really gotta holla at you," Micah said, as he stepped in the room.

"What's up, Micah?"

"Oh, what's up? I didn't know you were here. You spent the night?" Micah asked my boyfriend.

"Yeah, I came in last night. I guess you were sleep," he said.

"Yeah, I went to bed early last night. I had to catch up from my lack of sleep in Atlanta," Micah said.

"Shit, I feel you. Atlanta was loose!" my dude said.

"I bet it was," Micah said, as he turned his attention back to me.

"What you got to holla at me 'bout?" I asked.

"Yo, I think I will get at you later about it. I'll let y'all have some time together," Micah said, as he walked back to the door.

"Ight then, Micah," I said.

"Ight, Micah," my boyfriend said.

"Ight, y'all. Be safe," Micah said, as he closed the door.

"He seemed a little shocked to see me."

"Yeah, he did," I said. "He'll be ok though."

"And he will," he said, as he came over and gave me a kiss. I wanted to push it further, but he said, "C'mon, baby. I gotta get to class."

I sighed, "Ight, let me hop in the shower and I will be on my way."

"Ight."

*Umm, hmm, catch that nut, Shawty," he said.*

*"Shhittttttttt, aw fuck!" I yelled, as my dick erupted and I came all on his sheets.*

*Simultaneously, he yelled, "I'm cumin," as he released his seed deep in his condom, deep inside of my bowels.*

*"Damn, I love yo' ass," he said, as he pulled out.*

*"I love you, too," I said.*

*"So that thing with Eric is done, right? You're with me now, right?"*

*"Yeah, I'm with you now," I said.*

*"Good," he said as he reached down as kissed me. "Let's go shower."*

"WOW," I said to myself as I got in the shower. "That shit was mad crazy. Mad crazy."

*****

# *Rozi*

I still couldn't believe that shit that I saw in the mall.

How in the world was my brother and the real father of my baby roommates? I told Eric a long time ago that I couldn't tell him who the guy was because he might have known him, but who would have thought that he was his fucking roommate. They seemed kinda close, and if Eric was to find out that I was fucking Amir, then that might mess up their friendship. I don't wanna have anything to do with that.

And then Micah—who would have thought his ass was gay? I know I didn't. That shit is still bothering me.

"Let me just get confirmation from him first," I said, as I picked up the phone to call Micah.

"Hello?"

"Hey, Micah," I said.

"What's up, Rozi?" he said agitated.

"You don't sound too happy to hear from me," I said.

"I'm just on my way to class," he said. "What's up?"

"Can I ask you a question?" I said.

"Go ahead, Rozi."

"Are you gay?"

He didn't say anything.

"Did you hear me? I asked you were you gay?"

"Why does it matter to you?" he asked.

"Because that could have been big, Micah. How were we gonna raise a child if you were gay?"

"What I do in the privacy of my bedroom has nothing to do with how I would have raised my child," Micah said.

"So, you're telling me that you are in fact a homosexual," I stated.

"Yes, I am!" Micah sternly said.

"So, was that Kris boy your boyfriend?" I asked.

"Yes, he is," Micah stated.

"Oh, he's cute, Micah. At least you got good taste," I said.

"Are you finished? I have to get to class," he said.

"Yes, I am. Well, it was nice seeing you again. Maybe we will all get up someday and have tea."

"Whatever, Rozi," Micah said, hanging up the phone.

*This shit is crazy,* I said to myself, as I left my apartment, got in my car and started to make my way over to Spelman's campus. I rubbed my stomach and sighed. *What the fuck am I doing?* On the way to school, Eric called.

"Hey, Eric," I answered my phone.

"What's good, baby sis?"

"Nothing, heading to class," I said.

"Oh, I just got out," he said.

"Ok."

"Rozi, how do you really know Amir?"

"I told you I met him at some event a lil while ago and we just kicked it off."

"Rozi, don't lie to me," Eric said.

"I'm not lying, Eric," I said, lying.

"Was Amir the real father of that baby?" he asked.

"No. Amir is just my friend," I said, touching my stomach. I wasn't ready for Eric to know the truth yet. Hell, Amir doesn't know the truth.

"Are you sure, Rozi?" Eric asked.

"I'm positive. Amir was not the father," I said.

"Because I've been thinking and everything adds up," Eric said. "From the times that he went to Atlanta over MLK Weekend, to the random trips he took back to Atlanta during the spring semester and how he was home in Atlanta the entire summer—the pieces just seem to line up in his favor."

"Well, that is just a curse of luck, because Amir is not the dude, Eric," I said, arriving on campus.

"Ok, Rozi, if you say so. But I'ma let you go," Eric said.

"Ight, Eric, I will call you later."

"Ok, Rozi," he said, as he hung up.

As soon as I got off the phone with Eric, I called Amir.

"Answer the phone!" I said, listening to the ring tone. "Answer the damn phone!"

I hung up.

I had to let Amir know not to tell Eric that we were fucking around. Hopefully, he's already on the same page as me.

*Hopefully...*

# 84

# *Zach*

As I walked in the house after practice, I saw Micah sitting in the living room. I spoke and said, "What did you have to talk to me about?"

"You can't tell Eric," Micah said, as I grabbed a bottled water.

"Ok. What's up?"

"This shit is crazy. Real crazy," Micah said.

"What happened?" I asked.

"I was in the mall with Kris this past weekend in Atlanta. Amir, one of the dudes that Morgan was fucking was in the mall. Eric, too. *Damn, Morgan was fucking Amir? I knew his ass was gay.* I said, "Eric told me he saw y'all in the mall, but what's up?"

"Well, I saw this girl at the mall who turned out to be Eric's sister," Micah added.

"Ok, what's wrong with that?"

"Kris was with me, too," Micah said.

"Ok, I'm not following," I said.

"ZACH—ERIC'S SISTER IS THE GIRL I GOT PREGNANT!" Micah confessed.

"Are you fucking serious?" I asked, eyes wide.

"Yeah, she was standing right there next to Kris and then Eric and Amir walked up. It was crazy when I found out that was his sister."

"Damn, that shit is fucked up," I said.

"She called me today and asked me if I were gay," Micah stated.

"What did you say?" I asked.

"I told her the truth. There wasn't a need to lie. She had kinda

413

figured out that Kris was my dude when we were standing there talking," Micah said.

"Damn, this shit is crazy," I said.

"Yeah, please don't tell Eric," Micah said.

"DON'T TELL ERIC WHAT?" Eric said, as he walked in the crib.

"Nothing, baby," I said, as I kissed him.

"Is this what you had to tell him this morning, but then you saw me in the room and you couldn't because you didn't want me to know?" Eric asked.

"Yeah," Micah said. "I mean I know Zach tells you a lot of shit, but I just need this one to stay between us. It's kinda personal."

"That's understandable," Eric said, as he went to the room.

When I got in the room, Eric and I watched TV and just hung out. As the night went on, I got hungry, so I went in the kitchen and made some cheeseburgers and fries for us to eat. I couldn't clear my mind of what happened between Dwight and me in Atlanta. When I got back in the room, Eric's phone started to ring.

"What's up, Amir?" I heard Eric say. "ARE YOU SERIOUS? OK, I'M ON MY WAY," Eric said as he jumped up.

"What happened?" I asked.

"Amir said that my scores came in from the med school test and I also have a letter in the mail from Howard University," Eric said.

"They've made a decision already?" I asked.

"I guess so. We're about to find out," he said. "I'ma be right back. I'ma go get the mail then I'ma come back."

"Ok, baby," I said, as I kissed him and he ran out the house.

I was nervous for him. This was big.

After I finished the rest of my food, I went to the bathroom, cleaned out myself and hopped in the shower. When I got back out the shower Eric was sitting on the bed looking nervous.

"What did it say?" I asked.

"I haven't opened them yet," Eric said.

"Why not?" I asked.

"Because I'm scared," he said, as he handed the two letters to me. "You do it."

"Ok," I said, as I took the med school exam letter first.

I examined the score card, reading what it said.

I smiled, "Wow, baby!"

"What? How did I do?" he asked.

# Life of a College Bandsman 2: Is This Love

"Out of 36 possible points, you got a 32. This paper says that is right between a good, competitive score and a stellar score. It says that you can pretty much get into a good school."

"ARE YOU SERIOUS? I GOT A 32?" he said excited, as he took the paper. After seeing this results for himself, he ran through the house yelling, "Oh, my God. Oh, my God!"

I brought him back in the room and said, "Eric, you've still got one more letter."

"Ok," he said, as he sat down. I opened the letter from Howard University. "Based on your application, your interview and completion of your scores on the MCAT, we are pleased to conditionally accept you into the Howard University School of Medicine for the Fall 2004 Semester. You will be fully admitted into our program upon completion of a Bachelors' Degree. Below is more information—"

"Baby, I got accepted?" he said, as he looked at me.

"Yeah, Eric, you're in," I said, as I walked over and kissed him.

"DAMN!" Eric said, as he kissed me back.

Before I knew it, we were into it. Clothes had come off and we were deep into our foreplay.

"Shit, Zach," Eric said, as I took his dick into my mouth. "Damn, baby."

I was proud of my man. I wanted to make him happy because he deserved it. Soon after, we switched positions. I was now on the receiving end of the stick.

"DAMN, ERIC!" I yelled in pleasure as I heard my phone ring.

"You deserve this," Eric said, as he stopped what he was doing and walked over to my nightstand.

"What are you doing?" I asked, wondering why he stopped sucking my dick.

"Something that we should have done a long time ago," Eric said, as he grabbed the condom and lube.

"ARE YOU SERIOUS?" I asked.

"Yeah, baby," he said as he ran came down, lifted my legs and started to lick around my ass.

"Oh my, God," I said to myself. I looked down at Eric and asked, "Are you ok?"

"Yeah, baby, I'm great," he said, as he ripped the condom open and poured the lube on my ass. "Damn, I love you."

"I love you, too," I said, as I felt Eric at my entrance. "Slow, baby."

"Oh, shit. You feel so damn good," Eric said, as he slowly entered my ass in the missionary position.

"DAMN, BABY," he said again. "WHAT THE FUCK WAS WRONG WITH ME?"

He inched more of his dick inside me causing me to exhale in ecstasy. "Fuck, Eric. That feels damn good."

When he was fully inside, he paused for a second before he started to really work. A few seconds later, he started to move in and out, in and out, slapping his balls up against my ass.

"Damn, baby," I said in excitement.

"This shit feels so good," Eric said, as he continued to make love to me. "Damn, I love you, Zach."

I heard my phone ring again.

A few minutes later, we changed positions and I ended up on top of Eric. He held on to my hands as I gave him the ride of his life.

"Oh, shit!" Eric said. "Don't stop. Please, don't stop!"

In between our love making, I'd lean down and kiss him. That shit only made the night more magical. We ended up in the doggy style position with Eric beating the fuck out of my ass. I know he was getting close because his breathing became more intense all while he picked up the pace.

"SHIT, BABY I'M BOUT TO NUT!" he yelled, as he made one last plow into my guts. I felt his body shake which caused me to shoot my nut as well. When all the excitement died down, he rested his body on top of mine.

"Damn, that shit was great!" he said.

"Yeah, it was," I said. "See, it wasn't that bad."

"No, it wasn't," he said. "I don't know what my problem was. I just hope you can handle this shit 'cause we've got to play catch up for all the time we've missed."

"Shit, you ain't said nothing but a word," I said, as Eric lifted himself off me and went to the bathroom.

"You coming?" he asked, as he peeped his head out the bathroom.

"Yeah, I'm coming," I said, as I walked over to my phone. I had three missed calls. *"What does he want?"* I asked myself, as I made my way to shower with my baby.

*****

# Life of a College Bandsman 2: Is This Love

# *Dwight*

I really enjoyed myself with Zach this past weekend. We really had a festive time and we bonded on a totally different level.

The more time I spend with Zach, the more I realize how much I need this dude in my life. Zach is a different kind of dude and I like that shit.

That nigga respects me for the person that I am, flaws and all. That's why I chill with that nigga.

I know he needs to drop that pussy ass nigga, Eric. I don't see what Zach sees in that bitch nigga. I wanna fuck Eric and Chaz asses up so bad. Both of those niggas foul as hell.

I wanted—I needed—to hear his voice, so I picked up my phone to call him again but he didn't answer.

*What the fuck that nigga doing?*

I really needed to holla at him. I have something important to say. I waited a few more minutes and tried him again. That was the fifth time I've called and got no answer.

"I know Eric ain't fucking him, so what the fuck he doing?" I asked myself, as I felt on my hard dick.

"One more time," I said, as I called Zach again. No answer.

"Oh, well," I said, as I called my *other* friend.

"What's up, Dwight?"

"I wanna get up again," I said.

"Right now?"

"Yeah, right now!" I said.

"Ok, let me get in the shower then you can come through."

"How long is it gonna take?" I asked.

"You can come in like thirty."

"Ight, I'll be there," I said.

"Ight."

I called Zach again. No answer.

*Damn, Zach. What the fuck are you doing?*

"Oh, well, I guess I'll get him later," I said, as I prepared to go fuck the shit out of my *other* friend.

# 85

# *Zach*

*Wednesday, October 22, 2003*
*Homecoming Week*

Life has taken a turn for the best—kind of. Things are going really good right now. It has been about three weeks since the Atlanta trip and things are progressing quite well— sort of.

My mind has been all over the place. I don't know what to believe and what not to believe anymore.

Ever since Eric and I had sex, it has been a nonstop thing. That fool wants it all times of the day. It was cute at first, but damn boy, calm down a bit.

Dwight is still pissed at me because I didn't break off things with Eric, but he will be alright. It ain't like he's giving me the dick—or is he?

This was the most dreaded week of weeks—homecoming. All we did was practice. I hated this shit.

"Yo," Jared said, as he called the upperclassmen over. "Tonight at eleven-thirty, we're gonna start the process to cross the freshmen."

"We beating ass?" another upperclassman asked, being stupid.

Jared ignored that statement and said, "Peanut is gonna be the Dean of Pledges for the 2003 class. Please be on time."

"Peanut is the D.P.?" another upperclassman asked, upset.

"That's what I said," Jared replied.

"Where are we gonna meet?" Dwight asked.

"At the usual spot," Jared said. "Any more questions?"

Nobody responded, so Jared said, "Ight, I'll see y'all at eleven-thirty."

When I turned around, Chaz was standing on the sideline talking to Devin, Ian and some of the other drum majors. I hadn't talked to Chaz in a while. He was still looking damn good.

Dwight interrupted my thoughts when he said, "You're not about to talk to that nigga are you?"

"I can be cordial to the man. We were close this time last year."

"You never seem to amaze me," Dwight said, as he shook his head.

"Hey, Zach," Chaz said, as I approached him. "What's up, Dwight?"

"Sup, man?" Dwight said.

"What's going, Chaz? I haven't seen you in a minute," I said.

"I'm just trying to get it done. I've been extremely busy with the kids and grad school. Life is kinda hectic right now, but I'm just trying my best to do the best I can."

"Shit, I feel you on that. I think I'm so stressed, I don't even know what to believe," I said.

"What do you mean by that?" Chaz asked.

"My mind is all fucked up," I said, as I looked at Dwight. "I don't know what to believe sometimes."

"Damn, that's crazy, lil nigga," Chaz said.

*Damn, he hasn't called me lil nigga in a long ass time. I loved the way he used to say that shit.*

I smiled and said, "It's good to hear that you and Eric are back on good terms."

"Yeah, you know after *that night,* things went downhill for us. But everything worked itself out. I love my cousin. Despite what happened, I'm happy to have him back in my life," Chaz said.

"That's good to hear. It sounds as if you have really moved on with your life," I said.

"Yeah, it was hard but sometimes you just gotta face facts and takes things are they are," he said.

"I feel you on that shit," I said.

"Yeah."

"Well, it was nice seeing you again," I said.

"Same here, lil nigga. Take care of yourself," Chaz said.

"I will and you do the same," I said, walking away with Dwight.

"I still don't like that nigga," Dwight stated, as we approached his car.

# Life of a College Bandsman 2: Is This Love

"Dwight, who exactly do you like?" I asked, getting inside the car.

"Nobody that's gonna fuck yo' ass over," he said.

"I guess."

"And why are you still with Eric's bitch ass? I've told you on numerous occasions to let that nigga go," Dwight said.

"Yeah, but," I said.

"But nothing, Zach. You're gonna do what the fuck you want anyway, so there's no need for me to keep talking," he said, as he turned up the radio.

"Oh well... he will be alright," I said to myself, as I thought back to Atlanta:

*"Yo, Shawty," he softly said.*

*"Yeah?"*

*"Why we playing with each other?" he said, as he took his fingers and gently ran them up and down my arm.*

*"I don't know."*

*"How long has this shit been going on?" he asked.*

*"Too long," I replied.*

*"I love yo' ass and I know you love me," Dwight said. "I know you were feeling me that day we met at band camp before we came to FAMU."*

*"Yeah, I was," I said.*

*"So, why are we playing with each other, huh?"*

*"I don't know."*

*"Look, I've never felt this way about no other dude before, but this shit just feels right. Being with you just feels right and I can't hide that shit no more," Dwight said. "I love your ass, Zach."*

*"I love you, too."*

"WHAT?" Dwight asked, as I looked at him.

"What happened, Dwight?" I asked.

"Hold on," he said, as his phone started to ring.

Ironically, every single time I ask him about Atlanta, something comes up. That shit is starting to piss me off.

"Get at me later, Big Z," Dwight said, as we arrived at my place. He was still on the phone.

"Yeah, man," I said, as I got out the car. "I'ma ride with Kris to the spot tonight."

"Ight," he said, as he pulled off.

*This shit is crazy...*

*****

421

# Jaxon Grant

# *Raidon*

Tony and I have gotten pretty close over the last month or so. We haven't done anything sexual, but the tension is definitely there. Tony has been spending the night at my house for the past two weeks. I know he wants to go there with me sexually. It's bound to happen at some point.

However, I'm scared.

I'm scared because I like him. I'm scared because I want to do something with him, but I have HIV. I can't do anything with him. I'm scared to tell him.

I exhaled, as I saw him heading for my car. I tried to put on a straight face, but I guess he saw right through it. Once he got in the car, he looked to me and said, "You straight?"

"Yeah, I'm good."

When we got to the house, Tony put his things down and went to the bathroom. When he came out, he only had on his basketball shorts. His dick looked so damn good through that shit. Being that I was fully versatile, I could enjoy the best of both worlds.

"What are you looking at?" Tony asked, as he walked over to my couch.

"Shit, I ain't looking at nothing," I said.

"Yes, you are. You're looking at my dick," Tony said.

"No, I'm not," I said.

He stared me in the eyes and said, "Raidon, I like you because you're older. You're mature. You're not like the young ass dudes I used to mess with. You're different. To be honest, I never thought that I would fall for an older dude, but you're different. I know and you know that we're both feeling each other. We have chemistry."

"Yeah, I'm feeling you, too. That shit is obvious, but—"

"No buts," he said, as he leaned over and kissed me. "Let's just be real for a change."

"Tony," I said, as I tried to break away from the kiss.

"No. This is right—me and you, right here, right now," Tony said, as he kissed me again. He took his hand and placed my hand to his dick. *Damn, his dick felt good.*

I wanted to stop. Everything inside of me told me to stop, but I couldn't. I needed this. God, I wanted to stop but I couldn't.

# Life of a College Bandsman 2: Is This Love

Before we knew it, we both were out of our clothes, kissing and licking all over each other. It felt so good to be here with him. It had been a long time for me. My body needed this, too.

After all the licking and kissing, we headed to the room and undressed. We skipped the sucking and eating and got straight to the point.

"Damn, I wanna feel you," Tony said, as he attempted to put his raw dick at my entrance.

I knew what I was doing was bad, but I was not gonna let him fuck me raw. Not in the condition I was in.

"Umm, go get a condom," I said.

"We don't need a condom," Tony said. "I know you're clean and you know I'm clean. Besides, it doesn't feel right with condoms."

"Get a condom, Tony."

"Ok," he said, as he walked to the dresser and got that and some lube. I watched him as he put the condom on his dick. He put some lube on my ass. He fingered me, opening me up a little bit. I was so ready for some action that my body was already accepting of his penis before he even entered me.

It took a little second but when he finally entered me, it was the best feeling in the world. For that moment in time, all my pain and worries went away as I was taken to a place called heaven. Tony had me in heaven.

He did me long and hard the entire night. He wouldn't stop. It felt good to be there with him as he gave me the fuck of my life.

We went at it for about forty-five minutes that round. We went at it again when we woke up the next morning.

Tony gave me my life back…

\*\*\*\*\*

# *Blackwell*

I've thought about and I've thought about it. I've even taken another trip up to Tallahassee. Eric doesn't know it, but I know he's still fucking around with dudes.

I don't know what else I can do to stop him from doing this shit. *It ain't right!*

I rented a car and watched Eric for two days. I know he's fucking with that dude. I ain't crazy, but it looks like the dude that came here with Tony a few months ago. I know this was a little on the crazy end, but I had to find out for myself, so I called him.

He answered, "What's up, Black? It's kinda late."

"Eric, we've been through a lot together and I'm really proud that you got accepted to medical school. I'm proud of all your accomplishments, but this shit gotta stop!"

"What shit, Black?" Eric asked.

"Eric, don't play stupid," I said upset that he was insulting my intelligence. "We both know that you're still fucking with dudes."

"No, I'm not, Black," he said.

"Eric, why do you continue to lie to me? I've seen you. I've watched you go into that man's house and not come out until eight and nine o'clock the next morning. Eric, I know."

"Black," he said.

"You gave me your word that you were gonna stop fucking with dudes," I said.

"I know, but—"

I cut him off, "You gave me your word! I guess that shit doesn't mean too much of nothing anymore."

"No, Black, it's not like that!"

"So, why are you still fucking with men? You're my fucking brother! McDaniel's aren't gay!"

"It's just—I love this dude, Black. It's hard to drop him like that," Eric said.

"Well, it's either gonna be that dude or your family because you know if I tell mama, you're done. Is that what you want? You're gonna lose your family over some fucking dude?"

"No," Eric said, as he started to cry. "I love him and I love my family!"

"Blood is thicker than water, Eric. Never forget that."

"I know," Eric said.

"Family comes first. And you know this family doesn't condone homosexuality. It's not what we believe in."

"I know, Black," Eric said.

"Well, the next time I talk to you I would have hoped that you made the right decision. If not, you know where you would stand in this family," I said.

"BLACK, DON'T DO THIS!" Eric yelled.

# Life of a College Bandsman 2: Is This Love

"I'm not, you are," I said, as I hung up the phone.

*Eric needs to stop this shit! He has too much to live for than being a damn faggot.*

# 86

# *Zach*

*Thursday, October 23, 2003*

Being that this was homecoming week, most professors cancel class on Thursday and Friday. There's just too much stuff happening on campus to hold class. Luckily for me, all of my classes were cancelled. That allowed me to catch up on some much needed sleep that I've been missing, especially since I didn't in until about five this morning.

Last night was crazy. It really felt different to be on the other side. I know how the kids felt last night, because I was in that position last year. Being that we weren't the ones getting our asses beat this time made things a little easier. Crossing the section is no easy feat. I still have my eyes on Keli, the gay one. Something about him warms my heart.

The atmosphere in that house was crazy. It seems like everyone turns into completely different people. I know the Dwight that I saw last night was not the Dwight that I knew. Kris, Omar, Peanut and George was different. Everyone was different. I guess my freshmen brothers were taking their anger out on the freshmen, based on what happened to us last year when we were in this position. I know I was. When it was my turn to paddle the kids, I was a little nervous at first, but once I got the hang of it, it was cool. I wanted those fucking freshmen to feel the same shit I had to feel last year. I know it's wrong, but that's just how it is. Quinton got his licks in, too, even though he wasn't marching anymore.

I was a little hungry, so I made my way into the kitchen. I looked around the kitchen, but it wasn't too much of nothing in there.

"I need to go to the grocery store," I said, as I grabbed a banana and took a seat on the couch.

"What are you doing?" Jared asked, as he and Omar entered my house.

"Do y'all know how to knock?" I looked at them.

"Lock your damn door," Omar said, as he took a seat.

"Anyway," Jared said, as he sat down. "What's up with you?"

"I'm just thinking," I said.

"About last night?" Omar asked.

"Yeah and some other stuff, too," I said.

"Last night was crazy," Omar added.

"Yeah, it was, but what is the other stuff?" Jared asked. "Does it have something to do with Dwight?"

"Yeah," I said. "My mind has been going crazy lately."

"What happened now?" Omar asked.

"You remember when we went to Atlanta?" I asked.

"Yeah, you stayed at his house," Omar said.

"Yeah, his parents and his lil brother were out of town," I said.

"Did y'all fuck?" Jared interjected.

"Damn, fool, can I tell my story?" I said.

"Omar, get me a drink because this is gonna be good," Jared said, as he took off his shoes and got comfortable.

"Damn, nigga," I said.

"Shit, I'm waiting to hear this one," Jared said.

"Umm, hmm," Omar added.

"Well, I was a lil confused. Hell, I'm still a lil confused," I said.

"How?" Omar asked.

"Because things were kinda crazy," I said.

"Ok, start from the beginning," Jared said.

"Ok... from the beginning? Well, we went to practice."

"Skip all the mumbo jumbo! Get to the juicy shit," Omar stated.

"I got a call from my homeboy from high school. He lives in Atlanta now. Dwight and I went and had lunch with him. Dwight was acting a lil funny, kinda like he was my man or something. He was very protective of me. He sat really close to me at the table. He stared the boy down. It was just kinda awkward," I said.

"Umm, hmm," Jared said.

"After we left the restaurant, Dwight showed me around Atlanta. He took me to his high school. The people there are in love with him. We left there and went to visit his grandmother. She was a real nice woman but she's blind."

"Oh, ok," Jared said.

"The entire time we were in the car he was just saying random shit, like how much he needed to get his life together and shit," I said.

"Ight," Omar added.

"Well, we stopped by the liquor store and picked up some liq. We were gonna be in the house and we weren't going nowhere, so we were free to drink a little."

"Y'all ain't twenty-one yet. How y'all get some liq?" Omar asked.

"Dwight's homeboy worked at the liquor store. That's how he got it," I said.

"Oh, ok."

"So, when we got back to his house, he started fixing drinks and we were getting right. It wasn't nothing too bad, but we were right. We talked about a lot of shit. I really got to know more about the dude I call my best friend. We really bonded," I said.

"Umm, hmm," Jared stated.

"But, this is where I'm starting to get confused," I said.

"What do you mean?" Omar asked.

"I don't know exactly how to say it," I said.

"Just speak," he added.

"Ok, soon after, Dwight went and took a shower. I stayed in the room and watched television. He eventually came out the room, sat on the bed and asked me some questions about something that happened in high school that me and my boy were talking about. When I finished explaining what happened, I went and took a shower. Something about the atmosphere in the house was telling me that something was gonna go down that night."

"OH, SHIT!" Jared said. "Here we go!"

"Yeah, so being the person that I am, I cleaned myself out. You know you gotta always be prepared," I said.

"Ain't that shit the truth," Jared agreed.

"But when I got back out, Dwight was walking around in his boxer briefs and tank top. Damn, he looked so fucking good," I said.

"Hell, look at him when that nigga got on clothes. I can only imagine what it's like when he's damn near naked," Omar said.

"But we talked some more and he said some shit about me not being able to sleep in his brother's bed or on his mom couch. I told him I wasn't sleeping on the floor, so it was discussed that we were just gonna sleep in the bed together. Dwight then went back outside to the living area and he called me back. I was feeling a lil funny. I think the liquor was starting to take effect. When I got out there he was pouring another drink. Me being the stupid person that I was took another one and another one. I wasn't drunk but I was right. We played some basketball on his brother's gaming system. I took another drink and then we ended up getting in the bed."

"Oh, shit," Omar stated.

"It took Dwight a lil while to come in the room and get in the bed, but he did eventually. I was really feeling out of it now, but I knew that I wanted Dwight right then and there. My dick was hard. I was overdue for some sex. I needed it. But we laid in the bed. My mind was all over the place. When I realized that nothing was gonna happen because I couldn't get the courage to try him, I fell asleep."

"Damn, bruh," Omar said. "I would have gone for the dick."

"But, when I woke up, or at least I thought I woke up, Dwight was holding me. His head was on my head. He said some shit about why we were playing with each other and he kissed me."

"HE DID WHAT?" Jared said.

"He kissed me—or at least I think he kissed me."

"Either he kissed you or he didn't," Jared said.

"Let me finish!"

"Ight, man," he said, as he waited for me to finish my story.

"Anyway, we ended up having sex. The shit was hot! I still have the images in my head, or at least I think I do. That was the best fuck ever. When we finished, I remembered him vividly telling me to drop Eric and come with him and that we were gonna be together. Then we took a shower."

"So, y'all really fucked," Omar said amazed.

"Well, when I woke up in the morning, we were still in the bed. Dwight was on his side. I was on my side and I had on new clothes. I only had on my basketball shorts when I went to bed. Now, I had on a t-shirt and some new shorts. The sheets on the bed were changed."

"Well, if y'all fucked then of course he would change the sheets," Jared said.

"Yeah, and if you showered afterwards, you would change clothes," Omar added.

"Yeah, Dwight had on new underwear, too," I said. "Before we went to sleep he had on boxer briefs, but when we got up he had on some regular boxers."

"Sounds like y'all fucked to me!" Omar said.

"When I woke up, I had a crazy headache," I said.

"I remember that," Jared added. "You had a nasty, NASTY attitude at the parade that morning."

"Yeah, but if we fucked then I would think Dwight would've acted differently," I said. "But he wasn't. He was still acting like his normal self. I started to ask him questions about what happened and he would never completely answer them. All he would say is that I was wild. He said that I threw up all over the bed and that's why we had to shower again and change the sheets. But I don't remember that shit. I don't remember throwing up."

"So, you're saying you don't think the fuck happened?" Jared asked.

"See, I'm confused and have been ever since it happened. I can see the images in my head. That shit is vivid. I've never had a dream that was that vivid before. But Dwight hasn't acted any differently since that night. He's still Dwight. He's been telling me to drop Eric since forever now, so when he tells me to do it now, it doesn't really hold much clout. I try to ask him what happened that night but all he gives me is that I was wild and I threw up on his shit."

"Damn, so you don't know what happened," Jared said.

"Exactly. I don't know if the shit was real or was it a dream. My entire body was in pain so I can't say that my ass was hurting. Everything was hurting. I felt awful when I woke up that Saturday morning," I said.

Jared said, "So, in your mind, you have these vivid images of you and Dwight fucking. But you also were fucked up that night. When you woke up the next morning, both of you had on different clothes and the sheets on the bed had been changed. Dwight says that you threw up on everything, so that would explain the clothes and sheets. You say that you don't remember throwing up. You remember having sex with Dwight, but when you woke up, nothing had changed. He was still being himself. You try to ask him about that night, but all he says is that you were wild. And now nearly a month later, you don't know what to think or believe. Is that right?"

"In a nutshell, that is correct," I said.

"Damn, Zach, I don't know what to say," Omar said.

"Well, what do you honestly think happened?" Jared asked.

"I wanna believe that we had sex, but that's something that I want to happen. I was fucked up, so the whole thing could have been a figure of my imagination. I don't know what to believe and since I don't know what to do, I just went on with my life with Eric. When we got back to Tally, Eric got his results from the MCAT and his acceptance letter into Howard's Med School. We had sex that night and now he can't stop. The sexual aspect of our relationship has really taken us to newer heights. I just know the Dwight shit is really fucking my mind up."

"Damn, Zach," Omar said again. "I don't know what to say."

"Yeah, that's makes two of us," I said

"Well," Jared said, as he put his shoes back on. "I'm sure things will become clearer in due time. Sometimes we just gotta be patient and let things take its course. When we rush things, we rush them because we want instant gratification. Only trouble comes from that. Just be patient and let the pieces fall as they may. You know my mom told me that when you ask for something and you ask for something, you ask because you want it. You want it right then, but when you get it, it's not what you wanted it to be. It doesn't work out the way you want it to happen and you leave mad or upset, and sometimes confused. Zach, it looks to me that you got what you wanted, but because you didn't let the pieces fall where they were supposed to, you're confused and you still gotta wait to figure out the truth. It's kinda like you were just thrown a curve ball. You've still gotta get to the end of the road, but you gotta take the new route to get there now. The saying 'patience is a virtue' is so true," Jared stated as he got up. "Just be patient and everything will happen when it's supposed to."

"Hell, I see that shit now," I said "My mind is all fucked up."

*****

# Life of a College Bandsman 2: Is This Love

# *Eric*

I couldn't stop thinking about the conversation that I had with Black last night. "FUCK!" I yelled. "Why is he doing this shit?"

Luckily, Zach had something to do with his section because if he would have saw me last night, I don't know what I would have done.

I love my family. They are everything to me and I can't lose them. But I know how my family is. My family hates homosexuals—especially my mom.

She's told us numerous times the way she feels about them. If my mom found out that I was gay, I would never see or hear from her again. I love my mom too much. I can't have that.

I can't lose my family over no gay shit. Who the fuck says that I'ma be with dudes ten years from now? If I lose my family, there's no turning back.

But I love Zach. We've come so far together. I can't do this shit to him.

"FUCK!" I yelled.

What the fuck am I gonna do?

Do I lose my family and keep my relationship with Zach, or do I keep my family and lose my relationship with Zach?

God be with me...

# 87

## Zach

*Saturday, November 1, 2003*

I don't know what has been going on with Eric these last few days, but I don't like it. It was just like he just up and changed overnight. One day we were cool and the next he's acting funny.

I don't wanna talk to Dwight about it because I don't wanna hear what he has to say. I don't feel like hearing the *I told you so* bullshit. Not right now anyway.

"Yo, Zach," Micah said, as he stepped in my room.

"What's up?"

"What's up with you and Eric?" he asked, sitting on the bed.

"I don't know. I thought things were good, but he's acting funny."

"You don't think he went and did nothing crazy do you?"

"I don't know, Micah. I don't know what to think nowadays."

"You still don't know what happened in the hotel room with Dwight?" he asked.

"Naw," I said. "I don't have a clue."

"Well, I think y'all fucked," Micah said. "It ain't no way in hell that you got that fucked up where you don't know what happened, or in other words you can't separate dreams from reality."

"Well, until you step into my shoes, then you don't really have much to say about it," I said, as I started to get agitated.

"My bad, man. I didn't mean to make you upset, I'm just saying," he said.

"It's cool," I said. "I just wish I had answers. Dwight's ass is sticking to his story that I threw up and shit."

"Have you told him what you think what happened?" Micah asked.

"No, I haven't said anything. I mean, what the fuck I am supposed to say—'umm, Dwight did me and you fuck in yo' mamma house or was I just dreaming?' How the fuck does that shit sound?"

"I guess you've got a point," Micah said. "Have you told Eric?"

"HELL NAW!" I said. "What the fuck I look like?"

"I don't know what could have triggered the way Eric has been acting lately," Micah said.

"I don't know, either. I've asked him what was wrong and he always tells me that he's fine, or that it's just some family stress. This shit is unlike him," I said.

"You know I thought that when y'all started fucking and shit that would only take y'all to higher heights, but I guess not," Micah stated.

"Yeah, shit was good at first but then he just changed. It's like he's always upset. His patience is short. He has a look of *don't fuck with me*. I just don't know," I said. "I guess sex doesn't solve everything."

"Obviously not," Micah said as he got up.

"Where is Kris?" I asked.

"He has a study group for one of his classes. We're going to the movies tonight and I wanted you and Eric to go, kinda like a double date, but I guess that shit is out the window."

"I'll ask him," I said. "He may be in a better mood today."

"Well, I hope so," Micah said. "Just let me know what's up. We're gonna catch something to eat around eight or nine and the movie starts at eleven-thirty."

"Ight, I'll let you know," I said.

"Yep," Micah said as he walked out.

\*\*\*\*\*

# Life of a College Bandsman 2: Is This Love

## *Eric*

I cannot believe that I'm being forced to choose between my love life and my family. This shit is crazy.

I love my family and I love Zach. I fell for that dude the first time I met him. I had to wait on the side while he fucked Chaz. When Chaz fucked him over, he came to me but only to realize that he was still feeling Chaz, and it wouldn't be fair to me. I was there for him when Chaz told him that Genevieve was pregnant with their second child. I was there for him when he needed a shoulder to cry on. Then I finally got my chance. We chilled out for a second and then we got together. I felt like the happiest man on earth. Zach was the one for me. I love that dude. Even though his best friend doesn't like me, and that's fine because I don't like his ass either, but Zach still stuck it out with me. He listened to me deal with my issues. He was just the dude for me. Now, I'm forced to choose between my lover and my family.

I know I've been acting strange the last week or so, but I can't help it. I'm close as hell to my family. Everyone looks up to me. I'm about to go to medical school! I'm gonna be a fucking doctor, the first in the family!

I think about my mom and my brother. My mom has been my foundation since I can remember. I know how she feels about homosexuality. If she found out that I was fucking around with dudes, she would disown me, then probably die of a broken heart. And then there is my brother Black. We've been through so much together. That man has taught me so much. He stepped in and became the man of the house when our dad died. Black literally raised me and my sister. He didn't always make the best choices, but he has given himself a good life. How could I repay someone back who gave so much to me by being a person that they hate the worst.

Even though I know my relationship with sister will not change, I just don't want her to have to deal with the family. Rozi is gonna be put in the middle of this shit because she would be on my side and not on the side of the family. She doesn't deserve to be put in that stressful shit. She has her own issues to deal with.

Then when Black says something he means that shit. He's always been like that since we were lil kids. I know that he is gonna tell my mom if I'm really not done with dudes. I'm scared as shit.

This is the main reason why I didn't get involved with dudes despite how I felt about them. I didn't want to risk the chance of being exposed to my family. Maybe this gay shit ain't for me.

The first dude I fell in love with, Raidon Harris, just up and left me out the blue. That nigga just dropped me like I was shit. He didn't even give me notice that he was going back home, that nigga just up and left. It took a lil time and I eventually got over it. Then there was the other one. I wasn't in love with his ass, but I was feeling him— until that nigga shitted on my dick. That had potential to be something, but his mind was elsewhere. That's when I went back to pussy. I knew I was guaranteed some play going out with females. All the ladies love me. But while I was fucking pussy, I was feeling dudes, but scared as hell because of my family. I didn't want Chaz's ass to know what was really up with me. There was just too much for me to lose. Then I met Zach and everything changed.

Now, a year after I met his ass, I'm forced to choose between him and my family.

I can't win in this gay shit.

Maybe this really ain't for me.

# 88

## Ra'Jon

We loaded three charter buses left Orlando this morning, headed east to Daytona Beach for the Bethune-Cookman College homecoming game. Our high school band marched in the parade this morning and now we were at lunch getting ready to go to the football game. Bethune-Cookman was playing Johnson C. Smith University, who was based in Charlotte, NC. We were invited to do a performance once the game was over for the Bethune-Cookman Wildcats crowd.

As I watched the kids eat, I sighed and thought about my family. Something is going on and I don't like it. I don't know what the fuck it is, but I just got a feeling that the shit ain't good—not by a long shot.

My mom has been calling me a lot recently. But each time she calls, I can tell that there's something she really wants to say, but can't get the words out of her mouth.

I wonder if it is about pops. I know they're separated, but something else has to be going on. Or maybe it's Raidon. I know he has shit in his damn closet, too. Or what if it's Morgan or Micah. Or what if Michelle's fast ass done came up pregnant. Hell, I don't know but I know something is up.

My mom tells me that she's proud of me for moving to Orlando and starting over fresh, but I can hear that *something* in her voice.

"Mr. Harris!" one of the high school band members yelled, as she came up to me.

"What's up," I said.

"I think I wanna go here," she said.

"Why?" I asked. "FAMU is better!"

"I like Cookman," she said. "There's just something about their band that is impressive to me."

"Well, regardless of what school you go to, you just make sure you get an education," I said.

"I know, Mr. Harris. I was just saying because I know you were gonna get mad," she said, as she started to laugh. "You're crazy bout FAMU."

"Y'all gonna stop messing with me," I said, as my phone started to ring. I walked out of McDonald's and answered the call.

"Hey, baby," my mom said.

"What's up, Mama."

"Nothing, what are you doing?" she asked.

"We're in Daytona Beach at B-CC's homecoming," I said.

"Oh, if you're busy with the kids then I can call you back later," she said.

"No, we're at lunch. You can talk."

"Oh, ok," she said, as she took a breath.

"Mama, what's really going on?" I asked. "I can tell that you have something that you wanna say."

"Ra'Jon, I love you, baby."

"I know that. I love you, too," I said.

"Well, there's something that I have to say. It's been bothering me for years now," she said. "It's time that you know the truth."

"WHAT TRUTH?"

"Baby, it's a long story and I know you don't have time for the long version," she said.

"Just spill it, Mama," I said. It was bothering me now.

"Well, you know that me and Michael aren't together right now."

"Yeah, I know that you and pops aren't meshing," I said.

"Well, part of that is my fault. Michael had his problems, too, but were not talking about him."

"Why do you keep calling him Michael?" I asked. "You usually say *your father*."

"Because he is Michael to you," she said.

"I'm not following," I stated.

"Michael isn't your father," she said.

"What?" I said.

"I'm sorry, baby, but he isn't your birth father," she said. "I know I've been lying to you, to all of you, but that was my secret and I couldn't hold on to it anymore."

"Are you serious?" I said, in disbelief. This had to be a joke. I know she was playing a game.

"Yes, Ra'Jon, this is the truth," she said.

"Well, who is my father?" I asked, not believing a word that was coming out of her mouth.

"Alonzo," she said.

"UNCLE ALONZO?"

"Yeah, but he isn't your uncle," she said.

"Ok, now I'm confused," I said.

"I'm surprised that you're taking this lightly," she said.

"Mama, nothing surprises me anymore. Besides, I've done a lot of growing up since I've been in Orlando. If what you're saying is true, then I have no choice but to accept it. I've learned that we all make mistakes and we all hold secrets, but in the process, I've come to accept things for what they are. There's no need for me to get upset. As far as I'm concerned, Uncle Alonzo may have donated the sperm, but Michael Harris is my father. He is the man who raised me. He's the man that showed me how to be a man. He gave me my education. He taught me right from wrong. He is my father, not Uncle Alonzo," I said, as I digested the information that she gave me. "But how is he not my uncle? They're brothers."

"Oh, boy," she said, as she took a breath. "This is what happened…"

\*\*\*\*\*

# Zach

Eric showed up to the house crying. I didn't know what was going on. When he stepped in the house, I said, "Eric, why are you crying? What's wrong? What's going on?"

He didn't say anything, but just looked around the apartment. I closed the door and stared at him. He pointed to Micah's room and asked, "Are they here?"

"No. Micah and Kris are out."

"Well, we need to talk," he said, wiping his tears.

"What's wrong? What happened?"

He said, "Can't nobody tell me how much I love you. I love you more than life itself."

"I love you, too, Eric," I said, as I really was becoming nervous. "What's going on?"

"I have been put in a tough situation and it's fucking up my life. You've been wondering what's wrong with me, well this shit is what's been wrong. I'm in a tough place and I don't know what to do," he said, as the tears fell.

"Eric, what are you talking about? Stop talking in circles. What's going on?"

"I love you, Zach. Oh, my God, I love you, but we can't do this anymore," he said.

"Eric, what are you talking about?" I raised my voice.

"Zach, I don't wanna do this, but I have to. I have no choice." He sighed and said, "I've gotta end things with you."

"Excuse me? You're breaking up with me?"

"Zach, let's just be friends. This ain't gonna work. I love you, but it's for the best," he said, as he stared me in the eyes.

"WHAT THE FUCK, ERIC?"

"I'll come back for my things," he headed for the door. "Bye."

"IT'S LIKE THAT, ERIC? HUH? IT'S LIKE THAT?"

As Eric walked out, Dwight walked in. Dwight saw me and then looked back at Eric. Dwight slammed the door and yelled, "What the fuck that fuck nigga do? What the fuck did he do?"

I looked at Dwight with tears falling from my eyes.

Dwight stepped in my face and said, "Zach, I'm about to go fuck his ass up! What the fuck did he do to you?"

I looked Dwight dead in his eyes and said, "He just broke up with me. That nigga just broke up with me."

"Oh, shit," Dwight said, as his tone of voice changed. "My bad, Big Z."

"That nigga just broke up with me," I said again, looking at Dwight, trying to control the tears.

"Damn," Dwight sighed, as he turned and stared at the door. Then in a sudden unexpected move, he stepped in closer to me, placed his arms around me and gave me a hug. He whispered in my ear, "Man, fuck that nigga. Don't be crying, wasting tears over that pussy nigga."

He hugged me again, a bit tighter this time. He said, "Fuck that nigga. I got you. I GOT you. Fuck that nigga, I got you."

# 89

# *Zach*

*Saturday, November 8, 2003*
*Tallahassee, Florida*

This last week has been kinda tough. I was really feeling Eric and he just dropped me like that, just dropped me with no explanation or anything.

When he came to the house to get his clothes, he really didn't say much of anything other than that he was sorry. I could tell that he had still been crying, as I'm sure that he could tell that I had been crying.

But like my best friend, Dwight, says, "Life goes on. There's no need to dwell in the past."

I just wish I had some kind of closure on the situation.

Micah and Kris have been really supportive, but there's nothing they can really do for me right now.

Dwight has really been a good friend, too. He's been trying his best to keep my mind off of the situation, but regardless of what we do, it's still in the back of my head.

Today, we have a football game in Orangeburg, South Carolina, against South Carolina State University and the SCSU Marching 101 band. Taking this trip is something that I need. I think that it will help to clear my mind of my issues with Eric.

We got out of practice late last night, so I know that everyone is gonna fall asleep as soon as the buses start rolling—especially since it's three in the morning. I hope no one oversleeps and get left in Tallahassee.

"Yo, Big Z," Dwight said, as he approached our seats.

"What's up?" I replied, yawning.

"Dawg, stop stressing 'bout that shit. That nigga chose his path," Dwight said.

"Dwight, I ain't stressing about that any more. It's over and done. I'm over it."

"Yeah, if you say so," Dwight said, as he took a seat. "I think you should be grateful that the punk ass nigga is gone."

"Why is that?" I asked.

"Because it opens the door for a real nigga—a real nigga who's really feeling you to come into your life. Everything happens for a reason, so look for the positive in the situation," he said.

"So, who is supposed to be the real nigga?" I asked.

"Shit, you tell me," Dwight stated. "You know what kind of dudes that you like."

I didn't say anything.

"But, then again, maybe you should look for a different type of dude," Dwight stated.

"Like who?" I asked.

"Shit, I don't know. But the two dudes that I know you were fucking with wasn't good for shit. Chaz and Eric were both some soft ass, pussy ass, bitch ass niggas. Maybe you should leave them soft ass niggas alone and find a dude who's gonna be a real nigga to you," Dwight said.

"Like who, Dwight?" I stared at him, waiting for him to say his name.

"I don't know, but I'm sure he is out there—somewhere," he said as he got up. "Damn."

"What?" I asked.

"I'm cold and I left my blanket under the bus. Let me get run and get it before they take off," he said, as he hurried off the bus.

*Oh, my God. I love Dwight. Damn, I love him!*

This whole Eric thing is making the Dwight situation worse for me because I still don't know if anything happened in his house. Based on the way things are playing out, I'm starting to believe that it was just my mind running wild. But now I'm free to be with Dwight and I'm scared to say something.

I just wanna tell him how much I love his ass. Not that play-play love I had with Eric, but that real shit. I'm in love with Dwight. *I'm in love with him!*

This shit is eating me up inside. I wish he'd just man up and tell me how he feels about me. Things would be a lot easier.

He was always telling me to drop Eric's ass and now that Eric is gone, he hasn't stepped up to the plate. My thing with Eric has been over for a fucking week now. That's more than enough time for him to step up. But I guess that shit is too gay for him.

"Ight," Dwight said, as he got back to the seat. He threw me the blanket over me and said, "I know you're cold, too."

"I guess I can use it, too," I said, as Dwight sat down. "Get my pillow from up there, please."

"Ight," he said, as he stood up and retrieved my pillow from the overhead bin.

"There you are," he said, as he gave it back to me and sat back down.

"Thanks."

"I'm tired and I haven't been to sleep, so I'm about to call it a night. I'll see yo' ass when we wake up. Hopefully we'll be in South Carolina then," he said, as he got comfortable under the blanket that we both shared.

"Yeah, I'm about to call it quits, too," I said, as I positioned myself to go to sleep.

"Fuck you," Dwight said.

"I love you, too."

"I know you do," Dwight said, as he put his head on my shoulder and prepared to go to sleep. "I know you do."

# 90

# *Micah*

I heard my phone. I sighed.

*"Who the fuck is calling me at nine o'clock on a Saturday morning?"* I said to myself, as I reached over to grab the phone.

"HELLO!" I stated, wanting the person to know that they were interrupting my damn sleep.

"I'm sorry for waking you, Micah," Rozi stated.

"Oh, what's up, Rozi?" I said, clearing my throat.

"There's something that I need to tell you," she said.

"What's up?" I asked, wondering if Kris had made it to South Carolina yet.

"I know that you're gonna be mad at me, but I've got to get this shit off my chest. It's really fucking me up. I'm not that type of person. My friends have been down my back about this and it is really tearing me up inside," she said.

"What going on, Rozi?" I asked concerned.

"I did something that I'm not proud of," she said.

"What's bothering you?" I asked.

"Look, at first I thought that you were, but as time passed, I later learned that it wasn't you," she said. "I'm sorry."

"I'm confused," I said. "What are you talking about?"

"The baby," she said. "You weren't the father."

"What did you just say?" I asked, sitting up in the bed. I had to make sure I heard what I thought I heard.

"You weren't the father of the baby," she said.

"You're lying, right?"

"No. I mean I thought you were at first and that's when I told

447

you. But when I found out how many weeks along I was, I knew that the baby wasn't yours," she said.

I yelled, "So, you just let me go along with this shit! Do you know how much shit was fucked up and could have been fucked up over a fucking lie! *A fucking lie!* I almost fucked up my relationship over this bullshit and you're now telling me that you knew the damn kid wasn't mine! I had to tell my fucking mother about this shit, Rozi!"

"I'm sorry, Micah, I really am. I didn't mean to cause you any harm. I'm sorry."

I continued, "And I worked my damn ass off this summer so I could support what I thought was my seed. I saved up money for that baby! And you still let me send you the money for the fucking abortion knowing damn well that kid wasn't mine? I want all my fucking money back!"

"I'm sorry, Micah," she said again.

"I can't believe this shit," I stated.

"I'm sorry," she said, as she hung up.

*****

# *Amir*

I was lying in bed, playing with my dick when I saw my phone light up. I looked at it and exhaled. What the hell did she want now? I answered, "What, Rozi?"

"Look, I've got something to say," she said.

"Why are you crying?" I asked.

"Because I have something to say!"

"What's up?" I said, feeling my dick getting softer.

"I've hid something from you."

"What are you hiding?" I asked, as I sat up in my bed. I was getting suspicious.

"This is hard for me to do, ok," she said.

"Rozi, just talk. It's too damn early on a Saturday morning for games and shit."

"I was pregnant," she said.

"WHAT?"

"I was pregnant with your child," she said.

# Life of a College Bandsman 2: Is This Love

"You're carrying my baby?" I asked, as I got excited. I always wanted a lil Amir. He would be fly just like his daddy.

"Was pregnant," she said.

"What do you mean you *were* pregnant?"

"I had an abortion," she said.

"YOU ABORTED MY CHILD?" I yelled. "WHAT THE FUCK GIVES YOU THAT DAMN RIGHT?"

"I wasn't ready for no fucking kids!" she stated.

"YOU KILLED MY BABY?" I yelled. "YOU FUCKING KILLED MY CHILD WITHOUT LETTING ME KNOW?"

"I'm sorry," she stated.

"What the fuck, Rozi? That was my blood. What kinda fuck shit is that?"

"I wasn't ready for no damn kids! Besides who knew what kind of father you would have been. I didn't wanna put my baby though that drama," she said.

"Don't you ever fucking judge me! You don't know the kind of life I had to live to get to this damn point in my fucking life! I didn't have a fucking father that loved me. So, I knew whenever I had my own kids, I was gonna be the best damn dad that is. Don't ever tell me that kind of man I was gonna be with my kids! You don't know shit about me!"

"Well, I just wanted you to know the truth," she said, agitated.

"Rozi, I can't believe you'd do this."

"Well, it's done now, so just stop, ok."

"When was this?" I asked.

"When was what?"

"When were you pregnant?"

"I got pregnant back in the earlier part of the summer. I had the abortion at the end of August," she said.

"And you're just telling me this shit five or six months later."

"I'm sorry. I just thought you'd have liked to know."

"Maybe this is the one thing you should have kept to your damn self," I said, as I hung up the phone.

I exhaled, as I thought about what life could have been with a lil shawty of my own.

*I could've been a father.*

"What gives her the right to do that shit without letting me know first?"

*What gives her the right?*

# 91

# Ra'Jon

*Orlando, Florida*

I was excited because I was gonna spend some time with my buddy, Black, today. After I started working and helping out the W. P. Foster High School band, I really haven't had much time for a lot of shit.

Deep down, I was still feeling Black. I wanted to be with him, but I knew that Black wasn't gay, so that shit was out of the question. But it is ok to dream, right?

My mom still has been calling to apologize for lying to me my entire life, but I keep telling her that it's ok. I was a little upset, but like I told her, Michael Harris is my father, not his lover, Alonzo. I love my mom and we all make mistakes, so what can I be mad at her for? I mean who knows how my life would have been if Alonzo raised me.

"What's up, Black?" I said, as he approached the table. He was decked out in some black jeans with a fly ass brown Sean Jean sweater. He was looking good. He dreads were pushed back and he was smelling good as fuck. Damn, I wanted this dude.

"Chillin, man," Black said, as he took his seat. "What's going on with you?"

"Nothing, really," I said. "To be honest, I was kinda looking forward to this day all week."

"Is that so?" Black asked.

"Yep. I missed hanging out with you and shit," I said.

"That's what's up," Black said, as he started to laugh. "You're something else, RJ. Something else."

"I'm just me. Either you like me or you don't," I said.

"Well, I like you," Black said. "You're good people."

When the waitress came over, she took our order. When she left, we caught back up on time missed. We discussed the various things that was happening in our lives. I told him about my paternity issue and he told me that I was better than him. He couldn't have let his mother off the hook like that.

Being around Black again was good for my soul. I needed to be in his presence again. The shit just felt right.

I was a little sad because our lunch was coming to an end.

"Yo, what you about to do?" Black asked.

"Nothing, really. I guess just go back to the house and chill out there. I mean it ain't shit for me to do," I said.

"We should go bowling or something," Black said. "You up for that?"

"Shit, that's cool. I'ma follow you though," I said, as I paid for the meal.

We drove for a lil minute, but we eventually got to the bowling alley. It was kinda packed, but that was to be expected since it was in the middle of a Saturday afternoon. We had to wait for a few minutes, but a lane eventually opened up and we got right into the game.

The competition was good and I think I surprised Black. I was good as hell at bowling. That was one of my favorite activities.

After we finished bowling, we ended up going back to Black's place. We ordered pizza, talked some more and watched TV. I could tell that something was on his mind and it was bothering me because I wanted to know what it was. So, I asked, "What's wrong, Black?"

"Nothing. Why you ask that?"

"It just looks like something is bothering you," I said.

"Well, something has been on my mind for the longest now, but I don't know," he said.

"What's up?" I asked. "Ever since I've known you, you've been pretty straightforward. What's going on?"

"Well, I want to ask you a question," Black said.

"Ok."

"Don't take this the wrong way, ok," he said.

"Ok, what's up?"

He took a deep breath and blurted, "Dawg, are you gay?"

*"Oh, shit,"* I said to myself. That was the last thing on my mind—

the last thing. I know how he feels about gay dudes and if I tell him that I am gay that could possibly be the end of this *relationship*.

"Well?" he said.

"Just put me on the spot, huh?" I said, as I tried to make light of the situation.

"I mean, I just wanna know," Black said, as he kept his serious look on me.

I took a deep breath and said, "Yes, I am. I am a proud gay, black man."

"I see," Black said.

"Is that gonna be a problem?" I asked.

"No, I just wanted to know," he said. "I kinda already knew though."

"You did?" I asked.

"Yeah, I mean I wasn't too sure, but I kinda thought that," Black said. "I just wanted to see what you were gonna say."

"So, if you knew that I was gay, why did you still hang out with me?"

"I don't know," he shrugged his shoulders. "I guess you're different. Something about you is different. Even from the first day I met you at the diner, something was different about you. In my mind, I knew that you were, but I always brushed it off."

"So, you're saying that you're cool with my sexual preference?" I asked.

"Yeah, man, you're cool," he said. "I mean you ain't tried me or no shit like that, so you're good."

"I see."

"What are you thinking about?" Black asked.

"I'm just wondering why you're so cool with me being gay but when it's other people, like your brother, then it's different," I stated.

"Well, I don't like faggots, and you're are not a faggot," Black said. "And my brother is family. I mean that whole situation is just complicated. It's a lot to that story and I really don't wanna talk about it."

"What happened?" I asked.

"I said I don't wanna talk about it!" Black aggressively stated.

"My fault," I said.

"I'll tell you one of these days, but right now ain't the time," Black said, as he stood up. "You want something to drink?"

"A Coke is cool," I said.

"Nigga, I ain't talking about no damn Coke," he smiled. "Do you want something to drink?"

"Well, if I drink, then I can't drive home," I stated.

"You can crash here," Black stated. "That ain't a problem."

"Oh, ok, well get me whatever you're getting," I said.

"I like my shit strong," Black said.

"That's cool with me. Just get me what you're getting."

"Ight," Black said, as he went into the kitchen.

"Damn," I said to myself, as I thought about what just happened. "That was a strange turn of events."

*Strange…*

# 92

# *Zach*

*Orangeburg, South Carolina*

It was a little after nine-thirty at night and another successful game was in the books. We came into that stadium and did our thing. South Carolina State's band never stood a chance.

As my freshmen brothers talked about the game, I took the time to check my phone. After reading my text messages, I focused my attention back to the group.

Peanut looked at Dwight and asked, "What y'all doing tonight?"

"Nothing, really," Dwight said. "I've got some bio-chemistry homework to do so that's where I'm gonna be."

"On a band trip?" Omar said to Dwight. "Nigga, do that shit back in Tally."

"Umm, this pharmacy school shit ain't no joke—soooo, I need to have my head in these books," Dwight said.

Peanut added, "Well, I know this party that's going down. The Que's from SCSU are throwing it. It's not that far from the hotel, so I'm gonna hit that shit up."

"How far from the hotel is it?" Kris asked.

"The dude at the game said that it was about a fifteen or twenty-minute walk," Peanut answered.

"Oh, ok, that's what's up. I think I'ma hit that shit up," Kris said.

"Hell, me, too," Omar added. "I think we all should go."

"You coming, Zach?" Kris asked.

"Naw, I'ma just lay low in the hotel. I've got a lot of shit on my mind," I said.

Kris said, "Coming out tonight will get yo' mind off that

problem."

"I know but I just ain't in the mood," I said.

When we got to the hotel, we immediately rushed across the street to go to the Waffle House. Eating without being in long lines was a hassle in this band. We had to wait about twenty minutes, but we eventually got served.

After we ate, we headed to the room. I rushed to the shower. Once I finished, Dwight was still in his uniform sitting at the table looking at his textbook. Kris then went in the shower. When Kris finished his shower, he said to Peanut, "Yo, I'm about to run down to 414 right quick. Come grab me when you're ready to go."

"Ight," Peanut said, as he went in the shower.

"You sure y'all don't wanna go?" Kris asked Dwight and me.

"I've gotta get this done," Dwight said.

"I'm good, man," I said, as I flipped the channel on the TV.

"Stop stressing about Eric, that nigga is gone," Kris said, as he walked to the door. "I'll see y'all when we get back."

Once Kris left, Dwight looked to me and asked, "Are you ok, Shawty?"

"Yeah, I'm good," I said.

"Kris made a good point, and I've said it a thousand times—stop stressing 'bout that nigga," Dwight said.

"I ain't thinking about him."

"Yes, you are," Dwight replied. "Let that nigga be. He made his choice."

I didn't say anything back to Dwight. I rolled my eyes and continued to watch TV. Eventually, Peanut came from out of the shower. After he got himself together, he walked to the door. As he stepped out, he said, "See y'all boys later."

A few minutes after Peanut left, Dwight went to the bathroom and turned on the shower water. He then came back out and put his suitcase on the bed. He looked through his suitcase and said, "We're gonna get up when we get back to Tallahassee."

"Ok," I said.

"What do you wanna do?" Dwight asked, as he started to take off the rest of his uniform.

"Whatever you wanna do."

"Well, shit, I have a lot in mind," he said, as he was now in his tank top and boxers.

"Like what?"

# Life of a College Bandsman 2: Is This Love

"Hold on," he said, as he went to the shower. He came back in the room and said, "I had to make sure the temperature was right."

I looked at Dwight stand before me in his boxers. He had removed his tank top. I collected myself then said, "Yeah, but stuff I like what?"

"Shit, a lot of stuff," Dwight said, as he walked back into the bathroom. He carried his change of clothes this time.

When he came back out, I said, "Dwight, you're talking in circles."

"Well, first, I need to get my homework done," he said, as he took off his boxers.

*What the fuck? Is this nigga standing in front of me naked? Ok, Zach. Hit yourself on the face to make sure this shit is real.*

"What the fuck you hit yourself for?" Dwight asked, as he stood in front of the bathroom door, naked. His dick was just hanging.

"HUH?"

"Why did you hit yourself? Dwight asked, as if he wasn't standing in front of me without clothes.

"Why are you naked?" I asked.

"Because I'm about to go take a shower," he said. "C'mon, Shawty. I know you're smarter than that."

*This nigga is really naked. Oh, my God, he's really naked.*

"Well, let me run in here before the water gets cold," he said, as he closed the door.

As soon as Dwight closed the door, Peanut opened the room door. I was so startled that I jumped.

"What's wrong with you?" Peanut asked, as he walked in the room. He gave me a suspicious look. "Where is Dwight?"

"He's in the shower," I said.

"Humph."

"What are you doing back?" I asked.

"I forgot my wallet," he said, as he went to his bag. After he grabbed his wallet, he walked to the door and said, "Ight, I'll get at y'all boys later. By the way, please tell Dwight he's not fooling anyone. You, too."

"Wait…what's that supposed to mean?" I asked.

"Shitttttt—you tell me, freshman bruh," Peanut said, as he walked out, slamming the door.

*Fuck, that was close.*

What if Peanut would have saw Dwight standing in front of me naked? What would he have said? What would he have done? Peanut was suspicious of us in Detroit and in Mississippi. If he would've saw this—fuck! That nigga knows something is up because he always has something slick to say when Dwight is involved.

As I moved my attention away from Peanut and back to Dwight's very large package, I sighed. The picture I had in my mind of Dwight's naked body and dick are very similar to what I just saw.

So, the real question is—did we or did we not have sex that night in Atlanta? Was this Dwight's way of telling me, without telling, me that we did have sex? What is he trying to prove? Eric has been gone for a week and he still hasn't stepped up to the plate. What gives? What the fuck is really going on?

What I do know is if Dwight doesn't say something soon, I'm just gonna have to tell him how I really feel. I can't keep this shit to myself. Whatever happens after that will just happen. I'll just have to let the pieces fall as they may.

I'm sick of playing this game...

# 93

## Eric

*Thursday, November 20, 2003*

I miss him.

I don't know why I just couldn't stand up to Black. I love my brother and I love my family, but I *love* Zach. I feel so damn stupid right now. How could I let Black have that kind of control over my life?

The last couple of weeks have been hard as hell. It was tough enough to tell Zach that I had to end it, but getting my things from his house was the worst. The look on his face killed me. I fucking love that boy!

I haven't been myself lately. I just don't feel like doing shit anymore. I'm not motivated to go to class. I've spent quite a bit of time crying. Not sleeping next to Zach kills me. I don't know why I just couldn't stand up to Black.

"What the fuck have I done?" I asked myself, as I wiped the tears. "What the fuck have I done?"

I really fucked up this time—BIG TIME.

As I arrived back at the complex after driving around town for a while, trying to clear my mind, I tried to collect myself. I couldn't let my roommates see me like this. I walked in the house and saw Quinton. He was looking through the mail on the kitchen counter. Amir was sitting at the breakfast bar. Quinton placed the mail down, looked at me and asked, "Nigga, where the fuck have you been?"

"I was doing me," I said.

"If you say so. Anyway, I'm about to be out. I'll get at you dudes later," Quinton said, as he walked out the house.

Once Q was gone, Amir stared at me and said, "Yeah, where were you, dawg?"

"I'm just doing me right now," I said, looking through the mail, grabbing mine.

"Eric, what's really going on?" Amir asked.

I placed my mail back down on the counter, sat down next to Amir and said, "I fucked up!"

"What did you do?"

I knew that Amir was down and I'm sure he knew that I was down. Even though we never told each other, we knew it. Everyone in this house was down. I needed someone to talk to and for some reason, Amir seemed like he could help me clear my mind.

"I ended things," I said.

"Ended things with who?" Amir asked.

"My boy."

"Who?" Amir asked.

"Zach."

"What do you mean you ended things?" he asked.

"I broke up with him," I said. "Look—we all know that we're all down in this house, so we can just skip all the bullshit."

Amir smiled and nodded his head. He asked, "Who is Zach?"

"The dude that I brought here. You were talking to him on the couch that time," I said.

"Oh, yeah. Wait—y'all were together?" he asked, shocked.

"Yeah, eight months," I said.

"Damn, I didn't know that shit. I knew you were out with some dude, but I didn't think it was him."

"Yeah."

As if a lightbulb went off in his head, he said, "Yo, that's Dwight's homeboy!"

"Yeah, they're best friends."

"Humph, but what happened?"

"A lot of shit," I said, as I told him about the sex issues that we had and the situation with Black.

"Damn, your brother put a gun to your head?" Amir asked.

"Yeah."

"Wow, that's crazy."

"Tell me about it," I sighed.

"But it seems like you're still feeling this dude," Amir said.

"I didn't wanna break up with him. I did that shit because I was scared. I was scared of losing my family. I didn't wanna be put out there. I regret that shit. I knew I should have stood up to my brother. I can see that shit now that I've ended things with Zach. All I want is my dude back. If my family can't love me for me, then fuck them! I want my dude back!"

"Well, go get him," Amir said. "It sounds to me like he wants you, too."

"Yeah, but I don't know how to approach him. I didn't even give him a reason as to why I ended it," I said.

"Well, call and talk to him. Get him to see your point of view. All you can do is try," Amir said. "All you can do is try."

"Thanks, man," I said. "I think I'ma do that. I just gotta get my words together."

"Well, you get your shit together and go holla at him. If you wait too long, he might move on. Just go holla at him ASAP," Amir said.

"Ight, thanks, Amir," I said, as I got up to go to my room. "Thanks a lot."

"No problem, Eric."

*****

# *Chaz*

As we walked inside the mall, Ian asked, "Why did you have me meet you here?"

"Because I want you to help me."

"Help you do what, Chaz?"

"I've gotta get something and I need your opinion," I said.

"Ight, but I've gotta head to practice in a lil bit," Ian said. "This Florida Classic week and we've gotta get this show together. Are you coming to Orlando?"

"Yeah, I'll be there. I'm leaving Friday after I get finished with something up here," I said.

"You know Zach and Eric broke up," Ian stated, as we walked through the mall.

"They did?" I asked, shocked.

"Yeah, a few weeks ago," Ian added.

"Wow, I didn't know that."

Ian looked at me and said, "Yeah, so does that mean that you're gonna try to get back into Zach's life?"

"Why would you ask me that?"

"Because I know how you operate," Ian said. "You got what the fuck you wanted so I just know you're gonna go after it. I know you want some more of that ass."

"It ain't even like that, Ian," I said, as I thought back our sexual encounters. I smiled. We had good times—and damn good sex.

"Nigga, stop thinking with your dick," Ian said.

"What?"

"Stop thinking with your damn dick!"

"It ain't even like that," I pleaded.

"Yes, it is," he said, as he looked down at my shit. "You're hard!"

"Whatever, fool," I said, as I tried to adjust myself as we entered the store. "I'm done with Zach and this gay shit."

"What was that?" Ian asked.

"You heard me! I said I'm through with Zach and that gay shit. I'm ready to move on with my life. That's why I had you meet me here."

When Ian realized what I was doing, he stared at me and shockingly said, "Are you serious? Chaz, are you fucking serious?"

"Dead serious," I said, as the associate approached us. "Dead fucking serious!"

# 94

## *Zach*

I needed a job and I needed one badly. I had been looking for a job for the last few weeks, but I wasn't successful. I told Micah about it and he said that he would talk to his supervisor for me.

Before practice started, Micah drove me over to his job. I was a little nervous, but he told me that I would be fine.

I looked at Micah and asked, "Are you sure I'm gonna get it?"

"Yeah, man. I already talked to her for you. Just go fill out the application and you'll be straight," Micah stated.

When we got in the clothing store, he told me to start filling out the application and that he would go get the manager. A few minutes later, a middle-aged white woman came out.

"Zach?" she said, as she extended her hands.

"Yes?" I said.

"I'm Diane. It's finally nice to meet you. Micah has said so much about you."

"It's nice to meet you too," I replied, smiling.

"Are you done with the application?" she asked.

"Yes, ma'am," I handed it to her.

She looked at it for a second then said, "I can interview you right now if you have a few minutes."

"I have the time," I said, knowing that I had to get to practice. But practice could wait. I needed to get this job.

"Good. Follow me to the back."

When we got to her office, she went over the application with me. She asked me a lot standard interview questions, but she seemed to be more interested in my major and how the band works than

463

what I can do for the company.

"Well," she said, as she looked at me. "Right now we can offer you $7 an hour. I know it's not much, but that's all we can afford at the time."

"That's fine," I said.

"Good," she replied. "So, I take it that you will accept my job offer."

"YES!" I said.

"Great! Welcome to the team! I will give you a call after Thanksgiving to get you worked in. That way you can finish out the band season and go home and enjoy the Thanksgiving holiday. But when you come back I expect you ready to work. The holidays are our peak season," she said.

"I will be ready!"

"Good. I'll give you a call with your orientation date and work schedule."

"Thanks," I said, as I walked out of the office.

"How did it go?" Micah asked, as he approached me with some other sexy ass dude.

"I got the job," I said.

"That's what's up," Micah said. "Oh, this is Will. He's one of the team leaders in the store."

"Nice to meet you, Will," I said, as I shook his hand. *Damn, he had a firm grip.*

"Same here," he said, as he looked at me.

Will was just my type—tall and light. His caramel colored skin turned me the fuck on. I don't know what it was about me and light colored dudes but that shit drove me up a damn wall. He had a clean shaved face and a fresh, sharp haircut. And from the clothes that he wore, I could tell that his body was on point. He looked like he played basketball.

"Ight, Will," Micah said, as he dapped him up. "See you tomorrow."

"Ight, man," Will said to Micah. Will looked at me and said, "I look forward to working with you."

When we got in the car, Micah smiled and said, "Ain't that nigga hot as hell!"

"Hell, yeah," I said. "What's his deal?"

"Oh, that nigga ain't like us, Zach. He's far from gay. But, he's cool people though."

# Life of a College Bandsman 2: Is This Love

"He know about you?" I asked, heading for practice.

"Hell, naw! I ain't crazy," Micah said. "I don't put my shit out there for them gossiping ass females at the job—and you better not either."

"I got you man," I said. "But that nigga was hot though. Just my type."

"Well, you make sure you keep that shit in your head because he's straight."

"Ight, Micah. I got it," I said, as we continued on to practice.

"But congrats, man."

"Thanks, Micah," I smiled. Thanks for everything."

\*\*\*\*\*

# *Chaz*

*Ok, Chaz. You can do this. You can do it!*

I had thought long and hard about this shit. I had to make sure that this was the direction that I wanted to take my life. I had done a lot of shit in my past, but now was the time to man up and get real. I had to let the dudes go and create a life with Genevieve.

She really is phenomenal. I love her with all my heart and she deserves the best from me. Hell, she gave birth to my boys, Xavier and Elijah. We were one happy family.

I booked a private booth at one of the more expensive restaurants in Tallahassee. I had Genevieve's sister to watch the kids, so I could take this night out with her. I knew that Genevieve was excited because she kept asking me all day what was going on. I couldn't tell her. *I couldn't.*

We were escorted to our booth once we arrived at the restaurant. We ate and talked about everything. I told her how much I loved her and how she changed my life.

"Excuse me," I said, as I stood up. "I have to use the restroom."

"Ok, baby," she said, as I walked away.

I stepped outside to call Ian.

He answered, "What do you want? We're in practice!"

"I don't know if I can do it," I stated.

"Nigga, just do it. You've gone this far. Just do the shit," Ian said, as I could hear the band playing R. Kelly's song, Step in the Name of Love.

"What if—"

"Stop second guessing yourself! Just do it!" Ian said, as he hung up.

I gathered my composure and walked back into the booth. *Ight, Chaz.*

As I sat down, she asked, "Are you ok?"

"Yeah, I'm good," I cleared my throat.

"Is something bothering you?" she asked.

"No. Yeah. I don't know," I shrugged my shoulders. "I guess I'm a little nervous."

"Nervous for what?" she asked, concerned. "What's going on, Chaz?"

"There's just something on my mind."

"What is it?" she asked, staring me in the eyes.

"Look," I said, as I grabbed her hands. "Genevieve, you've changed my life. You've made me a better person, a better man. I owe all that shit to you. Genevieve, you are my everything. My world evolves around you and our kids. I've been through a lot of shit and you've been the person by my side the entire time."

"Chaz, what are you trying to say?" she asked.

"Genevieve," I said, as I reached in my suit pocket and grabbed the box. I got down on one knee.

"CHAZ!" she yelled, as she started smiling. "OH, MY GOD!"

"Genevieve, I know it's not gonna happen right now. It might even take a few years, but I want you to be my wife. I want you to be the mother to all of my kids. I want to grow old with you. I love you. Genevieve, would you do me the honor and become my wife? Will you marry me?"

"OH, MY GOD, CHAZ! YES! YES, I WILL MARRY YOU," she yelled, as she jumped up and gave me the biggest kiss known to man.

Everyone around us started to clap and cheer.

"I love you," I said, as I put the ring on her finger.

"I love you, too, Chaz. I love you, too."

# 95

# Zach

*Friday, November 21, 2003*
*Orlando, Florida*

It was finally here! It was the biggest game of the season, for both the football team and the band. It was the annual Florida Classic football game against our in-state rivals, the Bethune-Cookman College Wildcats.

This is what we wait for all season. This was like Auburn and Alabama. This was like Florida and Florida State. This was like Michigan and Ohio. Everything was on the line for this weekend. Whoever football team wins the game and whichever band wins halftime carries bragging rights for the next three-hundred and sixty-five days.

Of course, there is no doubt that halftime will belong to us, the Marching '100', but after last year upsetting loss to Cookman, I'm a little nervous about the football team. Regardless of whatever happens, I'm happy that I'm at home in Orlando to enjoy the festivities.

We had returned to the hotel about thirty minutes ago after our performance at the annual battle of the bands. It was close to midnight. I had already showered and was ready to go.

"You ready, Shawty?" Dwight asked, as he stepped out the shower.

"Yeah," I stated. As I grabbed my overnight bag, my phone started to ring. I looked at the name and sighed. *What does he want?* I thought about not answering the phone, but something told me to go and do it anyway. I motioned to Dwight that I would be right back. I stepped out of the room and answered. He said, "I didn't think you were gonna answer."

"Well, I did. What's up, Eric?"

"I wanna holla at you," he said.

"About what?" I asked.

"Us," Eric said

"Eric," I said, as I was cut off.

"Zach, just hear me out—please," Eric begged.

"Yeah," I sighed.

"Thank you. I just got to the hotel that y'all are staying at. Can you meet me downstairs?" Eric asked.

*For someone who attends Florida State, he's always at a lot of FAMU functions.* I sighed and said, "Ight, I'm coming."

I hung up the phone and headed back to the room. I said to Dwight, "I gotta step out for a quick second."

"Why? I thought we were leaving?" he asked.

"We are but I just gotta handle this right quick," I said.

"Ight, Zach. Don't be gone too long. I'm ready to go," Dwight stated.

"Ight, I'll be right back," I said, as I walked out the room.

When I got to the elevators, I thought about what Eric could possibly have to say to me. Some of everything flashed across my mind while I waited to be taken to the first floor. I haven't talked to Eric since that night he broke up with me, three weeks ago tomorrow.

There were a lot of people downstairs in the main lobby. Everyone was excited about the performance that we had just got finished doing, and was equally excited about the game tomorrow. There was nothing like being in the environment of black college football.

I looked around for Eric, but I didn't see him. I was gonna call him, but walked outside. That's when I saw him leaning against one of the walls leading into the hotel. As I approached him, he stared at me and said, "What's good, Zach? It's good to see you."

I rolled my eyes, "What's going on, Eric? What do you have to say?"

"Can we go talk in my car where it's private?" he asked.

"That's fine, but I don't have much time. Dwight is waiting on me. We're heading somewhere."

"Dwight," Eric said, sarcastically chuckling.

# Life of a College Bandsman 2: Is This Love

"What's funny?" I asked.

"Nothing, man," he said, as we got to his car. "Nothing."

It felt a little awkward to be in his car again. The entire situation felt a bit strange.

"Look," he said, as he took a deep breath. "I'm sorry. I fucked up. I fucked up big time," he said. "I'm so sorry, Zach."

"Is that what you had to tell me?" I asked, looking at him.

"Zach, hear me out," Eric pleaded.

"I'm listening."

"I know I've done some stupid and crazy shit in my life, but I think breaking up with you had to be the most fucked up one yet. I really fucked up, Zach."

I didn't say anything.

"Zach, I love you. I love you! You just don't know how much I really love you."

"I love you, too, Eric. I always will."

"Just hear me out," he said.

"I'm listening," I stated.

"What I did wasn't right. I didn't even give you a reason as to why I abruptly ended things with you and for that I'm sorry," he said, as my phone started to ring.

"Hold on," I said, as I answered the phone.

"Where you at?" Dwight asked.

"I'm kinda busy right now," I said. "I told you I'd be back up in a second."

"Yeah, but it's been longer than a second," Dwight stated.

"I will be there in a little bit," I said, as I hung up the phone.

"Where y'all going?" Eric asked.

"Out!" I quickly stated. It wasn't his business what I did anymore.

"Okay, then," Eric said, getting the hint.

I just stared at him.

"Ok, well like I said earlier, I fucked up and I let the actions of others control me," Eric said.

"I'm not following," I replied.

"My brother," Eric said. "My brother did this."

"What does your brother have to do with our relationship?"

"Remember that night when you said that your grandmother called you and told you to be careful and stuff," Eric said.

"She has told me that a lot of times," I replied.

"Well, the time when you called me and told me to be careful, too," Eric said.

"Yeah, I remember that. I asked you was everything ok and you told me yes," I said.

"I lied," Eric confessed. "Your grandmother was right. I didn't want you to worry about me."

"What happened?"

"Well… a lot of shit happened that night," Eric said, as he began to explain the situation with his brother, Black.

As he talked, I realized that I was with Tony when I met Black the night before I came back to school.

Eric said, "I don't know how Black found out, but he knew that I was fucking with dudes. He threatened for me to quit. He threatened me to leave you alone. And to get his point across, he put a loaded gun in my face. That's when Quinton came home and that only caused a bigger problem. Quinton and Black got into a lil shuffle and the gun went off."

"Oh, my God! Are you serious? Was someone hurt?" I asked.

"No, everyone was fine. Quinton left upset and that's when Black got a chance to talk to me. Long story short, he told me to leave men alone or he was gonna out me to our family. You know I told you how my family was, how they think about homosexuality."

"Yeah, I remember," I sighed.

"I didn't want to be put out there like that so I agreed to his terms. At the time, I would say anything for Black to leave and go back to Orlando. But in the back of my head, all I could think about was you. After Black left, Chaz talked to me."

"Chaz? How does he come into play?"

"He came after Quinton left. I guess Quinton called him over there," Eric said.

"Oh."

"You called me after Chaz left that night. I didn't want you to know what was going down, so I told you everything was ok. I knew that once things cooled off, that everything would go back to normal, and I could continue my thing with you," Eric said

"But," I said. I just knew a *but* was to be placed there.

"But Black called me about three weeks ago," Eric said.

"What did he say?" I asked.

"He basically told me to end things with you. He told me that he knew that I was sleeping with you and that I wasn't holding up my end of the bargain. Black said that if I didn't stop, he was gonna tell my mom and that would pretty much be the end of me."

"Wow," I said, as I took in everything that Eric was telling me. "That's crazy."

"Yeah, it is. But I say all of that to tell you that I fucked up. I let my brother control my actions and I've made the biggest mistake in my life."

"So, Eric, what are you trying to tell me?"

"I thought about a lot of shit and I've thought about the consequences that will happen as a result of it. But I'm willing to risk all of that for you."

"Oh, wow," I said. "Are you sure about that?"

"I promise I am, Zach," Eric pleaded. "If my family can't accept me for who and what I am, then fuck them! I want to be with you. I want you back in my life. I love you, Zach. I fucked up, but I'm begging you to work this out with me. I know it was my fault, but I just hope that you can find it in your heart to forgive me. Forgive me and come back to me. Please, Zach. Let's try this again, please!"

"Wow, Eric," I said stunned at his confession. "Wow."

"Please, Zach. Please let me back into your life," Eric begged.

I took a second to gather my thoughts. The feeling in the car was strange. I could feel and hear the sincerity in his voice. I knew he meant every single word.

He looked over at me with concern in his face when I took a deep breath and said, "Eric, I love you. I really do. And like I said earlier, I will always love you. You have that place in my heart. The time that we shared together was great. Even though everything didn't work out how I wanted it to, I enjoyed my time with you. I have grown so much because of you. You were there for me when I was going through that whole Chaz fiasco. You were always on my side and for that I thank you."

I took another breath and continued, "Eric, I forgive you. I understand the pressure that you were under. I don't know what I would do if I was faced with that situation. I love my family, too. I know some of them already suspect shit, but for them to actually find out that I'm fucking with dudes would do some major damage—damage that I don't know I'm ready to fix. So, when I say I understand, I honestly do. But you hurt me, Eric. That shit you pulled really hurt me. I'm mad that you didn't believe in me to tell me the truth then. I thought that we were in this together. If you would have told me what was going on, then maybe we could have worked through this shit together, but you didn't trust me and I hate that. The way you ended things with me still plays in my mind constantly."

"I'm sorry," Eric said, as tears started to flow from his eyes.

"Eric," I said as I took a deep breath. "Eric, I forgive you."

"REALLY? Oh, my God. I knew that we could work this out. I KNEW IT!" he said, as he reached over and French kissed me.

Oh, it felt so good, damn good, but I had to break apart.

I broke away from the kiss and said, "I'm not finished."

"Oh," he said, in a low tone as he gathered his composure.

"Like I said, I forgive you. I'm sure we can be friends or something but I'm not going backwards in my life. I'm progressing forward."

"What are you trying to say?" Eric asked, with a serious look on his face.

"Eric you made that decision to end things with me—for whatever the reason. You did that, not me. I've done a lot of thinking over the last three weeks and I'm starting to realize that things really happen for a reason."

"What reason?" he asked.

"You know how much I love the soap opera, Passions," I said.

"Yeah," Eric said. "But what does that have to do with us?"

"My favorite character, Theresa Lopez- Fitzgerald, does a lot of things out of love. Despite what results, she follows her heart. She lets her heart lead her in the right direction. It doesn't matter how bleak the outcome may turn out, she follows her heart. She has this thing and she believes everything happens because of it," I stated.

"What is that thing?" Eric asked.

"It's simple," I said. "It's just a four letter word called FATE. Things are happening around me and I can't control them. I've done a lot of thinking and I'm starting to see that maybe fate is taking its course. When I think about the things that my grandma tells me, to the instances with Chaz, the things with my homeboy from Orlando, to your recent break up with me, and then I think about things that are happening on the other side, maybe fate *is* taking its course. Like Theresa, I'm not gonna go against fate. All the stars are aligning itself up in my favor and I'm gonna go with my gut."

"So, you said all of that to say what?" Eric asked.

"I'll have to pass. I can't take you up on your proposal. I loved my time with you, but it's over, Eric. That chapter in my life is closed and it will never be reopened again."

"Are you serious?" Eric asked.

"Eric, we can be friends, but that's all we can be. Our relationship is over."

"Are you sure?" Eric pleaded. "I can make this right!"

"Eric, I'm done. I love you but I'm done."

He took a breath and called my name.

"It's over, Eric. Just accept it and move on."

No words were spoken for what seemed like an eternity.

He cut the tension by saying, "Can I have one last kiss?"

"Sure," I said, as I reached over and kissed the person that I loved so much.

The kiss was very passionate, very intense. Because of the circumstances, I let him enjoy this kiss; it would be his last. After a few moments, the kiss concluded.

"I love you," Eric said, as the tears started to fall again.

"I love you, too," I replied. "But it's what I need to do right now."

"Are you sure we can't work this out?"

"It's done, Eric. It's over," I said, as I opened the door.

"Ight," he said, as he took a deep breath.

"Don't be a stranger, Eric. Keep in touch," I said, as I walked out the car and prepared to go back into the hotel.

*Damn, that shit was hard.*

Dwight was sitting in the hotel lobby. He looked at me and asked, "Are you ready now?"

"Yeah. I need to get my stuff," I said.

"I already got it," he said. "Let's go."

We were going to see my grandmother and then we were going to spend the night at my mom's house, like we did last year. One of my uncle's picked me up from the hotel when we got into Orlando this afternoon and that allowed me to go get my grandma's car. Both Dwight and my grandma said that they wanted to see each other, so who was I to stop them.

"I hope Ms. Carrie is still up, being that you've been missing for the past thirty fucking minutes," Dwight said, as he got into the car.

"I had to take care of something," I said, as I looked at him.

"You've been talking to Eric?" Dwight asked.

"Yeah," I said.

"What does he want?" Dwight asked, agitated.

"He told me what happened, what caused the break-up and how

sorry he was. He expressed how he wanted to get back with me," I stated, as we headed for my grandmother's house.

"Please tell me you didn't get back with that pussy ass nigga," Dwight said in a serious tone.

"No, I ended things with him for good."

"GOOD!" Dwight said, as he started to smile. "Good."

"What's so good about it, Dwight?"

He stared at me.

"What's so good about it?" I repeated.

"It's good because you're finally coming around," Dwight said, he looked at me and licked his lips. "You're finally coming around."

# Part Six:

## End of Semester

# 96

# *Morgan*

*Thursday, December 11, 2003*
*Tallahassee, Florida*

Life has been good. I finally worked things out with Devin and we are on the road to a successful relationship. That period when he *left* me really did a number on me. I really saw things for what they were and I realized that I needed to get my act together.

Devin is the first dude that I can say that I really loved. I have liked a lot of dudes, but no one has captured my heart the way that he did. We still have a lot to work on, but this is where I need to be.

I've have put all the hoeing and fucking around with dudes to the side; Devin has done the same thing. People say that homosexuals can't have successful, monogamous relationships, but I'm here to prove them wrong.

Both Devin and I will be graduating in April 2004. I want to stay in Tallahassee for graduate school, but Devin wants to move to Atlanta. He says that he will have better job opportunities in Atlanta versus Tallahassee. And to be honest, he is correct. I want to be with Devin and because of that, I can go to graduate school anywhere. Despite how I may have acted in my personal life, I maintained at 3.84 GPA all throughout college, with mathematics as my major. I think that says a lot about me. Any school would be lucky to have someone of my caliber. I'm gonna apply to grad school at Georgia Tech next week. That way, both Devin and me can still be together all while we pursue the different venues that life has to offer.

*****

477

# Devin

Being with Morgan has changed me for the best. I'm sure that he won't say the same thing, but he really has. I've grown a lot as a person since I've been with him. That time when I had to leave him really brought us closer together.

I'm at the point in my life where I want to be with Morgan—forever. I wish we could get married, but maybe that opportunity will present itself in the future when the mainstream world becomes more accepting of this alternative lifestyle.

We have discussed telling our parents about our relationship. I'm a little nervous about it, but as long as we have each other then we can do it. Morgan is ready to come out. He already thinks his mom knows about his rendezvous with people of the same sex. Mine doesn't. I think I will take a little more time to figure out if I'm ready for that, but I do know that Morgan is where I wanna be.

After we graduate in April, we will be moving to Atlanta together to start a new life. I thought about saying here and going to graduate school so I could march one more year in the band, but after a long fight with myself, I decided that it was time to let it go. I love the band and I love being a drum major. My college years has been the best of my life and being a drum major in the Florida A&M University Marching '100' band has been the highlight of that experience.

These past four years have been something I will never forget; and now I have Morgan to help me relive these memories for the rest of our lives.

*****

# Ian Goodley

Well, it is finally here. Tomorrow, I will graduate with my master's degree from the Florida Agricultural and Mechanical University. It has been a long journey, but it is here.

You never know where life takes you, but one thing I have

# Life of a College Bandsman 2: Is This Love

learned is that you just have to be prepared for everything it throws. You can never be caught off guard.

I'm gonna miss everyone; but it's time that I go and live my life. Being the head drum major of the FAMU band is something I will never forget. That was one of my ultimate goals and I'm honored that Dr. Hunter saw a leader in me—a leader to be the head of leaders to lead his great unit of musicians. I will be forever grateful for him.

I don't know what to say about Chaz. That's my best friend and nothing will change that. I'll continue to love him regardless of the stupid shit that he does. We have been through so much together.

I will continue to take my strong stance on him and show him tough love. I think it's finally starting to pay off. Proposing to Genevieve was a huge step for him. I can only hope that he is positive that this is the direction that he wants to take his life.

This thing with Quinton is gonna be tough. Quinton is my heart. I loved that nigga since the day I met him. We went through that Ra'Jon shit together and that only made us stronger.

He is graduating, too, with his bachelor's degree. He has a job offer to be a band director at a new school in Orlando. I received a job offer in Jacksonville, Florida. So, I know that we're gonna move apart.

I don't know where life is gonna take us, but I know that I love him and hopefully we can do the long distance thing.

*****

# Quinton Washington

I've done a lot of shit while I was up here, but I don't regret any of it.

I was that bitch on the practice field, but when I look at my band kids like Kris, Zach and Dwight, I know that the shit paid off. Those dudes are gonna make a name for themselves in the band and I am proud to say that I was their band father.

They may not have liked the things I did, but all that mattered was the results. When the fire was lit under their ass, they produced.

I love those kids and I will never forget them. I'm sure one of them has the potential to be a section leader and I know whoever it is, will be a great one in the process.

Zach and I have been through a lot. The kid never liked me, but I saw something in him the day I met him. I wanted to push him to be great. I just wanted the best for him. That mouth of his can get him in trouble. But nonetheless, I like the kid and I only wish the best for him.

I'm fucked because my baby and I are about to go in different directions in our lives. I'm moving to Orlando next year. I got a teaching job at a brand new high school. I'm looking forward to building this new music program up from scratch, but Ian can't be with me.

He has job offer in Jacksonville. Although Orlando and Jacksonville are only two hours away, I don't know how long we can be in a long distance relationship.

Regardless of what happens, I love Ian and I value everything that he has brought to my life.

*****

# *Eric*

I could do a lot of things to get Zach back, but it wasn't worth it. I love Zach, but he made his decision and I'm gonna have to live with it. Like I said when the whole thing was going down, maybe this gay shit ain't for me. Maybe in supposed to be with a woman.

I haven't seen or heard from Zach since that night I talked to him in Orlando in the hotel parking lot. It was sad to see him go, but I'm glad that we at least ended things on a good note.

I will be graduating in April from Florida State University with my degree in Biology/ Pre-med. After graduating I will be moving up the nation's capital city to attend medical school at Howard University. Despite how things turned out with Zach, I'm excited about my life and the future opportunities that lie ahead for me.

The vibration of my phone caught my attention. I smiled when I saw the name. When I answered, my baby sister said, "Hey, Eric."

"What's up, Rozi?"

"Nothing, really. I was just checking in on you to see how you were doing," she said.

"I'm ok, just packing my things to go home for the break," I said.

"Oh, ok."

"Did you ever tell Micah about the baby?" I asked. I had been wrapped up in my own situations that I stopped thinking about Rozi's issue.

"Yes," she said. "And I told the real father."

"You never told me who it was," I said.

"I know that. But you know Eric, that entire situation made me realize a lot of things," she said.

"If we don't grow from our trials and tribulations, then what purpose did they serve in the first place," I stated.

"True," she said. "But the dude was Amir."

"I kinda figured that, Rozi."

"You're not mad?" she asked.

"I probably would have been at the time, but what's the purpose now? All I would be doing to you and Amir is the same thing that Black did to me. We all make choices and we've got to live by them."

"That's true," she said. "I'm glad that you took it so well."

"I've grown a lot in these last few weeks, Rozi. You'd be surprised that way I view things now," I stated.

"Yeah, I can somewhat hear it in your voice," she said.

"But look, let me get off the phone and finish packing while it's on my mind. I will see you when you get home to West Palm Beach."

"Ok, but Eric, I won't be coming home this Christmas."

"Why not?"

"I have to work."

"When did you get a job?" I asked.

"A few weeks ago," she said. "Besides, I'm really busy up here."

"Rozi, what's going on?"

"Nothing. I'm just working."

I exhaled and said, "Ight. Take care of yourself."

"I will and I love you."

"I love you, too, Rozi."

# 97

# Ra'Jon

*Orlando, Florida*

My friendship with Black has gotten even better ever since he asked me was I gay. I was a little scared to say anything to him, but I'm glad that I did tell the truth. He has become very interested in the lifestyle by asking me a lot of questions.

I'm glad that I could be a source of information to him. I'm glad that I could be the one to inform him about this lifestyle and how it's not as bad as everyone makes it out to be.

I'm really enjoying my job teaching the little middle school kids. Being around those kids everyday has brought a sense of realism back to my life. As much as I hated leaving FAMU, I realized that was the best thing for me. I didn't see it at the time, but you can never question God. He has his reasons for doing everything and I'm starting to see why I had to leave.

I am an educator. I went to school to become a music educator. Teaching at FAMU wasn't giving me the satisfaction that I'm getting around these middle school kids. I feel like I have a purpose again in life and I believe these kids brought that back to me.

The more I hang around Damien Duvel, I realize how much of a nice, sincere dude he is. I know that something is troubling him, but I can't figure out what it is.

I can't lie, my heart is with Black. I learned a lot dealing with Chaz and I don't wanna force anything on Black. I think that he likes me, but this time, I will let him come to me. I won't fuck this up how I fucked up my thing with Chaz.

Speaking of Chaz, I haven't forgotten about getting my revenge back on him. Actually, this is the perfect time since he is now engaged to Genevieve, but I'm better than that. That shit is over. There isn't a need to go back in my life. I'm moving forward. But mark my words—I heard that girl named KARMA is a true bitch! And before the fat lady sings her last note, I'm sure karma will pay Chaz a visit and make his life a living hell, plus some. But this time I won't have anything to do with it.

*****

# *Blackwell*

Who would have thought that I, Blackwell F. McDaniel, would be friends with a gay dude. I know I didn't—never in my wildest of wildest dreams.

But this gay dude, Ra'Jon Harris, has been more of a friend to me than my *true* friends. I don't know where he came from, but I'm glad that he is in my life.

He is really getting me to open up my mind about a lot of things dealing with homosexuality. While I'm still not partial to it, I respect him because he is still a man first.

I learned a lot about this alternative lifestyle because of him and I'm sure I still have a long way to go. I'm still not too pleased with my brother being gay, but it is what it is.

Because of RJ, I will be starting community college in January. I'm so grateful to him. He is really helping me to become a better man.

I still have some stuff in my past that I need to address and I'm happy that Ra'Jon is here to help me with them. Words can't express how much I've come to care for him.

*Words can't describe…*

# 98

## *Tony*

I completed my first year of college football, and I know, without a doubt, I'm gonna make it to the pros.

I have a son, Tony Jr., that I love so very much and I have a mentor that I love as well. When Zach told me that we would never be, that shit crushed me to my core. But I am Antonio Marquis Shaw. I always bounce back. Nothing can and nothing will hold me down for long.

When Raidon came into my life, I didn't know how to take him. But as time went on, I realized he never wanted anything from me, but to be a mentor and for that I respect him. I have a lot of people on my dick—males and females. Shit, can you blame them? Look at me.

But the difference between those groupies and Raidon is that Raidon actually cares for me. He wanted to know the real me, not how big my dick was.

As time passed, I fell for Raidon. I never thought that I would fall for someone older than me, but I can't control my feelings for him.

That night when we finally had sex was magical. We've had sex a few times since then, but Raidon is always skeptical to do it. I don't understand why. I know he's feeling me as much as I'm feeling him.

He won't suck my dick and he won't kiss me in the mouth. The few times we had sex was great, but something is missing. Something is not allowing him to fully give himself to me. I don't like that shit.

I know he has something that he wants to say, but he won't say it.

Maybe after the Christmas break we can start the new year off with everything out on the table. I want to make this thing work. I'm falling for Raidon and I want this to work.

*****

# *Raidon*

I feel so bad, but I can't tell him. I've tried to tell Tony about my status, but I can't get the words out.

That shit is killing me inside because I'm not that type of person. Whenever we have sex, I make sure that it is safe. Still, I know that shit ain't right. He deserves to know that the person he is sleeping with is living with HIV.

To this day, no one knows of my status other and my mom and the dude who gave me this shit, Phil.

I'm doing everything that I'm supposed to do to live a healthy life. I'm going in the right direction to receive my Ph.D. These classes are kicking my ass, but the payout will be worth it.

I actually enjoyed having Zach in my class this semester. He is a very smart dude and once he realized that his relationship with Eric had no bearing on my class, he opened up and became one of the better performing students in the class. I just got finished grading his final exam and he deserves the "A" that he is gonna get from my class. He really isn't that bad of a dude. I can see why Eric fell for him.

My phone started ringing. *Who is this?* I asked myself. I was trying to finish grading these papers. Tony was in the living room watching TV, so I had the room to myself to concentrate on getting this done. I didn't recognize the number.

"Hello?"

"May I speak to Raidon," I heard the familiar voice say.

"This is he," I replied.

"Raidon, I know you said that you didn't want to hear from me but—"

"PHIL?"

"Yeah, man, it's me," Phil said.

"It's been a long time," I said.

# Life of a College Bandsman 2: Is This Love

"Yeah, it has. But I don't want to talk long. I understand how you feel about me but I just wanted to call you to tell you once again that I'm sorry. I'm sorry for what I've done to you. I know that I'm not the best person in your eyes right now, but one day I hope that you can find the courage to forgive me."

"Oh, wow," I said. Listening to Phil talk made me think about my thing with Tony and how I was basically doing the same thing to Tony that Phil did to me—but only worse. Phil didn't know that he was positive—I do.

"I don't wanna hold your time, but maybe one of these days we can be friends again. I'm really sorry, Raidon. I'm sorry," he said, as he hung up the phone.

When I got off the phone with him, I knew that I had to tell Tony the truth—right then. I had prolonged this for too long. It was time for him to know the truth.

*"Ight, Raidon,"* I told myself, as I gathered my composure and headed out to the living room. *"Just say it."*

"You finished grading the papers?" he asked, as I walked over to him.

I exhaled.

"What's up, baby?" Tony asked concerned. I guess I looked on the outside, how I felt on the inside—scared and nervous.

I took a seat next to him and said, "Tony."

"What's up, baby?"

"There's something important that I have to say."

"What's wrong, Raidon?" Tony said, as he cut off the TV.

*"Ok, Raidon, just do it,"* I said to myself.

"Raidon, what's going on?" he asked.

I took a deep breath and exhaled. I said, "Tony, I'm—"

# 99

## *Micah*

I peeped my head in the room and said, "Kris, are you ready?"

He said, "Yeah, baby, I'm coming right now."

I was taking Kris out to dinner. Kris was the love of my life. Luckily for me, that thing with Rozi never leaked out. If it did, I'm sure this dinner wouldn't be happening tonight.

We would be going our separate ways for the Christmas break and I don't know how I'm gonna live without Kris for three whole weeks.

I had to work over the break, so I wouldn't get a chance to go home to Norfolk until after Christmas, but it's cool. I love my job. Zach is fitting in very well. I'm proud of him.

*****

## *Kristopher Simms*

I didn't wanna have to leave Micah over the break, but I needed to go home to see my family. I love Micah to death and I'm glad that we have been together for as long as we have.

Micah has always been faithful to me and I have been to him. I think that is one of the reasons why our relationship has been so successful.

I can only image what the next few years have in store for us. As long as we are together fighting what battles may come our way, we will be ok.

I know it.

*****

# *Dwight*

Amir walked in the house and asked, "Nigga, what are you doing?"

"Chillen. Where are you coming from?" I asked.

"The house. I'm still a lil upset about Rozi and the abortion. She killed my seed," Amir said.

"That was fucked up man, but everything happens for a reason. You've just got to look for the positive in everything," I said.

"That's true. Dallis told me to tell you to holla at him," Amir stated.

"Ight," I said, as I made mental note to call his brother.

"But what's really going on with you?" Amir asked.

"What do you mean?" I asked.

"You've been a lil distant lately," Amir said. "What's up?"

"I'm just trying to sort out some things in my life, just trying to see the direction I want to go in, if I really wanna do this or do that. I have so many options open for me right now. I just don't know what to do."

"This shit might sound gay, but follow your heart," Amir said. "Your heart ain't gonna lead you in the wrong direction."

"Shit, I'm scared. My heart is telling me one thing, but I know that ain't what I'm supposed to do. Not me!"

"Nigga, just do the right thing. I don't even know exactly what you're talking about, but I do know to do what feels right. It will work itself out in the end," Amir said.

"Yeah, we'll see," I said.

"How is your lil brother?" Amir asked.

"Oh, that nigga," I said, as I started to laugh. "Ced is good. He's fucking up a storm. He'll be here at FAMU in the fall."

"Shit, that's what's up. Is he gonna join the band?"

"I don't know," I said. "But whatever he does is cool with me."

"That's what up," Amir said, as my phone started to ring.

I answered, "Hello?"

# Life of a College Bandsman 2: **Is This Love**

"What's up, Dwight?"

"Nothing, just sitting here talking to my boy," I said.

"Zach?"

"No, Amir."

"Oh, ok, that's what's up."

"Why, what's up?" I asked.

"I want you to come through, you know to take care of this shit one more time before we leave for the break."

"Ohhhhh, ok. Shit, that's what's up. You ready?" I asked.

"Yeah, I'm ready when you are."

"Ight, let me hop in the shower and I will be over in a lil bit," I said.

"Ok, see you then."

"Yep," I said, as I hung up.

"You're about to go fuck, huh?" Amir asked.

"Yep. Gotta keep my dick happy," I said.

"Ight then," Amir said, as he started laughing. "You take care of that shit and get at me later."

"Ight, Amir," I said, as I let him out of my apartment.

*****

# *Zach*

Jared and Omar wouldn't let this Dwight thing go. Omar said, "Y'all just need to make this shit official and stop playing with each other."

"Whatever," I said, sipping on some water.

"You still don't know if y'all had sex or not?" Jared asked.

I rolled my eyes.

"Anyway, how is the job working out?" Jared asked.

"It's cool," I smiled. "I have a co-worker. His name is Will. That nigga is fine as fuck, but Micah says that he's straight."

"What the hell does Micah know?" Omar asked. "That nigga doesn't know shit! Has Micah tried Will and been rejected or something? I don't think so. That nigga doesn't know shit!"

"Well, I just know that nigga is just my type," I said. "Will is so fucking sexy."

Jared added, "Excuse me—Dwight is the type! Stop getting

sidetracked with all these other dudes. If you keep on, you're gonna let Dwight walk out for real."

"I didn't say I wanted to sleep with Will, all I said was that the nigga is fine and he's my type," I said.

"Umm, hmm," Jared said.

"I'm serious," I stated.

"Whatever," Omar said. "You're just scared as shit to approach Dwight. Nigga just do that shit."

"I've been thinking," I said. "This is the perfect opportunity. I'm just gonna do it."

"We will believe it when we see it," Jared stated.

"Umm, hmm," I said, as I got my things. "I'll see y'all at commencement tomorrow."

"Ight," Jared and Omar, said as I left their house. I had borrowed Kris' car since he was out on the town with Micah.

I've been thinking about it and I know that this is what I need to do—and I will do it.

*Dwight will be mine!*

# 100

## Chaz

*Friday, December 12, 2003*

My life could have gone in so many directions, but I'm happy that it is where it is now. Tonight, I am graduating with my master's degree and I'm engaged to the woman of my life.

I have been offered an administrative position at a high school in Tallahassee and I will being work there in January. Genevieve will finally put her degree to use, when she starts teaching next August.

Ian is leaving me today. I'm gonna miss having my best friend around. The positive is we can still see each other being that he is only going two and a half hours away to Jacksonville.

Ian has been there for me, keeping my ass in check. He's always kept an honest view of everything. I loved that man.

I'm happy that my relationship with Eric is back on track. I do feel sorry about that things that I've done, but he can never know that. I'm glad that he is gonna go to Howard for med school. He's always wanted to be a doctor, so I'm happy that he is living out his dream.

I can't even lie, I miss Zach. I loved that lil nigga. But I'm sure that he is gonna pursue things with Dwight. That's where his heart is really at anyway. I hope everything works out for them.

It's gonna be hard, but I'm through with dudes. I still have an attraction to them, but Genevieve is where I need to be.

We've discussed the wedding plans, and while we are engaged, it's not time for us to be married just yet. We are still working on some things to make sure that this is the best decision for us. Right now, she's looking at a date in 2005 or 2006. Whatever she chooses is fine with me. I will be ready.

"Quinton Washington," I heard the lady say, as I watched Quinton walk across the stage to get his bachelor's degree.

*"Do that shit,"* I said to myself. I was proud of Q. He has come a long way since that that day he came here as a freshman, four and a half years ago.

As the night progressed, they eventually got to the graduate degrees. Hearing my name being called as I walked across the stage was a great feeling. I had two degrees down—one more to go. *Chaz McDaniel, Ph.D., has a nice ring to it.* Getting that Ph.D. is my next goal. I want my sons, Xavier and Elijah, to have someone positive to look up to. I want to show them what an education can do for you.

I passed the band as I walked back to my seat. I saw Zach sitting next to Dwight. Zach had a big smile on his face. He pointed at me and nodded his head when I walked past him. I knew he was proud of me and that made this night so much more special. When I got back to my seat, I saw Ian taking his place getting ready to walk across the stage.

"Ian Goodley," the lady spoke. I was so proud of my best friend. He had been through so much stuff, especially dealing with some stuff in his family, and his cousin, Christian Goodley, the last couple of years. He really deserved this shit. When commencement was over, I caught up with Ian and Quinton.

"I'm so proud of you boys," I said.

"I'm proud of you, too," Ian said, as he gave me a hug.

"Quinton, I know you're gonna do that shit down in Orlando. Make your mark man," I said.

"Thanks, Chaz. I really appreciate that," Quinton said. "Yo, Ian, I'ma go catch up with my family. Call me so we can get up later."

"Ight, baby," Ian said, as Quinton walked away.

While Ian and I talked, some people recognized us as former drum majors and they wanted to tell us congratulations.

"IAN!" I heard a dude say as he walked over to us. When he was in front of us, he said, "Congrats, Ian. I'm proud of you."

"Thanks, man," Ian said.

Ian looked to me and said, "Chaz, this is Cordell, Cord for short, my cousin from Orlando. He's Christian's brother. He graduates high school in May."

"Oh, you're the Cord that I hear so much about," I said, as I shook his cousin's hand.

"Nice to meet you," Cord said to me.

"Where is everybody at?" Ian asked Cord.

"Everybody is waiting on you," Cord replied.

"Ight, I'm coming," Ian said, as Cord walked away.

"Ight, Chaz," Ian said, as he gave me a hug. "Get at me."

"Ight, best friend. I'll see you later," I said, as he ran off to join his family.

*"Now to my family,"* I said to myself, as I went to join them.

*****

# *Zach*

My mind was occupied. I know what I needed to do and it needed to happen tonight. I had to get this off my chest.

Dwight turned down the radio and said, "I can't wait until I graduate."

"That makes two of us," I said, as Dwight drove back to my place.

"Are you ok, Shawty?" Dwight asked.

"Yeah, man, I'm good. Just thinking," I said.

"Oh...ok," he said, as he turned up the radio.

We rode in silence the entire ride to my house. I was nervous and scared, but I knew that I had to let Dwight know how I felt.

"Ight, Big Z," Dwight said, as we got to my house.

I didn't get out of the car.

"What's wrong, man?" Dwight asked again, as he put the car in park.

*"Ight, Zach,"* I said to myself.

"What's up, man?" Dwight asked, concerned. "Yo, let's go in the house."

I didn't say anything. I just got out of the car and made my way up the stairs. As I was walking in, my co-worker, Will, was walking out.

"Oh," he said, as he saw me walking in the house. "What's up, Zach?"

"Sup, man," I said, as I continued the walk to my room.

*"What is he doing here?"* I asked myself. *"NAW,"* I said, to myself as thought about it. Micah had the house to himself because Kris was at commencement. *"NAW, you're thinking too much into it."*

"So, what's up, Zach?" Dwight asked, as he walked in the room and closed the door.

"Look, Dwight," I said, as I started to cry. I didn't mean too, but this shit was eating me up.

"What wrong, man?" he said, concerned.

"I've tried to hide this shit from myself, but I can't. I can't help the way that I feel. I've been fighting this shit since the day I met you, but I can't hold it anymore," I said, as the tears flowed from my eyes.

Dwight didn't say anything.

"Dwight, I don't know what's gonna happen after this, but I've got to tell you how I feel," I said.

He still didn't say anything. He just looked at me in my eyes.

I took a deep breath and said, "Dwight, I'm in love with you. I want to be with you. I can't help this shit. My heart is with you—YOU DWIGHT! I love you!"

*Oh, it felt damn good to get that off my chest. Felt like the weight of the world had been lifted from my shoulders.*

Dwight looked at me for a few moments without saying anything. I guess he was processing what I had confessed.

He started to open his mouth to say something but stopped. He took a deep breath.

My nerves were going to get the best of me.

He exhaled.

"I love *you*!" I said again.

"Zach," he finally said in a very serious tone. "I'm shocked. I honestly didn't think that was what I was gonna hear tonight."

He took a deep breath and said, "But I love you, too. You know that. But the love that you have for me and the love that I have for you are two different types of loves. I love you as a friend. I love you as a brother," he admitted.

"What are you saying, Dwight?" I wiped my face.

"Zach, I want you to be my best friend, not my boyfriend. I'm not gay, Shawty. I like pussy. I'm not gay."

I stared at him, speechless.

He walked to the door and said, "I do love you though—just not like that. Call me tomorrow."

# Life of a College Bandsman 2: Is This Love

I stared at him as he walked out of the room and disappeared down the hall.

*What the fuck, Zach?*

*What the hell did I just do?*

*What did I just do?*

*~To Be Continued~*

# Life of a College Bandsman
## Upcoming Titles:

Life of a College Bandsman 3: Stuck on Stupid

Life of a College Bandsman 4: Hell on Earth

Life of an EX College Bandsman 5: Starting All Over

Life of an EX College Bandsman 6: Lovers and Friends

Life of an EX College Bandsman 7: Nobody's Perfect

Life of an EX College Bandsman 8: Growing Pains

Life of an EX College Bandsman 9: Nothing Lasts Forever

Life of an EX College Bandsman 10: Is He the Reason

Life of an EX College Bandsman 11: The Finale

# About the Author

Known mostly as BnTasty by his online reader-base, Jaxon Grant started his writing conquest in June 2008, on Da Site, which was a popular stories website for gay and bisexual men. With his initial publications, Jaxon captivated his audience and created a healthy following that urged him to move outside of the confines of those who flocked to Da Site to read his material. Now, after many years of growing and understanding his skills as a writer, he's brought his work to a national audience.

Jaxon has written with compelling thoughts that tackle the issues we face as Americans, not just in the LGBT community. In his unique style, he uses the elements of drama, mystery, suspense, romance and tragedy to further the depth and scope of his work.

Jaxon was born and raised in Orlando, Florida. He attended Florida A&M University (FAMU) and majored in Social Science Education with a concentration in Political Science. While at FAMU, Jaxon was a member of the marching band, the world renown FAMU Marching 100.

Please be sure to visit his website, www.jaxongrant.com, and sign up for his newsletter to receive important updates from Jaxon. You can follow Jaxon on Twitter @jaxon_grant. Finally, you can text Jaxon to 88202 to receive new release alerts directly to your phone.

CPSIA information can be obtained
at www.ICGtesting.com
Printed in the USA
LVHW110337271021
701667LV00001B/19

9 781518 740541